# THE VANIS

# THE VANISHING

Venezia Miller

THE VANISHING

Copyright © 2024 by Venezia Miller.

All rights reserved. No part of this book may be used or reproduced in any manner whatsoever without written permission except in the case of brief quotations embodied in critical articles or reviews.

This book is a work of fiction. Names, characters, businesses, organizations, places, events, and incidents either are the product of the author's imagination or are used fictitiously. Any resemblance to actual persons, living or dead, events, or locales is entirely coincidental.

For information contact: Venezia.Miller@gmail.com
ISBN : 9798879989410


Book and Cover design by V. Miller, images taken from www.pixabay.com and adapted using GIMP.

First Edition: May 2024

# CHAPTER

# 1

**SLOWLY, LIKE WAKING FROM A DEEP SLEEP,** he began to regain consciousness. Confusion clouded his mind as he struggled to make sense of his surroundings.

Where was he?

He didn't remember. Everything was so muddled.

Rain beat down relentlessly, chilling him to the bone, while each breath felt like a burden.

Panic.

He couldn't move. He had arms and legs, but now they seemed strangely numb, unresponsive to his commands, while he could feel the cold droplets trickling down his skin.

His vision blurred, adding to his disorientation. Blinking only worsened the confusion.

In the distance, a faint moan hinted at distress.

There was someone close by.

Help. Help.

But his attempts to call for help fell flat.

His voice was barely a whisper.

The rain persisted, its cold penetrating deep into his very core.

And then, amidst the downpour, the sound of approaching footsteps shattered the silence. Straining to discern friend from foe, he felt a surge of anxiety. Memories flickered, but remained just out of reach, fueling his fear.

As the footsteps drew nearer, accompanied by the rustle of leaves, desperation consumed him. Trapped within his own body, he could only wait for the approaching figure to reveal its intentions.

The distant moans now turned into unsettling gurgles, heightening his unease.

Then, laughter cut through the air, triggering a sudden recollection.

He remembered everything.

# CHAPTER

# 2

CELESTE DREW THE CURTAIN ASIDE, catching sight of the conductor signaling the orchestra to tune their instruments. The brass occupied the rear, strings flanked both sides at the front, and right in front of the conductor, the woodwinds were in the midst of their warm-up.

Closing her eyes, she envisioned the music that would fill the concert hall. Sections tuned, and she strained to locate the violins. Her stomach tightened as the sharpness and brilliance she was once known for had faded. Distinguishing between the different sections had become a challenge. The music morphed into a homogenous noise, a painful reminder of how much she had changed over the past five years—a tumultuous period of ups and downs. A heavy realization struck her; the musician she once was seemed irretrievably lost.

She couldn't do this.

It was too early.

"Ready?" a man's voice pierced the moment. She turned to find her manager, Lukas Stendahl, in a tuxedo, offering a warm smile. In her simple black dress with short sleeves, she suddenly felt underdressed.

Lukas was a young man in his mid-twenties, possessing a slight frame that bordered on frailty. His appearance wasn't conventionally handsome, yet there was an air of gentleness about him that softened his features. And despite his unassuming demeanor, there lingered a subtle hint of confidence and shrewdness in his eyes.

"Celeste?"

"Uh... I suppose," she whispered, her gaze shifting to her hands, clutching her cell phone.

Lukas placed a comforting hand on her shoulder. "Are you okay?"

She nodded.

Pointing at the stage, Lukas raised his eyebrows in an encouraging gesture. "Look, I know it's scary. It's like starting all over again, but you got this. We've been practicing for months. Your comeback."

"I think...," she began, then sighed. She couldn't let him down—the only person who believed in her when everyone else had given up.

Disappointing him was not an option.

He smiled, cupping her head in his hands. "Breathe. It'll be fine. You'll see."

A faint smile and nod followed. He was right. This opportunity needed seizing—to demonstrate that her skills were intact, that she was still the great Celeste Westerberg.

Taking a deep breath, she declared, "Yeah, you're right. It's time to go back to what I'm best at."

Lukas smiled, delivered another reassuring pat to her shoulder, then shifted his focus toward the orchestra and walked away.

She closed her eyes once more. Now, she could hear the notes, each one dancing in front of her.

The next moment, her phone buzzed. Lowering her gaze to the screen, her eyes widened in shock—it was an unknown number. Her heart raced, and with a trembling hand, she answered the call. "Hello?"

A crackling noise echoed through the speaker. It looked like someone was playing an old record.

"Who is this?"

Then, amid the static, the notes of a familiar song reached her ears, played on a guitar unfamiliar to her but unmistakably known. The phone almost slipped from her trembling fingers, and she glanced around.

Again.

It was the same song as she had received in a message days ago.

He had returned.

Panic coursed through her veins.

She stared at her phone in horror, grappling with the unsettling darkness that closed in around her like a creeping fog.

The progress she had painstakingly made vanished in an instant.

"Celeste, are you ready?"

Voices whispered, mocked, and taunted in her ear. Louder and more insistent, they came from inside her head now. She covered her ears, trying to block them out, but it was futile.

"Celeste?" Lukas said and touched her arm.

"No!" she screamed, pushing him away. With each uttered word, she slipped further into the madness.

"Celeste, what's wrong?"

She was losing her grip on reality, a terrifying experience. To reclaim what she had long fought for, she needed to dismiss the imagined reality.

The phone showed the connection had been broken. Maybe it was just a wrong number and her mind was filling in the blanks.

She counted slowly to ten. "I am safe," "I'm loved," "I am not crazy." Gradually, with each repeated phrase, she reclaimed her composure amidst the relentless drumbeat of fear echoing in her head.

"It's time," Lukas said, turning to her. "Are you going to be okay? You need to tell me now."

"I'll be okay," she whispered, looking at the stage. The orchestra, the choir, the audience—they expected magic, a masterpiece, her brilliance. Yet, it was all gone, taken from her. He had stolen her sanity.

But the show had to go on. For the next two hours, she would deliver what they came for—a magistral Bach concert in the Philharmonic Hall in Gävle with one of Sweden's oldest orchestras.

The Gävle Symphony Orchestra featuring Celeste Westerberg.

\* \* \*

The room fell into a momentary silence as Celeste scanned the audience, then the music stirred to life. She closed her eyes, letting the melody's beauty envelop her soul. With a deep breath, she took a step forward, locking eyes with the conductor. Positioning the violin beneath her chin, she felt a surge of confidence, though it wavered as the impending moment, where all eyes would be fixed on her, drew near.

Celeste's hands trembled as the bow touched the strings. The audience held their breath, their gaze fixed on her. Yet, she couldn't shake off the memories—the cold, lifeless eyes; the haunting footsteps; his hot breath on her neck. He had returned. The phone calls, his unsettling knowledge of her whereabouts and activities—every detail flooded back.

He knew it all.

She forced herself to concentrate on the music. It almost flowed through her—a soothing current that momentarily eclipsed the haunting memories. Then, as abruptly as it came, the feeling passed, and Celeste returned to herself.

The first song concluded, and the audience erupted in applause, yet

Celeste remained still. In the front row sat her stalker, shrouded in a hoodie, his eyes piercing through the disguise. She held her breath.

He shifted his gaze toward the band, releasing a chilling laugh. An icy shiver ran down her spine. Why did no one react? Couldn't they see him? What was happening to her?

The conductor looked at her, signaling the start of the second piece, but Celeste's arm froze mid-air. She couldn't go on.

The voices intensified.

*He's here. He's coming for you. Run. Run.*

The violin dropped.

A buzz rippled through the audience.

She couldn't bear to stay there a moment longer, so she fled the stage, leaving behind a bewildered crowd. Celeste's only concern was escape. She raced through the backstage until she found a door leading to the rooftop.

Bounding up the stairs, she burst onto the roof, gasping for breath as the wind threatened to push her back. She grasped onto the railing, her heart pounding in her chest as she scanned her surroundings.

As she gazed at the city below, its twinkling lights and bustling traffic resembling tiny ants, a fleeting sense of dizziness washed over her. But fear swiftly replaced it, causing her to hyperventilate.

Footsteps approached, and she spun around, terror widening her eyes.

"Who's there?" she cried, gasping for air. "Show yourself!"

A blurry figure appeared in the distance, just outside the door.

"I'm coming for you. You can't hide," a voice whispered.

"Celeste, it's me," Lukas screamed.

"Get away from me!"

The dark figure drew nearer, its form shifting and morphing, from ghostly apparition to menacing beast, taking on an unsettling array of shapes. She continued edging closer and closer to the part of the roof

11

where there was no railing anymore. More ghosts came through the door. She heard their otherworldly voices.

*I want you. There is no escape!*

"Celeste," he repeated, his voice now laced with fear. He reached out and touched her arm, but she shrugged him off.

"Don't touch me!" she screamed hysterically. "You're just like the others! You're after me! Leave me alone!"

"It's me. Lukas. No one tries to hurt you." He gasped for air.

*Help me! Help me!*

She lashed out, her emotions spiraling into a maelstrom of guilt and self-blame. Why had she kept it all a secret? She grappled with an overwhelming sense of responsibility for the chaos that had enveloped her life.

Then, as her turmoil intensified, the masks fell off, and a chilling realization came over her.

"It's you," she whispered, her voice trembling. Her gaze flicked to Lukas, who stood so close that she could feel the warmth of his breath. His face contorted into a gruesome, bloody distortion, and she saw something in what was meant to be his hand—a knife, a butcher's knife.

"Celeste, please," he pleaded, but it was too late.

She turned and ran towards the edge.

The next moment she felt so light, so free, the air surrounding her like a warm blanket. All her problems were gone.

And then gravity pulled her down.

* * *

"I'm telling you, she was not herself," Lukas said for what felt like the hundredth time. "She was rambling on about someone trying to hurt her. And then she just jumped. If you don't believe me, there are a dozen other people who saw it."

He shook his head, still struggling to believe what he had just witnessed. It had all unfolded so swiftly—one moment, Celeste had been right beside him, and in the next, she was hurtling towards the ground, far below. He wished he could have intervened, but Celeste had been so fast, leaving him powerless to stop it.

Sergeant Varg Mårtensson leaned forward in his chair, a young man with vibrant red hair and a smattering of freckles across his face. No one would have pegged him for a police officer if he hadn't been cladded in his crisp police uniform, and that had been the frustration of his life so far. People had always thought he was much younger than he actually was, a misconception that seemed to persist no matter how many birthdays passed. His mother had tried to reassure him, telling him it would be an advantage as he grew older, but Varg didn't quite see it that way.

He had only recently been promoted to the investigation team, and Chief Inspector Isa Lindström had taken him under her wing, which only added to his sense of insecurity. This was the first time he had been tasked with interviewing a witness on his own.

His youthful features creased with concern as he fixed Lukas with a penetrating gaze. "You're sure that's what happened? She didn't say anything else before she jumped?"

Lukas swallowed hard, a bead of sweat forming on his brow, and shook his head once more. "No, nothing else."

Varg let out a weary sigh, massaging his temples as he contemplated the bizarre turn of events in the case.

"I'm so sorry, inspector," Lukas said, his voice shaking. "I just can't believe she would do something like that." Then Lukas put his hands over his ears and leaned forward, his head down. The next moment, Varg heard the man sobbing.

"I know this is hard, Mr. Stendahl, but we need to get as much information as possible," Varg said with a firm voice. "What can you tell me about her?"

"It was supposed to be her comeback," Lukas continued, his eyes fixed on the floor before him. "Oh, God, maybe it was too soon. Maybe I pushed her too much. And that's why..."

"Her comeback?"

Lukas looked up, his face red with tears. "She... uh," he tried to order his thoughts and find the words. "She had a breakdown... burn-out five years ago. She was in therapy and... this concert was supposed to announce her comeback."

"Okay. You're sure there's no possibility that this could have been an accident? That she slipped or lost her footing somehow?"

Lukas shook his head before burying his face in his hands once again and letting out a loud wail.

Varg looked at Lukas with a mixture of pity and disbelief. "Did she try to kill herself before?"

Lukas nodded, wiping the tears from his eyes. "Yeah, but that was five years ago, when she was really in an all-time low. That's why she went into therapy."

"But she was fine at the start of the concert?" Varg said.

"At least that's what I thought."

"And the weeks leading up to today?"

"She was full of energy and confidence," Lukas said and then suddenly frowned. "No, now that I think of it... she started to become anxious a few days ago."

"Did something happen?"

"She was going through a divorce and there was some trouble with her family... some disagreement, but I thought that was all behind us and she could concentrate on her music from now on. I'm not sure if that was the reason. I know it sounds crazy, but I swear to you, when she was standing on that roof, she was delusional... scared... like she had seen a ghost."

He shook his head in confusion.

"Do you think she had a relapse?"

He ran a hand through his hair. "Could be, but why now?"

"The stress of the concert."

Lukas closed his eyes and then ran his hands over his face. "Then it was my fault. Oh, God, I need to tell her family."

Varg put the notebook in the pocket of his jacket, got up and put his hand on the man's shoulder.

"I'm so sorry," Varg said and went toward the exit.

* * *

Celeste Westerberg's lifeless body sprawled across the pavement, limbs twisted in unnatural angles. A disheveled halo of long, brown locks framed her head, and her once-bright blue eyes now stared lifelessly into the distance. She had landed on her front, and a pool of blood had spread out from beneath her face, which was turned to the side.

Meters away, a crowd had assembled, their morbid curiosity drawing them to the scene. But police officers quickly intervened, cordoning off the area with yellow-black tape and urging the onlookers to step back.

Sergeant Sylvia Ahlgren walked past them and then crouched down beside the body, but as she suddenly realized who she was looking at, shock washed over her.

"Celeste?" she whispered.

She needed a moment to compose herself, her mind racing to make sense of the tragic scene before her. The shock of seeing someone she had once known lying lifeless on the pavement was overwhelming.

Celeste must have died instantly upon impact with the ground—a tragic end for someone so young and full of life.

Why? What had driven Celeste, someone in her mid-twenties just like herself, to take such a desperate measure? Life was supposed to be at its beginning for both of them.

A heavy breath escaped her, and she looked away in disbelief.

With a sense of sadness, Sylvia donned a pair of plastic gloves and began to search through the pockets of Celeste's black dress, hoping to find some clue as to why the young woman would choose to end her life this way. But all she discovered was a handkerchief and a key, which she carefully placed in a plastic bag.

As Sylvia rose to her feet, her gaze fell upon Dr. Einarsson. Instantly, her annoyance surged. She couldn't stand him; he had no sense of humor, and his demeanor was mechanical, devoid of any emotion or warmth. It was such a stark contrast to his predecessor, Dr. Ingrid Olsson, who had been a ray of light in comparison. But she wasn't there anymore. Ingrid was now teaching at the university. Sylvia found it a pity they had let Ingrid go, without offering any explanation whatsoever.

Dr. Einarsson was now standing next to her, looking at the corpse with his usual stoic expression, his glasses perched on the end of his nose.

He stood tall, a man in his mid-forties, with a head of blond hair that was gradually thinning on top. His face, clean-shaven and angular, briefly cast a glance in her direction. Pale blue eyes, once filled with life and humor, now revealed only a trace of the enthusiasm he had mustered each day since his painful divorce. It had all unraveled after he discovered his wife's infidelity with a close friend. Rumors circulated that years ago, he had been an entirely different person, capable of delivering the most hilarious jokes when in good spirits. But the divorce had taken its toll.

Her gaze remained fixed on the lifeless form. "I knew her."

He frowned, then knelt beside the body. "Should you even be here?"

"I mean... I knew her a long time ago," she stammered. "We were in the same class in secondary school for years, but she's not a friend."

"I see," he responded, his tone measured, as he carefully turned the body.

"What do you make of this?" she asked as she gestured towards the open wound on Celeste's head.

Dr. Einarsson remained focused on the body as he answered, "Everything I heard so far points to suicide. The body position is consistent with someone throwing themselves from a great height."

"But isn't it strange that she would decide to kill herself in the middle of a concert?" Sylvia said.

The wind was blowing strands of her long blond hair across her face, and she took a moment to put the hair in a bun.

"People in a psychosis do not make rational decisions," Dr. Einarsson said and continued his examination. "And I'd appreciate it if you could step aside and give me some space to conduct my investigation."

But she ignored him. "So, one moment she is clear of mind and the next she's in a psychosis and jumps off a building? I don't buy it."

Einarsson looked up at her and gave her a stern glance. "I'm sorry, but what you think is not important. I'm the one drawing the conclusion here."

She furrowed her brow. "I'm sorry, but what I think does matter. We, the police, have the final say, and I'm telling you, there's something suspicious about this entire situation. She was incredibly bright and successful. Everyone admired her in school. Do you remember 'Aria 25'?"

He arched an eyebrow. "Aria 25? No, should I?"

"It was a huge hit about four or five years ago," she explained. "Imagine being at the peak of your career at twenty-two and then suddenly dead at twenty-seven. Why?" She brushed the hair from her face and, with deep brown eyes, stared at him.

Dr. Einarsson turned back to the body and then said without looking at Sylvia, "The woman was clearly troubled, she had a history of mental illness, and all the witnesses say that she jumped off the building deliberately."

"But what would cause her to suddenly snap like that?" Sylvia argued.

"Well, since you so passionately disagree with me and think you know better, why don't you find the evidence?"

Sylvia fixed him with a steely glare, "Prick!" And then she ran off.

A faint smile appeared on his face as he leaned over and carefully touched Celeste's face with his gloved hands.

# CHAPTER

# 3

INSPECTOR ISA LINDSTRÖM GAZED out the window, her fingers wrapped around the warm mug in her hand. It sent a soothing sensation coursing through her body, yet an inner chill clung to her. Beyond the glass, the rain continued its ceaseless assault—a persistent downpour that seemed never-ending. Just rain, relentless and cold. Surprisingly, she yearned for the simplicity of snow, now a rarity in this unusually warm season—a quiet reminder of climate change erasing the bitter winters of her childhood.

As Isa continued to stare out of the window, an unexpected melancholy descended upon her, casting a shadow over her thoughts. She couldn't pinpoint the cause, but a profound sadness welled up within her. It was as if an intangible weight had settled on her shoulders, a premonition of change lurking in the recesses of her mind.

The silence was interrupted by the sudden ringtone of her cell phone. Isa reached for it on the table, glancing at the screen to confirm that it was Viktor, her ex-husband.

"Hey, what's up?" she said.

"Just wanted to tell you that the meeting with Felix's teacher is confirmed for Thursday."

"Okay," she stammered.

"You're going to be there, right?"

Isa hesitated for a moment. She hadn't been a part of her children's lives for so long, and the prospect of attending a parent-teacher meeting was both heartening and disconcerting. It was almost like what a normal family would do.

But they were hardly a normal family.

"Yeah, I'll be there," she replied.

There was a pause on the other end of the line, and then Viktor's voice softened. "I think Felix will really like that."

"I'll be there," she repeated, as if she needed to affirm it for herself.

"Shall I pick you up?"

"No, it's fine," she said.

After their conversation ended, she set the phone back on the table, her mind drifting back to Viktor. Unacknowledged feelings for him still lingered within her, hidden away like a secret she couldn't bring herself to admit, even to herself.

She sank into the chair with a sigh, her gaze momentarily tracing the white walls. The minimalist surroundings only seemed to amplify her sense of solitude. Despite her successful career, she felt adrift and isolated. Thoughts of Viktor, the loss of Alex—her deceased lover—and the weight of past choices left her overwhelmed by an enduring loneliness she couldn't shake.

At that moment, a soft knock on the door interrupted her thoughts.

"Sorry, am I disturbing you, ma'am?" Sylvia stood in the doorway, hesitating to step into the room.

"It's fine," Isa said and signaled her to come in. "And please don't call me ma'am... it makes me feel old."

Sylvia nodded.

"What's on your mind?" Isa asked.

"Celeste Westerberg."

"The suicide?"

"You see... I'm not convinced it is," Sylvia said.

She motioned for Sylvia to come further into the room.

"Tell me," Isa urged, her voice low and measured. "Why do you doubt it's a suicide?"

"I... have no evidence. It's just a feeling. Why would someone, targeting a comeback, suddenly end her life... in the midst of a concert? That doesn't make any sense."

"But sometimes, the pressures people face can drive them to irrational decisions."

"Yeah... but... I knew her."

"Have a seat," Isa said and gestured Sylvia to sit down, sensing the internal struggle the young woman in front of her was going through. She empathized with Sylvia's disbelief, knowing how difficult it must be to accept that someone she had known had chosen to end their own life. "How do you know her?"

"I didn't know her that well. We were in the same classes in secondary school. She was one of those people who would go on and do great things... you just knew it. She was already special. They all were."

"They?"

"I never interacted much with them. Celeste and her friends... they were the high potentials. The artists, the creatives. They were always together. You just knew they were destined for better and greater things. But..."

"Look, Sylvia, Dr. Einarsson's report supports the theory of suicide. And there is Celeste's personal history, and her struggles with anxiety and depression. I understand that it's difficult to accept, especially when you have personal memories of her as a vibrant and talented person."

Sylvia sighed, her shoulders slumping. "I know what the report says. I don't... I know Dr. Einarsson is a professional, but he's no Dr. Olsson. She used to be more open-minded. Why did she leave anyway?"

Isa felt Sylvia's frustration and skepticism. The absence of her friend, Ingrid Olsson, who had relocated to Uppsala, weighed heavily on her as well. Despite Uppsala being nearby, Ingrid's sudden departure had created a void within the team, a gap that proved challenging to fill.

Isa chose her words carefully. "Dr. Olsson left the department for personal reasons. Dr. Einarsson is experienced, and we have to trust his judgement."

"I know, but... it just doesn't sit right with me. I can't let it go."

"We'll wait for the toxicology report and then likely close the case," Isa added.

"Okay, if that's..."

"If I were you, I'd concentrate on the inspector's exam at the end of January. It's not that far," Isa continued.

"I'm ready," Sylvia said with confidence and got up.

"Don't underestimate this," Isa said in a stern voice. She couldn't tell Sylvia she had failed the exam the first time. "We need more people like you."

But she felt tired and couldn't really bring up the energy to give the young woman a peptalk.

Sylvia walked to the door and then suddenly turned around. "This feels good."

Isa frowned. "What do you mean?"

"You behind that desk."

"It's only temporary, until Inspector Paikkala is back."

"He's still out?"

"Still? It's the first time this year he took a break for more than a week. He'll be back in two days."

"Where did he go?"

"I don't know... some ice climbing in Abisko."

"Ice climbing?"

"Paikkala is a bit... crazy."

"Not sure if the weather is that ideal. Is there even any ice?"

"Up north you'll never know. Anyway, he'll be back in a few days and then I'm out of here."

She didn't regret it. The room was bare, its white walls devoid of any personal touches, giving off a sterile and unwelcoming vibe. The neat desk in the center held only essential documents, lacking any warmth or character. It seemed as though Paikkala's no-nonsense approach had left its mark on the space since he joined the team two years ago.

"It does suit you though," Sylvia said. "Being the superintendent."

And with a small smile on her face, she left the room.

Superintendent. Isa had never seen herself as superintendent. She was too accustomed to the fieldwork, the gritty investigations, and the adrenaline of the chase. The title of superintendent had always felt a bit too formal, too removed from the action.

But there was a part of her that longed for the recognition and status that came with this kind of job.

She shook her head and took the file from her desk. Einarsson's report of Celeste Westerberg's death. She didn't expect to find anything new, but maybe, just maybe Sylvia was right.

*\*\*\**

As Timo Paikkala sat in the dimly lit pub, his well-trained body settled comfortably into a wooden chair, he leaned forward, elbows resting on the scarred surface of the round table before him. The soft glow of overhead lights cast a warm, amber hue over the room, creating an atmosphere of relaxed camaraderie. The low murmur of conversation and clinking glasses surrounded him, providing a comforting backdrop to his evening.

His eyes were fixed on the large flat-screen TV mounted on the wall across from his table. The television emitted a soft, muted glow as it broadcasted a live news program, the anchor delivering the day's headlines and updates with a serious demeanor. He could hardly understand the woman. Prime Minister Olav Hult was interviewed about his new health legislation. Amidst the political discourse, there was a brief mention of the geopolitical tensions between China and the US, and then the news program seamlessly transitioned to the weather report, predicting a chilling outlook for the next couple of days.

His fingers idly traced the condensation on the side of his half-empty glass of coke. His leather jacket hung casually on the back of his chair.

From time to time, Timo would take a slow sip from the glass. His gaze remained fixated on the TV screen, though his thoughts wandered in and out of focus, his body yearning for rest after the demanding day on the ice.

Ice climbing was not just a hobby for him; it was a way to reset, to challenge himself in a different way than he did in his role as chief inspector. Usually, although exhausting as it was, it energized him, but not this time.

He took the cell phone from his jacket and searched for the number. He hesitated for a moment before pressing the call button. The phone rang, and he anxiously waited for the voice on the other end to answer, his exhaustion momentarily forgotten in the anticipation of the conversation to come. But it moved to voicemail, as it had done so many times in the past six months.

He took a deep breath and then said, "Hey, it's me again. I'm in

Abrisko. I miss you."

He put the phone down for a moment and sighed. "Look, George, I don't know what happened between you and auntie Lilia, but it can't be that bad. Whatever it is, it has nothing to do with our friendship. I was climbing today and the only thing I was thinking was how much I miss my friend, my buddy. Please... talk to me. Call me. Don't let mom or anyone else..."

His voice trailed off for a moment as he struggled to find the right words to convey the depth of his disappointment. "Don't let this silence ruin our friendship, George. I'm here whenever you're ready."

With a heavy heart, Timo ended the call. As he put the phone down, the exhaustion returned along with a sense of melancholy, and he sighed, hoping that his message would eventually reach George, his mentor. The man who had helped him through his most difficult moments.

"Do you need anything else?"

The unexpected interruption snapped him back to the present, and he looked up, straight into the blue eyes of a young woman. She radiated youth and energy, a stark contrast to his feelings of melancholy and exhaustion. Her beauty was undeniable, with short brown hair framing her face and a vibrant, youthful aura about her. He offered her a small, appreciative smile and shook his head. "No, thank you. I think I'm good for now."

She didn't go and continued to look at him. "I've seen you here before."

Timo's tired eyes met hers again, and he noticed the spark of interest in her gaze. "You might have. I come here from time to time after a day of climbing."

Her lips curled into a friendly smile. "I know. You used to come here with an older man."

George. The mention of his friend's name brought a wave of sadness crashing back over Timo.

"You seem to know a lot about me," Timo said.

The woman's smile widened. "I've been working here for a while, and I've seen you two come in together on several occasions. You always seemed like great friends."

Timo reflected on the change in their friendship, the silence that now stretched between him and George. "We were. But things change."

She nodded. "Sometimes they do. And sometimes, it takes just one conversation to set things right again." She leaned in a bit closer. "But there is something more... you seem sad. Really sad. I'm Emma by the way."

She put the tray with glasses down on the table and extended her hand. Timo shook it, and for the first time in a while, he felt a glimmer of connection and a sense of warmth that had been missing from his day. "Timo Paikkala."

She quickly looked around and when no one was calling for her, she turned her attention back to Timo.

"So, I'm a great listener," she continued.

"I don't know... Aren't you supposed to..."

"No worries," Emma reassured him. "The owner is my father, and it's pretty slow today."

He appreciated her offer, but he still wasn't sure if he was ready to delve into the complexities of his thoughts and emotions. He glanced at the now empty glass on his table and decided to change the subject. "Actually, a cup of coffee would be great. Thank you, Emma."

"Of course. I'll be right back with that cup of coffee for you."

As Emma headed back to the bar, he felt overwhelmed. He leaned back in his chair, his gaze drifting to the surroundings of the pub. It was quiet like she had said. Aside from himself, there were only three other customers.

Emma returned with a cup of steamy black coffee, placing it gently on the table in front of him. "A woman. That's what's bothering you."

He looked up and knew immediately the expression on his face had betrayed him. And more than ever, he didn't want to talk about it. Not with her, not with anyone.

With a polite but somewhat distant smile, Timo nodded. "You're right, but it's something I'd rather not talk about at the moment."

He had put an unspoken boundary.

"Of course. But whenever you're ready to talk or if you just need someone to listen, I'll be here."

She flashed him another radiant smile, a subtle trace of flirtation gleaming in her eyes, before gracefully retreating to fulfill her duties. His gaze lingered on her as she vanished into a small room behind the bar. She seemed no older than twenty. Technically she could have been his daughter.

As he brought the cup of coffee closer to his lips, he contemplated the twists and turns that had led him to this moment, where an unexpected connection with a young woman had momentarily brightened his evening but left him pondering the complexities of his life.

# CHAPTER

# 4

**ISA STROLLED INTO THE OFFICE**, nonchalantly dismissing the disapproving glare from Timo.

He sighed, "When the door is closed, it means..."

"I know, I know, you don't want to be disturbed. But I can't sit around waiting for you to bless me with your presence after your vacation," she interrupted.

Timo raised his eyebrows, "You do remember who's in charge, right?"

With a cheeky grin, Isa tucked a wayward curl behind her ear and plopped down into the chair across from his desk. "Well, I hope you enjoyed some downtime."

"I did," he uttered, pausing as though to add more, but ultimately choosing to remain silent.

"What's your take on the Westerberg case?"

"I was under the impression that case was closed," Timo responded, his striking blue eyes meeting hers directly.

Timo, at thirty-seven, had a charisma that earned respect from both peers and suspects. With dark hair and piercing blue eyes, he had a unique knack for truly listening, making others feel at ease enough to confide in him.

As he lounged in his chair with crossed arms, the powerful muscles of his biceps peeked out from under his black T-shirt. This never failed to distract Isa.

"So, you're thinking it's suicide too?" she asked.

"That's what the evidence and the witness statements tell us."

"I'm not completely convinced that this was a suicide," Isa said, her hands clasped tightly on the table in front of her. "Celeste Westerberg was one of the most promising violinists in Sweden. She had everything to live for."

"I know. I heard her play once, a long time ago. She was fantastic. The way she moved her bow across the strings, drawing out each note with such feeling and passion. Unbelievable."

Isa frowned. "I wasn't aware of your interest in classical music."

"There's a lot you don't know about me," Timo said and looked embarrassed he had shared this musing with her.

Isa continued, "Still something seems off, and I want your permission to investigate it further. By the way, the family doesn't believe it either."

Timo sighed and rubbed his temples. It had been a long day, and he was getting tired of these little chats with Isa Lindström. Every time she came into his office, it seemed like there was another problem that needed to be dealt with.

"Since when is the family of a victim dictating us what to do?" Timo said in a stern voice. "Look, I know you're trying to do your job, but sometimes people just snap. That's all there is to it."

"We came across something odd on her phone, though," Isa hesitantly revealed.

"Who's 'we'?"

"Sylvia and I."

"Your apprentice can be headstrong."

A grin appeared on Isa's face. "I thought she was your apprentice. She loves working with you."

She knew she might have gone overboard with the emphasis on 'loves', but Isa couldn't ignore the peculiar fascination Sylvia Ahlgren seemed to have for Timo. She suspected her of having a little crush on him.

Ignoring her statement, Timo asked, "So, what did you discover?"

"A message. Celeste didn't delete it. We tracked her calls and found she got multiple calls from an unidentified number in the last weeks before her death."

"Unidentified number?"

"Sivert, our resident IT wizard, couldn't trace it. He'll try again."

"Interesting," Timo mused. "What did the message say?"

"Actually, it's a song."

"A song? What type of song?"

"I knew it," Isa shouted and jumped up. "I knew you would be intrigued."

Timo scowled in annoyance, his mouth folding into an irritated expression. "It's not that difficult, since you're telling me the story anyway."

"So, you'll let me look into it," she said, almost out of breath. "We don't have many new cases anyway."

"Fine, fine... at least someone will be doing something interesting," he muttered, sighing as his eyes scanned the stack of papers on his desk.

"Is it really that bad?"

"I don't know what possessed me to take this promotion." He threw his pen down. "It's nothing but paperwork and politics. I miss the days when I could just go out and catch the bad guys."

"After all you went through to get this job. I can truly say that I speak on behalf of everyone when I say you're doing a great job. Paperwork is a small price to pay."

Timo rubbed his temples again. "I know, I know. But sometimes, it feels like we're making no progress amidst all this bureaucratic nonsense."

"I'm planning to talk to the Westerberg family tomorrow. Care to join me?"

"Maybe," he said, gracing her with a subtle smile. "After all this paperwork is done."

Isa made her way towards the doorway, but then hesitated, pivoting to face him. "Timo, I know you're swamped, but I have a favor to ask."

He glanced at her from the corner of his eye, furrowing his brow slightly. "Should I be concerned?"

"No, no, it has nothing to do with work. Just a friendly request."

"What is it?"

"My parents are throwing a party to celebrate their fortieth wedding anniversary in two weeks, and I was wondering if you could come along. See it as a late Christmas party."

Isa paused. Maybe it hadn't been such a great idea after all to ask her boss for this kind of favor.

Another frown appeared on his forehead. "Why?"

"I don't want..." She stopped and sighed. "Okay, they invited Viktor."

"Your ex-husband?"

"I can handle Christmas parties and birthdays. It's just me and them, but here... there are expectations. My mom still holds onto the hope of us getting back together again. She's absolutely thrilled now that Viktor and the kids are back in Gävle, thinking that maybe we could reignite those feelings... but..."

"You're not interested," Timo said.

She shook her head. "Too much has happened for that."

"And who or what am I supposed to be or do?"

"What do you mean?"

"Why do I have to come along?" he asked.

"Well... I just need a buffer."

"I have to play your boyfriend?"

"No. You're good at talking to people and maybe you can talk to my parents and Viktor a bit."

"So you don't have to," he said with a stern look on his face.

She really wanted him to come to the party—not just because her ex-husband would be there, but because it would show her parents that she had moved on. And maybe Timo could help smooth things over between Viktor and herself. It was complicated. There were still many feelings, but a romantic relationship she couldn't muster anymore. For that, they had grown too far apart.

"Please," Isa begged. "It would mean a lot to me."

She watched as Timo considered her request for a moment before finally nodding his head in agreement. "All right. I'll go, but on one condition."

"Name it," Isa said determined.

"If I ever need help with my mom... going to a party, concert, whatever, you'll help me."

"Sure, no problem," she smiled.

"Without grumbling," he said, raising his finger like a scolding parent.

Her smile became wider. "Maybe a bit of grumbling... but it's a deal."

"When's the big event?"

"Two weeks from now, Saturday at 2 p.m."

"Okay."

"And wear something different," she said, standing in the doorway.

"Why? What's wrong with what I wear?"

She sighed and before leaving she said, "I don't have all the time in the world."

* * *

Timo and Isa wandered through the Westerberg family home in Söderhamn, enveloped by its spacious luxury. Unexpected wafts of lavender danced in the air, a scent that triggered memories of Celeste, as her brother Max had told them. Max, tall and slender like Celeste with the same curious blue eyes, led the way with a solemn demeanor. Despite the sun's rare appearance outside, an aura of gloom clung to the air like winter clouds on a chilly evening.

The grand halls stretched before them, polished marble floors gleaming underfoot, adorned with an array of captivating paintings. Max guided the inspectors past these treasures until they reached the imposing double doors of their destination.

Upon entering, Mr. and Mrs. Westerberg greeted them, though their eyes betrayed their recent tears. Isa sensed their grief, yet the scene felt almost staged, as if meticulously choreographed to capture the essence of tragedy.

Mr. Westerberg, a stoic figure with piercing blue eyes and graying temples, exuded an air of quiet strength despite the defeat etched on his face. Beside him sat Mrs. Westerberg, renowned in Sweden's artistic circles for her crime fiction and media presence. Despite her age, she radiated vitality, her youthful appearance belying her true years.

"I'm sorry for your loss," Timo said after introducing himself and Isa.

"Thank you," Mrs. Westerberg replied softly, tears glinting in the corners of her eyes.

"We understand this must be difficult for you," Isa began, "but we need to ask you some questions."

"Are you finally going to treat this as anything but suicide?" Mrs. Westerberg interjected, looking directly at Timo and Isa.

"No one seems to take us seriously," she continued, frustration evident in her voice. "They write it off as suicide, an easy explanation to avoid digging deeper. But I knew my daughter better than anyone. She would never do this to herself."

"Annalisa," her husband interjected, then turned to the detectives without waiting for a response from his wife. "We'll assist you in any way we can."

The inspectors sat down opposite them, and Isa pulled out her notepad. "Can you tell us about Celeste?"

"We just don't understand it," Mr. Westerberg said, shaking his head. "Celeste was happy."

"But she wasn't always that happy," Isa said. "Five years ago, she went into therapy. Can you tell us about that?"

"She was always so driven since she was a child," Mr. Westerberg said after a long silence. "When she started playing the violin, there was nothing else in the world that mattered to her. She used to practice for hours every day, even when she was sick or tired. At first, we were proud of her dedication and talent, but then it became too much, especially when she started having success."

Tears welled up in his eyes now, and Mrs. Westerberg put a hand on his arm. "We tried talking to her about slowing down, taking some time for herself... but she wouldn't listen." He shook his head. "It got so bad that she began talking to herself, hallucinating, and becoming delusional. We had to act. She even turned violent."

"I remember reading about her involuntary admission to a mental hospital," Timo remarked.

"This was a year after her big success 'Aria 25'," Isa added.

"Yeah... the pressure was enormous to deliver another hit, and she couldn't handle it," Mr. Westerberg said.

"Celeste was released after just a month in the hospital, and the problems resurfaced. She believed someone was following her," Mrs. Westerberg explained.

"She was perfectly fine until the incident," Mr. Westerberg interjected, causing Max Westerberg, who had been standing by the window silently, to suddenly turn and look at his father with wide eyes. Up until that point, Max had been the epitome of composure.

"The burglary," Mr. Westerberg said and threw his son a quick glance, after which the young man seemed to relax a bit. "Our house got burgled. It happened in the night when we were at home. Celeste woke up and found someone in her room. The man attacked her. She could fence him off, but he escaped and until now the police never found who did it. After that, she didn't feel safe anymore and her mental health problems got worse."

"She went into therapy again, voluntarily, for a year, and then she started to rebuild what was left of her career," Mrs. Westerberg said.

"And was she doing okay?" Isa asked.

Mrs. Westerberg nodded and wiped away a tear.

"Coming back to the burglary," Timo said, "what was stolen?"

"Uh... nothing," the father said, "I guess Celeste caught him before he could take anything."

"Do you think it was real?" Timo continued.

"What do you mean? That she imagined it?" Mr. Westerberg let out.

"Did anyone else see the attacker?" Timo said calmly.

Isa noticed her boss was in full detective mode, freed from the burdensome paperwork on his desk, at least for a few hours.

"No, but...," Mr. Westerberg stuttered, glancing down at his hands. Perhaps the notion had crossed his mind before, but he had dismissed it

35

as irrational.

"It was all in her head, Dad," Max Westerberg asserted. "I've told you before, but you weren't willing to listen until it was too late."

"Too late? What happened?" Timo asked.

"Nothing in particular," Max replied, a tinge of sadness in his eyes. His voice remained steady and low, though he fidgeted subtly with his hands and avoided eye contact when Timo gazed at him. Isa could tell that this man was hiding something from them.

"We should have intervened earlier... now she's dead," Max continued.

In the next instant, doubt began to gnaw at Isa's thoughts. She felt a pang of empathy for Max's pain. His expression mirrored the agony of someone grappling with a recent and profound loss.

The ticking of the clock on the wall seemed to amplify the unfillable void they all shared. Max gazed out of the window, his eyes distant and tinged with sadness, as if on the brink of tears.

"She was doing fine," Mrs. Westerberg said.

Max turned to his mother and yelled, "No, Mom, she wasn't! But you and Dad were so obsessed with having her on that stage again that you didn't notice what was going on!"

He was ready to walk out the door when Mr. Westerberg jumped in front of him and said, "You don't get to speak to your mother like that. Apologize!"

Max sighed, looked his father straight in the eye, and then turned to his mother on the sofa, "Sorry... Mom."

Then he walked to the door and left.

"Did she appear depressed or anxious before she died?" Isa asked.

Mrs. Westerberg shook her head. "No, nothing unusual."

Then Mr. Westerberg interrupted, "Well, in that aspect Max was correct... she was enduring a difficult divorce."

"Alright, we'll speak with her husband," Isa declared. "What is his name?"

"Ex-wife," Mr. Westerberg responded with a hint of sarcasm in his tone. "I suppose it was just a phase she had to go through. I warned her from the start that woman was trouble. And look, I was right."

"What happened?"

"Her wife had an affair. I had a feeling something was going on, so I hired a detective to follow her. The pictures confirmed it."

"It seems you don't like your daughter-in-law," Timo said.

"A gold-digging vulture," Mr. Westerberg continued. "She was after our money."

"Please, Robert," his wife attempted to intervene and reach for his hand, only to be swatted away.

"Stop being a hypocrite," Robert said to his wife. "You didn't like her either. I wouldn't be surprised if that woman had something to do with Celeste's death!"

"And who exactly is that woman?" Timo asked.

"Alva Stendahl," Robert answered, sinking onto the nearby sofa beside his wife. "She's Lukas Stendahl's cousin. He's Celeste's manager. They're quite the cunning pair."

Puzzled, Timo pushed for answers, asking, "And what are they up to, you think?"

"Working their way into our family. He's less conspicuous than she is. He has charm and consideration, but both of them were manipulating Celeste. I believe she finally caught onto their true intentions."

"Are you insinuating that she terminated Lukas as her manager?"

Robert responded, "Yes... no... I'm uncertain. If she hadn't already, it was imminent."

"According to the other musicians she worked with, Lukas and Celeste had a superb working relationship. There were no indications that your daughter was planning to stop their partnership."

"Oh, he's a charlatan, just like Alva. They are responsible for her death."

Isa let out a sigh, glanced at the notepad in her hands, and then spoke, "Mr. Westerberg, there was no evidence suggesting anything other than suicide. I understand it's difficult to accept, but…"

"Then you idiots haven't looked hard enough," Mr. Westerberg spilled.

Timo got up. "We've thoroughly examined your daughter's case and unfortunately, the evidence points to suicide. That's it."

"I demand a new investigation!" Robert yelled.

"If you wish to file a complaint, I encourage you to consult your lawyer," Timo replied calmly, motioning for Isa to join him.

"I offer my deepest condolences once again for your loss," Timo said, nodded and then led the way to the exit with Isa by his side.

* * *

As they descended the steps towards Timo's parked car, a light but steady rain began to fall. Tiny droplets clung to their faces like teardrops.

"What do you think?" Timo asked, casting a thoughtful glance at his partner, before raising the collar of his coat to shield himself from the chilly breeze.

Isa paused for a moment before responding, "I'm not sure. Now, I'm leaning towards thinking Celeste's death might just be a suicide." She gazed at the sky, its gray clouds muffling her voice, and continued softly, "The Westerbergs were quick to place blame."

"Yeah," Timo agreed, pressing the car key to unlock the doors.

Isa settled into the car and added, "The son clearly disagrees with his parents' perspective on what triggered his sister's illness."

"It's easier for them to shift the blame onto others instead of accepting their own contribution to their daughter's mental health issues. But there's something about this family."

"Yeah," Isa replied from her seat next to him. "It doesn't sit right; we should investigate further."

Timo nodded in silent agreement.

"Why didn't you ask them about the message on her phone?"

"Not yet," Timo said, his gaze fixated on the darkened view outside. The rain relentlessly pounded against the car's windshield, creating a mesmerizing display of cascading water droplets that made it difficult to see outside. The occasional lightning illuminated the area briefly, casting a bright white light before fading back into darkness.

"Wow," Isa said, startled by the sudden burst of thunder.

"Besides... there's nothing really strange about that message."

"You think so?" she asked. "Why would anyone send her a recording of her own song?"

"A fan," he said.

A sudden burst of lightning illuminated the winter sky.

"Isn't it peculiar?" he mused, gazing out of the window once more.

"What do you mean?"

"A storm with lightning in the heart of winter."

She offered a faint smile. "This year has indeed been filled with strange things."

"Do you often think about Lars and Berger?"

She paused for a moment before answering, "Yes, I do, from time to time."

"How we let them down... how we couldn't bring the true culprits to justice."

"Timo, you can't dwell on that. Let it go. This is challenging enough. We need to move on. You'll see, things will get better in the coming year, in 2020."

Just then, Isa's phone vibrated in her pocket. Glancing at the caller ID, she swiftly powered it off.

"Aren't you going to answer that?" Timo asked.

"No... it's Ingrid."

Timo's stomach tightened, and he found himself momentarily speechless as he stared at Isa.

"I didn't think you would like it," Isa commented, returning the phone to her pocket.

"No, no, it's alright," Timo shook his head, his gaze fixated on the steering wheel as if he had never driven a car before and didn't know how to start it.

"By the way, she's doing well," Isa added.

"It's alright... really."

"I can see that," she said, a touch of sarcasm in her voice.

"I'm sure she's doing great. Teaching is her calling, after all. I assume she's excelling at it."

"You two are doing a fantastic job at pretending not to care," Isa remarked.

"Has she been talking about me?"

"What do you think?" Isa sighed. "You can call her, you know. I don't want to be the middleman all the time."

"No, no, I need to move on from Ingrid Olsson," Timo said firmly, inserting the key into the ignition. "Let's go back to the station."

CHAPTER

# 5

**SYLVIA FOUND HERSELF PERCHED** at her desk, eyes fixed on the computer screen. The article on Celeste Westerberg commanded her attention. The disconcerting feeling, lingering since witnessing Celeste's lifeless body on the pavement, refused to dissipate. There was an unsettling disconnect in the case.

As she delved into Celeste's history, Sylvia discovered she had been a young prodigy, playing and composing music from as early as four years old. Memories cascaded back—nostalgia from an era of carefree days with the creatives, a group of self-proclaimed artists on a mission to revolutionize the world. A smile escaped her.

Then her thoughts drifted to her time with the group, especially her connection with Bulgari, a young man she had once called her boyfriend.

United by a passion for the arts, they had shared creative aspirations. Despite their current divergent paths, Sylvia cherished warm memories of those days, discovering her artistic voice, and embracing her love for writing.

A lingering question emerged—was there a connection between Celeste's case and the creatives?

Her focus shifted to another article, which described an incident involving Dancho Krastev, Bulgari's brother, during a hiking trip organized by the creatives. The story unfolded, detailing the mysterious disappearance of a student in the same area where Dancho, injured but alive, was eventually discovered.

As Sylvia continued, she learned that Dancho and a friend encountered trouble while descending a treacherous cliff. The circumstances suggested the missing student might have sought help when the accident occurred. The rest of the group was absent during the incident.

"What are you doing?" Varg asked, leaning over her shoulder to peer at the computer screen.

Sylvia jolted in her seat. "Oh, just reviewing the Celeste Westerberg case."

Varg's expression grew serious. "I thought this one was already closed."

Sylvia hesitated. "I'm not entirely sure... maybe."

Raising an eyebrow, Varg settled into the chair on the other side of their shared desk. "I understand you want to impress Paikkala, but is this the right approach?"

"What do you mean?"

Varg gave her a sarcastic grin. "It's obvious. You've been working tirelessly on this case, as well as others in recent months, all to make a good impression. It's not just the cases; I've noticed the way you look at him and how you behave around him."

Sylvia's face flushed with embarrassment. "It's not like that. I simply want to do my job, and I don't appreciate your insinuations."

Varg chuckled, attempting to lighten the mood. "Relax, I was just joking. But he's an attractive guy if you're into that sort of thing. I mean, for you as a woman, not me... I'm not into..." Varg's words tumbled out, and his face turned red.

Instead of allowing Varg to dig himself deeper, Sylvia's embarrassment turned into anger. "That's not the point. This is my career, and I take it seriously. I don't want to be labeled as the detective trying to win favor with the boss. I want to be recognized for my dedication and my work."

There might have been a time when she had been interested in Timo Paikkala, just like some of the other women in the police station who found him attractive and had developed small crushes on him. But those feelings, if they had ever existed, had long been buried beneath her commitment to her profession. Now, her focus was solely on proving herself as a capable detective.

Varg closed his eyes, attempting to calm down, then raised his hands in surrender. "Alright, alright. I didn't mean to upset you."

Sylvia took a deep breath, trying to steady herself. Observing Varg, she sensed a sudden seriousness in his expression. "What's wrong?"

Varg hesitated before replying, "I just got an email about the inspector exam."

"I know," Sylvia said. "Isn't it exciting?"

Sylvia's heart surged with anticipation. This was it—the moment she'd been tirelessly working toward. With unwavering determination, she had poured countless hours into her detective career, studying, reviewing materials, and honing her skills. Now, poised and prepared, she stood on the brink of the next milestone: the exam to become an inspector.

"I know, but the thing is... I've never been a good student. I've always struggled with tests and exams," Varg admitted. "I know I'll screw up and fail. Maybe I'll just stay a sergeant. That's okay."

"What do you mean you don't want to take the exam? We've been preparing for it for months."

Varg looked at her with an awkward expression. "I know, but I just don't think I'm ready for it. I don't want to fail and make a fool of myself."

Varg clenched his fists under the table. Dyslexia had dogged him throughout his life, and the looming exam only intensified his anxiety.

He cursed his condition. Dyslexia had always been his closely guarded secret, buried beneath layers of shame and embarrassment. He couldn't bear to admit it to Sylvia or anyone else, not when his career was at stake.

Sylvia gazed at him with furrowed brows. "Varg, you're a great detective. You have a lot of experience and knowledge. That will help you in the exam. If you don't take it, you'll always wonder what could have been. You need to man up and seize this opportunity. Besides, you don't want me as your boss!"

A faint smile escaped him, and he turned to the screen of his laptop.

Isa strode in, sharp gaze scanning the room before settling on Sylvia and Varg. "And what did you find out?"

Varg looked up, confusion clouding his face. "Are we seriously going to look into this case?"

Isa crossed her arms, giving him an inquisitive look. "And you think we shouldn't?"

"Uh... it was suicide... no?"

Isa's gaze continued to linger on Varg, who grew more nervous by the second.

"Or maybe not?" he stammered.

"I'm not asking you to think, but to do what I ask you to do," Isa said. "So, what do you have?"

"I... uh," Varg stammered.

Sylvia intervened. "Celeste started to play the violin from a very young age. Four. It's unbelievable. I never knew, but by the time she was ten, she was already performing at cultural events and garnering attention for her exceptional talent. It's remarkable how someone so young could captivate audiences with such mastery. It was in her DNA. Her father was the conductor of the philharmonic orchestra until two years ago. She has played at the most prestigious venues all over the world, but it seems that the pressure to be perfect took a toll on her mental health."

"I was told it was a burn-out of some sort," Isa said.

"I don't have a lot of details. It happened just after her big hit, and the tabloids mentioned that it was likely the pressure of success. It might be good to get a court order to obtain her medical records. But what I do know is that five years ago, she ended up in a psychiatric hospital."

"Doesn't that suggest she had underlying issues?" Varg remarked.

"But the recent relapse was rather sudden," Sylvia countered.

Isa nodded. "Alright, we'll get a court order to access her medical records. In the meantime, let's talk to her friends and colleagues. See if anyone noticed any changes in her behavior recently. We need to figure out if this was truly a suicide or if there's something more going on."

"We won't get it that easily," Varg blurted.

Isa's eyes narrowed and a look of irritation appeared on her face. "Let's try it anyway. And what about her personal life? Any enemies?"

Sylvia shook her head. "From what I can gather, she kept to herself mostly. She had a few close friends in the classical music world. And as far as enemies go, there doesn't seem to be anyone who had a motive to harm her."

"And her marriage?"

"Alva Stendahl. They got married three years ago, but Celeste recently filed for divorce."

"And what about the message on her phone?" Isa asked.

"IT is still busy with it," Varg said. "But Sivert said he won't be able to trace them."

"Them? There is more than one?"

Varg acknowledged, "She received five of them in the weeks before her death. These were phone calls. Most of them were incredibly brief, except for the final one. It came from a different number, but Sivert couldn't trace that number either. They were all sent from prepaid phones. The only thing he can still do is try to locate where they came from."

Isa sighed, massaging her temples. "Alright, let's talk to Alva as well. Celeste's parents weren't too fond of their daughter-in-law. See if there were any issues in their marriage that could have contributed to Celeste's state of mind. And let's also look into her financials, see if there were any money problems that could have added to her stress." She turned to Varg, "Keep digging. I want to know everything there is to know about Celeste Westerberg."

"What's the boss' take on the amount of time we're spending on this case?" Varg suddenly interrupted.

"Let me handle the superintendent. Your job is to find out where those messages on her phone originated from."

"But Sivert said...," Varg stammered.

"I'm sure Sivert can work his magic." Isa met Varg's eyes with a serious expression. "And Varg, when I ask you a question, I expect a direct answer. Don't interrupt or question me... ever."

Varg nodded, his face flushing with embarrassment.

Then Isa turned to Sylvia. "You come with me. We're going to talk to some of Celeste's friends and colleagues. Maybe somcone knows something that can shed some light on this case. Let's work quickly, but thoroughly. Paikkala doesn't want us to spend a minute longer on the investigation than necessary."

\*\*\*

Timo stared at the towering pile of paperwork that seemed to mock him with its sheer size. It seemed to be never-ending. He missed the days when he was an inspector in Stockholm, working on cases that kept him on the edge of his seat. Now, as superintendent, he felt like he had become a paper-pusher. He felt a twinge of jealousy when he thought about Isa and the team out there, actively working on the Celeste Westerberg's case. He knew it was irrational, but he couldn't shake the feeling.

He remembered the interview with Celeste's parents and how energized he had felt by being out in the field, talking to people, trying to piece together what happened. He missed that sense of purpose, the feeling of making a difference. Now, he was stuck in his office, signing off on reports and delegating tasks to his team. It wasn't what he had signed up for.

But Timo knew he couldn't let these feelings consume him. He was in this position for a reason, and he needed to make the most of it. He couldn't let his personal desires cloud his judgement. He would focus on his work and find a way to make a difference in his new role. He reminded himself that there were still people who needed help, and that he had the power to make a change. It was just a matter of finding the right way to do it.

He let out a sigh of frustration, rubbing his temples to alleviate the building tension in his head. Just as he was about to dive into the endless sea of forms and reports, his phone rang.

He recognized the number as that of his old colleague, Kristina Rapp. Back when he had served as an inspector in Stockholm, they had been part of the same team—he as an inspector and she as a profiler. Throughout their time working together, their relationship had always been cordial, though Timo couldn't ignore the lingering, unspoken feelings Kristina had for him. He had made it clear to her on various occasions that he only thought of her as a friend, but it seemed that her feelings had never truly faded.

He picked up the phone, trying to keep the unease out of his voice. "Kristina, how are you?"

There was a moment of silence before she said, "Good."

Silence again.

There was a sense of dread building in his stomach as the silence stretched on. Timo knew Kristina well enough to realize that she was not one to engage in small talk. Whatever she had to say was likely significant, and the prolonged silence only heightened his concern.

Finally, she spoke up. "Timo, it's been a while. I was thinking... I'll be in Gävle in a few weeks from now. Maybe we could have dinner together."

"Of course. When and where do you want to meet? Let me invite you to my house. I'll cook."

Kristina hesitated for a moment before replying, "Uh... I'm not sure that's such a good idea."

Maybe she was right. He remembered the last time he had cooked for her, and the outcome hadn't been great. Moreover, he wasn't entirely certain if inviting her into his home was the wisest decision. A knot tightened in Timo's stomach as he attempted to decipher the unspoken subtext behind Kristina's words. It was clear that there was something she was holding back.

"Is everything okay? Is there something you need to talk about?" he asked.

"Everything is fine," Kristina said quickly, but Timo could hear the hesitation in her voice. "I just wanted to catch up with an old friend, that's all."

He wasn't convinced, but he didn't press the issue. He didn't want to make Kristina feel uncomfortable.

He made plans to meet with her and then hung up, but he couldn't shake the feeling of unease that had settled in his stomach. Every time they met it ended in some sort of drama.

Then he quickly glanced at his watch. With a drive to Uppsala that would take approximately 1.5 hours, he realized he needed to get moving. He quickly gathered his belongings and made his way to his car. Another meeting, courtesy of Police Commissioner Eriksson, loomed on the horizon—this time about budget allocation. His lack of thorough preparation weighed on his mind as he slid into the driver's seat.

As he drove to Uppsala, Timo thought about Kristina and the strange phone call, but he tried to push the thoughts out of his mind. He'd better focus on the upcoming meeting with the Police Commissioner, but his mind drifted back to the slender woman with sad eyes.

Kristina and he had a lot in common. Their shared love for hiking and climbing had brought them closer. She stood as the only person who hadn't condemned him when he had turned to racing to cope with the pain following his girlfriend Caijsa's death. But after her heartfelt confession of love, he had made a conscious effort to keep his distance.

The windscreen wipers swept back and forth, battling the relentless raindrops on the car's windshield as he navigated through the stormy weather. Gävle was no stranger to rain, but today it felt especially bleak, mirroring his somber mood. Anticipation weighed on him as he approached the meeting with the Police Commissioner, well aware that the ongoing budget reallocations had become a contentious issue among the departments.

Rumors had been swirling for months about significant reductions affecting some departments, and he found himself unprepared for the potential outcomes. To make matters worse, he was aware of the animosity brewing between him and Eriksson. It wasn't just the Police Commissioner; he suspected the entire administration under Prime Minister Olav Hult held some resentment toward him, and there was a valid reason for it. Timo knew Eriksson's secret. It was a double-edged sword hanging over him, as Eriksson could potentially use it against both Timo and the Gävle police department if their differences escalated any further. The uncertainty made every interaction with Eriksson feel like walking on a tightrope, and Timo knew he had to tread carefully in the meeting.

The fact that Eriksson hadn't removed him as superintendent remained a puzzle to him. Perhaps he still served a purpose, but he felt that there was more to the story, especially after the tumultuous events of the past year.

He looked at the road in front of him. It was busier than usual, and he sighed. He was going to be late. Stress. He knew that it would take all his negotiating skills to try and secure the budget for his department.

But maybe it was pointless. Eriksson probably had made up his mind already.

# CHAPTER

# 6

ISA AND SYLVIA ARRIVED AT THE Royal College of Music in Stockholm and proceeded to the room where Zelia Flodin was conducting a class.

"Isa... Inspector Lindström," Sylvia stammered as they walked through the corridor.

Isa furrowed her brow and fixed Sylvia with an inquisitive gaze. Sylvia appeared nervous, and her hesitation raised Isa's curiosity. "What's on your mind, Sergeant Ahlgren? I thought we were past calling each other by rank."

Sylvia took a deep breath, gathering her thoughts. "Sorry. It's just... I didn't tell you everything about my connection to Celeste and her friends.

I knew them better than I let on."

Isa stopped in her tracks and looked at the young woman. "What didn't you tell us?"

"I was part of the creatives for a short while. One of Celeste's friends, Boris Krastev, was my first boyfriend, but we broke it off after a few months."

"And is this going to be a problem?"

Sylvia shook her head quickly. "No, it happened a long time ago, and I don't see how it could be relevant to the case. But I thought you should know."

Isa studied her for a moment. "Fine. We'll talk about it later. Right now, let's focus on finding out what Mrs. Flodin can tell us about Celeste Westerberg."

Isa and Sylvia continued down the corridor in silence until they arrived at the classroom. They paused, peering through the glass panel in the door. Inside, they saw a room filled with students, each with their instruments in hand, all under the watchful eye of Zelia Flodin.

Zelia was a remarkable figure, middle-aged, tall, and thin with a stern expression that commanded respect. She stood at the front of the room, her arms crossed, as she listened to the young girl playing the piano. The girl was talented, but she made mistakes, and Zelia stopped her immediately.

"No, no, no! You're playing it wrong," Zelia scolded the girl. "You need to pay more attention to the score, or you'll never get it right."

The little girl was no more than twelve years old, with curly brown hair and bright blue eyes. Her hands shook as she tried to play her piece on the piano, but Zelia Flodin was quick to spot another mistake.

"Stop, stop, stop!" Zelia slammed her hand down on the piano, making the little girl jump in her seat. "What is this, Antonia? I expect better from my students. Do you want to be a mediocre pianist for the rest of your life?"

Tears were now starting to form in Antonia's eyes, but she tried to hold them back as she stammered an apology.

"I... I'm sorry, ma'am. I... I'll practice more."

Zelia sighed. "Practice is important, but so is passion. You have the talent, Antonia, but you lack the drive. You must want it more than anything. Do you understand? You need to put more effort into it. Otherwise, you're wasting my time and yours."

Isa and Sylvia watched as the girl tried again and again, her hands shaking with fear. Zelia was relentless in her criticism, never letting up until the girl finally got it right.

"Much better," Zelia said, her voice cold and unfeeling. "Now, let's move on. You've already wasted enough of my time."

"Wow," Sylvia whispered as she continued to watch the girl, who returned to her seat among the other pupils. None of them offered any sympathy or support. It was clear that Zelia Flodin ran a tight ship, leaving no room for compassion among her students. They saw each other as competitors.

"Yeah, there's a thin line between constructive criticism and bullying," Isa said. "Not sure what this one is. And I can see how Celeste Westerberg became such a successful musician, but it's a tough world. It can break someone."

"You might be right," Sylvia said, her eyes still fixed on the young pianist. "Talent alone isn't always enough in these competitive fields. It takes resilience and a strong spirit to endure the pressures. Maybe that's something Celeste and her friends learned the hard way."

"So, let's talk to Mrs. Flodin," Isa said and opened the door.

The classroom had emptied by then.

As they entered the room, Zelia turned to face them. "Can I help you?" she asked, her voice a mixture of annoyance and curiosity.

The women introduced themselves. Zelia listened carefully, but she was clearly not happy about being disturbed. "I have another class in fifteen minutes."

"I'll make this quick," Isa said. "We'd like to ask you a few questions about Celeste Westerberg."

Zelia's expression darkened at the mention of Celeste's name. "Celeste? What about her?"

"She died recently," Sylvia added.

"Yes, I saw it on the news. But it was suicide, no?"

"We're investigating the circumstances surrounding her death," Isa explained. "We'd like to gather any information you might have about her time here at the Royal College of Music."

Zelia hesitated for a moment, her eyes darting away as if contemplating her response, "She was a student of mine many years ago, but she was never quite up to par."

Sylvia looked surprised. "Can you explain what you mean by that? It's quite surprising since Celeste Westerberg was regarded as one of the shooting stars in classical music."

"Celeste was talented, there's no denying it," Zelia said. "But she was weak. She didn't have the drive or the passion that a real performer should have. She was never meant to make it in this business."

Isa raised an eyebrow. "What happened to her?"

"She had a burn-out," Zelia said, without a hint of empathy in her voice. "But that was to be expected. The world of classical music is tough. It's not for the faint of heart."

Isa was not satisfied with Zelia's answer. "Do you think Celeste's burn-out was because of the pressure you put on her?"

Zelia's eyes narrowed. "I push my students to be the best they can be. If Celeste couldn't handle the pressure, that's on her, not on me."

"And this happened about five years ago?"

"Indeed, five years ago. She left the college and disappeared from the public eye."

"After her great success 'Aria 25'?"

"If you can call it a success... it was an abomination. No classically schooled violinist would ever consider that pop-infested nonsense as a legitimate form of music. If Celeste had chosen to stay true to the classical genre, I might have respected her choice. But no, she had to involve her friend, Freya Younggren—an artist of mediocre talent who eventually faded into obscurity."

"It did achieve considerable popularity, though," Sylvia pointed out.

Zelia scoffed. "Popularity doesn't equate to quality. Celeste may have fooled the masses with her gimmicks, but true musicians know the difference."

Isa decided to change the subject. "You mentioned that Celeste disappeared from the public eye after leaving the college. Do you have any idea what she was up to during those years?"

"No idea. But there were several incidents before and after her alleged burn-out. Some believe she may have fabricated it to stay in the spotlight."

"Incidents?" Isa asked.

Zelia sighed, clearly annoyed. "Celeste was always a difficult student. A diva. She tended to break down and make a scene. It was all quite embarrassing, to be honest. I'm sure you understand."

"What scenes?" Sylvia asked.

Zelia rolled her eyes. "Oh, she would start crying in the middle of a performance, or she would have panic attacks before a concert. She was a mess. I'm not sure what she thought was going to happen."

"And was there anything particular that triggered those scenes?"

Zelia sighed and glanced over at her class. She noticed a group of students standing in the open doorway. With a subtle wave of her hand, she signaled for them to stay outside a moment longer. The students exchanged puzzled glances but obediently remained in the hallway. "There was one incident where Celeste claimed she was being stalked," she said. "I considered it nonsense at the time."

"Stalking? Do you know more?"

"Celeste claimed that someone was following her and even broke into her room," Zelia said. There was a hint of amusement in her voice. "But I never saw any evidence of it."

"Did she report the break-in to the police?" Isa asked.

"She did. But nothing was ever found. They concluded that it was probably just her imagination."

Sylvia scribbled a few notes in her notepad as Isa continued to probe. "Did you ever see anyone suspicious around the college or in Celeste's neighborhood?"

"No. It was all just a figment of her imagination. I told her that many times, but she never listened. She was always so emotional, always overreacting."

Zelia glanced at the students lingering in the hallway.

"Celeste wasn't like her father," Zelia continued with a sigh. "She had the talent, but not the drive. Her father, on the other hand, was mediocre at best, but he had the ambition to make it to the top. He was known to be the most successful conductor in Sweden, and even beyond. He was a hard man, but he knew what he wanted, and he wouldn't let anyone get in his way. He pushed Celeste to be the best she could be, but it was all for his own gain. Her success was his success."

"And how did Celeste feel about that?" Isa asked.

"She hated it. She wanted to make a name for herself, to prove that she was more than just her father's daughter. But in the end, she couldn't handle the pressure. She was weak."

Isa's frustration and anger towards Zelia grew with each passing moment. "What about friends? Did Celeste have many friends?"

Zelia shrugged. "There are no friends in this world. Everyone is too busy competing against each other. Celeste may have thought she had friends, but they were just using her for her connections or her talent. She was a fool to trust anyone in this business."

Isa thought about how lonely this must be. To be constantly surrounded by people, but never really having anyone to turn to for support or comfort. It was a harsh reality of the music world, and it made her grateful for the close-knit relationships she had in her own life.

"The creatives," Isa mentioned, quickly glancing at Sylvia. "Have you ever come across that name? Did Celeste ever mention that?"

"Creatives? What's that? No, should I have?"

While Sylvia continued to make notes in her notepad, Isa shot Zelia a stern look, and ignoring the woman's questions, she said, "Alright. Thank you for your time, Mrs. Flodin. We won't keep you from your class any longer."

As the detectives exited the room, Zelia turned to the students waiting in the doorway. "Don't just linger there. Come inside. We've wasted enough time as it is."

\* \* \*

As Isa and Sylvia made their way to their car, they shared a moment of contemplation about their interview with Zelia Flodin.

"That was quite an experience," Sylvia remarked. "I can't believe how harsh she was to her students."

"No wonder Celeste struggled with mental issues," Isa added, still feeling the frustration from their conversation with Zelia. "Being in such a cut-throat environment all the time must be incredibly isolating."

"But it does seem to yield results. Celeste became one of the most successful classical musicians of her generation."

"At what cost, though?" Isa asked. "Success loses its meaning if you can't enjoy it."

As they settled into the car, Isa's mind buzzed with lingering questions. Was Celeste's burn-out solely due to her weakness, or did Zelia's pressure play a role? And could the dismissed stalker incident be linked to her time at the college? Their investigation had suddenly spawned more questions than answers.

With her hands on the wheel, Isa turned to Sylvia before starting the car. "Dig into the stalker incident. Mrs. Flodin brushed it off, but it might be crucial. We need to determine if Celeste was genuinely being stalked and if it played a role in her death. But I must admit, I'm not entirely convinced we have a case here. Pressure and competition are present in every profession, and not everyone can cope."

Sylvia sighed. "I understand. Thank you for considering my perspective. I'll respect your decision and Inspector Paikkala's, should you decide to close the case."

With that, Isa started the car, and they drove away.

* * *

"You shouldn't have called me," Ingrid said.

"I know, but I just wanted to hear your voice," Timo sighed. "I just wanted to know how you were."

Silence followed.

"The whole point was that we wouldn't see each other anymore."

He knew that. He knew all of that, but he couldn't deny that he woke up every morning with a deep sense of loss and longing for her. It was almost like she had died, and that he had to live with the knowledge that he would never see her again. He couldn't bear the thought.

"I miss you," he finally said.

"I miss you too. But we can't do this. We can't keep torturing ourselves like this. Why are you calling? Is there something wrong?"

"Everything is so different. Einarsson is great, but he's not you."

"I know," she said. "I am irreplaceable."

A faint smile appeared on his face. "Yes, no one can replace you."

"Timo... my life is at peace now. Every time you call, it takes me days to recover. That's what you do to me. It takes so much energy."

Silence.

She continued, "I saw you sitting outside my house again. Timo... this has to stop."

He knew she was right. He knew that what they were doing was wrong, and that it would only lead to heartbreak... again. But the pull of their connection was too strong to ignore. He longed to hold her in his arms again, to feel her skin against his, to lose himself in the warmth of her body. But he knew he couldn't have her, not like that. Not now.

"You're right," he said. "I'm sorry."

"It's okay. I understand. But we must be strong, for both our sakes. We can't keep doing this to ourselves."

They couldn't keep living in the past, holding onto a brief affair that was never meant to be. They had to move on, to let go of the past and embrace the future.

But it was easier said than done.

"Maybe you just need to go out there," she said. "Start dating again."

It was like a knife to Timo's heart. He had tried dating after their breakup, but it only made him feel more alone and it reminded him of what he had lost.

"Isa is alone," she continued. "You two are good friends."

He frowned. "Are you trying to set me up with Isa?"

Silence followed.

"I need to go," she said softly. "Take care of yourself, Timo."

He said goodbye with sadness in his voice and put the phone down.

Then he walked over to the big floor-to-ceiling windows of his house overlooking the lake. He wrapped his arms around himself, trying to keep warm in the chilly winter air that seeped in through the glass. Although it was winter, this year had been unusually mild, with hardly a glimpse of snow and temperatures rarely dipping below freezing.

The lake lay before him, still and serene, with only the distant cawing of crows and the occasional rustle of branches in the unseasonably warm weather. Despite the absence of snow, the view remained enchanting. The lake seemed to stretch out endlessly, as far as his eye could reach. Above, the sky was an expansive canvas of gray, its clouds thick and laden with the promise of more rain rather than snow.

He felt a sense of calm come over him as he gazed outside. The world was so still and quiet, it was almost like time had stopped. For a moment, he forgot about his worries and fears, about the pain of longing for someone he could never have.

For a moment, he was at peace.

\* \* \*

The school building was an old, imposing structure, with tall brick walls and large windows that let in a flood of natural light. The floors were made of polished wood, and the walls were adorned with colorful posters and artwork made by the students.

As Isa and Viktor walked down the hallway, the sound of their footsteps echoed off the walls, adding to the feeling of nostalgia that was already building inside Isa. The smell of chalk and pencil shavings filled the air, bringing back memories of her own school days.

It wasn't the same school Isa had attended as a child, but the familiar sights and sounds made her feel like she was thrown back in time. She could almost hear the sound of the school bell ringing, signaling the end of class, and the chatter of students as they made their way to their next class.

She glanced over at Viktor walking next to her. It was strange. After one year being back in her life, it still surprised her how she wasn't used to seeing him with the gray hair. He was still a beautiful man, but he was more reserved, guarded as if she had to cross a barrier to reach him. The memories of their marriage and the hurt that came after still lingered in the air, like a heavy fog that refused to lift. Yes, there was still something about him that stirred up old feelings inside her.

She remembered the days when they were married when they had been happy and in love. But those memories were tainted by the pain and hurt that had come later. She had left him and their children. Viktor had taken the children to the UK and had tried to build a life there for five years until it had all come crashing down.

She had loved him once, and a part of her still did. But she knew that it was too late to go back to the way things had been.

She felt a twinge of guilt and regret. She had hurt him deeply by leaving, and she knew that the wounds would never fully heal. But they had both made their fair share of mistakes, and Isa knew that they had a long way to go before they could truly move forward. But the fact that they were here, together, walking down the hallway of their son's school, was a small step in the right direction.

As they approached the classroom, Isa pushed all those lingering feelings and emotions aside.

The teacher greeted them warmly and invited them into the classroom.

"As you know, I've been keeping a close eye on Felix," the teacher started. "He is a truly gifted child. Based on his IQ test and the school evaluation from his time in the UK, which Mr. Clausen has provided to us, we've already advanced him. Today he's in the fourth grade, just as Olivia. But his intelligence and passion for science and mathematics are remarkable. I believe he has the potential to achieve great things, and I want to make sure we are providing him with the appropriate opportunities to foster his growth."

"What are you saying?" Isa asked.

"I'm proposing we advance Felix another year in his studies and place him in a new group of children of different ages who share his interests and can challenge him further," the teacher explained.

Viktor and Isa exchanged a look.

"That sounds like a great opportunity for Felix," Viktor said. "What would this imply?"

"Well, it would mean that Felix would be studying more advanced material and interacting with children who are older than him. But I believe he is up for the challenge," the teacher replied.

"I'm not sure," Isa said. "He's so young. And what about Olivia? How would that affect her when she sees her younger brother being ahead of her?"

The teacher nodded. "It's important to consider the impact on both children, which is why we've carefully assessed Felix's readiness for advancement. We'll also provide additional support and resources to help Olivia continue to grow and learn at her own pace."

Viktor interjected, "What kind of resources are we talking about? And how will Felix interact with the other children in the advanced class? He might feel out of place or isolated."

The teacher, Mrs. Anderson, was a middle-aged woman with a warm and reassuring presence. Her hazel eyes sparkled with enthusiasm as she spoke about Felix. "We have a plan to introduce Felix gradually to the new environment and ensure that he feels supported and included. As for resources, we have several programs and partnerships with universities and research centers that can provide him with challenging opportunities and access to advanced technology."

"Universities? He's only nine." Isa looked at her hands. She felt proud and sad at the same time. Felix was growing up so fast. She could hardly keep track of him. She had already missed five years, and now she couldn't catch up. Felix with his gentle and angelic features. Never a bad word, no arrogance or frustration in his demeanor. Patient, polite and understanding.

He was the perfect kid.

Olivia was another story. The progress she had made with her daughter had been disappointing. Olivia still held it against her that she had left them. It would take time. A lot of time.

The teacher continued, "I understand your concern, but believe me I know Felix's potential. We won't overwhelm him, but rather, we'll create an environment where he can thrive academically while still enjoying his childhood. Next to that, I also wanted to mention that Felix showed a keen interest in artificial intelligence. He even looked up an article and webinar by a certain... Alexander Nordin. I was impressed by his curiosity and passion for the subject."

The rest of the words Isa hadn't heard anymore. She felt like she was in a daze. The mention of Alexander Nordin had thrown her off completely. She tried to focus on what the teacher was saying, but her mind kept drifting off to memories of Alex.

Why was she there again? In that dark place full of pain and heartache. This couldn't be a coincidence. Felix had deliberately searched for Alex's work. But how did he know? She couldn't remember if she had ever mentioned his name to Felix. Every memento she had of him, she kept in her bedroom, close to her.

"Isa?" Viktor's concerned voice cut through her distraction.

"Uh... okay. Yes."

Viktor leaned closer to her. "Is everything okay?"

Isa took a deep breath and tried to compose herself. "Sorry. I just got lost in thought for a moment. What were you saying?"

"We should first talk to Felix about this," Viktor said.

Isa nodded, but she already knew her son would be over the moon. It was she who still had so many questions and doubts weighing on her mind.

"You look distracted," Viktor said as they walked back to the exit.

"Uh... sorry," she whispered.

He looked at her with doubt in his eyes, not sure if he wanted to talk about the subject on his mind. "So, Felix knows about Alex Nordin."

She stopped in her tracks and quickly turned to him. "Alex? How do you know?"

"Your mother," Viktor said.

"Mom? Since when..."

"Look, Isa, I don't want to meddle. But are you okay? You seem down."

"Yeah... I'm okay."

"If you want to talk, I'm here," he said.

She nodded but didn't say anything.

"Your mother invited us to their party. If you don't want me or the kids to be there, then I'm okay finding an excuse not to go," he said.

She smiled and put her hand on his arm. "No, you should come. She's been looking forward to spending more time with Felix and Olivia, and she really wants to see you."

Then she looked at her watch. "Shit. It's that late. I have to run. I have a meeting with Timo."

"Isa...," he said, watching as she disappeared around the corner.

He was alone now, with nothing but his thoughts. He felt a pang of sadness and frustration, knowing that there was still so much distance between them. The steps they had taken were small, maybe too small. But he had to be patient. He couldn't risk overwhelming her and having her run away as she had so many times. He was happy to see that she was building up a relationship with Felix, although it had largely been initiated by Felix himself.

He sighed, buttoned up his coat and walked to the exit with a steady pace.

* * *

"So?" Timo asked.

"I'm not sure," Isa replied, sinking into the chair.

Timo leaned against his desk, arms crossed. "What did you find out?"

"Not much," she sighed.

"Isn't it time to close this case?" Timo looked annoyed.

"That message on her phone is still playing through my head."

"No one was able to trace it. Likely it was some sort of prank."

"But the other messages?" she stammered.

"They might not be linked, and we have no reason to assume they had anything to do with her death."

"Zelia Flodin, Celeste's teacher, talked about a stalker. He could have sent the message."

"I looked at her file. There was nowhere mentioning of a stalker."

"People don't always report these things."

"She went into therapy five years ago. We got parts of her medical file. Her psychiatric report talks about a burn-out attributed to her perfectionism and self-imposed stress, nothing about a stalker."

"Sylvia and I want to talk to Alva Stendahl, Celeste's wife or rather ex-wife," Isa said.

"No, Lindström, I'm closing this case."

"But Timo..."

"Move on," Timo said and dropped into his chair. "We have a burglary and an assault that need your attention."

It was useless to argue with him. Timo had always been a no-nonsense guy, and once he made up his mind, it was difficult to change it.

She walked toward the door.

"Is everything okay?" Timo asked suddenly.

Isa turned around, her hand on the doorknob. "Yes, everything's fine," she said with a smile that didn't quite reach her eyes. "Just a little tired."

As she stepped outside, she turned back. "You won't forget my parents' party next Saturday, right?"

He looked up and then said, "No, I won't. We still have some time to

65

decide, but shall I pick you up?"

"Yeah... that would be nice," she said.

"At one or is that too early?"

"That's okay," she said and walked to her desk.

Why was she so irritated? Was it Celeste Westerberg or just the fact that after meeting with Felix's teacher she almost had a meltdown? Being reminded of Alex, Viktor's considerate words, Felix's progress. Everything felt like it was slipping away from her. For once, she could do without men in her life.

She thought of Timo. Maybe it was a bad idea to ask him to her parents' party. Who was she kidding? He wasn't interested in her.

* * *

The man's heart raced as he meticulously arranged the array of medical instruments on the cold, stainless-steel table. The glinting surfaces of scalpels, clamps, and drills seemed to whisper promises of agony and suffering. His gloved hands, trembling with anticipation, caressed each tool, relishing the malevolent power they held. Weeks and months of meticulous planning and skill honing had brought him to this moment. The imminent torment filled him with a thrilling dread, the anticipation almost unbearable as he braced himself for what was to come.

But this was not just about the thrill. It was about revenge. Deep-rooted and consuming, a need to make someone pay for the sins committed. He closed his eyes, letting the haunting memories flood his consciousness.

Celeste had been a mistake. A miscalculation in his pursuit of retribution.

This time, he couldn't afford any mistakes.

Ascending the stairs, he sealed the door to the basement, his satisfaction unmistakable at the sight of the neatly arranged instruments.

Returning to the living room, he gazed out the window, raindrops cascading down like tears from the heavens. He sighed, enjoying the calm that hid the darkness inside.

He then seated himself at the table and reached for the recorder, pressing play. The room echoed with the haunting notes of 'Aria 25'. He shut his eyes, envisioning the guitar strings dancing. Yet, when a man's emotionally charged voice emerged, cracking with raw intensity, he couldn't bear it and turned it off. A deep sadness enveloped him. How could his mood shift from freedom and joy to these unsettling thoughts of anger and pain in the blink of an eye?

No, this wasn't his fault.

They made him do it.

Opening his eyes, hands steady now, he smiled. The stage was set for his twisted work, but patience was his ally. He couldn't rush this, he had to wait for the best moment, the perfect chance to unleash his vengeful masterpiece.

CHAPTER

7

**TAMARA ENTERED THE BUSTLING** emergency call center, where a constellation of calls lit up the wall monitors—a map of medical crises, fires, and pleas for police assistance across the city. Phones rang incessantly, voices melded in a chaotic symphony, making coherent thoughts elusive. Committed employees navigated the cacophony, handling calls with a blend of concentration and compassion.

It was Tamara's first night shift, and a hint of nervousness tinged her anticipation. She approached two colleagues wrapping up their shifts—a guy typing away and a woman finishing tasks under the harsh fluorescent lights.

"Hey there," Tamara greeted with a warm smile. "How's

everything?"

The woman responded with a bright smile. "Hey, Tam. Good to see you. It's been tough this afternoon. We're short-staffed."

Tamara scanned the room. "Isn't Orvar here?"

The woman sighed and shook her head. "No, he called in sick."

"Damn," Tamara muttered, hanging her coat on a peg. She settled into a chair beside the woman, feeling a twinge as the armrest pressed against her side. Had she gained weight? The chairs seemed smaller. She glanced at the chocolate in her bag, hesitated to take it out, and then decided to place the bag on the floor.

Unease about her appearance crept in. Her relationship with Pelle, her boyfriend, was strained, and she found refuge in food. Despite her conviction that looks didn't matter in love, Tamara faced the harsh reality that they did. She still saw herself as the chubby girl struggling to keep up.

She often wondered why Pelle, with his striking looks and bright mind, hadn't left her yet.

She gave in. The chocolate bar called to her, but just as she reached for it, her phone buzzed. Pelle's name lit up the display. She hesitated but chose to ignore it. They had a massive fight, fueled by pent-up frustrations. Tamara needed time and space to sort things out.

"Tamara, we're waiting for you," the supervisor called out.

"I'm coming," she replied, tucking her phone back into her bag.

* * *

Tamara rubbed her eyes. The quiet night shift had lulled her into a drowsy stupor, but an unsettling energy now hung in the air, as if a storm were gathering.

Dimmed lights barely revealed the figures next to her; even her friend Amanda's face was shrouded in shadows, deep lines etched on her forehead as she listened intently to the caller. Thoughts of Pelle crossed

Tamara's mind. Was he still angry? She took a sip of coffee and stifled a yawn.

How would she stay awake through the night? This was harder than she had anticipated.

A sudden ring pierced the silence, snapping Tamara back to reality. Her headset pressed close, she curtly answered, "Emergency services. What is your crisis?"

Fatigue tinged her words.

Silence on the other end—a void filled only by unsettling heavy breathing and crackling static.

"Hello?" Tamara asked, a sense of danger crawling over her.

No response. The crackling noise intensified.

"Hello? Is anyone there?" Tamara repeated, her anxiety rising.

A distorted voice broke the silence, "Help me... please."

The voice sounded familiar.

Fear gripped Tamara. "Sir, where are you?" Her fingers raced to trace the caller's location.

"Help me... help me."

In the background, a song played.

"Tell me where you are! What's your name?"

A chilling scream echoed, replaced by another one and then laughter. Tamara's stomach turned. "Who is this?"

A deep voice mocked, "Well, well, it's you, Tamara. Too bad. It would have been so much more fun if it were Amanda." The screen displayed the caller's location: Hälsingegatan in Gävle.

Tamara turned to Amanda, who was staring at her. "Isn't that where you live?"

Amanda quickly looked at the screen and stammered, "Yes... that's where I live."

"Tell Amanda Jukka says hi," the man said, and the connection snapped.

Tamara was paralyzed. It took her a few moments before she could think straight again. "I have to tell you that... Jukka says hi," she mumbled, removing the headset.

"Jukka? My husband? What's wrong with him?" Amanda demanded.

Tamara shrugged, unable to explain. Amanda turned the chair to face her. "Tell me!"

"The man... he told me... Jukka says hi... there were screams," Tamara stammered. She still couldn't wrap her head around it.

"What happened?!" Amanda yelled. The desperation was clear in her trembling voice.

\* \* \*

On a crisp winter morning in Gävle, Varg arrived at the scene. His car glided to a slow stop outside an elegant home on Hälsingegatan. Stepping out, he surveyed the surroundings before heading towards the door with determined strides. Snowflakes descended gently from the sky, resembling tiny white feathers as they lightly brushed against his face and vanished into the air.

At last, there was snow, making it feel like winter had truly arrived.

The door to Amanda and Jukka Ulfsson's house stood wide open, its bright red paint stark against the dull gray exterior walls. The area around the house bustled with activity, as police officers worked diligently, collecting evidence.

It all felt somewhat surreal.

As Varg entered, he nearly collided with some of his colleagues who were busy dusting for fingerprints, taking photographs, and measuring various aspects of the scene. He stepped aside and observed their meticulous work. Someone handed him plastic shoe covers and gloves, mentioning that he should wear them if he didn't want Dr. Einarsson to kick him out of the house. It made him feel like a rookie again. He complied, donning the shoe covers and gloves before making his way through the hallway to the kitchen.

There he found Dr. Einarsson, who looked up quickly when he heard Varg enter. The doctor was kneeling beside a blood smear on the floor, next to a small black table. One of the two chairs was tucked neatly under the table, while the other was oddly placed in the center of the room, where most of the blood appeared to be concentrated.

Varg didn't know for sure but there was a slight hint of disappointment in the doctor's face when he saw Varg.

The kitchen was in chaos. Pots and pans were strewn about the floor, blood spattered everywhere. It was clear that a struggle had taken place here.

"What did you find, doctor?" Varg said.

"I hope you didn't mess up my crime scene," the doctor said and then put his attention back to the blood. He ran a swab over the bloodstain and put the sample in the forensic kit next to him.

A second time, Varg felt stupid and inadequate.

"There is so much blood," Varg said.

Dr. Einarsson stood up. "Mr. Ulfsson was probably attacked here. The rest of the rooms are unscathed."

"What's going on with the chair?"

Dr. Einarsson looked at it for a moment and then turned to Varg. "He was likely standing behind the cooking hub, given the mess over there, when he was attacked and then he was put on this chair and..."

"Tortured? There is a lot of blood."

"Might be."

Varg scanned the room and then let out a sigh. "This looks like a normal family. A young couple without children. Why would anyone do this?"

Dr. Einarsson straightened his back, his sarcastic grin still in place as he replied, "What I've learned in all these years on the job is that nothing is ever normal. These people have secrets."

"Maybe whoever did this chose a random victim," Varg ventured.

"Less than 10% of crimes that occur in the victim's home are committed by strangers," Dr. Einarsson countered.

"But it's still 10%."

Dr. Einarsson shook his head. "As far as I understand, the man who abducted Jukka Ulfsson knew his wife and where she worked. This was no stranger."

* * *

Tamara's hands were shaking, trying to make sense of what had just happened. She felt sick. All she wanted to do was go home and forget about it ever happening.

"Tamara, I understand you're in shock," Isa said, taking a seat beside her.

Everything in Tamara's head felt hazy, with few details remaining from the disturbing phone call, even though it had happened not so long ago.

"It's okay," Isa reassured her, placing a comforting hand on Tamara's arm. "We know this must be difficult for you, but we need your help to catch whoever abducted Jukka Ulfsson."

Tamara nodded, still struggling to find words amidst the chaos in her mind. She then asked, "How's Amanda?"

"My colleague Sylvia is talking to her. Don't worry. So, you started your night shift at 11 p.m. Is that correct?" Isa inquired.

Tamara confirmed with another nod.

"Was there anything unusual that night?"

"No," Tamara let out. "Well, it's my first night shift."

"Why is that?"

"I... need the money. My boyfriend and I have plans to renovate our house, and this pays a lot."

"Who else knew you'd be answering the calls tonight?"

Tamara shrugged. "My supervisor, some of the colleagues." She let out a sigh and then said. "But it doesn't matter. There was no way the man could have known who'd answer the call."

"How are these calls dispatched?"

"Calls are typically dispatched in the order in which they are received, with more serious emergencies being dispatched first, but it was a quiet night so all the people who were free at that moment could have gotten the call."

"You told my colleagues he knew your name."

"Yes, he did." A chill swept through her as she recalled the way the voice had spoken her name.

"Did you recognize the voice?"

Tamara narrowed her eyes. There was something, but she couldn't quite pinpoint what it was. The voice itself wasn't familiar.

"No, but it was like the voice wasn't real, like it was twisted," she explained.

"Was it altered with a voice modulator?"

Tamara shook her head. "No, but it did feel like he intentionally changed his voice."

"And the other man?"

Tamara swallowed a few times, the memory of the screams still vivid in her mind. "That man sounded terrified. He kept screaming for help, over and over again. I didn't recognize him at first, but I think it was Jukka."

"Can you remember anything else that Jukka or the other man said? Anything at all that might give us a clue about where they were or who the other man was?"

Tamara swayed her head slowly from side to side. "I'm sorry. It all happened so fast, but I can bring up the recording."

"Then let's hear it," Isa said and closed her notebook with a snap.

Tamara turned to the screen and waited a few moments before pressing the keys on the computer. She opened a folder, and a long list of recordings were displayed.

"Let's see... it was around 1 a.m.," she said and let her gaze go over the files. "This one must be it."

Suddenly she turned to Isa. "Should I be worried? Maybe he'll come for me. My parents, Pelle..."

Isa gave her a reassuring smile and then said, "Look, Tamara, there is no indication that it was targeted to anyone else than Jukka Ulfsson."

"But what if... he knew my name," Tamara stammered.

"He used you to draw attention to what he was planning to do. Like you said, it could have been anyone else in this room."

"But then he knows us," Tamara said.

Isa straightened her back and looked at the young blonde woman who was sitting a few meters away from her, talking to Sylvia. "That tells us he's familiar with the call center and the people who work here. Tamara, let me hear the tape."

Tamara turned to the screen and pressed the button. Her own voice echoed through the room, "Emergency services. What is your crisis?"

Silence lingered, and then her repeated questions if someone was there. The desperate cries for help from the man sounded through the speaker, causing Isa to jump up.

"You're right," Isa said. "The voice seems unnatural. Like it's been altered or distorted in some way."

Tamara nodded, her own sense of unease deepening. The atmosphere in the room had shifted from confusion to something more unsettling.

"What's that in the background?" Isa exclaimed. "Can you replay?"

Tamara quickly pressed a few buttons, and the recording played again. As they listened attentively, the faint sound of music, like someone playing a guitar, became more apparent in the background of the call.

Tamara hesitated, her brow furrowing. "That's strange. I didn't notice it at the time. I know this song."

Isa leaned in closer to listen. "Me too." Then she turned around and called for Sylvia.

When Sylvia joined them near Tamara's desk, Isa requested the emergency dispatcher to replay the recording. "We need to get this analyzed as soon as possible," Isa stated. "It reminds me of the message we found on Celeste's phone."

Sylvia's face turned serious, and she began, "I have to tell you something."

Isa met Sylvia's gaze, her eyes filled with concern, prompting her to go on.

"Jukka Ulfsson was part of the creatives. He knew Celeste Westerberg very well."

"And only now you're telling me this," Isa said in a stern voice.

"I'm sorry... I didn't think it had anything to do with Celeste."

Isa's irritation was evident, but she swiftly regained her composure. "Play it again," she directed Tamara.

Tamara, still feeling perplexed by the unexpected revelation, nodded and replayed the recording as Isa instructed. The eerie call played once more, with the unnaturally altered voice and the haunting background music. The deep voice of the man filled the air around them and then the recording stopped.

"Sylvia, do you recognize this man's voice?" Isa said.

"I... he sounds strange," Sylvia said. "I don't think so, but..."

Isa got up and walked over to where a frightened Amanda Ulfsson was sitting.

"Celeste Westerberg," Isa said. "Does that name sound familiar to you?"

"Uh... yes," Amanda said and wiped a tear from her face.

"How do you know her?"

"I don't, but she used to be one of Jukka's best friends."

"Used to be?"

"They're not so close anymore. Not that they had a fall-out. They just grew apart. But they used to be very good friends at one point. It was before my time. And... it's strange but Jukka got a call from Celeste weeks ago, before she died."

"Do you know what it was about?" Sylvia asked.

"No, he didn't say, but he was cranky after that... for days."

Isa turned to Sylvia. "You were right. There is more to the Westerberg case than we know."

# CHAPTER

# 8

"**ATTENTION EVERYONE!** We have an abduction on our hands," Timo declared, addressing the room filled with police officers. "The next 24 hours will be crucial. We don't know what the abductor's intentions are, but we need to assume they're not good. We want to find this man alive."

Isa placed a picture of Jukka Ulfsson on the whiteboard and swept her gaze around the room, taking in the assembly of Varg, Sylvia, and a group of uniformed police officers. Varg occupied the seat beside Sylvia, who was completely engrossed in her note-taking, meticulously capturing every detail Timo provided.

Varg admired her dedication, even finding himself briefly entertaining the notion of a certain fondness for Sylvia. Pushing aside these fleeting thoughts, he refocused his attention on Timo, who continued to recount the events from just eight hours ago. The weight of fatigue hung heavily over everyone; it was already 9 a.m., and they had all managed precious little sleep the night before.

Varg observed Isa, noticing the tension in her demeanor. He knew she and Sylvia had clashed a few hours earlier, though the details remained unknown to him.

"Jukka Ulfsson, 27 years old. He lives in Gävle with his wife Amanda, and he was abducted from his home last night," Timo explained and pointed at Jukka's picture. The image portrayed a happier time, with Jukka smiling alongside Amanda. He was a blond man with a neatly trimmed beard that lent him a somewhat older appearance than his actual age. In the picture displayed on the whiteboard, his blue eyes looked directly into the camera. Many would say he was handsome.

"So, the call came in around 1 a.m.," Isa interjected. "There's a witness who saw a white van parked in front of the house around that time."

"Who's the witness?" Varg asked.

Isa's attention was momentarily drawn to Dr. Einarsson, who had quietly slipped into the room and now leaned against the wall. His sharp gaze scanned the space, lingering briefly on Sylvia, who remained unaware of his presence, her back turned to him. Varg, however, had noticed.

The mere presence of Dr. Einarsson always stirred feelings of inadequacy in Varg. He harbored a distinct aversion to the man. In contrast, memories of Dr. Ingrid Olsson, his predecessor, brought forth warmth and fondness. With Einarsson, Varg often found himself at a loss for words, struggling to find common ground.

In Sylvia, Varg saw a stark contrast to himself. She fearlessly challenged Dr. Einarsson and asserted her own perspective without hesitation. While their differences sometimes led to tension within the team, Varg admired Sylvia's strength and determination secretly wishing he could embody the same traits.

"One of the neighbors came home from a party," Isa said. "He was drunk, but I think we can use him as a credible witness. And no, he didn't recall the license plate number."

"Do we know when the van was parked there?" Varg asked.

Isa shook her head. "The neighbor arrived home around 1 a.m. Soon after that, he heard the car leave. So, we don't know how long the vehicle must have been there."

Dr. Einarsson interrupted, "When I investigated the bloodstains in the kitchen, some were partially dried up. Given the amount of blood and the fact that the kitchen floor is made of ceramic tiles, I'd say Mr. Ulfsson was attacked hours before the call was made."

They all looked at him in surprise.

"The amount of blood in the splatter, the surface where it fell, and the temperature and humidity of the crime scene all influence how rapidly this occurs," he continued as if he felt the urge to give them a lecture about bloodstains.

"Dr. Einarsson, that's interesting but...," Isa said, but he interrupted her again.

"But the bloodstains in the middle of the room, next to the chair, were more recent. It supports the idea that the victim was sitting in the chair and then likely was tortured."

"Or he continued bleeding from the wounds he sustained when the attacker overpowered him," Sylvia said with a straight face.

Dr. Einarsson furrowed his brow and gave her an air of arrogance before saying, "Regardless... the attacker spent at least a few hours in the house before abducting Mr. Ulfsson in his van."

Timo sighed. "There was a lot of blood. Do you think he's still alive?"

"I don't want to speculate. It depends on what injuries he sustained, but yes, he might still be alive. I only don't know for how long."

"So, we need to be quick. We need to know if the van was picked up by any of the cameras in the area. Before and after Jukka Ulfsson was kidnapped. Which direction did he come from? Which direction did he go? We need to check with neighbors, family, colleagues. Was there anything unusual the last days, weeks and even months? Varg, Sylvia, that's for you. And don't forget the wife's colleagues. The kidnapper knew where she worked and when she would be at work. Meanwhile, police in Sandviken and Uppsala have been warned about the abduction. I want the perpetrator caught. I want him held accountable. We're going to move fast, and I know we're going to catch him. And Isa, you and I need to talk to the wife again. This case might be linked to Celeste Westerberg's suicide. We need to know how."

After Timo's words they got up and scattered to each of their areas.

"So, it's going to be you and me," Isa smiled. "I knew you couldn't stay behind your desk."

"A man's life is at stake," he said with a serious expression.

* * *

The interrogation room was a cramped, windowless chamber, its stark white walls enclosing a solitary table and three chairs at its center. Silence hung thick in the air, broken only by the voices of Amanda and the detectives as they exchanged words. Unseen but ever-watchful, a camera perched on the ceiling recorded the scene silently.

"Where is Jukka?" Amanda let out. "Did you find him? What happened?"

Amanda was a few years older than her husband Jukka. She possessed a striking presence. Her blonde hair cascaded in loose waves down to her shoulders, framing her face with a touch of maturity. She had expressive hazel eyes that carried a mix of fear and determination.

Despite her age, she exuded a sense of strength, a testament to the resilience she had built over the years. Amanda had harbored great dreams and hopes when she was younger, but the passage of time had left her in a monotonous, low-paying job. Life had turned out to be far less exciting than she had imagined.

She loved her husband, but both had experienced their fair share of disappointments in life, which had tempered their once-bright aspirations into more subdued realities.

"We're doing all we can to find him," Isa tried to reassure her. "I understand this is incredibly difficult for you, Amanda, but we need to gather some information. It might help us locate your husband. Every detail you can provide, no matter how small, could be crucial in bringing him back safely." Isa's eyes locked onto Amanda's.

"Ask me anything, and I'll do my best to help."

"Did you notice anything unusual in the days leading up to the abduction?" Isa asked, casting a quick glance at Timo beside her.

Amanda pondered for a moment and then shook her head. "No, nothing out of the ordinary. But Jukka was on edge, more nervous than usual."

"Why was that?" Timo inquired.

Amanda shrugged. "I don't know... well, Jukka always had arguments with his dad. His dad owns the garage, but Jukka wanted to sell it. His dad doesn't want to."

"So, this created a lot of tension?" Isa probed.

"Yeah," Amanda admitted with a sigh. "But not to the point that... Do you think his dad and brother could be involved in this somehow?" Her voice quivered with worry as she considered the possibility. "They are family."

"How is your financial situation?" Timo interrupted.

Amanda hesitated. After a moment, she reluctantly confessed, "Uh... not good. Jukka had debts. Some wrong investments and gambling debts.

That's actually why I had to go back to work." She couldn't hide the anxiety in her voice as she revealed this aspect of their lives.

"Can you tell us who Jukka might have owed money to?" Timo leaned back in his chair, his icy blue eyes fixed intently on the woman sitting in front of him.

"Just some people down south... in Uppsala," Amanda stammered. "Oh, God, did they abduct Jukka?"

"Who?" Timo pressed.

"A guy called Andreas," Amanda replied hesitantly. "Andreas Lundqvist. But I didn't know it was that serious."

Timo's expression darkened as he recognized the name. "Andreas Lundqvist. He leads the Mörkbroder gang in Uppsala. He's a very dangerous man."

"Amanda, how did Jukka get involved with that man?" Isa said. "And did Jukka ever mention receiving any threats or demands from them?"

"I don't know much, but it must have been two weeks ago when Jukka came home. He had a black eye and scratches on his face. He didn't want to talk about it at first, but after a while, he said he owed Andreas Lundqvist and the Mörkbroder gang money."

"Did you ever meet Andreas Lundqvist? Could it be his voice Tamara heard during the call?"

Amanda shook her head. "I don't know him. I never met Lundqvist. Until the moment Jukka told me about him, I didn't even know he owed him money."

"How much money does Jukka owe him?"

Amanda gazed at her hands. "I don't know."

"Can you tell us who knew you'd be working the night shift on the day Jukka was abducted?"

"My supervisor, Tamara, and of course, Jukka knew."

Isa pressed further, "No one else?"

"I guess most of my colleagues knew. The timetables are distributed among everyone a week in advance."

"Amanda, can you tell us about your relationship with your colleagues? Is there anyone who might have had a grudge against you or Jukka?"

"No... of course not. I don't know all of them that well, but I have no fights with anyone."

"You consider Tamara a friend?" Timo asked.

"I wouldn't call her a friend, but she is a nice colleague. She's always very helpful. It's sometimes hard on her."

"Why?"

Amanda hesitated for a moment. "Tamara has been going through a tough time. Her boyfriend, Pelle, doesn't respect her. They've been renovating a house together, but Tamara's the one who has to take care of everything. They don't have a lot of money, so it's been a real struggle for her."

"They don't have a lot of money?" Timo repeated.

"Yeah," Amanda said with surprise in her eyes. "Do you think she... no, it can't be. Why would anyone..."

Timo disregarded Amanda's questions and shared a fleeting glance with Isa, signaling the necessity to redirect the conversation. Isa then positioned her phone on the table and started the playback.

"Help... help me," a man pleaded, accompanied by the playing of music in the background.

Amanda's complexion turned pale as she absorbed her husband's distressing appeals for help. The mixture of fear and concern etched across her features, and she grappled to restrain the tears. "That's Jukka. I already told you. Why do you play this again?"

But Isa shifted her focus to the music. "Do you recognize it?" She pressed the replay button.

Amanda shook her head. "No."

"This is a guitar rendition of Celeste Westerberg's 'Aria 25.' It's quite unique. No one seems to have ever heard this particular version of it," Isa said.

As the conversation unexpectedly turned toward Celeste Westerberg, Amanda's initial sadness morphed into annoyance. A frustrated expression etched itself across her features.

"What do you know about Celeste Westerberg?" Timo intervened.

"Nothing," Amanda replied curtly.

Timo's probing continued, "What about the creatives? Ever heard about them?"

Amanda's response was punctuated by a mocking laugh. "The creatives? Oh, my God, seriously. That's ages ago. Jukka told me about it. They were all so young and naive."

Timo maintained his stern gaze, his features locked in an expressionless mask.

"Are you serious?" Amanda stammered. "Do you think the creatives have anything to do with Jukka's disappearance?"

"What do you know about them?" Timo pressed.

Amanda's irritation with the line of questioning was unmistakable as she answered, "You see, they were all just teenagers back then—unbelievably naive on one hand and ruthlessly ambitious on the other. But... Celeste was the only one who really made it and look where she is now. Dead. They all had dreams of success and fame, but... Jukka ended up working in his dad's garage. That Bulgarian guy—I met him only once—is working for his family in a supermarket. His brother, well, he's like a plant... half dead. One of them just disappeared, vanished without a trace. And that woman Celeste shared her biggest hit with? She ended up a drunk and a drug addict, and no one has any idea where she is now."

"So, Jukka had no contact with his former friends anymore?" Isa inquired.

A dry chuckle escaped Amanda's lips. "Friends? In the end, I very much doubt if you could still call them friends."

Timo leaned forward, his hands resting on the table. "Why was that?"

"From what Jukka had told me," Amanda began, "it seemed they had a huge fall-out after the drama."

"What drama?" Timo probed.

"I mean... after Celeste's success. They were young and dreaming of the big time. But then the disagreements started, egos clashed, and friendships turned sour. Money came into play."

"I see," Isa interjected. "You mentioned Celeste called Jukka a few weeks ago. What was it about?"

Amanda looked down at her hands, then shook her head. "I don't know, but Jukka was upset."

"What did he say or do?" Isa pressed.

"He didn't say much. But he ran off, took the car, and only came back in the middle of the night. He never told me where he went. And he never spoke of it anymore."

"Okay," Isa offered Amanda a sympathetic smile. "If you remember anything else that could help us to find Jukka, please don't hesitate to contact us."

Amanda nodded, her eyes reflecting a mix of emotions. "I will. I hope... you find my Jukka."

Isa nodded, rising to open the door as Amanda exited the room. Timo and Isa remained behind in the silence.

Timo broke the quiet first. "Did you get the feeling that Amanda was holding back something?"

"Definitely. Her reactions, especially when we mentioned the creatives and Celeste Westerberg, were unusual. She knows more than she's letting on."

Timo leaned back in his chair, deep in thought. "We need to dig deeper into this creative group and Celeste's history. There is a connection."

"I'm on it. But first, there's something you should know," Isa said.

Timo frowned. "What?"

"Sylvia... she was once part of the creatives. She knows them. I can take her off the case."

Timo contemplated the dilemma for a moment, then sighed reluctantly. "Or?"

Isa leaned in. "Or we can use her knowledge to our advantage. She can help us navigate this group and gather information. It could be crucial to the investigation."

Timo sighed, considering the potential consequences for a moment, but then relented. "Alright, but... don't make me regret this."

Isa flashed him a bright smile. "Of course you won't regret it."

But deep down, he wasn't so sure.

# CHAPTER

# 9

JUKKA SLOWLY OPENED HIS EYES, and immediately regretted it. His head throbbed with a sharp pain shooting through his temples. He groaned, attempting to lift his hand to soothe the ache, but the realization struck—his hands were bound to the chair's arms. Panic surged as he struggled against the tight ropes.

Trying to take deep breaths to calm himself proved challenging with the pain and confusion clouding his thoughts. His vision blurred, his eyes swollen from the beating he had endured. Vague memories of being attacked in his kitchen floated in his mind, hazy and disjointed.

Surveying the dimly lit room, Jukka heard muffled voices in the distance, resembling a TV. The source seemed elusive, perhaps emanating from above. Was he trapped in some sort of basement?

The room was stark except for the chair he was sitting on and a table in front of him, adorned with a small lamp. Another table stood against the wall, its contents unclear in the dim light.

Footsteps echoed, and Jukka tensed. He tried to turn his head, but the pain in his neck was too much to bear.

As the footsteps grew louder, a figure appeared, shrouded by bright light, obscuring the face.

"Hello, Jukka," the figure greeted.

He didn't recognize the voice, but there was something eerily familiar about it. Fear overwhelmed him. He had never felt so alone and vulnerable in his life. The realization that he was at the mercy of someone willing to hurt him was too much to bear. The pain in his head and neck paled in comparison to the horror he felt. "Who are you? What do you want?"

"Don't play dumb. You know what you did."

Bewildered, Jukka had no inkling of the man's accusations. "I really don't know."

Then the music began. Familiar notes and a voice, slightly different than he remembered, triggered a rush of memories.

A puzzle piece clicked into place.

And then it stopped.

"Do you now know what I'm talking about?" the deep voice asked.

"I don't understand," Jukka stammered.

"I want you to tell me."

Jukka shook his head. His words sent a shudder down his spine. Still clueless about his supposed wrongdoing, he pleaded, "I swear, I don't know what you're talking about."

But frustration surged as the man accused him of lying.

"Fine. We'll do this the hard way, then."

The man turned, walking back towards the door, muttering

something under his breath.

Jukka slumped back in the chair, his head spinning with confusion and fear. He had no idea what was going to happen now, but he knew it wasn't going to be good. He tried to calm himself down, to think of a way out of this situation, but his mind was a jumbled mess.

The room echoed with the clinks of metal as the man rummaged through the tools on the nearby table. Jukka strained to see, but the neck pain thwarted his efforts. The distinct sound of a blade being unsheathed sent a jolt of terror through him, realization dawning on the impending horror.

He screamed out in terror as the man approached him with the blade, and he heard the man laugh in response. The sound chilled him to the bone. He knew that he was in for a world of pain, and there was nothing he could do to stop it.

"Jonathan!" Jukka cried out in desperation. "Please."

As the other man stopped and Jukka sensed his shock, the sudden silence was broken only by the sound of heavy breathing. It was a tense moment, with adrenaline surging through both of them. Jukka could hear the rapid rise and fall of the other man's breath.

Jonathan. He didn't even know why he had called that name.

The next moment, the blade sliced through the air, and Jukka felt a searing pain as it cut into his skin.

He felt his consciousness slipping away.

The pain became too much to bear.

\* \* \*

As the officers filled the meeting room, tension hung clearly in the air. Isa took her seat at the head of the table, her gaze scanning the faces of her team. Timo sat to her right, his jaw set in a firm line. Varg and Sylvia flanked the other side of the table, their expressions equally grave.

The meeting room itself was austere, with plain white walls and a long table in the center. The only decoration was a large whiteboard mounted on one wall, currently empty besides a hastily scrawled timeline of events. The lighting overhead cast an unflattering glow on the officers, highlighting the bags under their eyes and the tension lines around their mouths.

Isa cleared her throat. "All right let's get started. As you all know, Jukka Ulfsson has been missing for 24 hours, and we need to find him."

The room grew even quieter if that was possible. Varg shifted in his chair, his eyes darting around the table. Sylvia sat with her arms crossed, her gaze fixed on Isa.

"So far, we don't have much to go on. Varg, where are we with the white van?" Isa continued.

Varg took a deep breath and leaned forward, resting his elbows on the table. "The neighbor was correct. Traffic cameras show that a white van was seen driving away from the neighborhood around 1 a.m. The CCTV showed that the van likely arrived there around 11 p.m., just after Jukka's wife had left for work."

He paused for a moment, letting the information sink in. "But we've also checked the days before the abduction, and it seems the van was already seen in the neighborhood."

"Do we have a license plate?"

Varg nodded. "We do. But the owner had reported it stolen months ago. And the face of the driver isn't visible on the footage."

Isa reclined in her chair, her forehead creased. "That doesn't provide us with many leads. What about witnesses?"

Sylvia spoke up, "We've spoken to everyone in the area, but besides that one neighbor no one saw or heard anything unusual."

Isa let out another deep sigh. "We need to broaden our search. I want every centimeter of this neighborhood canvassed, and I want everyone on high alert. We don't know what we're dealing with, but we need to be prepared for the worst."

"Why would anyone abduct this man?" Sylvia started. "Ransom?"

Isa quickly looked at Timo. "We've scheduled a press conference in an hour from now. Inspector Paikkala will be present to address the public and provide updates on the investigation. We'll also have Amanda making a plea to the captors to release her husband."

"I doubt it'll help," Varg let out.

"We need to try."

"I'd look into the wife again," Timo said. "It's not the first person who hires someone to get rid of an annoying husband."

"She looked genuinely upset," Sylvia said.

"Einarsson said Jukka was attacked hours before the call. She could have attacked him just before going to work and an accomplice could have called the emergency center," Varg interrupted.

"Maybe, but why the drama? There are other ways to get rid of a husband."

Varg looked at Sylvia with confusion on his face.

Then Timo said in a stern voice, "I'd have another chat with her regardless."

"Jukka is relatively tall and well-trained. What I don't understand is how one man can overpower him and put him in the van... alone?" Varg asked, glancing at his colleagues to gauge their reactions.

"You're suggesting there was more than one abductor?" Timo inquired.

"Exactly."

"It's a valid route to look into," Timo acknowledged.

"Maybe organized crime? Jukka Ulfsson was arrested six years ago for possession of drugs," Isa said. "Their financial situation is bad. A huge number of debts. Gambling according to his wife, and he owes Andreas Lundqvist a lot of money. Andreas Lundqvist runs the Mörkbroder gang in Uppsala. They are involved in various criminal activities, including drug trafficking, extortion, and money laundering. I wonder if Jukka's involvement runs deeper than we initially thought."

"We can talk to Andreas Lundqvist," Varg suggested.

Timo frowned. "Talk to Lundqvist? You don't engage with that man without risking more than just a conversation. He's not exactly renowned for his chattiness. Plus, you'd need to locate him first. He's on the list of the most dangerous criminals in Sweden. No, we should approach this situation differently. But I fear that if Lundqvist has Jukka, he might already be dead."

A moment of uneasy silence settled in the room.

"What about the recording?" Varg said. "The music. That doesn't sound like a criminal gang would do."

Isa's attention shifted to the man who had just stepped into the room. It was a rare sight to see Sivert not clad in his usual stained T-shirt adorned with Darth Vader, the fabric straining over his growing belly. Instead, he sported a sharp look: a pristine white shirt paired with sleek black pants and shoes, a laptop bag casually slung over his shoulder. He looked almost unrecognizable. Was he off to a job interview? Then it hit her—he had been invited to deliver a lecture at the forensic conference in Uppsala.

Everyone in the room was as surprised as she was, but she stopped herself from making a joke about it. Instead, she said, "Tell us what you found."

Sivert pulled out his laptop and set it on the table. "I managed to enhance the audio from Celeste's phone," he said while opening a file. "But it's still pretty garbled, and I can tell that it's been manipulated."

He paused for a moment, glancing around the table at the faces of the other officers. "Parts have been left out. I did manage to retrieve some metadata, but it's been intentionally scrubbed clean. There's no way to trace where the recording came from or who tampered with it. Not yet." He looked up at Isa. "I'm sorry, I wish I had more."

Isa sighed, running a hand through her hair. "Thanks for trying. We appreciate it." She turned to the rest of the team. "We'll have to work with what we have. Keep digging, keep looking for any leads or evidence."

Then she said, "Sylvia, can you stay for a moment?"

\* \* \*

"Jukka, Jukka, I'm not sure what game you're playing," the man's voice sliced through the tension. "But you can't keep this up. Sooner or later, you'll break."

Jukka felt like his hand was ablaze, waves of agony coursing through his entire being. It was nearly unbearable. Desperately, he tried to maintain steady breaths, but the pain was overwhelming, pushing him towards hyperventilation. His gaze fixated on his hands. Where once there was a finger, now remained only a gruesome, bloody stump.

Drawing closer, the man's presence loomed over him, breath hot against Jukka's face. "Tell me what I want to know," he growled, twisting one of Jukka's remaining fingers.

"I've told you everything!" Jukka's scream pierced the air.

"Nine more to go... and then, your wife..." The man's threat hung in the air, chilling Jukka to his core.

"Leave her out of this!"

"Then you know what you have to do."

\* \* \*

"You knew Celeste and Jukka," Timo said, looked down at Sylvia and crossed his arms.

Sylvia had been working long enough at the police station to know that he wasn't happy.

Before she could answer, he continued, "Why didn't you tell us before?"

"I did," she stammered. "As soon as I realized there could be a link between them, I told Inspector Lindström."

Isa moved closer to where Sylvia was sitting. "Tell us everything you know. They were part of the creatives, right?"

Sylvia nodded. The name just sounded so naive and ridiculous now.

"How long were you part of the group?"

"Just a few months. Bulgari and I..."

"Bulgari? Like in the fashion company?"

Sylvia gave her a faint smile. "It's a joke. We called him like that because his family came from Bulgaria, and he was always loaded with jewelry. He took good care of himself. He was... good-looking. He wanted to be an actor. Now he's working in his father's grocery store." She quickly looked at her hands. "Not all dreams come true, I guess."

"You and Bulgari were a couple," Isa continued. "When was that?"

"It was only for a few months. He was a bit of a player. I was sixteen and pretty naive. After we broke up, I remained on the periphery of the group."

"Who was in the group?" Timo asked.

Sylvia could tell he was losing his patience.

"Celeste, Jukka, Freya Younggren, Celeste's best friend at that time, uh... Bulgari—his real name is Boris Krastev—his brother Dancho, Celeste's brother Max and... Jonathan Gedman. Yeah... Jonathan."

As she spoke Jonathan's name, her gaze drifted into the distance, as if drawn by the pull of a long-forgotten memory. She hadn't thought of Jonathan for a long time, not until she had pulled up the article about his disappearance.

"So what happened?" Isa asked.

"I don't have all the details, but there was definitely a fair share of drama," Sylvia said.

95

"What kind of drama?"

"Both small and big drama," Sylvia explained. "Celeste, she was always at the heart of it. She had this magnetic quality, drawing people toward her. But she was incredibly hard on herself, fiercely dedicated to her ambitions of becoming a classically trained musician. I remember her performing the violin in school plays. It was sheer magic. After graduating from secondary school, she went on to compose that incredible hit, 'Aria 25,' blending pop and classical music. It was a massive success."

"And then she disappeared from the scene," Timo added.

"Yes. But what still surprises me until this day was that she asked Freya to take the vocals. Freya was a good... no, mediocre singer, but not brilliant. Strange choice. Anyway, Freya moved away. I don't know where she is right now."

"And what about Bulgari?" Isa quipped, a sly smile quirking the corners of her lips, a reaction that seemed to be universal whenever the name was brought up.

"As for Bulgari, I told you already. He had dreams of becoming an actor, but besides a few plays with the local theatre group, he never quite succeeded. His brother Dancho is a few years younger, and he always looked up to his older brother. Their childhood was tough. They were both born in Sweden. Their father had come to this country with his wife and her sister about ten years before Bulgari was born. Tragedy struck when they lost their mother in a horrific car crash, and since then, their aunt has been looking after them."

She remembered the aunt, a stern, severe-looking woman, who had been aged by both the weight of tragedy and the passage of time. The aunt had a reputation for being tough, unforgiving, and highly judgmental. It seemed that, in her eyes, no one was ever good enough for the family she had devoted her life to. Her protective nature and exacting standards had cast a long shadow over the lives of Bulgari, Dancho, and their father, making their upbringing even more challenging. And Sylvia had experienced it first-hand. She still believed that because of her she and Bulgari had broken up.

"Jukka?"

"Jukka," Sylvia said and frowned. "I never quite figured out why he was there. It took him two years more to graduate than all of us. He wasn't particularly smart."

"He was convicted for dealing drugs when he was twenty," Timo said. "Can there be a link?"

"You mean... if he was supplying the group with drugs?" Sylvia asked.

Timo shrugged.

"I don't think so," Sylvia said. "But I don't know much about him."

"Tell me about Jonathan," Isa interrupted.

Sylvia drew in a deep breath, memories of Jonathan Gedman flooding her thoughts. "He was a writer and a composer—poems, books, songs. He's... no longer with us."

"How?"

"It was a terrible accident. You can read the news clippings. The group was on a weekend trip in Höga Kusten. It was an incident involving Dancho, Bulgari's brother, and Jonathan. They went off on their own in the morning and encountered trouble while descending a cliff. Nobody knows what really happened, but Jonathan vanished. Just like that."

"What about Dancho? He's still alive, right?"

"He's in a coma since the accident. He has never spoken about it. At that time, everyone thought Jonathan might have ventured off to seek help and that something happened to him. His body was never found."

Timo turned to Isa. "Check with Västernorrland County. They likely have the full case file."

Isa nodded and then turned to Sylvia again. "You said Max Westerberg was part of the group?"

"Yes and no," Sylvia said calmly. "He was there to keep an eye on

Celeste. That much was clear."

"Why did she need a chaperone?"

Sylvia's voice held a hint of uncertainty as she continued, "I don't know... it was a weird relationship, I must say. It was almost like he was... jealous. He wanted to have Celeste all for himself."

"Older brothers can be overly protective sometimes," Isa said.

But Timo's stern expression hinted at his disagreement. It was a well-known fact around the police station that he had a troubled relationship with his own brother, Fredrik. The mention of sibling dynamics seemed to touch a sensitive nerve for him.

In a sudden rush of memories, Sylvia found herself thinking of her own brother. It caught her off guard, and she wished it hadn't surfaced so unexpectedly. Erik, her younger brother, had displayed an exceptional sensitivity, unable to navigate the pressures of life. He had always been a gentle soul, easily overwhelmed by the world around him. His struggles with his sensitivity led him down a dark path, ultimately succumbing to the grip of addiction. Despite desperate attempts by family to intervene, his addiction tragically spiraled, culminating in a fatal overdose at a young age.

Only seventeen. For some it seemed ages ago, as if he had never existed. For her, it was like yesterday that someone had torn a piece of her heart away, leaving a void that time couldn't seem to fill.

As Sylvia reflected on the cherished bond she had shared with Erik, she reclined in her chair, lost in memories of their childhood and the inseparable connection they had forged. As confidants and best friends, they had spent countless hours delving into their passions and aspirations.

But the weight of Erik's premature passing lingered heavily on Sylvia. She couldn't shake the feeling of guilt for failing to recognize the signs of his silent struggle until it was too late. The burden of her past mistakes weighed heavily on her mind as she pondered Max and Celeste's situation. Perhaps, she mused, Max had only wanted to support and protect his sister. Like she should have done with Erik.

Maybe, that was all there was to it.

"Timo, it's time," Isa's voice suddenly cut through her thought process.

"Shit, the press conference," Timo said, quickly grabbing his jacket from the chair.

"What do we do in the meantime?" Isa asked.

Timo paused for a moment. "Investigate them... all of them," he said, before rushing out of the room and into the hallway.

\* \* \*

Amanda was constantly looking at the man next to her. Timo was nervous too, although he should have been used to it, given the events that had happened in the last year and a half. The room was filled with reporters, cameras, and a sea of expectant faces. He began with a general description of the ongoing investigation, providing an overview of the case's developments and the efforts made by the police force to solve it. His words were measured, delivered with a sense of purpose, and a backdrop of urgency. He knew exactly what to say without saying anything.

As he continued, the room remained hushed, the collective attention of those present focused on the updates. He talked about the van and requested the public to come forward if they knew anything or had seen anything that night. The possible link with Celeste's suicide was left untouched.

Then Timo added, "And now his wife Amanda Ulfsson would like to say a few words."

Amanda approached the podium, her voice already quivering as she began to speak. Tears welled up in her eyes, and her voice trembled as she addressed the room.

"I... I can't even begin to express the pain our family is going through right now... his parents, his brother... me," Amanda managed to say between sobs. "Jukka is a loving husband. He's the anchor of our family, and without him, we are lost. Please bring him back to us."

She paused to wipe away her tears. She couldn't go on and Timo took over again.

As Amanda's emotional plea hung in the air, the room erupted with a cacophony of questions from the press, and Timo tried to answer them as best he could.

But it was a bit out of his league.

*  *  *

The man sat alone in the darkened room, intently watching the press conference on his television screen. His eyes fixated on the images being broadcast, and a sinister, knowing smile slowly crept across his face.

He leaned back in his chair, calmly lifting a fork to continue eating his meal. The eerie calm that enveloped him was a stark contrast to the chaos that Amanda's words had stirred in the room full of journalists.

With calculated poise, he reached for the remote control and silenced the sound. In an instant, the room was engulfed in a haunting silence.

It was quiet.

Too quiet.

## CHAPTER

# 10

THE PSYCHIATRIC HOSPITAL, with its imposing gray stone structure, dominated the landscape from its perch atop the hill. Surrounded by barren trees and under an overcast sky, it exuded an aura of solemnity.

As they neared, the automated gate, a modern marvel flanked by sturdy stone pillars, smoothly swung open, beckoning them in. The well-maintained driveway guided them toward the main building, revealing its sprawling, multi-winged form. Despite its age, the brickwork appeared clean, and the windows, fitted with sleek bars, hinted at modernity.

An unexpected shiver crept over Isa as they parked, the scent of dampness and decay clinging to the air. The recent snow had melted, and it seemed like nature couldn't quite decide between snow and rain. The temperature kept oscillating between an unseasonably warm and an uncomfortably familiar cold.

Timo cut the engine, and they sat in the car, enveloped in a moment of silence.

She let out a deep sigh.

Timo's words broke the silence. "Are you okay?"

She nodded, her gaze fixed outside. "Just knowing that he is in this building... somewhere..."

The memory of Alex's murderer loomed large, casting a shadow over her thoughts. Despite the passage of time, the anger and resentment remained intense, making her stomach churn at the mere mention of his name.

"I know it's hard," Timo said, removing the key from the ignition.

She glanced at him. At least there was no lecture about how she should face Alex's killer at some point. They had debated this countless times, but it always felt too soon, too raw.

"Come," Timo said, breaking her reverie as he opened the door.

While the rest of the team pursued their investigative tasks, Isa had suggested a different approach to Timo, hoping to give him a morale boost. Her boss, grappling with his own sense of helplessness, longed to be more directly involved in the investigation despite his superintendent role. And delving into Celeste's psychiatric history and its connection to Jukka's case seemed to make a lot of sense.

As they approached the entrance, Isa couldn't shake the sadness and anxiety. Even the grandeur of the place failed to lift her spirits. The entrance hall, though elegantly appointed with wood paneling and a modest chandelier, felt eerily quiet, resembling more of a mausoleum than a place of healing.

They made their way to the reception desk, where a middle-aged woman sat behind a dark wood counter, engrossed in her computer. She looked up as they approached, offering a polite greeting. "Good afternoon. How may I help you?"

"We're here to see Dr. Malin Holmberg," Isa stated.

The woman behind the desk maintained her stoic expression. "Do you have an appointment?"

"No, we don't," Timo responded. "But we were hoping to speak with her if that's possible."

The woman's eyes flicked between Isa and Timo. "I'm sorry, but visitors are not allowed without an appointment."

"We understand," Isa interjected quickly, flashing her badge. "But this is important. We need to speak with her."

There was a brief pause before the woman gave in. "Very well. I'll see what I can do. Please wait here."

With that, she disappeared through a door behind the desk, leaving Isa and Timo alone in the entrance hall.

After a few minutes, she returned. "Dr. Holmberg will see you in her office. Follow me, please."

Isa and Timo fell into step behind her as they navigated the hallway lined with closed doors. Passing a few nurses in scrubs who cast curious glances their way, they arrived at a door bearing a plaque that read 'Dr. Malin Holmberg, M.D., Ph.D.'

The woman knocked softly. "Dr. Holmberg, these are the visitors to see you."

"Come in," came the reply from within.

Isa and Timo entered the office, greeted by the sight of Dr. Holmberg seated behind a cluttered desk. Despite the chaos of files and textbooks surrounding her, she exuded an air of calmness.

"Good afternoon," Dr. Holmberg greeted them, rising from her chair. "How may I assist you?"

Isa wasted no time. "I'm Inspector Isa Lindström. This is Superintendent Timo Paikkala. We're with the Gävle police." She displayed her badge once more.

"Is something wrong?" Dr. Holmberg inquired, gesturing for them to take seats across from her.

"We wanted to talk to you about Celeste Westerberg," Timo explained.

"Celeste? It's tragic... but I thought she took her own life."

"We believe her case is linked to another case we're working on. We were hoping you could provide us with some information about her time here at the hospital," Isa added.

Dr. Holmberg settled back into her chair. "I see. Well, I can certainly understand why you would be interested in her case."

Pausing briefly to collect her thoughts, she continued, "Celeste was admitted to our hospital about five years ago. She was suffering from severe depression and suicidal thoughts. We provided her with the necessary treatment and medication, and her condition seemed to be improving. She was discharged a year later. However, about six months ago, she was admitted again, albeit briefly. She was suffering from severe hallucinations, depression, and anxiety attacks."

Isa and Timo exchanged a glance.

"Six months ago? Her parents didn't mention anything about that," Isa noted.

"I can imagine she kept it quiet from her parents. They are rather... opinionated," Dr. Holmberg remarked dryly.

"Did anything happen around that time that could have triggered her mental health decline?"

Dr. Holmberg took another moment before responding. "She didn't mention it during our initial conversation. It was difficult to break through to her, but I later discovered details about her divorce."

"Yes, we know. Alva Stendahl. She was a patient here too."

Dr. Holmberg looked at them and then said. "I'm sorry but I cannot discuss other patients with you."

Timo nodded. "Fair enough. Then let's go back to Celeste. She was admitted for depression and burn-out two times, correct?"

"Uh... yes."

"You are not convinced?"

The doctor looked at the hands in her lap and then said, "I was indeed not convinced. She was experiencing hallucinations. She was genuinely scared. Strangely, her family tried to steer my diagnosis in the direction of a burn-out."

"Was it because they wanted to keep up appearances?"

"Absolutely," the doctor said. "For her family, it could only be a burn-out. Other mental issues were off the table."

"So, what could it be then?"

"Anxiety disorder. She had panic attacks."

"In your expert opinion, could it be the reaction of someone who thought she was being stalked?" Isa asked.

"Stalking? So you heard about that." Dr. Holmberg stared at the window for a moment and then said, "Maybe. PTSD came to mind. I still don't know if the stalking was real. But strange things were happening."

"What exactly?"

"Celeste reported seeing a man standing outside her window at night. When the hospital staff investigated, they indeed found footprints in the flower bed below the window, but then it turned out we had a gardener who had been paid by journalists to take pictures of the famous violinist. He was fired. Then she started receiving strange letters and packages at the hospital."

"What kind of letters and packages?"

"They were poems, but... strange. Not the romantic kind. Weird. Almost... possessive, obsessive."

"Do you still have them?" Isa asked.

"No. I don't quite know what happened to them. This was five years ago."

"Could it have been a fan?" Timo asked.

"Maybe... but the letters were so disturbing. And they had no stamp or return address."

"So, someone delivered them," Isa said.

"The nurses probably just left them on her bedside table. So, it's difficult to say who delivered them. And we didn't realize the severity of the situation until later. After that, the staff increased security measures and we were on the lookout for any suspicious behavior. Unfortunately, we never caught the person responsible."

"Anything else?"

"A nurse reported seeing a man following Celeste around the hospital. When the nurse approached him, he quickly left the building. And Celeste reported receiving repeated phone calls from someone who would not speak."

"You never reported it to the police?"

"No, I wanted to, but her family was very insistent that we handle it internally. They were worried about the negative publicity it would generate for Celeste and her career."

Timo leaned forward. "Do you have any idea who could have done this?"

The doctor shook her head. "No, but... if there was any stalker at all, that person knew Celeste's daily routine. He knew when to call, when to leave the messages without being seen."

"Someone from inside the hospital?"

"Or her family and friends," the doctor added.

"And did this continue the entire time she was here?"

"I don't know," the doctor said and sighed.

"Why don't you know?"

"The family decided to take another psychiatrist, but what I do know is that Alva's presence helped a lot. The family might not have liked her, but she managed to gain Celeste's trust and provided her with emotional support. She also helped her confront her fears and anxieties. Celeste made a lot of progress under Alva's care and was eventually discharged. But Alva was struggling with her own demons."

"So, their relationship started here?"

"Correct," the doctor said.

"And after she started to befriend Alva, were there any incidents?"

"There was an incident involving Alva herself," Dr. Holmberg said with a sigh. "One evening, Alva was passing by Celeste's room and heard a noise. She went inside and found someone going through Celeste's things. She chased after him, but unfortunately, she fell down the stairs in the process. Luckily, her injuries were minor."

"Did she see who it was?" Isa asked.

"Yes, she managed to describe the man to the police, but unfortunately, they never caught him."

"So this incident was reported to the police?"

"Yeah... we had to. Someone got injured."

"You think this was the same person who had been stalking Celeste?"

"We don't know for sure," the doctor replied. "But it's definitely a possibility. Whoever it was seemed to know Celeste's daily routine and was able to access her room without being detected."

"Where employees of the hospital checked?"

Dr. Holmberg shrugged. "I think so... we were all very shaken and scared, but there were no incidents after that. Again, I cannot tell you if the calls or letters continued, but Celeste seemed more at ease after that."

"Who was her new psychiatrist?"

"Dr. Pedersen, but he's no longer here. He died last year."

"What happened?"

"He died in a car accident."

"I'm sorry to hear that," Isa said.

"It was a great loss for all of us. He was a brilliant psychiatrist and a good man."

"Did he mention anything to you about Celeste or Alva before he died?" Timo asked.

"Not that I can remember. He had many patients, and I never got the impression that he had any particular concern about Celeste or Alva."

Isa looked at her notes and then turned to the doctor again, "This happened five years ago. What about the second time she was admitted to the hospital?"

"She only stayed for two weeks. I was her physician... on her request. It seemed different though."

"Why?"

"It's hard to say for sure, but she didn't show the same air of paranoia. Celeste was calmer, more cooperative... stronger, yet vulnerable at the same time. There was no concrete evidence of any external threat or harassment like the first time. It was like she needed some time to reflect. There was talk about revamping her career and the pressure was high. It was a burn-out. After that, she also filed for divorce."

"Did Celeste ever mention a Jukka Ulfsson?" Timo asked.

Dr. Holmberg thought for a moment and then shook her head. "Not that I recall. Why?"

"Or the creatives?" Isa added.

Dr. Holmberg shook her head again. "Jukka Ulfsson... is that the man who was abducted?"

Isa ignored her question and then said, "Thank you so much for your time, doctor. We really appreciate it."

"Yes, thank you," Timo added. "If you remember anything else, please don't hesitate to contact us." He put his card on the desk and then got up.

But as they walked to the door, Dr. Holmberg suddenly blurted out, "Wait, before you go, there is something I should tell you. I saw Celeste a month before her death. She looked bad and scared again, just like she used to be when she arrived the first time at the hospital. I had the impression that her stalker was back."

"Did she say this explicitly?" Isa asked.

"No, she didn't mention a stalker. But her behavior was very similar to when she first came to the hospital. I tried to ask her about it, but she refused to talk and insisted everything was fine. She didn't look fine at all."

"Did you try to talk to her family about it?" Timo asked.

"I did. I hesitated at first since they had been so dismissive the first time. And just as I thought they didn't seem to take it seriously. They thought she was just having a bad day. I wish I had pushed harder, but I didn't want to violate her privacy or cause her any more stress."

"Okay, thank you, doctor," Isa said and followed Timo to the hall.

As they walked along the hallway, Isa said, "This changes things. The stalker was real."

"Yeah, it's definitely concerning," Timo agreed. "But without any concrete evidence, it's hard to know what to do next."

"I know," Isa said with a sigh. "But we can't just ignore this. We need to keep digging and try to find out who was Celeste's stalker."

"But it's not sure if this lead will help us to find Jukka Ulfsson who is our primary concern at this moment," Timo said. "Celeste and Jukka. Maybe these incidents are not connected at all."

"What about the music? There is a reason why this unknown version of Celeste's greatest hit was played before Celeste died and Jukka disappeared."

"Inspector Lindström," a voice sounded.

Isa and Timo turned around and saw an older man with a white coat and glasses on the tip of his nose looking at them.

"Dr. Wikholm," Isa stammered.

"It seems you found your way back to a hospital," Dr. Wikholm said with a sarcastic grin on his face, "but unfortunately not back to my office."

"Uh... I've been busy," Isa said. "What are you doing here?"

"Visiting a patient," he said, his eyes fixed on Isa. It almost felt like a staring contest. "Well, I'll be patiently waiting for your return... after you're not so busy anymore."

He turned around and after giving the nurse at the reception desk a quick nod, he walked away down the hallway.

Timo stared at him as he moved away from them, and then turned to Isa.

"Don't start," Isa warned him and with her mouth folded in an angry grin she walked toward the exit.

"I didn't say anything."

But Isa was annoyed. In an attempt to better her life, she had hired Dr. Wikholm to deal with her lingering traumas. Alex's death, her divorce, the strained relationship with her children and the betrayal of her old partner. But she hadn't been able to push through.

It was too confronting.

When Timo caught up with Isa outside of the hospital, he asked, "Are you okay?"

"Yeah, I'm fine. Sorry, I just don't like being reminded of things I'd rather forget."

"I get it," Timo said. "But don't let it get to you. We have work to do."

Trying to shake off the memories that had been stirred up, she said, "You're right."

But that was easier said than done.

* * *

Seated in his living room, a simmering fury pulsed just beneath the surface. He had pinned all his hopes on Jukka Ulfsson, convinced he held the key to everything, the solution to his dilemma. But Jukka had let him down, withholding the crucial information he desperately needed.

Staring at the blank wall ahead, a whirlwind of thoughts raced through his mind. Had Jukka deceived him? Was he in cahoots with someone else? The notion of being played like a fool fueled his frustration.

"Stupid, just stupid," he muttered, fists clenched. The weight of failure bore down on him—a critical error, a fatal misstep. Impatience had clouded his judgment, and now remorse gnawed at him.

He rose, repeating the self-reproachful mantra. His breathing was all over the place. He couldn't control it.

The pent-up rage demanded release.

Glancing at his distorted reflection in the mirror, he no longer recognized himself—anger contorted his face, eyes blazing.

Without hesitation, he seized the vase from the table and hurled it at the mirror, shattering it into countless shards. Then he sank to the floor, tears streaming down his face as he surrendered to the overwhelming surge of emotion.

Fury knew no bounds.

When he got up, the rage continued.

It was so overwhelming.

He recklessly flung anything within reach, transforming his once orderly living room into chaos. The TV crashed, the bookshelf toppled, books scattered. The sound of breaking glass and splintering furniture echoed through the house as his screams pierced the air.

The destructive rampage continued until exhaustion overcame him. Collapsing amidst the wreckage, surrounded by the remnants of his shattered living room, he embraced the deafening silence.

A profound emptiness and regret settled in. To regain control, to rectify his mistake, he knew he had to think clearly, act logically. Then, a realization struck, and he knew exactly what needed to be done.

# CHAPTER

# 11

*I AM HERE! WHY DOESN'T ANYONE HEAR ME?*

His voice vanished, leaving behind a heavy silence that pressed on his chest. He observed and listened, but the helplessness of his situation nagged at him. The quiet drove him mad, and he craved the simple touch of life.

In his dreams, he yearned for the sun's warmth on his skin, a pleasure he once took for granted. The embrace of a loved one felt like a distant memory. It drained him, day by day, a never-ending cycle of watching and longing.

He lived in a dream world he had created. There he was not a captive but a master of his own destiny. Boundaries blurred as he weaved stories and adventures, escaping into his mind's sanctuary. Despite being a prisoner, his spirit roamed freely through vibrant landscapes of imagination, finding solace from the harsh reality.

Yet, reality lingered like a persistent shadow, an uninvited guest. It intruded into his dreams, a stark reminder of his situation. In those moments, the walls of his mental refuge crumbled, trapping him between imagination and unyielding confinement.

It could be over at any moment.

But why was he so afraid? Death would be a blessing. Nothing was more tempting than the escape it promised. Yet, paradoxically, the idea of death also filled him with dread. It wasn't the end that frightened him; it was the unknown, the uncertainty of what lay beyond. The void between life and death seemed vast and uncharted. In the stillness of his existence, he grappled with the haunting question: What if there was nothing after, and all he knew was the torment of silence and isolation.

It was a terrifying thought.

There was sadness for the loved ones he had not been able to save.

Revenge. It was the only thing that kept him alive. The prospect of revenge. Even if he would never be able to exact it, the feeling was so strong. It was a fire that burned within him, a fierce determination to ensure that the ones who had brought him to this state would pay for their actions. In his darkest moments, this burning ember of retribution kept his spirit alive, a silent vow that he clung to amid his agonizing silence.

He would not be silenced.

He just needed to find a way.

If someone just listened, just realized that he was still here.

*I am here. Can't you see me?*

## CHAPTER

# 12

**BORIS STOOD IN THE DOORWAY.** Every time he saw the still figure in the bed, he was sad. The room felt like a time capsule, preserving the memory of that fateful morning when their lives had taken an irreversible turn.

He remembered that day vividly, how he had chosen to stay behind while Dancho and Jonathan went on a hike. It was a decision he regretted deeply.

As he watched his brother's motionless form, he wondered if he had been there, maybe he could have done something to prevent the accident.

The early days after the incident had been the darkest. The doctors had given up hope, advising them to end his brother's life support. The family, still grappling with the loss of their mother, had made the heart-wrenching decision. But then, against all odds, Dancho had clung to life. He had taken his own breaths, opened his eyes, and yet there had been no response, no flicker of recognition.

Five long years had passed since then, and the room had become a silent witness to the agony of waiting. The hope that Dancho would ever speak or sing again had dimmed with time. Boris' visits were a mixture of love, despair, and a relentless sense of responsibility. He couldn't abandon his brother, just as he couldn't let go of the guilt that tethered him to the room and the past. That was why it was so hard for Boris to move on with his life. He couldn't let anyone in. There was simply no room and energy left to care for someone else. And even if there was, the fear of losing someone he loved was too much to bear.

Boris remembered when Dancho was young. He was so full of life and boundless energy. He had been a free spirit, always singing and dancing, always with some strange songs in his head. Some were good, catchy tunes that would stick in your mind for days, and some were not so good, goofy little jingles that never failed to make everyone laugh.

Dancho, with his lust for life, had been a whirlwind of infectious enthusiasm. He embraced every moment, making the mundane seem exciting and the ordinary extraordinary. He had a talent for turning even the gloomiest days into something to smile about, and Boris cherished those memories.

Dancho had been so much like their mother.

But his brother had also carried a secret, a burden that he'd struggled to share with the world. He had never been able to tell their father that he loved men. The weight of unspoken words had cast a shadow over his joyous spirit. It was a truth that had remained locked away, a part of Dancho's identity that had been hidden from the world. Forever.

Boris wiped away a tear. He wished more than anything that he could have been there for Dancho, that he could have helped him find the courage to be his true self.

He stepped back and closed the door. Then he went downstairs and found his aunt in the kitchen, doing the dishes.

"You have a dishwasher, you know," he remarked.

She quickly turned around, her stern expression softening into a faint smile, and then continued her task. The clinking of dishes and the warm familiarity of the family home provided a brief respite from the heavy emotions that had filled the room upstairs. It was a simple moment, but it was a reminder that life continued, even in the face of adversity.

His aunt had weathered the storms of a life filled with hardship, and she was a complex figure. Her face bore the deep lines of experience, and her eyes held a mixture of weariness and a quiet, steely determination. On the surface, she often came across as hard and stern, her exterior masking the depths of her caring nature.

Her hair, though once vibrant, had now dulled with age, and she wore no-nonsense, practical attire that reflected her no-frills approach to life. Her demeanor could seem unfriendly to those who didn't know her, but Boris understood that beneath that stern exterior lay a heart of gold.

She had been a constant presence in their lives, always ready to lend a helping hand and provide unwavering support. Boris respected and loved her deeply, even though he still longed for his mother's softer touch. His mother had been a stark contrast to her sister, bringing warmth and gentleness into the family.

With her deep Bulgarian voice, she asked, "How was he?"

He didn't speak any Bulgarian. He understood it, but never spoke it. For him, that was enough to maintain a connection to his heritage while fully embracing the language and culture of his home country Sweden. His mother had always encouraged them to speak Swedish, both at home and at school, as a way to integrate into their new environment. Much to the dismay of his father. Aunt Stoyanka had always stayed neutral in the often heated discussions between his parents.

"As always," Boris said and reached out to take a towel from the kitchen counter but was met with an angry look.

"Leave it," she said. "You are a guest in this house."

"But...," Boris stammered. He knew not to oppose her and put himself in the chair at the table. He wondered if she would have said the same thing if he had been a woman. Daughters and sons were never treated the same way. Daughters were expected to help. Sons were expected to be providers, but doing the household was never one of those jobs. At least not in his father and auntie Stoyanka's mind.

He sometimes felt caught in this age-old division of duties and expectations. But he didn't have the strength to explain or counter them.

He turned his head to the window. Everything was so gray. Only now he realized winter had really set in, and it didn't help his mood.

"Sometimes...," he started, "I think he can hear me, understand me."

Stoyanka stopped and looked at him. "What do you mean?"

"I don't know. It's like he's following me with his eyes."

"I told you before: doctors said it's just a response to light and movement. Involuntary twitch. Don't get your hopes up."

"That was five years ago," Boris said. "Maybe we should get him examined again. I can't believe he's in a coma."

"Persistent vegetative state," she corrected. "And you'll have to talk to your father about it. I tried. He doesn't want to listen. I don't know what he thinks anymore. One moment Dancho is dead in his eyes, the next he's alive."

Boris took a deep breath. "Where is dad anyway? I hardly see him these days. He never comes to the shop. He leaves me and Janko alone to take care of the customers. What's going on?"

Stoyanka shrugged. "I don't know. He's probably in the lake house."

"The lake house? What is he doing there?"

"He wants to be alone. He's been going there the last six months almost every day, leaving me alone with Dancho."

"I'm so sorry. If there is anything I can do..."

She held up her hand. "No. I don't want to hear it. You have your own life. My job is to take care of your father and your brother."

A faint smile appeared on his face. "If we didn't have you..."

"Leave it," she said, finishing the last of the dishes and setting it aside.

As Boris was about to respond to Stoyanka, his phone rang. He quickly retrieved it from his pocket and looked at the caller ID. It was an unknown number. For a moment he hesitated but decided not to take the call.

He leaned back. "I'll talk to dad about Dancho. Maybe it's time to consider a fresh medical evaluation."

She didn't utter a word and maintained her gaze on the water, as if she hadn't heard him, the remnants of dishwashing disappearing down the sink.

With a sigh, Boris rose from the table and moved to where she was standing, but a second time the phone in his pocket rang.

Frustration creased his forehead, but curiosity nudged him to answer the call this time.

"Boris Krastev. Who is this?"

There was nothing but silence on the other end of the line, and Boris' brow furrowed in confusion. He repeated, now growing more impatient, "Who is this?"

"Bulgari," someone said on the other side of the line.

No one had called him Bulgari since high school. He recognized the voice. "Max?"

"Yes, it's me."

"Uh... I heard about Celeste," Boris said. "I'm sorry for your loss, and I'm sorry I didn't go to the memorial service, but..." Boris' voice trailed off, filled with regret for not being there to support his old friend during such a difficult time.

Max's voice on the other end of the line held a hint of understanding. "It's alright, Bulgari. It's been a tough time for everyone. I appreciate your condolences, but that's not why I called."

"How did you get this number anyway?"

"It doesn't matter. Did you hear about Jukka?"

"Yeah... it's been all over the news. Why?"

"I am... we are in danger."

Boris' frown deepened, and he glanced at his aunt, who was still in the kitchen with her back turned to him. Not wanting to alarm her with the conversation, he made a quick decision. He walked to the living room, where he could continue the conversation in private. Meanwhile, he heard Max's voice through the speaker, "I got a message."

"From whom?"

"I don't know. It was sent to my phone, but it's coming from an unknown sender. It's a recording."

"About what?"

"Never mind... Bulgari, you need to be careful. He's coming after us."

"I still don't understand. What does this have to do with me... us?"

Max's tone was a mix of urgency and desperation. "Listen, I can't explain it over the phone, but I think they know."

"They know what? I still don't get it."

"Let's meet tomorrow."

Boris' heart raced as he contemplated the gravity of the situation. He knew he had to help his old friend, even if he didn't fully understand the danger they were facing. "Alright, Max."

With that, the call ended, leaving Boris with a growing sense of unease and a deepening mystery in which he was now entangled.

Max, Celeste, Jukka, and the secrets of their past were about to resurface in ways he could never have anticipated. He didn't want to think of that time anymore. It was so loaded with mixed feelings. On one hand, his brother had been his cheerful self, and he regretted not having spent enough time with him. Only afterwards did he realize the significance of those moments and the value of the simple joys they had shared. On the other hand, the memories of their youthful indiscretions still haunted him. He had been so young, so naive. A prefrontal cortex still in development, making decisions without fully grasping the consequences. But the only thing he knew was whatever Max feared had nothing to do with him. He wasn't part of the drama. That had been clear for quite a while.

So why did Max involve him?

Nothing made sense.

Suddenly, a loud, startling noise echoed from the upper floor, jolting Boris from his thoughts.

Dancho.

He ran up the stairs to his brother's room. When he pushed the door open, he wasn't prepared to see what he witnessed.

Stoyanka sat on the floor, her gaze fixed on the man sprawled before her.

"What happened?" Boris asked surprised.

Stoyanka looked up at him, her eyes filled with a mixture of fear and confusion. "I don't know, Boris. I think he... fell out of the bed. I heard a loud thud, and when I came in, he was on the floor."

Boris rushed to Dancho's side, his heart pounding. His brother lay on the floor, his eyes open but unresponsive, as they had been for years. Boris gently checked for any signs of injury but found none.

"He seems okay," Boris said.

Stoyanka nodded, her face pale. "I don't understand how it could have happened."

Together, they lifted Dancho and placed him in the bed, covering him with a blanket.

"We'll need to keep a close eye on him, make sure that he's okay."

Stoyanka nodded, still visibly shaken by the incident. "I'll stay with him."

Boris left the room, his thoughts torn between the strange phone call from Max and the sudden incident with Dancho. It was turning into a day filled with unexpected and troubling events, and he felt a growing sense of unease about what might come next.

Something was lurking in the shadows, something that would soon demand his attention.

Everyone's attention.

## CHAPTER

# 13

**THE WOMAN WHO OPENED THE DOOR** was tall, slender and undeniably beautiful. Her medium-length brown hair was straight and fell effortlessly down her back, framing her angular features. Her brown eyes were bright and inquisitive, betraying her surprise at seeing the two inspectors standing at her doorstep.

She was dressed casually in a loose-fitting T-shirt and faded jeans that accentuated her slender frame. Despite her stunning appearance, there was something disheveled about her. She had flecks of paint in her hair and on her clothes, and her hands were covered in colorful smudges.

Isa observed the noticeable contrast between Alva and her cousin Lukas, whom they had encountered before. Lukas had presented himself as reserved and serious, whereas Alva radiated a more carefree and relaxed aura. Nevertheless, a subtle sadness lingered in her eyes.

"Yes?" she said with a surprisingly youthful tone.

Isa showed her badge and then said, "Inspector Isa Lindström and this is my colleague Inspector Timo Paikkala. We called."

She stared at them, her eyes jumping from Isa to Timo and back, and said nothing.

"Is there something wrong?" Timo asked.

"Uh... no, sorry. Are you really with the police?"

"Yeah," Timo said surprised.

"I didn't know police officers looked like that," Alva blurted.

A faint smile tugged at Isa's lips. "How are they supposed to look then?"

"Old, uninterested, stern, ugly," Alva said and smiled. "It almost seems like you two stepped out of a fashion campaign."

She continued to stare at them for a few moments.

Isa started to feel a tad uncomfortable under Alva's intense gaze. She cleared her throat and said, "Ms. Stendahl, we're here to ask you a few questions regarding your late wife Celeste Westerberg. May we come in?"

"Of course," Alva said and opened the door further to let them in. "Don't mind the boxes."

"Are you leaving?"

"I was supposed to... with the divorce and all... but not anymore. This is my house now."

"It's a beautiful home," Isa remarked and let her eyes go over the impressive entrance hall.

The high ceiling soared all the way up to the upper floors, creating an expansive, light-filled space that seemed to echo with the sound of footsteps.

The walls were painted a warm, creamy white, with intricate moldings and ornate carvings that added to the sense of grandeur. Large windows on either side of the entrance flooded the space with natural light, making it feel even more like a concert hall.

At the center of the hall stood a majestic staircase, its polished wooden steps gleaming in the sunlight. The staircase curved gracefully upwards, disappearing into the upper floors of the house. Isa was impressed by the sheer scale and beauty of it all.

The rest of the decor was equally impressive, with carefully chosen furnishings and tasteful decorations that spoke of a refined and sophisticated taste. A large chandelier hung from the ceiling, adding to the feeling of elegance and luxury.

"Yeah, it is," Alva mused and stood there for a moment, gazing at the hall. "From the first moment we saw the house, Celeste fell in love with it. I can still picture her standing on the stairs with her violin. The acoustics are so wonderful here that she would often play in the hall, even if it was just for herself. It was her and the violin. I would sit in my art studio and listen to her music filling the entire house."

Isa noticed a slight tremble in Alva's voice and realized how much the memories of her late wife must still be affecting her.

"I'm sorry for your loss," Isa said.

"Thank you," Alva said. "Would you mind if we talk in my studio, I'm busy with a painting?"

"That's fine," Isa said and looked at Timo who nodded.

Then Alva led them through the entrance hall and into the art studio, located on the ground floor of the house. The studio was a spacious, open area with high ceilings, white walls, and large windows that allowed ample natural light to flood in. It was stocked with various art supplies, including paintbrushes, canvases, and easels. Several paintings in various stages of completion were scattered around the room.

In the center of the studio, there was a large unfinished canvas. Isa noticed how different the paintings in the room were from the more traditional pieces she was used to seeing in galleries and museums. They were bold, colorful, and abstract, with wild brushstrokes and unexpected splashes of color.

The canvas that Alva was working on was a riot of colors, with swirls of pink, orange, and yellow blending together in a frenzied dance. Isa couldn't quite make out what the painting was supposed to be about, but she assumed that was the point. She wasn't much of an art connoisseur, and the modern style of Alva's paintings didn't really appeal to her. But she could appreciate the skill and talent that went into creating them.

Alva walked to the canvas and picked up the brush.

"Wow, really beautiful house," Isa said while wandering around the room. "I guess you're glad that you don't have to leave."

Alva stared at her for a moment. "Maybe... Celeste is dead."

Timo looked at Isa who was now standing in front of a bookcase, her eyes fixed on a thin book. "Beatris Ivenson?"

Then Alva turned her attention from Timo to Isa. "Do you know her?"

Isa took the book and let her fingers go over the blue cover. It was a better-preserved version than she had.

The winter poems.

"*In the silence, memories linger, of times long gone and people we miss. The snow covers all like a white shroud, reminding us of those we've lost and how,*" Isa said.

"You chose one of the saddest poems," Alva remarked, keeping her eyes fixed on Isa as she returned the book to the cupboard.

Isa sighed and then said, "I knew her grandson."

For months, after his death, the book had laid on the living room table. She hadn't been able to open it. The memories were too vivid. Alex had given it to her the morning of his death.

Now, it somehow gave her solace.

Alva nodded slowly, as if she understood the weight of Isa's words. "Loss is a heavy burden to bear. Especially in winter. The cold and the darkness seem to magnify the pain."

Isa couldn't agree more. The winter after Alex's death had been the hardest of her life. The days were short, the nights long and lonely. The snow had seemed to mock her with its pristine beauty, a cruel reminder of the ugliness that lay beneath the surface of her world.

"So, what do you want to know about Celeste?" Alva asked, her eyes still fixed on Isa.

Isa cleared her throat. She had to admit that the book had stirred more than she had anticipated. "We understand that you and Celeste were married for a few years before her death. Can you tell us a bit about your relationship?"

Alva's expression grew pensive, and she looked down at her hands, which were still covered in paint. "It was... complicated," she said after a moment. "We loved each other, but we had our issues. Celeste could be... difficult. She had a lot of demons she was struggling with."

"You had some troubles yourself," Timo said.

Alva looked up, and for a moment, Isa thought she would explode— anger quietly simmering beneath the surface. But as swiftly as it had emerged, it passed. "Fair enough... yes, I had." Then Alva moved her paintbrush in swift, confident strokes over the canvas.

"Dr. Holmberg wasn't too specific, but can you tell us why you were admitted to the hospital?"

Alva put the paintbrush down. "Alcohol, drugs. It was a hard time, but I've been clean for four years. I was in the hospital for four months. I learned to paint over there. Therapy. And I've loved it ever since."

"Dr. Holmberg was your therapist?"

"Only for a short while, then it was Dr. Pedersen. That's when I met Celeste. It clicked from day one."

"And you got married a year later?"

Alva nodded, a small smile on her face. "We did. It was a beautiful ceremony. We were happy, at least for a while."

"What led to the breakdown of your relationship?" Timo asked.

Alva's smile faded, and she looked away from them, her gaze fixed on the unfinished canvas. "Our marriage ended before it even began. Her family never accepted me. They didn't accept Celeste being gay. They tried to break us up from the beginning. And then..." Alva's voice trailed off.

"And then what?"

"And then she died," she said. "And now they don't want me to get what is rightfully mine. They'll fight me with everything they have."

Isa frowned. "Why?"

Alva raised her hands and explained, "Celeste paid for all of this—the house, everything. It was her money, but she wanted us to share everything when we got married. She left everything to me in her will, but her family is contesting it. They claim that I coerced her into leaving everything to me, that I took advantage of her. But I won't let them take this away from me. This is my home, my sanctuary. I won't let them destroy it."

Timo cleared his throat. "But Celeste filed for divorce. She wasn't so convinced anymore about your love."

"Years of poisoning her mind. I told you before, we had no chance."

Timo pressed on, "It's very convenient she killed herself before the divorce was finalized."

Alva's eyes narrowed, and she turned to face him. "What are you suggesting? That I made her take her own life?"

"No," Timo clarified, "but someone did."

Alva hesitated for a moment before speaking. "I don't understand."

Timo retrieved his phone from his pocket. "I'm going to let you hear a recording. I just want to know if you recognize it."

The music started, haunting and melancholic, accompanied by a man's voice singing an all-too-familiar song.

Alva's face stayed emotionless as she listened to it.

When the recording ended, Alva looked up at Timo. "So?"

"Do you recognize the song?" Isa asked.

Alva nodded. "Aria 25. Celeste's greatest hit."

Timo asked calmly, "And the man's voice?"

"Am I supposed to recognize it? Where does it come from?"

"We found it on Celeste's cell phone."

"And you think I had something to do with it?" Alva said, continuing to draw another line on the canvas. "How does this connect to her suicide?"

"After receiving this message, she jumped off the building," Isa explained.

"And?" Despite her best efforts to mask her emotions, Alva couldn't conceal her visible agitation. It took energy to keep her emotions under control. The brush strokes on the canvas were increasingly erratic. The smooth strokes had turned into jagged lines and Isa thought that she was about to throw the paintbrush across the room at any moment.

"Do you have any idea who might have sent it to her?" Timo asked.

Alva shook her head. "No, I don't. Can't you trace it?"

"It was sent from a prepaid phone. Did Celeste have enemies?"

Alva blurted, "Why don't you try her brother? He's a controlling, manipulative son of a... you know what. He wanted to control everything. Celeste's life, her money... He didn't approve of our relationship. But she finally saw who he really was. He was obsessed with his own sister. Just... creepy."

"What happened?" Isa echoed.

"He showed up unannounced at the most unearthly hours of the day. He had a key to our house. I caught him once in our bedroom, his shirt half-open, and his hands... on Celeste's breasts. She was deeply upset and didn't want to talk to me for days. That relationship was just... not right."

"Are you saying they had an incestuous relationship?" Timo asked.

"I don't know. I just know that he has been spreading lies about me. He said I was a gold digger."

"And are you?" Timo asked bluntly.

Alva's jaw clenched, her eyes narrowing into icy slits. "I'm not. I loved Celeste. I still do."

"Then why did she file for divorce?" Isa asked.

Alva sighed. "I told you; her family poisoned her mind. They convinced her that I was no good for her, that I was only after her money. They made her doubt me, made her think that I was cheating on her. It was all lies, but she believed them."

"And did you cheat on her?" Timo asked.

Alva shook her head. "No, I didn't. How many times do I have to say this? I loved her, and I was faithful to her. But she didn't believe me."

"Do you know Jukka Ulfsson?"

"Jukka? That arrogant prick who runs after the Westerbergs for his own benefit. Yeah, I know him. He used to harass Celeste. For some reason, he thought she was interested in him. He finally married a nobody. She is the real gold digger. She was engaged to a man, about to be married. After she met Ulfsson, she ditched her fiancé and moved in with him the next day. They got married six months later. Word is out that she has a lover and is thinking of leaving him. She was a bit disappointed about Jukka's financial situation."

"Jukka disappeared," Timo said.

"I wouldn't be surprised if his wife is behind it. Or that he's hiding somewhere. He owes people a lot of money... as I've been told."

Timo looked at the phone in his hands and said, "And what about the rest of the creatives?"

"The creatives? Oh, my God, that's a long time ago. I don't think I've talked to any of them in the last five or six years, except Jukka and Celeste, of course."

Timo frowned. "I thought you met Celeste in the psychiatric hospital. Now you're telling me you knew the creatives?"

Alva was suddenly at a loss for words. "Everyone knew the creatives in school. Lukas was part of the group... well, not really. He was just a good friend of Jonathan Gedman. I... actually never talked to them. I just admired them. They were always so... otherworldly, divine creatures, no one could touch. Only later, Celeste and I got to know each other better."

"And then the divine creatures fell off the pedestal," Timo added.

"Uh... what?"

"Jukka, Max," he said. "From what you told me, you don't like any of them."

"Because they hurt Celeste," she said, almost sounding out of breath. The emotions were getting the better of her again. "I'm sorry... I just miss her."

"We understand," Isa said and looked at the young woman who was staring at the swirls of paint on the canvas.

Then she turned to Isa, and for a moment, another lingering unease settled in the air as Alva's gaze held a subtle intensity that left her on edge.

"Okay, Ms. Stendahl, you were very helpful. I think we've taken up enough of your time," Timo said.

Isa walked up to Alva and reached out to shake her hand, but Alva stared at her.

"There is paint on the sleeve of your coat," Alva said.

"Oh, shit!"

Isa was staring at the big red stain. She had probably touched one of the paintings when she was walking around. She tried to quickly wipe it off with a tissue, but Alva stopped her. "There's a bathroom down the hallway, on your right. You can use it to clean up. Warm water and dish soap. You'll find some near the sink."

The next moment, Timo and Alva were alone in the room. She kept on staring at him with an intense gaze which made him feel uncomfortable.

Then she walked over to a smaller empty canvas that was on an easel a few meters away from where she stood and held up her paintbrush directed at him. "You never considered modeling?"

"Uh... sorry what?" Timo said with an expression of shock on his face.

"Modeling. You have the looks, the body and that certain sadness and melancholy in your eyes. It could make for a powerful portrait."

Timo cleared his throat. "Uh, no thank you."

"Naked," she blurted out with a grin on her face.

Timo felt his cheeks turn red. "That's not such an... appropriate suggestion. And aren't you supposed to be..."

"Gay," she continued and smiled. "I am bisexual. I love men and women. On the Kinsey scale I am a three. Equally homosexual and heterosexual."

Timo shook his head. "Kinsey scale?"

"The heterosexual-homosexual rating scale."

Timo nodded, still feeling uncomfortable with the turn in the conversation.

"Maybe you can ask your sexy colleague to join us," Alva said.

At that moment Isa entered the room.

"Are you ready to go?" Timo said quickly.

"Uh, yeah," Isa stammered, and then gave Alva a faint smile.

Then Timo said, "Thank you again for your time, Ms. Stendahl. We'll be in touch if we need anything else from you."

Alva gave him a teasing smile and walked him and Isa to the door. "Good luck with your investigation," she said as they left.

As soon as they were out of earshot, Isa turned to Timo. "What's wrong? You were in quite a hurry to leave. What did she say?"

He sighed and quickly glanced at the house. He was just in time to see the curtains move, as if Alva had been watching them. "It was strange. I think... she was hitting on me."

Isa raised an eyebrow. "Hitting on you? Isn't she supposed to be..."

"I guess not," he said.

The curtains moved again, and Timo felt a chill race down his back.

"It's probably nothing."

"I'm not sure. The bathroom was spotless. Clean as a whistle. Everything ordered, structured, put nicely into place. Just like the boxes in the entrance hall. I have never seen anyone who's moving be that organized. But then I passed by the living room, next to her art studio. The door was open. The place was a mess. Pieces of a broken... I think a vase on the floor. Pieces of glass."

"Maybe during the move?"

"But the person who cleaned the bathroom would never leave a mess like that," Isa said.

"Maybe that person is dead. That was Celeste, not Alva."

"Such a stark contrast," Isa said.

They reached the end of the street and walked a few meters to where the car was parked.

As they got into the car, Isa couldn't shake off the feeling that something was off about Alva Stendahl. "Do you think we should dig a bit deeper?"

"Maybe. But for now, let's focus on Jukka Ulfsson. Unless we think she has anything to do with his disappearance, I don't think we need to spend more time on her."

Isa nodded, but she wasn't quite convinced about Alva's innocence.

As they drove back to the station, Isa's phone rang. She picked it up and listened for a moment before hanging up. "That was Sivert. He has something for us."

He quickly looked at her. "What?"

"He didn't say, but we'll soon find out."

He turned the wheel and drove to the police station.

\* \* \*

"Tell me what you have," Timo said, took a chair and put himself next to

Sivert who was looking at the screen of his desktop.

Sivert's office was a small space, cluttered with computer equipment and cables. His desk was covered with papers, a keyboard, and a mouse, with a large monitor taking up most of the space.

Next to Sivert's desk was a small filing cabinet, which was overflowing with papers. A printer was situated on a nearby table, and there was a small coffee maker in the corner of the room. Despite the mess, Sivert seemed to know where everything was, and he was enthusiastically typing away on his keyboard as Timo and Isa joined him.

Timo took a seat next to Sivert and Isa sat on the other side of him, her arms crossed and a concerned look on her face. Sivert continued to type as he spoke, his eyes fixed on the screen.

"I've been going through the recording, trying to trace its origin," he said, "but it wasn't easy. Whoever made this was careful to cover their tracks."

"But you found something?" Timo voiced.

"The message was sent from a prepaid phone. The device is no longer in use, but I managed to locate where the message was sent from," Sivert replied, still typing away on his keyboard. "It's a rough estimate based on triangulation, a method of determining a location by analyzing signals from multiple sources."

Sivert turned to his printer and grabbed a piece of paper. He handed it to Timo, who glanced at it before passing it to Isa. "Downtown," she read aloud. "That doesn't exactly narrow it down."

"I only had two base stations to work with. But the last call she received is more interesting," Sivert said. "Read the bottom line. I could narrow that down a bit more."

"The area around the concert hall?"

"Her stalker was there the moment she died?" Timo asked.

"I would be cautious about drawing that conclusion," Sivert said, taking the paper back from Isa and placing it on his desk. "But he was in the neighborhood."

He turned his attention back to the computer screen.

"I also found some metadata in the audio file that might help us. Someone tried to hide it, but the original recording was made six years ago. Pieces have been removed as I already told you and then the rest was stitched together. The sound spectrum analysis clearly shows this."

And he brought up the sound spectrum of the recording. Timo and Isa leaned in closer to get a better look.

As the image came into focus, they could see a series of peaks and valleys that represented the different frequencies in the audio file.

"Whoever edited this did a pretty good job of covering their tracks," Sivert said, pointing to the screen. "But there are still some telltale signs. For example, the amplitude of the sound wave changes abruptly at certain points, which suggests that there was a cut."

He zoomed in on one section of the spectrum and highlighted a specific point. "See this?" he said, pointing to a sharp peak. "This is where the original recording ended, and a new section was spliced in. You can tell because the waveform doesn't match up perfectly."

"Was this recording made on a cell phone?" Timo asked. "You know, like... without someone having a clue they're being recorded."

Sivert shook his head and then turned to him. "I doubt it. This is of pretty good quality. You know what this reminds me of?"

"Enlighten me," Timo said with a grin on his face.

"I was watching a movie the other day about a music band... stupid movie by the way. Anyhow, it reminds me of an audio production in a studio."

"So, you are saying that this is some kind of mastered tape?" Timo asked.

"Not exactly," Sivert replied. "It's rather one of the multitrack recordings. These are separate tracks for various instruments and vocals, allowing for individual adjustments, edits, and mixing before they are eventually combined into the final audio recording. I think this is one of them. Even in an early stage. Maybe even one that was never used."

"Likely, because no one recognizes this version." Then Timo leaned back in his chair and rubbed his chin. "But why would someone edit this version? And what does the message mean?"

"We need to find the original recording," Isa said.

"That might be difficult," Sivert interrupted.

"I'd start with Celeste's record label," Isa said.

Timo sighed. "Why was there another version of this song anyway?"

Isa turned to Sivert. "You said the recording dates back from six years ago."

"Right," Sivert confirmed. "As far as I can see from 25 October 2013."

"This is almost a year before 'Aria 25' was released," Isa said. She got up and leaned against the wall. The pain in her back was killing her. She winced, realizing that perhaps her aching back was a consequence of a poorly chosen sleeping position. It made her feel old and weary.

"So, this is a very first version of that fantastic hit. Why don't we hear Celeste or Freya on this recording? Celeste's family told us she played violin and piano, but never the guitar. It's a man's voice, not Freya's voice. What does this mean?"

"It could be Celeste composed it and her friends were playing it."

"Then you don't make a professional recording of it," Timo said. "And what friends?"

"We also need to consider the possibility that this recording is fake, a hoax designed to mislead us," Isa continued. "We shouldn't jump to conclusions until we have all the facts."

"I agree but this is linked to Jukka Ulfsson in one way or another. It has a meaning. Celeste received it before she died. It is significant."

"Why did the abductor even call?" Sivert said. "He could have taken Jukka without any problem. Why the drama?"

"Good point," Isa said. "He wants us to know about this recording."

"We need to find the studio where this song was recorded in 2013," Sivert said.

"Let's start with Celeste's record label as Isa suggested," Timo said. "I'm beginning to think Celeste Westerberg wasn't the original composer of this song. We need to find out who it was."

# CHAPTER

# 14

**JUST A BRIEF TEN MINUTES HAD PASSED** since the call, the voice distorted by a modulator, imparting an almost surreal quality to the conversation that barely had spanned a minute.

They approached the ancient warehouse. Its imposing brick façade loomed like a relic from an industrial era long forgotten. Boarded-up windows, peeling paint, and a roof patched with rusted metal sheets silently chronicled the relentless march of time. A faint whistling sound whispered through the gaps.

Separated from the warehouse by a rusted and bent chain-link fence, the deserted parking lot stood as a testament to neglect. The pavement was cracked and potholed, and several abandoned cars, scattered without rhyme or reason around the lot, had windshields frosted over from the recent snow. Dim yellow streetlights flickered, casting eerie shadows across the desolate area.

The snow had melted, but its remnants remained—dirty slush, frozen puddles, and muddy footprints. Each breath materialized in the cold air. A fleeting cloud.

In the silence, occasionally punctuated by creaks and rustles, a white van stood out in the parking lot, its paint chipped and peeling with age.

Their footsteps echoed as the police officers approached, drawn to the van's partially open rear doors.

As they came closer a distinct musty odor emanated from within the van.

They advanced with caution, now and then throwing glances at each other. When their flashlights finally cut through the darkness, a grim scene was revealed: a battered man, his head twisted unnaturally, lay in a corner, blood staining his shirt.

The seriousness of the situation sank in, their stomachs turning at the sight. One of them paused, swallowing hard to suppress the rising nausea. This wasn't a sight they had seen before, and it rattled them to the core.

Their hands shook as they reached for their radios, urgently calling for backup.

*　*　*

Dr. Einarsson stood next to the dissection table, his gloved hands hovering over Jukka's body that lay naked on the table. The bright overhead lights illuminated every part of his body.

The doctor's expression was stoic as he took in every detail. His sharp eyes scanned Jukka's bruises and lacerations, noting the severity and location of each injury. He carefully probed the wounds with his gloved fingers, observing the depth and shape of each one.

The autopsy room was quiet, save for the occasional hum of machinery. The air was heavy with the acrid scent of chemicals and the metallic tang of blood. Though, that was something he was used to by now.

"Did you find anything?"

Dr. Einarsson jumped up. "Jesus, you scared me."

Sylvia wasn't impressed and looked at him with a steely expression. "Well, did you?"

Dr. Einarsson composed himself and adjusted his glasses before answering. "There are signs of blunt force trauma to the head and chest, as well as several cuts and bruises. The cause of death appears to be a combination of head trauma and blood loss from the lacerations."

Sylvia jotted down some notes in her pad. "And what about the missing fingers?"

The doctor furrowed his brow. "They were removed pre-mortem. It definitely contributed to the severe blood loss he suffered."

"He was tortured."

"Correct. Based on the injuries and evidence, it appears that Jukka was subjected to a violent and prolonged assault before his death," Dr. Einarsson confirmed.

"Anything else?"

Why was she feeling so hot? So weak. She hadn't eaten a thing that morning, and she knew that wasn't good.

"Are you feeling alright?" he asked.

Sylvia nodded. "I think I'm just hungry."

"Aren't we all," Dr. Einarsson said and then turned to the body. "I found pieces of glass in the wounds."

"He was cut?"

"Likely. There are stains on his clothes... the same as what was found on the kitchen floor of his house, but also others. Clay."

"Clay?"

Einarsson raised his brow and said, "Small particles of clay were found under his fingernails, and there are traces of it on his clothes as well. It's possible that he came into contact with it before his death."

Sylvia nodded, scribbling down some notes.

She then asked, "What about his shoes?"

Dr. Einarsson looked at her curiously and replied, "What about them?"

"Did they find any clay on his shoes? This could give us an idea where he has been."

"I'm not sure," the doctor said, walking over to the counter where a tray with evidence bags lay. He sifted through them and picked out a plastic bag containing a pair of sneakers. "Let's see," he said and examined them without taking them out of the bag.

Sylvia leaned over to get a closer look. She noticed something odd about the shoes—they were clean. Too clean. Something she was eager to point out to the doctor.

"You're right," he said, turning the shoes over in his hands. "These shoes have been cleaned. But there's something else..." He paused and sniffed at the bag. "There's a faint odor of gasoline. It's very subtle, but it's there."

"Gasoline?"

"Whoever killed Jukka might have wanted to burn them to get rid of any evidence but changed his mind," Dr. Einarsson said, putting the bag on the table. "We'll send them to the lab for analysis to be sure."

He walked back to the dissection table and Sylvia followed him, but she suddenly saw the room spinning around. She held on to one of the cupboards to steady herself.

This hadn't gone unnoticed to the good doctor. "Are you sure you're okay? I don't want another newbie throwing up in my examination room."

"I'm not a newbie."

Dr. Einarsson raised an eyebrow at Sylvia's outburst. "Well, you are new to this department, and you're still in training, so technically..."

Sylvia felt her frustration building. "I'm a sergeant, studying to be an inspector. I'm not a newbie."

"Okay, okay," Dr. Einarsson said, holding up his hands in surrender. "I apologize. You're not a newbie. You're a highly trained professional who happens to be new to this department."

The deep breaths were not enough to calm herself down, and irritation grew as she saw the sarcastic grin on his face.

"So, the shoes were drenched in gasoline, but also his clothes, his hair, his entire body," Dr. Einarsson continued. "Smell for yourself."

Sylvia leaned over and sniffed Jukka's body. She could barely detect the faint scent of gasoline, but it was definitely there. "Why would someone do that?"

"There could be a number of reasons," Dr. Einarsson replied. "Maybe they were trying to destroy evidence, or maybe they were trying to conceal the smell of something else. But..."

She stared at him for a moment. "What are you saying?"

"I think... whoever abducted him poured gasoline over him and likely threatened to burn him alive. There were urine stains on his trousers. He was scared."

"Jesus," Sylvia said.

"It's just a guess. I don't know for sure of course."

"Did you find anything special in the van?" Sylvia asked.

"Wrappers, leaves, and pieces of glass. They are being processed for fingerprints and DNA."

"The van was stolen. Likely we'll only find the prints and DNA of the owner," Sylvia said with a sigh. "But we'll see what the lab comes up with. What else..."

Suddenly everything started to spin before her eyes. She stumbled backward, grabbing onto the edge of the dissection table for support. She tried to steady herself but found that her legs were wobbly and weak. Her heart raced, and a cold sweat broke out across her forehead. She could feel her blood sugar dropping, and she knew she was in trouble.

Dr. Einarsson noticed her struggling and rushed over to her. "What's going on?"

She tried to speak, but her mouth was dry, and her throat felt constricted. She raised a shaky hand to her forehead and tried to take a deep breath. "I... I think my blood sugar is dropping," she managed to say.

Dr. Einarsson quickly grabbed a chair and helped Sylvia sit down. "Do you have diabetes?"

She hesitated for a moment before nodding. "Type 1. I was diagnosed when I was a child."

"Okay," Dr. Einarsson said. "Let me get you some juice or something to eat."

Sylvia nodded again, feeling embarrassed and frustrated. She had been so careful about managing her diabetes, but the stress and intensity of the case had thrown her off balance. She watched as Dr. Einarsson hurried out of the room and she heard him rummage through the cupboards.

A few minutes later he returned and handed her a glass of orange juice and a granola bar. Sylvia felt a mix of gratitude and shame. She knew that she should have been more open about her diabetes with her colleagues, but she had been afraid of being seen as weak and unreliable. Now, as she sat there feeling shaky and vulnerable, she realized how stupid she had been.

"Thank you," she said, taking a sip of the juice. "I'm sorry for causing a scene."

"Do they know?"

"Who?" she said confused.

"Your colleagues, do they know about your diabetes?"

She frowned and took a bite of the granola bar. "No. They don't need to know."

His face turned stern. "If you don't take care of yourself, you're putting yourself and your colleagues in danger."

"I know... it won't happen again," Sylvia said.

He got up. "I need to postpone Mr. Ulfsson's autopsy. You can stay here."

"No... I'll go," Sylvia said, but the moment she tried to get up, her head started to spin again, and she felt dizzy. Einarsson assisted her back into her seat.

"I don't think you are capable of going anywhere at this moment," he said firmly. "I'll send someone who can monitor your glucose levels... since you don't quite care about them... but I do. I don't want you to pass out on the floor of my examination room."

She nodded and then looked at the glass of juice in her hand. She should feel irritated by the way he had addressed her, but she couldn't.

Stupid, so stupid. How would she ever be taken seriously?

Especially by him.

*** 

Everyone looked at Dr. Einarsson when he entered the meeting room, and then looked at Timo who was standing in front.

"I asked the doctor to join us," he said.

Isa didn't look up from the file in front of her. Varg was leaning back in his chair. He seemed tired and uninterested.

Dr. Einarsson made his way to the table and took a seat next to Varg. Isa looked up at him and offered a polite nod.

Then he quickly looked at Sylvia who was sitting at the other side of the table, but she decided not to give him a glance.

"Varg, what have we got?" Timo asked.

"The van has been identified as the one that was used to abduct Jukka. The license plates were changed but we checked the vehicle identification number and it's the same."

"What I understood is that prints and DNA were found," Timo said.

"Correct," Varg said. "We'll expect the results in a few days or so. The prints only gave a match with the owner, and he has an alibi. We can rule him out."

"Do we know when the car was left there? Sylvia?"

Sylvia's heart raced as Timo's question snapped her back to attention. She still felt weak and shifted in her chair. Then she quickly flipped through her notes.

"I'm not sure yet," she finally answered. "But we're trying to gather the surveillance footage from the area to see if we can pinpoint the time the van was left there. Maybe... just maybe, we can see the driver."

Dr. Einarsson cleared his throat, and Sylvia felt her eyes involuntarily dart towards him. He was looking at her with a curious expression, as if he knew what she had been thinking. She quickly looked away, feeling embarrassed.

What was it about this man? Even when he didn't say a thing, he managed to irritate her. And she had to admit that the strange fascination, the pull-push between irritation and interest, had her being confused most of the time when they were in the same room.

After the incident in the morgue, she had looked him up. It was strange. She had met him before when Dr. Ingrid Olsson had overseen the forensics team and before she had decided to leave. A choice Sylvia still hadn't understood. Einarsson had now and then assisted Ingrid, but Sylvia had never really noticed him until now. He always blended in the background.

And only after their recent meeting, Sylvia had decided to do some more research on him. She wanted to know more about this man who seemed to be causing her so much stress. She had looked him up on the internet and in the police database. He had a long list of academic papers and seemed to be a renowned expert in the field of forensic anthropology. Nothing but praise for his scientific achievements. Somehow it didn't surprise her. The image of an intellectual without the proper social skills kept popping up in her mind. He was fairly black-and-white, no compromise, but if she had to be honest to herself, she actually liked his uncompromising image of integrity and honesty.

The picture that accompanied his biography on most of his papers had caught her attention. He had been a lot younger, but that wasn't it. He had been smiling, and for some reason he actually was handsome in a classic kind of way. Soft features, symmetric face.

Now he looked sad and stern most of the time. It shocked her that human beings could change so quickly over the years. Few people had told her he had changed after his divorce. The breakup had been tough and dramatic. His ex-wife had remarried one of his best friends. After that, he had withdrawn pretty much from social life. After he had taken Dr. Olsson's position, he was always the first to be there in the morning, and last to leave at night. He never talked about family or friends. He seemed to have no hobbies or anything remarkably interesting in his life. But still she found herself having a strange fascination for him.

"The autopsy took a bit longer than expected," Dr. Einarsson started and threw a quick stare in Sylvia's direction.

"What did you find?"

"The lacerations on his hands indicate that he must have been restrained for a long period of time. We found glue on his hands. Likely tape was used to immobilize him."

"What else?"

"Two of his fingers were removed. Cut. My guess is that cutting pliers were used. The rest of his body showed multiple cut wounds, and the killer slashed his wrists. That's what eventually killed him. The massive blood loss."

"Jesus," Isa let out.

"When did he die?" Timo asked.

Dr. Einarsson straightened his back and then said, "According to the liver temperature I'd put the time of death between two and four hours before we found him. But the amount of blood we found in the van was still substantial. He likely was still alive when he was put in the van. We also found traces on the floor that suggest he was still trying to find a way out, but he must have already been weak. Even if we had found him earlier, he likely wouldn't have survived."

"Thanks, doctor. Let us know when you have the DNA results."

Einarsson nodded, got up and then left the room.

A strange mix of relief and disappointment came over Sylvia.

"What do we know about the caller?" Timo said.

"The call came in yesterday at 10 a.m. We could trace the call back to a public phone booth near the central station," Sivert replied. "It's one of the very few that still exist. We've checked the footage from the security cameras in the area, but there's no clear image of the person who made the call. We're still reviewing all the footage and trying to gather more information."

"Did the caller say anything else besides giving the location of the van?" Timo asked.

"No, just that there was a van parked at that location and that we'd be very interested in the contents," Sivert said.

"I want a thorough check on his wife's whereabouts of the last three days. I want a report from each of you on my desk tomorrow morning."

They got up and left the room except for Isa who was still sitting there, lost in thought.

Timo noticed and asked, "Is everything alright? You were so quiet."

"Yeah, I know... I'm just a bit tired, and..." Then she quickly looked at her phone.

He put himself next to her. "This is not like you."

"Someone has been desecrating Alex's grave," she said, almost with tears in her eyes.

"I'm so sorry," Timo said and took her hand. "Do they know who did it?"

She shook her head. "First it was small things, like flowers and candles being moved or missing, but now... now it's worse. They've been leaving strange objects and symbols, and even writing disgusting messages on the gravestone."

Timo squeezed her hand. "Shall I have a look at it?"

"No, you are busy enough as it is with this case... it's probably some stupid teenagers."

"Were other graves damaged?"

She shook her head. "Just leave it."

Her phone started buzzing. She stared at it but didn't do anything.

"Aren't you going to take it?"

"Since yesterday I've been getting these strange calls. I've tried to block the caller, but it's always a different number. When I answer, it's just silence. Weird."

"You have these phishing scams going on all the time," Timo said. "Just ignore it."

She offered him a subtle smile.

"I have to go," Timo said and got up. "Are you sure you're going to be okay?"

"Yeah, I'm fine," Isa said.

But he wasn't so sure. Time and time again, he had been surprised by how much Alex Nordin had remained a significant presence in Isa's life, even though it had been almost two years since his murder. Then again, it had taken him eight years to move on from the death of his girlfriend, Caijsa.

"Oh... Timo, don't forget about my parents' party," Isa said and gave him a warm smile.

"Lindström... we're in the middle of an investigation," he started. "I cannot afford to go off and party."

"One or two hours won't make a difference," she said and frowned. "I just... need someone..."

She looked so fragile and down. Timo hesitated, torn between his commitment to the investigation and his concern for Isa's well-being. He sighed and finally relented, offering a reassuring smile. "Alright, Lindström, I'll be there."

Isa's face brightened. "Thank you, Timo. It means a lot to me."

He stared at her as she left the room. He didn't know what it was, but he suddenly felt a pressing need to take care of her.

* * *

He ran his hands through his hair. It was a mess. The floor was covered in blood. It was everywhere. It was his own fault. Why had he decided to kill him? It was so unnecessary. He could have kept him for a while until it was over, but no, he had to let the rage take over. The moment he had poured the gasoline over his victim he knew there was no way back, he had to pull through and he had given Jukka the choice: burn alive or bleed slowly to death. Jukka had screamed, but his mind had been made up. That night Jukka Ulfsson had to pay for what he had done, just like the others would. The smell of fear, the soothing surge of revenge, he felt it all again. And he would feel it once more. His task wasn't done.

The man tried to calm himself. He needed to think clearly. He knew he had to get rid of the evidence and fast. The police would soon be on his trail, but he couldn't let them catch him. Not now, not when he was so close to finishing everything.

He walked over to the sink and washed his hands.

He grabbed some cleaning supplies and started scrubbing the floor. It was a gruesome task.

And then it was time to move to the next phase.

# CHAPTER

# 15

AS BORIS CRADLED THE GLASS OF WINE in his hand, he gazed at the misty, snow-covered hill. He felt awestruck and a little jealous of his friend's house. As he continued to gaze at the tranquil scene outside, Boris' mind drifted to the tangled web of family ties that seemed to dominate his existence. His brother, who often demanded his time and attention, his father, with his unending expectations, and his ever-watchful aunt who seemed to always know what was best for him. Although he had a house of his own, it felt more like a place to rest than a true reflection of his life. He longed for a space that was authentically his, a refuge where he could escape the burdens of familial obligations and truly find himself.

"Beautiful, isn't it?" Max said as he stood next to him.

"Yeah... great," Boris replied, taking another sip before turning to Max. "But I gathered you didn't invite me here to admire the view."

Max quickly looked down at his hands, then sighed and said, "They found Jukka."

"What are you trying to say?"

"The body in the van... it's all over the news. It was Jukka."

"Jeez," Boris muttered, his mind racing as he processed the grim news.

"Bulgari..."

"Don't call me like that," Boris' tone grew steely. "We're not children anymore."

"Boris... I'm scared," Max stammered and put his glass down, his hands trembling as he glanced around the room.

"Max, what did you do?"

But Max remained silent.

Boris sighed and leaned in closer. "You can't keep hiding. You have to tell me what's going on."

Max finally looked up. "I... we, Jukka and I, owe someone a lot of money. Things got out of hand."

"Who? What did you do?"

"Andreas Lundqvist," Max said and looked at him.

"My God," Boris let out and ran his hands through his hair. "Andreas Lundqvist! I thought you were done with that stuff. Fucking hell!" Boris' brows furrowed in concern. "How much?"

Max hesitated, then whispered, "One million kronor."

Boris took a deep breath and shook his head. "Man, you're in deep. How could you be so stupid?"

"I needed the money."

"How come you need money? Your family is filthy rich."

"My parents are... I've made some really bad choices. Jukka, Freya..."

"Freya? Freya as well? How..."

"I don't know where she is. I tried to call her when Jukka disappeared. I think something happened to her."

But Boris ignored him. "How could you let this happen? After all she has been through."

"It was her idea," Max said and looked down.

Boris' frustration grew. "You dragged her into this mess. You should have protected her. Remember the hell she went through after our graduation."

"Yeah, and whose fault was that?" Max's voice hardened. "She was your girlfriend, and you made her an addict."

Boris' frustration now reached a boiling point. "Don't you dare blame this on me! Freya's suffering was a result of my mistakes, and I've regretted it ever since. I thought you had learned from that. Now, you've put her in danger again."

"Maybe, but she came up with the idea to cheat Lundqvist."

"What did you do?" He put his hands through his hair again. "No, wait, I don't want to know."

But Max started explaining anyway, "We thought we could outsmart him. We've been skimming off a percentage of the drugs we were supposed to distribute, keeping it a secret from him. We hoped that we could build up enough stash to eventually have financial freedom."

Boris' eyes widened with disbelief as Max continued, "But it didn't work out as we'd planned. We made some risky investments that went south, and we lost a lot of money. To cover our losses, we decided to sell a portion of the skimmed drugs at a steep discount, thinking we could recoup our financial losses that way."

Max's shoulders slumped, his face showed a deep regret as he confessed the full extent of their actions. "Andreas found out about our scheme. He demanded that we repay the full value of the drugs we'd withheld, along with the profits we'd cheated him out of. One million kronor. Jukka is dead. Freya disappeared. I'll be next if I don't pay."

He took a deep breath and asked Max, "So, why am I here?"

Max looked directly into Boris' eyes, desperation evident in his own. "I need your help, Boris. I don't know what to do. I'm trapped, and I'm afraid for my life. You're the only one I can turn to for help."

"You need my money," Boris said. "Why on earth would you believe I have money?"

Max's voice quivered as he explained, "I need money, Bulgari. My family's wealth is deceptive, and I can tell you, my father would rather kick me out of the family before helping me. Jukka, Freya... I know it all spiraled out of control. I told you I got a message."

"What message?"

Boris' confusion deepened as he listened to the symphonic music playing from Max's phone. He couldn't grasp the connection between the haunting melody and the dire situation Max was in. "What does this music have to do with anything? It doesn't make any sense. This is just a prank."

Max's hands trembled as he held the phone. "It's a code. I've received it twice now. The same song was played after Jukka's disappearance. They also found it on Celeste's phone. It's a warning from Andreas Lundqvist. Maybe he killed Celeste... to warn us. I need the money... fast!"

Boris was growing increasingly frustrated with Max's paranoia. "Max, this doesn't make any sense. Stop freaking out. This is just a song. Nothing more, nothing less. You're letting fear cloud your judgment."

Now Max's desperation turned to anger as he clutched his phone tightly. "You don't understand. I'm not making this up. I've seen what Andreas Lundqvist is capable of. He's ruthless, and he won't stop until he gets what he wants."

Boris, realizing that he needed to distance himself from this increasingly dangerous situation, made a move to leave. "I can't help you with this. I'm sorry, but I can't get involved in something that could get us both killed."

But as Boris turned to go, Max's voice turned cold and threatening. "You walk away now, Boris, and I'll make sure you regret it. I know what you did."

Boris remained frozen in place.

Max continued his threats, "Now you're listening. I know things, things that could ruin your life. Remember that day on the cliff when your brother fell? I know where you were, and maybe the rest of the world should know too."

Boris' face drained of color as the weight of Max's accusations bore down on him. He couldn't find his voice, his mind spinning as he grappled with the dangerous game Max was playing. "I don't know what you're talking about."

"You don't? Well, you and the world will know soon enough."

As tension thickened in the room, Boris felt an urgent need to distance himself from the spiraling situation. He moved swiftly towards his coat hanging by the door.

His hands, trembling with a mix of fear and resolve, fumbled for the coat, slipping it on with unsteady movements. Still avoiding eye contact with Max, Boris then took a deep breath to steady himself, each inhale a desperate attempt to regain his calm.

Finally, his voice quivering yet determined, he spoke, "I'll take my chances, Max. And you... will still be dead."

With those words, Boris opened the front door and stepped out into the cold night, leaving behind the looming threat of Max.

He knew all too well what Max had been talking about.

* * *

The man's voice on the other end of the line pierced the monotony in Varg's office. He leaned back in his chair. With a reluctant sigh, he reached for his pen and notepad, ready to entertain yet another call.

The man continued, "I'm calling regarding an email that was sent to us."

Varg suppressed another sigh. "Which email are you talking about?"

After the press conference, Timo had assigned him the unpopular duty of monitoring the tip line. It had proven to be a monotonous and often exasperating experience. Varg had grown tired of the never-ending parade of calls from attention-seekers and individuals with information unrelated to the case. He longed for the investigative work that awaited him, the pursuit of Jukka's murderer. It seemed as if some believed he wasn't capable, and it grated on his nerves.

But this call seemed something else entirely.

"We received an email with an attachment from the Gävle police a few days ago," the man continued. "Someone from the police station also reached out to us, although they spoke with my management assistant. I was away on vacation for a few days, and that's why I only had the chance to review the email yesterday. After reviewing, it's clear the song was recorded in our studio."

Varg's eyes widened, and he felt a rush of anticipation. "The song? The recording? Sorry... who are you again?"

The man hesitated for a moment before responding, "I'm Gabriel Orne, the owner of Harmony Haven Studios in Stockholm. I thought I should contact you directly after reviewing the contents of that email."

"That was the right thing to do," Varg said, still trying to gather his thoughts.

"The song was effectively recorded at our studio," Gabriel continued. "Also, the date is correct: 25 October 2013."

Varg's interest was piqued. "Do you know who was present during the recording? Can you tell me a bit more?"

Gabriel sighed, weighing his words carefully. "I can tell you who hired the studio that day, but my policy is to respect client confidentiality."

"I understand, but this is now a murder investigation. I can get a court order or..."

"Murder? No, that won't be necessary," Gabriel interjected quickly. "We'll do everything to help."

The next moment, Varg heard the distinct clattering of keys on a computer keyboard. Less than a minute later, Gabriel's voice broke the silence. "A certain Dancho Krastev—I hope I pronounce the name correctly—paid 20,000 kronor to record the song."

"Dancho Krastev," Varg repeated. He had come across that name before, tucked away in the file he had been reviewing. The connection was becoming clearer, but he needed more details. The creatives. Everything was linked, and some of the puzzle pieces were falling into place.

Or maybe not?

"Do you know if he was there alone or with other people?" Varg inquired.

"That I cannot tell you," Gabriel said with a hint of regret. "We provide the studio and a professional producer, but the details of the recording sessions are generally left to the clients."

Varg thought for a moment and decided to press further. "Can you at least tell me the name of the producer who was present during Dancho Krastev's session?"

There was a brief pause, and then Gabriel replied, "The producer who worked with him that day was Helena Håkansson."

"Can you send me the original recording?"

Gabriel paused for a moment and then said, "I understand the importance of your investigation, but unfortunately, I can't provide you with the original recording. Client confidentiality and copyright regulations prevent us from sharing recordings without the artist's consent."

Varg frowned. "Let me emphasize again that this is a murder investigation. Lives are at stake, and we have substantial reasons to believe that the song might hold critical clues to the case. We're dealing with something much bigger than privacy and copyrights here."

Gabriel hesitated, the weight of Varg's words sinking in. "I can try to reach out to Mr. Krastev, but I must be honest—it might be complicated. Protecting our clients' privacy is essential to us, and I believe he could be particularly protective of his work."

It was a problem. As far as Varg knew, Mr. Krastev was in a coma, unable to give his consent. He was essentially in a vegetative state.

As the call concluded, Varg's mind raced. On one hand, there was a growing sense of anticipation that they were making progress. On the other hand, the obstacle posed by Dancho Krastev's condition was a significant setback. The investigation was beginning to revolve around the creatives, and he felt it in his stomach that the song had a central role.

But how?

As of now, they had more questions than answers, and he felt like time was running out. Who said the perpetrator was going to stop?

* * *

The interrogation room crackled with tension as Timo and Isa sat across from Verner Blixt, the notorious right-hand of Andreas Lundqvist. With a mocking and self-assured demeanor, Blixt stared them down, flanked by his expensive lawyer.

Verner Blixt exuded an aura of sophistication and elegance that set him apart in the grim interrogation room. His tailored charcoal suit was impeccable, and his silver tie glinted with subtle opulence. He possessed the air of a man who was well-versed in the world's finer things. But his most striking feature was his eyes. Behind a pair of expensive designer glasses, they gleamed with a cold and calculating brilliance that seemed to pierce through everything and everyone. His demeanor made it clear that he was self-centered and focused on his own interests, despite his refinement.

Timo cast a concerned glance at Isa. She appeared utterly drained, and she needed to be at her sharpest. This wasn't your everyday criminal they were dealing with—this was a true master of deception. Timo couldn't afford any slip-ups.

Verner reclined in his chair, dismissing his lawyer's attempts to hush him with an indifferent glance. "How many times are we going to do this little dance, Inspector Paikkala?" he quipped, fully in control of the situation. The conversation was going to happen on his terms.

"As many as needed," Timo replied calmly, his features betraying no emotion.

"Well then... let's tango," Verner taunted, a mocking smile curling his lips.

Timo didn't know if he should return the smile or maintain his composure. The conversation had taken on a particular tone, and he had to keep control over it. He couldn't allow Blixt to worm his way into his mind, no matter what.

"Where is your boss?" Timo asked.

"Where is yours?" Verner was quick to reply. He leaned in, another sly grin playing on his lips. "You know, Paikkala, I've heard about your particular relationship with Commander Eriksson. The rumors suggest you've got something on him, something that keeps you in his good graces. I wonder..."

Timo tensed. "What are you getting at, Blixt?"

Verner chuckled, leaning back in his chair. "I'm suggesting that sometimes alliances are forged in unexpected places. Maybe our bosses are a bit more on friendlier terms than you might expect. We've all seen what Eriksson is capable of. If I were you, I'd start thinking about my own protection. You never know when your little secret might not be enough to save you."

*Stay calm. Be in control. He's playing with you.*

"That's all very fascinating, but what I am mostly interested in is... Jukka Ulfsson," Timo said and put a picture of Jukka's damaged body in front of Verner.

Verner studied the picture, his expression changing from mockery to something more calculating. "That's a mess. Likely done by an amateur."

Timo's jaw tightened. "Really? You seem to be an expert."

Verner shrugged.

"This wasn't the work of an amateur," Timo continued. "The extent of violence inflicted upon him suggests otherwise."

Verner raised an eyebrow. "You think I did this?"

Timo leaned in slightly, his tone low and measured. "Or your boss."

"I am a respectable businessman. I don't even know this man."

Timo shook his head and gave him a sarcastic grin. "I had expected more. You must know by now that we check phone history, financial records... the whole shebang. Do you think we wouldn't notice the frequent calls Jukka made to your office? What was this about?"

Verner's poker face faltered for a brief moment. He glanced at his lawyer, who seemed equally concerned by the turn in the conversation.

But Timo seized the opportunity. "Mr. Blixt, we have evidence linking Jukka to your business. His calls, his involvement, his debts... it all points to you. Where were you the night of 16 December?"

Verner cleared his throat. "I'll have to consult my... busy agenda. Give me a sec." And he took his phone from the pocket of his trousers.

After a few moments, Verner put his phone down, his composure somewhat restored. "I was attending an event at the Strandvägen Hotel that evening. A gathering of business associates and colleagues. They can vouch for my presence."

"Business associates? Right. You do understand that we will be verifying this with the hotel and the people you mentioned, right?"

Verner nodded, trying to appear unfazed. "Of course. As always, you'll be very thorough, Inspector Paikkala. Just like your chief inspector here, who has remained very quiet. Very quiet indeed. Something wrong?"

Isa was clearly taken aback by Verner's attempt to regain control of the conversation. His slick demeanor and evasive tactics were unsettling, leaving her somewhat off balance. But Timo felt a twinge of disappointment. He wondered where his usually assertive chief inspector, Isa Lindström, had disappeared to.

Verner gazed at her intently, and Isa's expression remained unreadable as he continued, "He's worried about you. Quite intriguing. Are you his latest interest? Are you fucking? For sure, you are an upgrade over that fat, ugly doctor he was chasing after."

Timo felt his blood pressure rise, his frustration simmering beneath the surface. How did Verner know about Ingrid? But then again, he shouldn't be naïve. The Mörkbroder gang kept tabs on anyone they considered a threat. But it was disheartening to realize that his brief relationship with Ingrid wasn't as secret as he'd hoped, and that he had, in some way, placed her in danger. But that was precisely what Verner Blixt wanted.

"Jukka Ulfsson," Timo said in a stern voice. "He was on your payroll."

Verner sighed and then said, "He was one of our business associates."

"He owed you money. Lots of money."

"Which he was paying back. I needed him alive, not dead."

Timo leaned in, fixing Verner with an intense gaze. "You expected him to pay back a million kronor in cash? That's quite an assumption."

Verner shifted in his chair, but his expression remained poised. "I never said it was in cash. We had other arrangements."

"Arrangements like what?"

Verner merely smiled, a sly and unnerving grin. "Inspector Paikkala, you're always full of questions. But maybe you should start asking the right ones."

"And what are the right ones?"

"You are smart enough. Smart enough to know the power of the Westerbergs."

"What does that mean?"

"The secrets of the Westerbergs are much bigger than you can imagine. And the song... it's just the beginning."

"How do you know about the song?" Isa said and looked him straight in the eye. "This information was not revealed to the public."

As she spoke, the overhead light blinked for a moment, casting an eerie, unnatural glow over the scene.

"I know more than you think. Now, this has taken far too much of my time. I'm going to get up, and so is my lawyer. I'm going to walk out of here and you will stay away from me, my family, my business. We have nothing to do with Jukka Ulfsson's death."

As Verner and his lawyer stood to depart, the room's oppressive atmosphere seemed to lift, but the unease remained. Somehow, Timo knew Verner was right. This was far more complex than a simple retaliation.

This wasn't about drugs or money.

This was far more personal.

# CHAPTER

# 16

AS ISA AND TIMO MADE THEIR WAY INTO the living room, the chatter of the crowded party filled their ears. The room was filled with a mix of family and friends, all dressed in their finest clothing. The sound of glasses clinking together, and the occasional burst of laughter echoed through the space.

Isa's eyes swept across the room, taking in the familiar surroundings of her childhood home. The plush couches and chairs were arranged in a circular formation, creating a cozy gathering space for guests. The walls were decorated with family photos, capturing memories of birthdays and holidays gone by.

Isa's gaze was drawn to the center of the room, where her parents stood surrounded by a group of friends. Her mother was wearing a bright red dress that hugged her curves, while her father was dressed in a sleek black suit. They both looked happy, basking in the love of their guests.

But Isa felt a twinge of sadness as she looked at them, knowing that her own family was broken. Her children, Felix and Olivia, were here somewhere, but she hadn't seen them yet. Felix was warming up to her again, but Olivia was still angry and distant, and it saddened her more than she was willing to admit.

"Hey," a familiar voice said, and she turned around.

Viktor stood before her, looking just as handsome as ever in his dark suit. She felt a pang of nostalgia as memories of their past flooded her mind. She forced herself to focus on the present and greeted him with a polite smile.

"Isa," he said. "You look... nice."

"Thanks."

"Hello," Viktor said and turned to Timo.

Timo nodded and didn't say anything. She looked at him, a bit annoyed. She had expected him to at least do an effort to change his clothing. The eternal black T-shirt and worn jeans were his signature look, but it didn't quite fit in with the elegance of the party.

She saw her mother waving at her and then making her way toward them.

"Isa," she let out and threw her arms around her daughter. "So glad you could make it."

Then she looked at the two men and the expression on her face turned slightly cold.

"Hello, Viktor," she said with a nod.

"Mrs. Lindström," Viktor replied politely.

"You can call me mom again," she said and gave him a bright smile. Then she looked at Timo. "And who is this?" her mother asked, eyeing Timo up and down.

"This is Timo," Isa said. "My..."

Her mother's eyebrows shot up in surprise, and she said, "Ah, the Timo Paikkala... your boss. Well, it's nice to finally meet you, Timo."

"Likewise," he said.

Isa's mother was a striking woman with green eyes that sparkled with intelligence and a mane of curly gray hair. She had beautiful features and a slender, athletic figure that belied her age. Her bright red dress accentuated her curves, and she moved with a graceful ease that suggested a life of physical activity and good health. She exuded confidence and warmth, but there was also a hint of steeliness in her gaze that suggested she was not to be underestimated. Despite her initial coldness towards Timo, Isa knew that her mother was a generous and caring person who always put family first.

"Where are the kids?" Isa asked her mother.

"They're playing in the backyard," her mother replied.

"Isn't it too cold?"

"They're kids. They don't mind the cold as long as they can play. Why don't you go join them? I'll come with you."

Isa nodded and turned to the men. "I guess I can leave you guys on your own for a while." And her mouth folded in a grin.

"Uh...," Timo tried, but he could only see her disappear, with her mother trailing behind her.

Navigating through the crowded living room, Isa felt a sense of relief. The familiar scent of her mother's perfume and the soothing hum of conversations formed a comforting backdrop. She followed her mother out onto the back patio, where she could hear children laughing and playing.

As they stepped outside, Isa saw her son. Felix was running around with a group of other kids, all dressed in their party clothes. Darkness was already setting in, casting long shadows across the snow-covered ground, a reminder of the short days that Isa disliked about Swedish winters.

Snowflakes were coming down and the children were trying to catch them. She smiled. No matter how smart he was, he was still a kid and somehow that reassured her. He was a lanky nine-year-old with tousled brown hair and bright green eyes, not the genius in the making.

"Mom!" Felix shouted, running over to give her a hug.

"Hey, kiddo," Isa said, wrapping her arms around him. "Where's Livvy?"

Felix pointed through the window to a corner in the living room, where Olivia was huddled over a pile of Legos.

She let her hands go through his hair and then saw him run after the other kids.

A warm glow met her as she opened the door and stepped inside.

"Hey, Liv," Isa said, walking over to her daughter. "What a building! What is it?"

Olivia looked up at her mother with a scowl. "Nothing."

Isa sighed inwardly, suddenly feeling the distance between them as she most of the time did with Olivia. "Well, I'm glad you're having fun."

Olivia didn't reply, and Isa felt a deep sadness. She knew that repairing their relationship was going to take time and effort, but she was determined to do whatever it took to make things right.

In the other corner of the living room, Timo was still not really feeling comfortable, and Viktor had noticed.

"So she dragged you along," Viktor said and took a sip of his drink.

With a subtle smile playing at his lips, Timo said, "Yep."

"She needs a buffer," Viktor said, almost like he said it to himself.

"A buffer?"

"Something like that. She's a master in avoiding the difficult topics. She doesn't want to talk to me. That's why you are here. She doesn't want to talk to her parents about us... me."

"Yeah... that's Isa," Timo said and looked at the crowd again.

For a moment he stood there and looked at the party goers and their interactions. Some people were engaged in deep conversations, while others were laughing and joking around. Some were drinking cocktails, and others were enjoying the delicious hors d'oeuvres that were being passed around. But Timo felt like an intruder.

"Can I ask you something?" Viktor said hesitantly.

Timo turned to him. "Yeah, sure."

"Alexander Nordin. What was he like?"

"That's before my time. Why do you ask?"

"She looks so lost and confused every time his name is mentioned."

"He was a witness in the Sandviken case. He died."

"Wieland?" Viktor said.

"Yep, Magnus Wieland."

"You're not a fan."

"I'm not. I have experienced firsthand how cunning and manipulative Magnus is. He tried to kill me."

"I knew his older brother Elvin," Viktor continued. "He works in Jämtland. I tried to reconnect with him, after Magnus got arrested, but... he doesn't want to talk to me. That family is... in ruins. It's just so devastating."

Anger flashed in Timo's eyes. "Magnus made that choice. There's no one else to blame than him."

"I know, but still... Isa can sometimes be so careless, unaware about the hurt she inflicts."

Timo sighed, trying to calm the anger that was exceedingly boiling inside of him. "Look, that is no excuse to take someone else's life. Never. Alex Nordin had done no harm to Wieland. And on top of that, Wieland tried to scheme he's way out of it. He made evidence disappear. And I still think he's responsible for Nina Kowalczyk's injuries. I just can't prove it. Nina doesn't remember a thing."

"Nina?"

"The police officer he teamed up with after Isa got suspended. She was once Isa's protégé, but later chose to leave her job and return to university to pursue a career in forensics. Her life has taken a downturn. No one knows if she will ever completely recover."

"She still loves him, you know," Viktor blurted out. "Alexander Nordin."

Timo cast down his eyes. "Yeah, I know. It's not easy to get over someone you loved... with all your heart."

And for a moment, Timo was shocked at his own thoughts. For years, he had been taken hostage in his grief for Caijsa, his murdered girlfriend. And after finding her real killers, he had been obsessed about proving her betrayal and finding an answer to the question if she had aborted their unborn child. But he had come to the realization that it was all in his head, that he had let himself swept away by the lies of a manipulator.

There was no betrayal.

Caijsa was a relic of the past. He knew that now, and he had his mother to thank for it. His mother and he didn't always see eye to eye, and he usually got upset by her overly dramatic and sometimes egocentric behavior, but this time she had been there for him, and she had talked sense into him. There was no proof that Caijsa had been unfaithful to him. He should just move on.

And that was what he was trying to do. Move on from Caijsa and Ingrid. Only that last thing turned out to be more difficult than they both had anticipated. An on-off relationship they had gradually taken one step further, and that had ended in a magical weekend. But Ingrid had wanted to save her marriage and taken the drastic decision to put distance between herself and Timo by changing jobs.

He saw Felix walking up to them. It was a needed intermezzo.

"Dad...," he started and then turned to Timo. "Hey, hello, mister Timo."

Timo gave him a radiant smile. "Felix."

He liked the kid. A lot. There was something about Felix's genuine interest in others that always made him stand out. It wasn't just the bright smile or the eager way he listened—it was the sincerity in his actions, the way he truly seemed to care about those around him. Friends. His mom and dad, but also people he had just met, like himself. And Timo found himself drawn to Felix's warmth and authenticity, qualities that were all too rare in the world they inhabited.

Then the young boy addressed his father again. "Can I go to the park with the others?"

"It's getting dark. Why can't you stay here?"

"There's not enough space. It's too crowded. Please, dad!"

"I could watch them," Timo suggested.

Viktor looked at his son and then turned to Timo. "You don't mind watching him?"

"Not at all," Timo replied, looking at Felix and giving him a friendly wink. "You want to go to the park, right?"

Felix's face lit up. "Yes, please! It will be so much fun."

"Alright, let's go," Timo said, taking Felix's hand.

As they walked towards the door, Viktor called out to them. "Thanks, Timo."

Timo turned back and gave Viktor a nod. "No problem."

Felix gathered his friends and joined Timo at the front door.

"Where are you going?" Isa said.

"To the park," Timo smiled.

"Paikkala, you are trying to escape," she said, with a stern grin on her face.

"That's exactly what I'm doing," he said and then opened the door.

"It's cold and dark outside. And it's snowing."

"I'll survive," he said and disappeared.

Outside, Timo and the children trudged through the snow towards the nearby park. The snow was coming down hard, blanketing everything in a layer of white. Darkness was already creeping in, the streetlights casting a soft glow against the falling flakes. Felix chattered excitedly about the snowman they were going to build and the snowball fights they were going to have, his voice echoing with the pure joy of childhood. Timo listened, enjoying the boy's infectious energy, grateful for this moment of respite from the stresses in his life.

As they arrived at the park, Felix let go of Timo's hand and ran towards the hill, his small form disappearing into the gathering gloom. Timo watched him for a moment, the darkness seeming to close in around them, before shaking off the feeling and joining Felix. They spent the afternoon building snowmen and having snowball fights, the laughter and camaraderie chasing away the shadows of worry and doubt.

This was how he imagined his life to be: filled with simple joys and moments of connection, even in the midst of the winter darkness.

* * *

Isa poured herself a drink and walked upstairs to her bedroom. She had mixed feelings about the day. On one hand, she was happy that Timo had accompanied her to her parents' party and had even taken her son Felix to the park. It was such a nice gesture, and she found herself enjoying his company more and more each day. On the other hand, her thoughts kept drifting to Viktor. She couldn't deny that there were still feelings, even though they had been divorced for years. They had shared so much together, and even though it didn't work out, she still had a soft spot for him. She shook her head, trying to clear her thoughts. She couldn't keep dwelling on the past. She took a sip of her drink and looked around her bedroom. It was neat and tidy, just the way she liked it.

But something felt off.

Suddenly, her phone rang. It was an unknown number. She hesitated for a moment before answering. Over the last days she had gotten plenty of them, but her curiosity got the better of her.

"Hello?"

Silence. She could hear someone breathing on the other end of the line, but no one spoke. She was about to hang up when she heard a strange cracking sound. She looked up. It was as if someone was in the room with her.

"Who is this?"

The breathing on the other end of the line grew louder, and then the line went dead. Isa was left staring at her phone in shock. She felt a cold sweat break out on her forehead. Who was this person? And what did they want from her?

Isa's eyes darted around the room, and suddenly she realized that things had been moved around. Her jewelry box was open, and the books on her bedside table were now lying on the cupboard near the door. She was certain she hadn't moved them, or had she?

A surge of fear coursed through her as she made another unsettling discovery—Alex's sweater was missing. She kept it on the bed and occasionally put her head on it at night. It was like he was still there.

Had she put it somewhere else? She was so distracted sometimes.

Standing up slowly, she clutched her phone tightly as she made her way to the door. A sound from downstairs caught her attention—it was faint but unmistakable. Someone was in the house. The increasing pace of her heartbeat fueled a sense of urgency; she needed to get out.

Tiptoeing to the door, she turned the handle quietly, opening it slowly to avoid any noise. She stepped into the hallway where an eerie silence enveloped everything. Frozen, her heart still pounding, she felt unsure of her next move.

Returning to her bedroom, she glanced at the chair in the corner. There, she found her gun in the holster and took it.

Isa's heart pounded as she made her way down the stairs, gun in hand. Every creak of the old wooden steps sent shivers down her spine.

She had always felt safe in her home, but now, with the strange phone calls and the evidence of an intruder, she felt like a sitting duck.

As she reached the bottom of the stairs, she paused, listening for any sound that might give away the intruder's position. The silence was deafening. She took a deep breath and slowly made her way into the living room, scanning every corner for a sign of movement.

Her eyes darted to the window as she thought she saw something move outside. She held her breath and aimed her gun at the glass, ready to defend herself against whatever was out there. But it was only a branch, swaying in the wind.

She let out a sigh of relief and lowered her gun. As she turned around to head back upstairs, she tried to shake off the feeling of being watched. But deep down, she couldn't shake the sense that something was off. She couldn't explain it, but she knew she needed to be extra careful from now on. With a heavy heart, she made her way back up to her bedroom, hoping that she was just being paranoid.

## CHAPTER

# 17

**HE WOKE WITH HIS HEART BEATING FAST** in his chest. For a moment he could still capture the dream and the heavy emotions that accompanied it. He hadn't had a dream like that for a long time. Back to when he was twenty. Back to that fateful weekend in Höga Kusten. It felt like a lifetime ago, yet the memories remained remarkably vivid. He could almost smell the crisp forest air, hear the rustling leaves in the wind, and feel the warmth of the campfire on his skin.

Boris glanced around and quickly realized that he had fallen asleep on the couch in his father's house. His neck and shoulders were sore. He slowly sat up, wincing as his stiff muscles protested the abrupt movement.

The room around him felt unchanged, frozen in time. The familiar scent of his father's house enveloped him, a mixture of aging wood, well-worn leather, and memories of family gatherings.

As he tried to shake off the drowsiness, Boris reflected on the contrast between his life now and the memories of his younger self, a time when his mother had been alive, when life hadn't seemed such a burden. A time of carelessness, a time of bad choices and responsibilities he hadn't taken.

The doorbell rang. He quickly looked at the standing clock. Already 2 p.m. He should have been in the store long ago to relieve Stefan. Purely out of pity, he had hired the boy a few months ago. A boy without a diploma, from a family that could barely make ends meet. But Stefan's work wasn't good. Sloppy. He often scared off people with blunt remarks and little sense of customer friendliness. Moreover, Boris suspected him of stealing from them.

He got up and quickly looked out of the window to see who the visitors were. And then he decided to stay, at least for a while, before heading to the store to confront Stefan. Through the curtains, he spotted the silhouette of a person he hadn't seen or spoken to in years. Someone he still held fond memories of, even though their paths had diverged, someone he hadn't treated right.

His aunt opened the door. The rooms weren't that well isolated, and he could hear everything they said.

"Inspectors Isa Lindström and Sylvia Ahlgren," the older woman said. "We would like to talk about Dancho Krastev. Is Mr. Radu Krastev home?"

He heard his aunt say in her dry, stern and almost uninterested voice, "No. Why do you want to talk to him?"

"As I mentioned we would like to ask him some questions about his son Dancho."

"You will not be able to talk to Dancho either. He's... in a coma."

"We are aware..."

Boris opened the door and stepped into the hallway. "Auntie... I think we can let the inspectors in."

It was a shock for both of them. Seeing each other eye to eye after so many years. It stirred up feelings. She was still as beautiful as he remembered her. Even more so. The years had given her a certain air of confidence and determination, even though he knew how hard it must have been to lose her brother like that. He practically had lost his brother as well.

"Mr. Boris Krastev?" Isa said and then quickly looked at Sylvia who was still looking at him with open mouth.

He nodded and signaled for them to come into the living room. Then he turned to his aunt. "Maybe you can make some fresh coffee?"

She gave him an angry look but disappeared into the kitchen anyway.

"How can I help you?" he asked.

"We would like to ask you about a certain recording that your brother Dancho made a few years ago."

He frowned and then took a seat across from them. It was evident that Sylvia felt uneasy; she tried to avoid meeting his gaze, diverting her eyes whenever possible, clearly uncomfortable in his presence.

Isa took her smartphone and played the song they had found on Celeste's phone.

He recognized it immediately. It was the same tune Max had received.

"Are you saying my brother made this?"

"Do you recognize it?" Isa asked.

"No... yes, I recognize the text. Celeste's song, but not this version." He continued to listen as Isa put the phone on the small table in the center of the room. And then it dawned on him. The voice on the recording was familiar, a voice he hadn't heard in a long time. The flood of memories overwhelmed him, and he struggled to hold back tears. When the song ended, he yearned to replay it.

So many memories, so many feelings locked away for years, suddenly flooding back into his mind. He had forgotten so many things. His smell, his voice. The way he walked up the stairs. The way he could suddenly start dancing to the melodies in his head, out of nowhere.

"It sounds like my brother." His voice broke. "He loved to sing and dance."

Sylvia threw him a concerned glance and then looked at the notepad in her hand.

"Dancho paid 20,000 kronor to record this," Isa stated.

"20,000 kronor? He didn't have that much money. How?"

Now he knew why his brother's bank account had been empty. After the accident, they found out that Dancho had taken money from his savings account in the year before the incident. They were baffled. Why did he need money? Some of it they had found in his backpack, but not all of it.

"Why did your brother record this song?"

Boris' breath caught in his throat. "I don't know."

"You don't know anything about it?"

He shook his head.

"This was recorded 25 October 2013 at Harmony Haven Studios in Stockholm."

"In 2013? Dancho was only seventeen." He didn't understand.

"Anyone he was close to? Who would know?"

"Dancho... never confided in me. At that age, we were each living in our own world. I wish I had paid more attention."

Why was he feeling so down? Unlike his father and aunt, he had often talked about his brother. He felt so exposed, as though a hidden part of his past had suddenly been thrust into the light. Here, in front of Sylvia. She had been the only thing decent in his life. But he had treated her so badly.

His stupid sixteen-year-old self.

"Tell us about the creatives," Isa said.

"I'm sorry, but what is this about?"

"This song is linked to the death of Jukka Ulfsson," Isa said without showing any emotion.

"Jukka? Dead? But why?"

"The creatives," Isa repeated.

"There isn't much to tell. We were a bunch of naive teenagers, thinking we could do anything. But reality hit us hard."

"You haven't been doing that bad. Five stores across the country."

Money. Everything he wanted, but his life had been put on hold after his brother's accident, and it was he who had pushed the pause button. Somehow, he felt he didn't deserve happiness. Not after Freya, not after Dancho.

"That's my father," he said. "Not me."

The door opened and his aunt came in with a plate full of cookies and a tray with coffee cups. She placed the tray on the table and began pouring coffee for everyone. "It's a family trait, that ambition," she remarked with a smile, handing the inspectors a cup. But before giving Sylvia a cup, she looked straight at her and said, "I remember you."

Sylvia looked at her in shock. The old woman's eyes lingered on her for a few moments longer before she handed her the cup of coffee.

It almost felt like a threat, and he saw how Sylvia leaned back in the chair, as if she was afraid of Stoyanka. He remembered they had never been friends. In fact, no girl had ever been deemed good enough by his aunt.

Boris sighed, his hand reaching out to claim a cookie from the plate. "Yeah, but sometimes I wish I could just... be a bit more carefree."

Then Stoyanka turned to him. "Life has a way of throwing challenges at us. That builds stamina. That makes you strong. It's good."

He mustered a small smile. "Thank you, Auntie."

He didn't want to be strong. He sometimes just wanted to break down. But he wasn't allowed. He never was.

"Mrs. Krastev," Isa said.

"Ms. Dimitrova," Stoyanka corrected.

"Okay, Ms. Dimitrova, do you know this song?" Isa asked and played the song again.

Throughout the entire song, Stoyanka remained stoic. Not a twitch or muscle moved in her face. When it ended, she said, "I don't know this."

She got up and left the room.

"I'm sorry for my aunt," Boris said. "She didn't want to be rude. It's just the way she is. She hasn't had an easy life."

"Oh, why?" Isa asked.

"She's my mother's older sister. My grandmother died at a very young age when they were still young. Their father never got over the death of his wife. He was a drunk. Beat the hell out of them. My mother escaped when she met my father and married him. Stoyanka stayed with her father until he died. Then my parents decided to come to Sweden. Stoyanka came along. I was born here. My mother died in a car accident when I was fifteen. Since then, Stoyanka has been taking care of us. If we didn't have her..."

"Did she get along with Dancho?"

"Yeah... I mean... there were arguments, fights... we weren't always so nice to her. We were two teenagers, thinking we knew everything."

He looked down at his hands before continuing, "Now she's his biggest supporter. She takes care of him. Day and night."

"What about your father?"

"Dad is... he has never been the same after mom died and Dancho got injured. Most of the time, he isn't really here. He doesn't know what's happening. He hides in his cabin... in a fantasy world."

"So, it is you who takes care of the business," Sylvia said. It was the first time she spoke. As if she had to acknowledge he was doing something worthwhile in his life.

"Yeah, maybe...," he said and cast down his eyes.

"Tell us what happened the day Dancho got injured," Isa said.

It wasn't something he thought about that often. In fact, he almost never let those memories resurface. Until today's dream.

"We arrived on Friday evening and the idea was to go back home on Sunday evening. But there was already tension in the air the moment we arrived in the cabin," he started. "It was supposed to be a relaxing weekend between friends, but it wasn't. Far from it."

"Why?"

"Jonathan and Celeste were bickering all the time. There was something going on between them. You could feel it."

"Jonathan Gedman? The man who disappeared?"

Boris nodded. "But I don't know why they were so angry with each other. Dancho was nervous. He wasn't supposed to be there, but he had been whining the entire week about how he was not allowed to go and that it wasn't fair. Dad finally gave in. Dancho was so... hyper. Excited and scared at the same time. I don't know what it was. Maybe that was why he misjudged the hiking trail that Jonathan and he took that Sunday morning."

This was so hard. He should have stopped him. He should have stood his ground and not allowed him to come along.

Isa put the empty cup on the table and then looked at him again, "Who else was there?"

"Jukka, Freya, and me. Max arrived the next day. That started another fight... with Celeste. Max and Celeste. That was always a strange relationship. I never understood it. He was always so protective of her, so... clingy... so jealous."

A jealous lover. He couldn't even take that train of thought. It was too stomach-turning.

"Did you ever see him cross boundaries?"

Boris shook his head. But there were rumors. Plenty of them.

"And Jukka and Freya?"

He didn't want to go there. He closed his eyes, his chest heavy with sorrow. When he finally spoke, his voice was low and filled with the grief he had carried along for so long. But he couldn't talk about it.

"Freya... Freya was fine. And Jukka too." The words were hard to say, and as he uttered them, a vivid memory of Freya's pale face, her lips tinged with blue, flashed before his eyes. He could remember the frailty of her form, the fragility of her life slipping away. It was an image that had haunted him since that day.

"And what happened that Sunday morning?" Isa asked.

"Jonathan and Dancho decided to go for a hike early in the morning. It wasn't until hours later that we realized they hadn't returned."

His voice wavered. "We went looking for them."

"Who found them?"

"Them? Max found Dancho at the bottom of the cliff. Jonathan was gone."

"An accident?" Isa said and quickly looked at Sylvia's notepad.

"That's what it looked like," he said and sighed.

"Oh? You think it was something else?" Isa looked at him with sharp eyes.

"No... I meant... that's what it looked like."

"Dancho's bag was found in the bushes not so far from where he was found. Full of clothes and food. Was he going somewhere?"

He frowned. This was new. No one had ever told him that. "Uh, not that I know."

Isa continued to pierce him with a sharp gaze. "Jonathan was never found. It's a very dense and treacherous area. What do you think happened to him?"

"I really don't know. People said that he likely went off to get help."

"There were partial footprints and drag marks found but it had rained and most of them were unusable."

"I don't understand... what does this have to do with Jukka and the song?"

"That's what we're trying to find out," Sylvia said calmly.

Boris leaned back in his chair. It was as if the past was coming back to haunt him in ways he had never anticipated. He took a deep breath and, while trying to mask his anxiety, he said, "I've told you everything I know."

"Was there anything out of the ordinary that morning?" Isa continued.

A car. A white car. Concealed in the bushes, not too far from the cabin. He hadn't seen it very clearly, but it had been there the evening before, and it was still there when Jukka and he had left.

Freya. He should have stayed with her, not dump her in front of the hospital entrance like the next addict. It was his fault. He should never have pressed her. She had gone too far because of him.

He hadn't been there for Freya and neither for his brother.

"No... yes, maybe. Lukas Stendahl showed up at the cabin that morning. Unexpected."

"Stendahl? Why was he there?"

"Lukas was always... annoying. He and Jonathan were good friends. He wanted to be part of the group, but..."

"But he became Celeste's manager."

"That's right. He became her manager. Everyone thought he had a thing for Celeste, but that obviously wasn't the case. He's good at what he does. But at that time, we didn't take him seriously. We thought he was just chasing after her."

Isa's eyes narrowed. "What happened when he showed up?"

Boris hesitated for a moment. "We let him hang around for a bit, but he was pushy, and kept asking questions, acting all worried."

Sylvia chimed in with a question. "Worried about what?"

"About Dancho and Jonathan... I guess."

"In your statement you mentioned that you took your car and drove around to look for Jonathan after Max found Dancho. The area is very impenetrable, hard to navigate. Not easy to get through by car. Why did you do that?"

Boris hesitated, trying to recall the events of that day. "We... we were desperate to find him. We figured he might have gone to get help, and we wanted to cover as much ground as possible. It was a big forest, and we were scared for him. Plus, Stendahl was there, and he was insisting that we should do something."

"What did you find during your search?"

Boris' face tightened. "Nothing. We didn't find any trace of Jonathan. It was like he had vanished into thin air."

Sylvia pressed further. "And how about Dancho? What did you do when Max found him?"

Boris looked down. "We called for help and tried to keep Dancho as comfortable as we could. We knew he was badly injured, and we didn't want to make it worse by moving him."

"And Dancho? He's in a coma according to the medical files."

"Brainstem injury," Boris said and let out a deep sigh. "He'll likely never regain true consciousness."

"Are you sure?" Isa said suddenly.

He was taken aback by the unexpected question. "The doctors were very clear about that. Why do you ask this? What are you suggesting?"

Isa exchanged a brief glance with Sylvia before continuing. "There have been rare cases where individuals in a coma have shown signs of improvement or even recovery after years of being unresponsive. It's not a common occurrence, but it has happened."

"Well, he isn't." He felt a strange flash of anger boiling inside of him. "If you don't believe me, I'll show you."

\* \* \*

He usually never stood so close. It was confronting. He didn't want to see the pale face, the thin, messy hair. The handsome features that had once been full of life, now masked by the stillness of his brother's condition. The rhythmic sound of the ventilator was a constant reminder of the fragility of life, and the room felt cold, despite the warmth of the medical equipment that surrounded them.

"His eyes are open," Sylvia said.

"That's normal." Boris' voice wavered as he continued, "His eyes open on their own. It's not voluntary. He doesn't respond to external stimuli. There is no observable sign of awareness." Memories flooded back, the countless times they had hoped for some sign of improvement, only to be met with the harsh reality of Dancho's condition.

Stoyanka came into the room.

Isa turned to her. "You take care of him?"

"Yes," his aunt said.

"He looks so awake," Isa said and looked at the man in the bed. "He..."

"Don't get your hopes up," Stoyanka said. "He doesn't realize we're here. We gave up hope a long time ago. Maybe it would have been better if he had died."

Isa frowned and then looked at Boris.

"When we found him, the doctors told us he wouldn't survive the night. We decided to switch off life support, but he started to breathe on his own and he pulled through."

"But now he's on a ventilator," Sylvia said.

Boris chimed in. "He's been in and out of the hospital many times with pneumonia and other complications. It's a constant struggle to keep him stable. He recently had breathing problems. This is to give him some relief."

"So he will never wake up?" Isa asked.

"Never say never," Boris said. "I've prayed for a miracle every day for years, but reality is harsh. I've had to accept that my brother may never regain consciousness, and that's a pain I carry with me every single day."

Boris felt a deep sadness, more profound than any other day. The weight of years of uncertainty, pain, and grief bore down on him as he stood by his brother's bedside, and he felt overwhelmed by the hopelessness of their situation.

"He will never be able to tell us about the song," Boris said.

The song. The song.

And then it suddenly dawned on him.

The song was a love song.

He looked at the man in front of him.

Dancho had been in love. That day he had been in love. If he only had listened to him and not disregarded him as his stupid teenage brother.

# CHAPTER

# 18

**LYING IN THE DARKNESS,** shivering from the cold, he began to stir. His senses slowly returned, and he felt the icy chill seeping into his bones. Panic welled up as he realized he had no recollection of where he was or how he had ended up there.

Was it the same room? It didn't feel like it.

It was so dark and cold. He couldn't see a thing. Usually, he could see some light coming from the outside. Now, it was pitch black.

And the familiar sounds he used to hear were gone.

His heart raced, and he strained to hear any clue about his surroundings. Then, from the impenetrable darkness, he heard it—a soft, rhythmic sound, like distant breathing. His fear intensified as he realized that he was not alone; someone was watching, lurking just beyond his sight.

The breathing drew closer, deliberate and menacing. He was paralyzed by the uncertainty of what would happen next. Every time had been different, and he had learned that survival was never guaranteed. As the unseen presence inched nearer, he knew he might not make it out of this darkness alive.

His vocal cords strained as he attempted to scream, but no sound escaped his lips. He was trapped in a silent nightmare.

Why didn't anyone hear him?

After all those years, why didn't anyone realize?

Please. Don't.

Then it started. He couldn't remember how many times he had gone through this. The last time he had barely survived.

As the seconds dragged on, the air grew thick with the presence of impending doom. He felt a suffocating pressure around his head, and panic surged through him. The plastic bag tightened its grip, clinging to his face, sealing off any hope of breathable air. Every frantic gasp was met with nothing but suffocating plastic.

He fought with every ounce of strength he could muster, but his limbs were unresponsive. His mouth and teeth tried to claw at the plastic, desperate for a single gasp of air, but it was futile. His vision swirled with spots of light, and he felt a pounding in his temples. His chest burned with the relentless need for oxygen.

Please. Please.

The seconds felt like hours as he teetered on the brink of oblivion, a sinister dance with death itself. The struggle for survival waged on.

Then it stopped. He felt the air on his skin.

Then the laughter and the insults came. They always did. But he didn't care anymore. He knew one day, very soon this would all end.

He wanted it to end. It had to.

## CHAPTER

# 19

"**I WAS A BIT SURPRISED WHEN** you called," Timo said as he placed a plate of food in front of her.

"Why?" Kristina asked softly, her gaze fixed on him.

There was a moment of silence. The way she looked at him unsettled him; it was a mixture of sadness and anger, and he couldn't quite fathom where it was coming from. She had been quiet the entire evening, which was unlike her. She seemed distant. Timo wondered if he should say something to break the tension but decided to hold back.

"We haven't talked since Berger's wedding."

"I was busy," she replied and took a bite of the curry.

"I hope it's not too spicy. I've practiced since the last time I used you as a guinea pig," he said with a smile.

But she kept staring at the plate, fork in hand. "It's fine."

Something felt amiss. She would have laughed at his silly joke before. He sat down and pulled the plate towards him.

"You have a lovely house," she said, giving him a forced smile.

"Well, some people might disagree with you, but I think it's very cozy and quiet. It has its charm, and I love living here."

The light from the fire illuminated her face. At first, he thought it was a trick of the light, but upon closer inspection, he noticed her eyes were filling up with tears. She turned away and began eating again. He watched her for a moment. She was clearly in distress, but he couldn't figure out the cause. For the first time in their friendship, he couldn't bring himself to openly ask her. He leaned back in his chair, allowing the silence to envelop them.

"So, what are you busy with?" Timo inquired.

Kristina folded her hands and piously considered her response. "A new case, and I started writing a book."

"A new book? Really? What about?"

"The Sandviken case," she replied.

"The Sandviken serial killer?"

She nodded and moved the fork to her mouth to take another bite.

Timo nodded slowly, as if he were digesting the information. "But the case is reopened. The investigation is still ongoing."

"I know. It's not entirely about this specific case. I use it to illustrate basic concepts of forensic psychology and killer profiles."

"I see, but using an ongoing case..."

"I have Eriksson's permission," she said in a stern voice.

Eriksson. That was the last person he trusted.

"Okay then... I guess," he said, turning his attention to the food he had barely touched. "And what about your new case? Anything exciting?"

"A dead boy. It's a complex case."

"The Malmö case?"

With her gaze fixed ahead, she gently laid her fork down, ignoring Timo's attempts at casual conversation. After a moment, she said, "This is probably going to be my last case."

"Why?"

She met his gaze, her eyes red but her voice steady. "After this case, I'll resign."

"But why?" Timo stammered.

She stared at the food for a moment, and then looked him straight in the eye. "I need to tell you something, I don't have much time. I'm dying."

"Dying? But... how?"

He felt the energy drain out of him. Everything froze.

"I... I took your advice and got myself tested." She shook her head, as if she couldn't quite comprehend it herself. "I received the result two weeks ago. I have the Huntington gene."

Timo sat up straight, shocked and speechless, feeling as though he were falling into a black hole.

"I don't have symptoms yet, but it won't be long. I'm thirty-six, a year older than when my mom became ill. Usually, onset starts earlier in subsequent generations, so I'm running on borrowed time."

"Jesus, Kristina. And now what?" he stammered.

"Nothing. There's nothing they can do. They can only monitor for clinical changes. It's like..." She bowed her head. He couldn't see her eyes, but he knew the tears were coming. He got up, moved to her side of the table, and took her hand. The next moment, he pulled her into his arms. He wanted to say something, but words failed him. There was nothing he could say to fix this, so he simply held her. And she cried.

"I'm here for you," he whispered.

She looked up, cupped his face in her hands, and kissed him on the lips.

"Kristina, I...," he stammered as he gently pushed her away. The next moment, he was overwhelmed with guilt and confusion.

How could he reject someone who was dying?

She stared at him with wide eyes, filled with sadness and shock. "You know I've been in love with you ever since we met."

"I... know, but I can't. I care for you and respect you... as a friend." He turned away, not wanting to see her tears.

"One night," she blurted. "Just one night. That's all I ask from you."

"What?" he said, stepping back and shaking his head. "You want me to sleep with you."

"Make love to me," she said and sighed. "After that, I won't ask anything of you anymore."

"But I don't love you," he said.

"What does it matter?"

He couldn't believe his ears. Of course, it mattered. It mattered a lot. Love and sex were intertwined for him. He didn't want to separate them.

"Is it because of that Caijsa lookalike? Ingrid? Is that it?"

He felt a surge of frustration and anger, but it was crucial for him to maintain his calm. "That's a matter between Ingrid and me."

"Of course, you're sleeping with her! Does Anton know?"

"Kristina, you're in shock right now. You've received devastating news. But this is not the way to..."

"Spare me your psychological mumbo jumbo! You owe me!" She shot him an angry glare.

"I owe you? I don't understand."

"It's because of you that I took the test," she said.

"I simply told you what I would do. I believe you're old enough to make your own decisions. I didn't force you to take the test. Don't blame me for this!"

The tears were streaming down her cheeks. "It's all your fault. You made me do it. You said that it was the right thing to do."

He walked up to her and tried to take her hands in his, but she moved away from him. "Kristina, please," he pleaded. "You're not thinking clearly. You need help."

She shook her head and turned away from him. "I hate you."

"You don't mean...," he said, but saw her walk to the door.

"Kristina!" He followed her into the hallway, where she was already putting on her jacket.

"I need to go," she whispered.

"Kristina, please," Timo said and grabbed her hand.

She looked at him, lips trembling. "You know what to do." Then she opened the door and walked out, saying, "I wish you could be more like your brother."

* * *

The sleek glass and steel structure of the advertising company's headquarters dominated the skyline of Uppsala. As one of the largest companies in the city, it had earned its prime location on the bustling street of S:t Persgatan. The building's exterior was a testament to modern design, with sharp angles and clean lines creating a striking contrast against the historic architecture that surrounded it. From the outside, the office building exuded an air of success and sophistication.

Max Westerberg rushed into the office, his agitation evident as he arrived late for his meeting. He berated himself for not leaving earlier, especially after Google Maps had warned him about the standstill traffic. The snow only compounded his worries. He had even exceeded the speed limits, and he suspected a growing collection of speeding tickets under his name.

This meeting was so crucial. It concerned a key client, and although his colleague Magda was already present and more than capable of handling it, Max hesitated to let her take credit for the proposal he and his team had painstakingly crafted.

As he stood waiting for the unusually slow-moving elevator to come down, his grip on the briefcase tightened. While waiting for the doors to open and take him to the fifth floor, his mind raced through recent events that had left him on edge.

His sister's death. The grief and unanswered questions surrounding her passing. The strange messages with that mysterious song, an enigma he couldn't decipher. Andreas Lundqvist kept echoing in his mind, along with the debts he owed the man. It was a financial entanglement that had started to feel like a noose around his neck. He was still convinced Andreas was behind the messages.

Then, the memory of his rather humiliating discussion with Boris resurfaced. Max had tried to push it to the back of his mind, wanting to forget the whole embarrassing ordeal.

But something was looming in the background, a persistent and unsettling feeling. He couldn't quite put his finger on it, but he knew he couldn't ignore it for much longer.

As the elevator doors finally slid open, a voice called out his name. He pivoted and saw Lukas Stendahl approaching. "Max, can we talk?"

"I don't have time," Max said, attempting to turn away from Lukas. But Lukas swiftly moved to block Max's path to the elevator, effectively preventing his escape.

"Max, you need to stop this lawsuit," Lukas yelled.

"I have nothing to say to you."

"It's going to destroy Alva. What did my family ever do to you?"

Max took him aside and then said, "Did she send you?"

"No, of course not," Lukas let out. "Please stop this."

"That's up to my parents. I have nothing to do with it."

"Why do they want to take everything away from Alva? The house, the money."

"That house, that money belonged to Celeste, my sister. Your cousin decided to betray her."

"And the record deal?" Lukas said. "That has nothing to do with Alva."

"How dare you?! Now my sister is dead, and you see money. You want to exploit her suicide."

Lukas looked taken aback. "What are you talking about? The money from this compilation album would go to charity."

"I know you... and I know your cousin, that manipulative bitch. That money will never go anywhere except in your pockets. You'll see."

Lukas stepped back and then stared at him. "Alva was right. You and your family are so entitled. You think you can just take whatever you want and hurt anyone who gets in your way. But you don't know the whole story, Max. You don't know what Celeste did to Alva. She was there to pick up the pieces, every time. You don't know half of it."

Max's irritation boiled over. "I've had my fill of your family's deceit, Lukas. I've no patience for more. Talk to the lawyers, or better yet, talk to my parents."

He jabbed the elevator button again, and as the doors parted, he darted inside before Lukas could obstruct him. He could sense Lukas' gaze locked on him as the doors sealed shut, but he was resolute.

His focus should be on the impending meeting.

Lukas and his cousin were nothing to him.

*\*\*\**

As Max made his way to the car in the growing darkness, a cloud of discontent loomed over him. True to expectations, Magda had once again stolen the spotlight, leaving him seething with frustration. He attempted to quell the bubbling anger in him, urging himself to let it go. He still had an hour's drive to Västerås ahead.

Max shook his head, trying to clear his mind, as he got into his car and started the engine. His thoughts kept drifting back to the meeting and then to the conversation with Lukas.

Why couldn't everything go his way?

He turned the wheel and drove direction west. He took a few deep breaths and turned up the radio to drown out his thoughts. Frustratingly, the traffic was still gridlocked, and there were no signs of it letting up anytime soon on this evening commute.

In an attempt to escape the traffic, he opted for a shortcut through the forest, although he briefly hesitated, given the darkness and snow. Yet, he forged ahead. As he drove through the winding roads, he noticed a car following him. He squinted to see who it was and thought he recognized Lukas' car.

Then a wave of anger rushed over him.

Why was Lukas following him? Had he been waiting for him all that time? Was he trying to intimidate him?

The car behind him came closer and closer, and Max could see the silhouette of the driver through the windshield. His heart started pounding in his ears. He tried to focus on the road ahead, but his eyes kept darting towards the rearview mirror.

He could hardly see the road.

The car behind him continued to tailgate him, and Max could feel the driver's impatience. He checked the speedometer and saw that he was going over the speed limit. He slowed down, hoping the other car would pass him. But the car stayed behind him, its headlights glaring in his rearview mirror.

Max's mind raced as he tried to think of what to do. He decided to take another shortcut through a narrow road, hoping to lose the car behind him. But as he turned onto the road, he realized it was a dead end.

Now he was looking at a bunch of trees in front of the car.

The car behind him came to a stop just a few meters away, and Max's heart skipped a beat. He looked around, trying to find an escape route, but there was none. He turned off the engine and waited, his hands gripping the steering wheel tightly.

Then suddenly he heard the engine of the other car roar. He saw in the rearview mirror how the car came straight at him. Max's eyes widened as he realized the other car was intentionally trying to hit him. He quickly unbuckled his seatbelt and tried to open the car door. The sound of screeching tires filled his ears as the other car came closer and closer. Max could feel his heart racing and his hands shaking as he struggled with the door handle.

It was too late. The next moment he felt a jolt as the other car crashed into his, pushing his car forward with great force. Max's head hit the steering wheel, and he felt a sharp pain in his chest. He gasped for air, trying to catch his breath.

The next moment, his vision started to blur, and his breathing became labored. He knew he was losing consciousness. The last thing he saw before darkness set in was someone opening the door at his side.

\* \* \*

"You don't look good," Isa said as she dumped herself in the chair at his desk.

Timo yawned and then leaned back in the chair. "I didn't sleep well."

"Me neither," Isa said. "But at least the strange phone calls have stopped. What's your excuse?"

"Oh, never mind." Timo rubbed his tired eyes. "I've just had a lot on my mind lately. Between work and.... some personal problems, it's been hard to switch off at night."

Isa's frown deepened, and she leaned forward, resting her elbows on the desk. "Are you okay? Do you want to talk about it?"

Timo avoided her gaze and stared at the paper in front of him.

"Thanks, Lindström, but I don't think there's much you can do to help. I just need to sort things out on my own."

"So, I guess you ask me here to talk about Einarsson's report," Isa said.

"Yep. What do you make of it?"

"Well," she said. "It's unexpected to say the least."

"I've sent a team over to his house to check what's going on."

"Gideon Younggren," Isa said. "Freya's father."

"If he's involved, and I say 'if', we've been looking at the wrong leads. Celeste's suicide has distracted us."

"But what is the connection to Jukka? I don't understand."

Timo got up and straightened his back. "The undeniable fact is that his DNA was discovered on the body and in the car. He has a history of assault, and it's not the first time he and Jukka Ulfsson had a confrontation. And where is his daughter? Freya Younggren appears to have vanished from the face of the earth."

"Some of her colleagues said she's taken a holiday, but at the same time they said Freya taking holidays is out of character. In the four years she worked in the library, no one has ever seen her socialize, take a holiday or so much mention anything personal."

"But then again who really does know his colleagues," Timo said.

Isa raised a brow. "Maybe you're right. Anyway, could father and daughter be involved in an abduction and murder? And why?"

"I'll call Varg," Timo said.

"You sent Varg?"

"Yeah, is that a problem?" Timo said and took his cell phone.

"No, but he seems a bit distracted lately. I don't know what it is, but Sylvia is a lot sharper and pro-active."

"A bit too pro-active," Timo answered and brought the phone to his ear.

"What do you mean by that?"

With the phone pressed to his ear, he responded, "I just think she's been pushing too hard. It's like she's on a mission to prove herself, especially since we discovered her involvement with the creatives. She's been taking unnecessary risks, making impulsive decisions that could jeopardize the entire investigation."

"What's the issue with ambitious women?"

"It's not about women or men. I think she's going to wear herself out before her career is even started."

Isa smiled. "And I think she wants to impress the boss. She always had a soft spot for you."

"Leave it. Two indecent proposals in one week are enough." And with the phone clutched to his ear, he turned his face to the window. It was raining again. The streets outside were wet and slick from the rain, with the occasional car splashing through the puddles. Gray clouds hung low in the sky, casting a gloomy pall over the city. People on the sidewalks were hunching their shoulders against the cold rain. It was a typical winter day in Gävle, but Timo felt like the weather was reflecting his own mood.

An endless cycle of rain and snow.

He was tired and stressed.

Isa was looking at him with furrowed brows. He knew he had to give her an explanation at some point, but not now.

Finally, he heard a man's voice on the other end of the line. "Sergeant Varg Mårtensson speaking."

"Varg, Timo here. What did you find?"

"Mr. Younggren is not home, neither is his daughter. The house is quiet, like no one has been there for weeks, months. What do you want us to do?"

"There's not much we can do. We need a search warrant. But keep an eye on the place. If you see any suspicious activity, let me know."

"Well, the garden is a mess."

"What do you mean?" Timo asked.

"It's like a truck ran over the flower beds and then backed up over them again. There are tire tracks all over the place, and very distinct ones leading to the back of the house. There is another door."

"Interesting," Timo said. "Take a picture. I want to compare it to the tires of the van."

"Okay," Varg said.

He hung up the phone and turned to Isa. "Looks like we might have something to go on after all. Varg says the garden at Younggren's house is a mess with tire tracks everywhere."

"What does that mean?"

"I don't know yet. We'll have to get a warrant and search the place."

"What if Freya or her father were his first victims?" Isa said suddenly. "They might be in danger or dead. After all, Gideon's DNA was found in the back of the van."

Timo started to pace around the room. "We cannot enter that house. It's not an emergency. We need to do this by the book."

"Timo, he could be in danger," Isa said firmly. "And Freya too."

"There is no indication that he is. According to her colleagues, Freya is on vacation, and her brother spoke to her a few days ago."

"These were text messages. Anyone could have sent it. And why can't we reach her? And what about her father?"

Timo stopped pacing and looked at Isa. "No, Lindström, we get a search warrant."

The next moment, they heard a soft knock on the half open door. Sylvia stood in the doorway, looking a bit uneasy.

Timo signaled her to come in.

"Sir, the white van that was used to abduct Jukka has been spotted several times in the neighborhood where Gideon Younggren lives. Traffic cameras show repeatedly how the car is driving on and off. The license plates were changed, but we believe it's the same car. Also here, the driver is not clearly visible."

Timo frowned. "Thank you, Sylvia. That's important information. We'll need to follow up on that too."

Isa spoke up. "Maybe we can use that to get the warrant. The van was used to kidnap Jukka and has been seen near Younggren's house. That's enough for probable cause, right?"

Timo nodded. "It's a possibility. We'll need to consult with the prosecutor, but it's worth a shot."

# CHAPTER

# 20

SYLVIA CUT THE IGNITION, turning to Isa. "You look worried."

Isa didn't know if she wanted to reply. Her colleagues had obviously noticed that she hadn't been herself in the last few days. After another mysterious visit from her stalker triggered several anxiety attacks, she had called a locksmith to change all the locks in her house. Timo had even requested the forensics team to check her home for fingerprints and DNA, but everything had come out negative.

She sighed. Was she going crazy?

The day after, she stood at Alex's grave and stared at another batch of obscenities written on the marble stone. It shook her to the core. Why would anyone desecrate the grave of a dead person, especially someone she had loved with all her heart? Someone who could no longer defend himself. Alex, who had been so unhappy his entire life, couldn't find peace even after death.

"Yes, I'm worried. I don't know who's doing this and why."

It was surprising how fast the anxiety had made her world so small. She was always looking over her shoulder. When she came home late in the evening, she practically ran from her car to the front door. She started to take her gun out when she entered the house, thinking there was someone inside.

Every crack, every sound. It made her jump up.

Where would this end?

"Are you still getting those messages?"

Isa looked at her cell phone. "No, but then again I changed my number."

"That's good. Have you spoken to Inspector Paikkala about all of this?"

"Yeah, but there is nothing he can do. It's like..."

Closing her eyes, Isa sought balance. "It's like facing a ghost. I'm scared for the kids. What if something happened to Felix and Olivia when they are staying with me? I would never forgive myself."

Sylvia placed a hand on Isa's arm. "Have you considered getting a security system installed in your house? It might give you some peace of mind."

"The earliest is a month away," Isa sighed. "By then, I might be dead."

Sylvia frowned.

Isa managed a faint smile. "Just kidding. I'll be okay. Let's go inside and talk to Mrs. Younggren."

"Looks like she has a visitor. That's not her car I'm assuming." And Sylvia pointed to the red Fiat that was parked haphazardly in front of Mrs. Younggren's house. The car wasn't parked properly, and one of its wheels was over the curb.

"Well, let's see," Isa said and opened the door of the car.

They walked up to the front door and Isa knocked. After a few moments, Mari Younggren, a woman in her mid-fifties with a tall and slender figure, opened the door. In her youth, Mari must have been quite a head-turner, and those who knew her today could see that her beauty had stood the test of time. Her graceful presence suggested where her daughter Freya had inherited her good looks.

"Mrs. Younggren...," Sylvia started, but Mari interrupted her and said, "I haven't been Mrs. Younggren for ten years. That's my ex-husband's name."

"Sorry," Sylvia stammered.

The woman beamed at her with a radiant smile. "That's okay. I'll survive. Please come in. I was expecting you. Inspectors Ahlgren and Lindström I presume?"

Sylvia and Isa nodded.

Mari led them down the hallway to the living room. The house itself was quite modest, with a cozy ambiance that immediately made everyone feel at ease. As they followed Mari to the living room, a few cats roamed about, seemingly accustomed to having strangers in the house. Isa couldn't help but smile as one of them brushed against her leg. She had always wanted to have a cat herself, and even now, it was hard to resist her son's pleas for getting a kitten. But her irregular hours and frequent absences made it challenging to provide a stable home for a pet. She often found herself working late into the night, and she didn't want to neglect the responsibilities of being a pet owner, even though cats were pretty good at taking care of themselves.

The living room was lit by the light pouring from the large window. The room was furnished with a couch and a few armchairs, all of them looking worn out and old-fashioned. The walls were painted in a dull beige color, and a few picture frames were hanging on them, showing some black and white photographs of her daughter and son.

As they entered the room, Isa's attention was drawn to a young man who was sitting on the couch, his head bowed down. He was wearing a black hoodie and worn jeans. It reminded Isa of Timo's favorite outfit. The man had a small, neat beard, was a bit chubby, and looked up when he saw the women enter the room. Isa guessed he was in his mid-twenties.

"This is my son Roffe."

He got up and reached to shake Isa and Sylvia's hands. "I just came here to see if my mother needed anything. She's not well these days."

Mari smiled. "Thanks, dear, but I'll be fine."

Her words were reassuring, yet Isa saw concern in Roffe's eyes.

The mother turned to her son. "I'm sorry but I'll have to talk to these detectives. I'll talk to you later this evening."

"He can stay," Isa said suddenly. "We're here to discuss a few matters regarding your sister, Freya, and your father."

Roffe frowned and took a seat again. "What's going on?"

Isa continued, "To start, could you tell us more about your sister's last known whereabouts and her state of mind before she disappeared?"

His frown deepened and before his mother could intervene, he said. "Freya didn't disappear. I talked to her a few days ago. She's taking a break."

"Then where is she?"

Roffe looked at his mom. "I... don't know. She was very vague. I only got a few messages that she needed a break, that she didn't want anyone to know where she was and that she was fine. It's nothing to worry about. This is how she always interacts with me. Few words."

"And have you heard anything from Freya?" Isa said and turned to Mari.

"No... but that's not a surprise. We don't get along. She made her choice ten years ago, and it wasn't me. Since then, we hardly spoke."

"What about her friends? Her colleagues?"

"She doesn't have many friends," Roffe said and then was

interrupted by his mother.

"Now I remember," Mari said and looked at Sylvia. "You are Sylvia. You used to be one of Freya's friends. How have you been? My goodness, you look good. And a police officer. Wow!"

Sylvia quickly looked at her hands and then mustered a faint smile.

Roffe tried to redirect the conversation back to the topic at hand. "Mom, please..."

But she ignored him and continued, "I never told you how sorry I was to hear about your brother."

It was as if a shock went through Sylvia's body. Isa could feel the sudden shift in the atmosphere, and her instincts urged her to steer the conversation back to Freya. "Was there anything strange in Freya's behavior before she left?"

Roffe leaned back, his gaze distant as he reminisced for a moment. "Well, Freya had been acting a bit... off in the days leading up to her departure. She was quieter than usual and seemed preoccupied with something. She didn't confide in me, but it seemed something was bothering her, but nothing specific. To think of it, Freya was just... Freya."

Then Isa turned to Mari and asked, "And what about your ex-husband Gideon?"

Mari frowned. "What about him?"

Isa took the file from her bag and placed it on the table in front of her. The pictures depicted the white van where Jukka had been found, both from the outside and the inside.

Mari picked up the photographs and studied them for a moment. "Is this blood? Did something happen to Gideon? Oh my God... and Freya!"

Isa locked eyes with her and delivered the unsettling news, "Jukka Ulfsson was discovered lifeless in this van, and we also identified your husband's DNA at the scene."

Mari froze. Her entire face blanched, and her hands trembled as she clutched the photograph.

Roffe was the first to speak. "Jukka Ulfsson? Dead? We don't know anything about that."

Isa and Sylvia exchanged glances, the room filled with a sudden surge of tension.

"I'm glad he's dead," Mari said suddenly.

"That's a strong statement," Isa said.

With eyes full of resentment, Mari continued, "That man destroyed my daughter's life. Drugs. My sweet girl is a drug addict. She had such a promising future. The success she and Celeste had should have been a new beginning, but the drugs kept pulling her back down. It all started so innocently, just partying and having fun, but after almost ten years, it turned into a path of destruction. I can't remember how many times Gideon took her to the hospital, every time thinking she would... I am so grateful he kept me in the loop, because even though she hates me, I don't hate her. I love her with all my heart." She paused for a moment to regain her composure, and then she continued, her eyes welling up with tears, "Jukka was her supplier, enabling her every step of the way. I blame him for leading her down that path. It broke my heart to see what she has become."

"But she seemed to be doing okay," Isa said. "A good job as librarian..."

"You don't know what you're saying," Mari lashed out. "These are the words of someone who never had to deal with addiction, but... you do."

Mari turned to Sylvia and a second time during the conversation the police officer found herself in the spotlight.

"Please, don't make it about me," Sylvia interjected firmly. "You, your husband, and your son had all the reasons to kill Jukka Ulfsson."

Mari gave her a sarcastic grin. "Kill him? That would be too easy. For years, my husband... ex-husband tried to hold him accountable for Freya's addiction. But no luck! Even more so, it got him arrested."

"Where is Gideon?" Isa asked.

"I don't know," Mari said. She tried to keep her eyes fixed on them. There was rage. A lot of it. "But I do care. He is a decent man. Whatever he does, it's always with the best intentions in mind. He would do everything to protect Freya, but killing a man..."

"And where were you the night of 16 December?"

Mari looked disappointed. "Here. In my house, in my bed."

"Anyone who can vouch for that?"

"No," Mari said.

"And you?" Isa tuned to Roffe.

"At home. My wife was with me."

Isa gathered the pictures from the table and carefully returned them to her bag. "If you hear anything from Freya or Gideon, you need to contact us," she said, placing her business card on the table.

Five minutes later, Isa and Sylvia were standing outside and made their way back to the car.

"She knows where he is," Sylvia said.

"And she is protecting him. She knows what he's up to. We need to put surveillance on both... immediately," Isa said. "I'll get in touch with the team and have them set it up."

"So, it's all about drugs," Sylvia said and there was a hint of disappointment in her voice.

"Looks like it." But Isa felt the same discontent. Somehow it seemed so easy. Too easy.

Then Isa's phone rang. It was Timo.

"Lindström, get back to the station. Max Westerberg is missing."

* * *

"A witness saw Max's car disappear into the woods near Enköping. We found the car, but Max is missing. There's evidence of a second vehicle and blood, indicating he might be injured or worse."

Varg stood before the room, locking eyes with everyone. Timo, Isa, and Sylvia sat at the back, joined by two more officers.

"Any leads on the second car or the person involved?" Sylvia asked.

"The witness mentioned a black SUV, no license plate," Varg responded. "We're checking CCTV, hoping to identify the car or driver. Max's phone is switched off. The last signal was picked up in the area where we found the car."

Timo asked, "Why was Max in Enköping?"

"Heading home to Västerås. Witnesses say he had an altercation earlier, likely with Lukas Stendahl," Varg explained.

"Bring him in," Timo ordered.

"Does Stendahl have a black SUV?" Sylvia asked.

"No, but Gideon Younggren does," Varg said.

Timo interrupted them. There was a certain urgency in his voice when he said, "Focus, people. This is the second abduction. Jukka died in three days. We can't afford another failure. What ties Jukka, Max, and Gideon? Sivert, check CCTV. Varg, Sylvia, interview the witness, find more. Get Lukas Stendahl here. Let's find Max before it's too late."

*  *  *

"I checked, and Lukas Stendahl was telling the truth," Isa said, signaling the waiter to take their order.

Isa and Timo were sitting in a pub, not far from the police station, seeking refuge from the cold, rainy weather outside.

Inside the air was thick with the smell of freshly poured beer, the sound of clinking glasses, and the murmur of conversation from other customers. In the corner, a fire blazed in the stone fireplace, casting a warm orange glow over the room. The crackling of the logs and the occasional pop of embers provided a comforting background noise.

Despite the weather outside, the pub was bustling with activity, with people huddled around tables, chatting and laughing over drinks and plates of food.

A young woman approached their table to take their order. "What can I get for you, Inspector Paikkala?" she asked and gave Timo the biggest smile Isa had ever seen.

Timo cleared his throat. "Uh, just a coffee for me, thanks," he said and then glanced at Isa. She ordered a glass of water.

As the waitress walked away, Isa turned to Timo with a smirk. "Looks like you've got an admirer."

Timo rolled his eyes. "I doubt it. She's just doing her job."

Isa chuckled. "Sure, Timo. Keep telling yourself that. You guys should go out."

Timo frowned.

She jokingly imitated the waitress' voice, saying, "Oh, Inspector Paikkala, what can I get for you? Is everything fine? Can I bring you another coffee? Cushion? Massage? Kiss?"

"Not funny," he said in a serious voice, but he couldn't hide his amusement.

"So, Lukas Stendahl. He has a blue Volvo. We checked and the traffic cameras showed that he was indeed in a different part of the city at the time of Max's abduction," Isa said, bringing the conversation back to the investigation.

"What were they arguing about?"

"The Westerbergs are suing the Stendahls. They want to prevent Alva from getting the house and the money. They weren't divorced yet. And they accuse Lukas of having withheld money from Celeste during the time he was her manager."

"Let's look into that. If Lukas was embezzling money from Celeste and Max found out, he has a motive for abducting Max."

"But he wasn't in Enköping," Isa remarked.

"His car wasn't, maybe he was. He could have changed cars."

"We'll keep looking but this case is... I don't know." Isa took a sip of the water and then leaned back in her chair. "There is something we don't see, and I think it's staring us in the face. I don't buy the drugs angle. It's too convenient. There must be a link to Celeste. The song. Why all this drama when you just want to punish a man for making your daughter an addict. Why now? He could have done it years ago. And what does Max have to do with it?"

"Max's financial situation is not great," Timo said. "Until a few months ago, there were regular deposits made on his account. Guess by whom."

"Jukka Ulfsson?"

"Indeed. Max has been in and out of rehab a few times. Alcohol according to his family. I'd say drugs. He and Jukka were working together."

"So, it is drug related."

"Maybe. I agree it doesn't sit well with me either. We need to revisit Celeste. By the way, did we ever speak to Celeste's closest friends? They might know something about the song. Dancho Krastev isn't going to tell us anything."

"Well, that's the thing. She didn't have any friends."

"How come?"

"I don't know. According to her parents she used to have a few good friends, but she hadn't seen them for years. They blame Alva Stendahl."

"It seems Alva Stendahl is to blame for all the bad things in the world."

A grin appeared on Isa's face. "Ms. Stendahl wasn't being entirely truthful. Turns out, she did have an affair. The Westerbergs hired a private detective. I've seen the rather juicy pictures. There's no denying."

"And do we know who the lucky one was?"

"They are not together anymore. It was a certain Stella—it's in the file. But the Westerbergs definitely used Alva's indiscretion to pull Celeste away from her."

"And what do we know about Freya Younggren?"

"Her problems with addiction started when she was a teenager, involving alcohol and drugs. She's been in and out of rehab more times than I can count on two hands. A few times, she nearly ended up dead. Interestingly, one of those occasions was the day Jonathan Gedman disappeared, and Dancho Krastev had his accident."

"Tell me more."

"The hospital nurses could only say that she was literally thrown out of a car, as the CCTV later showed. They found her on the steps at the entrance of the emergency room. She had an overdose and barely made it. The second time, her father brought her to the hospital. He was so upset he smashed some chairs."

"It looks like Gideon Younggren has a temper."

Isa took a sip of her drink and continued, "She leads a pretty reclusive life these days. She started working in the library four years ago. She pretty much keeps to herself. Her colleagues hardly know her. She has no friends and a pretty empty bank account."

"So you don't think she has anything to do with it?"

"I didn't say that. Her life is a bit too inconspicuous. She's on holidays, but no one has been able to contact her. She's hiding."

"Perhaps…" Timo said, his voice trailing off. "Maybe she just needed a break."

A brief silence settled between them as Isa, her thoughts lingering on Timo's words, observed him with concern. He looked nervous.

Breaking the pause, Timo decided to shift gears and suddenly asked, "Now, for something different… can I ask you for some advice?"

She took another sip of her water and replied, "Of course, go ahead. What's on your mind?"

He sighed, fiddled with the cup and saucer, and then confessed,

"Let's say you hear that a close friend of yours is dying and they have one final request."

Isa's expression turned to concern as she nodded, encouraging him to continue. "Alright, what's the request?"

"It's a bit embarrassing," he hesitated, "but let's say this friend has been in love with you for a while and wants to spend a night together."

Isa's eyes widened in surprise, caught off guard by the unexpected nature of Timo's request. She took a moment to gather her thoughts before responding. "Well, it's crucial to consider your own feelings toward that person. If you reciprocate their romantic feelings, then it's up to you to decide whether you want to fulfill their request. However, if you don't share those same romantic feelings, it's important to communicate that gently and respectfully."

"I understand what you mean and it's all logical, but it's just a challenging situation. I deeply care about this person, but I don't share their romantic feelings."

"It's not an easy decision to make, but ultimately, you have to do what's right for you and your own feelings," Isa advised.

"What would you do?" Timo asked.

"It's Kristina, isn't it? That's why you've been so quiet the last few days."

He hesitated for a moment. "Yes, it's Kristina."

"What happened?"

"Huntington's disease."

"I'm so sorry, Timo," she said softly, reaching out to touch his hand.

"I appreciate that," he replied, giving her hand a grateful squeeze. "This request has just made things more complicated."

"I can only imagine. But I think it's important to focus on what you want and need in this situation. Don't feel like you have to do something just because it's someone's dying wish."

"That's true. I don't want to do anything that I'll regret later on, but...

she put me in a difficult situation. What would you do?"

Isa shook her head. "I'm not in that position..."

"Lindström... please, I need your advice."

She looked at her hands and then said, "It's just sex. If it were me... I'd maybe consider it. But then again, I've always been good at separating love and sex."

He looked lost.

"But not you," she continued.

He gave her an inquiring look. "You don't know me that well."

"Yes, I do. Eight years to get over Caijsa, and now Ingrid. You're not the type of man who can switch off his feelings and just have sex with whoever."

He sighed and leaned back in his chair. "Whatever I do, it's going to end in disaster. If I don't sleep with her, I'm going to lose my friend. If I do sleep with her, I'm going to lose myself."

"I think you should talk to her," Isa said. "Tell her how you feel, that you care about her deeply, but that you don't have the same romantic feelings for her. Whatever you decide, just make sure it's something you can live with."

"It's not going to be easy, though."

She smiled and then took his hand.

"Thanks, Lindström."

"Anytime, Paikkala. That's what friends are for."

## CHAPTER

# 21

**MAX'S ENTIRE BODY ACHED** from the strain of being suspended in the same position for what felt like hours. His arms were numb, and his fingers were beginning to tingle from the lack of blood. The rope around his wrists dug into his skin, causing excruciating pain with every movement. He tried to move his arms, but the pain made him gasp in agony.

His fear was intense, his heart pounding so loud he thought it might burst out of his chest. He didn't know where he was or who had taken him. The darkness of the cellar only added to his terror, making him feel claustrophobic and helpless. He felt like a trapped animal, waiting for the predator to pounce.

But then a strange feeling of anger began to simmer within him, aimed at his captor. How dare they do this to him? What gave them the right to take away his freedom and inflict such pain? He wanted to lash out and fight back, but he knew he was powerless in his current state.

This wasn't good. He needed to stay calm and focused. He tried to take deep breaths and clear his mind, but it was difficult with the constant pain and discomfort.

As Max strained against the ropes, a creaking door pierced the silence. His eyes widened, catching a fleeting glimpse of a shadowy figure vanishing into the distant glow at the room's end. How long had that man been there?

Dread washed over him like a chilling wave, gripping his senses. The unknown, the unseen—his mind plunged into a pit of terror.

Why?

This wasn't Andreas Lundqvist.

But who?

\* \* \*

Gideon's hands came to rest on the table with a heavy sigh, his gaze shifting towards the man seated across from him. What had initially appeared as a promising idea now loomed over him as a grave mistake. With two lives claimed, the haunting question lingered: how many more would follow?

Remorse washed over him, a feeling that had arrived too late, after losing his wife, his family, and the descent of his daughter into the shadows of inner turmoil.

The man's proposal had seemed clear-cut at first, offering the allure of revenge. Jukka and Max were to face consequences for their role in Freya's addiction. Confessions were meant to expose their illicit deeds and secure their imprisonment. However, reality unfolded differently; Jukka's death exempted him from facing justice. Unwittingly, Gideon had provided a sanctuary for the man's plans.

He had just been a bystander as he had parked the van outside Jukka's house, had assisted in moving Jukka into the van, and had collided his SUV with Max's car. It was not planned; he was not to blame.

But the man's motives remained elusive, continuously shifting his focus between Jukka, Max, and Celeste, and perhaps even others unknown to him.

What did he want?

"We should put an end to this," Gideon urged.

The man slammed his fist on the table. "No, we should finish this. All the way to the end."

Gideon shook his head. "This has gone too far. More lives will be ruined. We need to reconsider. I want to do this the legal way."

"It's a bit late for that. If I go down, you're going with me."

"Why? Why are you doing this? This is cruel."

"What did you expect? That they would confess just like that? You're a coward. You have no idea what it's like to lose everything. This is the only way they'll pay for what they've done."

Gideon's face hardened. "I do know. Freya's life is destroyed."

A sarcastic grin twisted the man's mouth. "I'd say she had some part to play herself. Your daughter is weak, just like her father."

Gideon's anger flared. "Don't you dare talk about my daughter that way! This revenge won't bring back what we've lost. You're on your own."

"Don't walk away from me!"

As Gideon turned to leave, the man's desperation peaked. He grabbed a hammer from the cupboard, swinging it at Gideon with a sickening thud. The force sent Gideon staggering, pain radiating through his body. And in that moment, the thin thread holding their dangerous alliance snapped.

\* \* \*

Every time Sivert took the stage during a briefing, an air of unease surrounded him. He seemed to be trying too hard to impress, especially the women in the room, using overly complicated words and dramatic intervals. But Isa found herself strangely amused by it. Amidst the tense atmosphere, it brought a touch of normalcy.

But not everyone echoed her sentiment. Timo seemed preoccupied, his gaze frequently shifting to his phone, seemingly disengaged from the unfolding drama on stage.

"Is everything alright?" Isa asked.

Timo looked up from his phone, momentarily taken aback, before quickly regaining his calm. "Yeah, sorry about that. Just got a text from a friend," he said, slipping his phone into his pocket.

"Kristina?"

"Sivert, continue," Timo directed his attention to the young man standing in front of the room. "But keep it concise. I don't have all the time in the world."

Sivert cleared his throat before saying. "Based on the evidence we've collected so far, the black SUV started to follow Max's Mercedes all the way from Uppsala when he left his office. The license plates were replaced by false ones. We believe Max's car then disappeared in the woods around Enköping. He never arrived in Västerås."

He started flipping through the notes on his tablet. "Fifty minutes after Max's car was last seen we see the black SUV driving north via route 70 to Sala and Avesta and then to Sandviken. Then no trace of the car anymore."

"So he stayed in the neighborhood," Timo said.

"Exactly. We've been analyzing CCTV footage from gas stations and rest areas along that route, and we found some interesting footage at a gas station in Sandviken. The black SUV stopped there, and we can see a man getting out of the car. He fills up the tank and goes inside. There are no signs of Max. It's hard to see if someone is sitting in the backseat, but for sure no one is sitting on the passenger side."

"Can you display the CCTV footage?" Timo requested, glancing at his phone once more as another beep indicated a new message.

Isa observed him closely.

The persistent buzzing of Timo's phone began to distract the rest of the team, and Isa could sense Sivert's growing frustration as he tried to present his findings.

Timo glanced up at the team and suddenly realized they were all watching him. "Sorry, continue," he said and put his phone in silent mode.

Sivert nodded and initiated the playback of the CCTV footage on the large screen at the front of the room.

"Is that the best you can do?" Isa asked.

"We've enhanced the footage, but the image quality remains insufficient for identification," Sivert replied.

"It might be Gideon Younggren," Varg suggested.

"It could be anyone," Isa countered.

Sivert paused the image and elaborated, "We've also scrutinized Max's phone records and found something intriguing. He had frequent contact with Verner Blixt, but that's not the most interesting part. In the days leading up to his abduction, he received numerous messages from unknown numbers. We couldn't trace them; they're all from burner phones, much like we found on his sister's phone."

"The recording?" Isa inquired.

"It's a possibility," Sivert confirmed.

"Damn... We need to establish the link between the recording and these abductions," Timo exclaimed, letting out a frustrated sigh. "Weeks of work, and we're still grappling for answers."

Isa empathized with his frustration. Despite their prolonged efforts—examining evidence, analyzing data, and conducting interviews—they had yet to uncover a breakthrough.

"Dancho Krastev was the one who recorded this song," Sylvia interjected. "Helena Håkansson, the sound producer, remembered him. She found the song intriguing and asked Dancho about it. He revealed it was a surprise—a declaration of love for someone special. A year later, she heard the same song on the radio. This time, it featured Celeste's violin as a central theme and Freya's vocals."

Timo raised an eyebrow. "A love song? Did he tell her who it was for?"

"Yes," Sylvia said. "Jonathan Gedman."

Isa frowned. "What? Jonathan Gedman who disappeared?"

"It makes sense," Timo said and turned to Isa. "Dancho and Jonathan were planning to run away that Sunday."

"But why so secretive?"

"Someone didn't want them to be together," Timo added. "Maybe the accident wasn't an accident."

"Then who would try to stop them?"

Timo shook his head. "I still don't understand how this is linked to Jukka and Max."

"They were there during the hike trip," Sylvia said.

"Why would Jukka, or Max for that matter, have anything to do with this?" Then Timo turned to Varg. "I want everything there is to know about Jonathan Gedman. His life, his family. Everything."

Varg gave him a quick nod.

"We should go to Höga Kusten," Isa intervened.

"Why?" Timo asked.

"I have a feeling that what happened there is central to the whole mystery."

"And what makes you say that?"

"Think about it," Isa began. "Jonathan composes a song. He

disappears without a trace. A year later Celeste and Freya score a world hit. But Celeste has mental issues. Freya disappears from stage. Could it be remorse? Guilt?"

"Are you saying Celeste and Freya got rid of Jonathan?"

"Freya was in a hospital with an overdose," Sylvia pointed out. "She couldn't have been there."

"But Celeste was... remember she went to look for them but never found them," Isa said. "And the others covered it up."

"And someone wants to take revenge now?" Timo asked.

Sylvia nodded in agreement. "It's worth exploring."

Timo considered their words. "Alright, let's gather what we have on Jonathan Gedman. Isa and I will head to Höga Kusten tomorrow. Varg, coordinate with the local police there. We need full access to any records tied to Jonathan."

The room gradually emptied as everyone dispersed to carry out their assigned tasks. Sylvia and Sivert left first, then Varg headed out to make the necessary arrangements with the local police, leaving Timo and Isa alone.

"I hope this journey to Höga Kusten gives us something concrete to work with," Timo said.

Isa kept her gaze fixed on the files and evidence spread across the table. "We need to talk to his family. This feels more and more... personal."

But Timo was distracted again. He looked at his cell phone and frowned.

"What is it?"

"Uh... nothing," he said and put the phone down. "Text messages from Kristina. She wants to talk to me."

"Did you tell her?"

"I didn't have the time yet."

"You'll have to talk to her eventually," Isa said and threw her legs on the table.

"I know. I just don't know how to tell her. It's going to crush her."

"The longer you wait, the worse it'll be."

"I know. I'll do it soon."

They sat in silence for a moment, both lost in their own thoughts.

"Do you ever think about quitting?" Isa asked suddenly.

Timo looked at her, surprised. "What do you mean?"

"I mean, do you ever think about quitting this job? All the stress, the long hours, the emotional toll... the danger."

Timo sighed. "Sometimes. Why? Do you?"

She looked out of the window.

Outside, the wind was howling, and rain was pouring down in sheets.

"Yes... now that the kids are back, and everything is going well with Felix. And I know Olivia and I will get there as well. I sometimes wonder what will happen if I get hurt or die. The job is not without its risks."

"I didn't know you felt that way."

She gave him a faint smile. "Relax, I won't quit. Not just yet. I just... sometimes think about it."

"I understand," Timo said. "But you're a great detective, Lindström."

"I'm not irreplaceable."

"Well, you are to me," Timo said.

Isa smiled. "Thanks, boss."

"Now, back to work. We need to catch this guy before he strikes again."

*  *  *

He tasted the blood in his mouth. Max felt like he was being torn apart. The pain was excruciating, and he couldn't even scream. He had lost count of how many times the man had hit him or shocked him with the electric prod. He had tried to keep quiet, to endure the torture without giving his captor the satisfaction of hearing him scream, but it was becoming harder with each passing moment.

He realized he had broken several of his teeth. He felt dizzy and disoriented, and he couldn't focus on anything except the pain. He wondered if this was how it was going to end for him, if he was going to die here, alone and in agony.

But then he felt a surge of anger. He couldn't let this monster get away with what he had done. Jukka, Celeste. He had to stay alive and find a way to escape.

Max gritted his teeth and tried to push away the pain. He closed his eyes and focused on his breathing, trying to stay calm and centered. He didn't know how much longer he could hold on, but he was determined to fight until the very end.

But what came next was hard to imagine.

\* \* \*

"Timo, I need to talk to you," the message on his phone sounded. He had ignored the ten messages Kristina had left throughout the day, unsure about confronting her. If he were honest to himself, he had made up his mind from the moment she had asked him, but he had been postponing the answer hoping that the problem would disappear on its own. But it hadn't.

"Just answer your phone," Isa said annoyed.

"No, it's fine," he said. "I'll talk to her later."

"You'd better concentrate on the trail," Isa said, her voice muffled by the persistent rain.

The unpaved path had transformed into a muddy obstacle, making each step a precarious venture. Timo struggled to maintain his footing as he navigated the slippery trail.

The rain showed no signs of mercy, drenching them both.

Isa cast a sideways glance at him, concern etched on her face. "Just deal with it before it becomes a bigger problem. And just... keep your eyes on the trail! I'd rather not scrape you off the ground."

Timo sighed, realizing the truth in her words. The trail ahead seemed endless.

The forested area of Höga Kusten stretched out in a lush expanse, shrouded in mist from the persistent rain. Towering pine and spruce trees stood tall, their branches forming a dense canopy overhead. The air was permeated with the earthy fragrance of wet moss, and the forest floor was a carpet of fallen leaves and needles.

As they continued hiking, the trail got tougher, eventually bringing them to a cliff that offered a stunning view of the High Coast. Towering high above, the cliff overlooked the Baltic Sea, with the sound of waves crashing filling the air. The wind carried the scent of the sea mingled with the aroma of pine, a refreshing blend after their arduous journey.

Timo, an experienced climber, felt a mix of excitement and concern. His eyes followed the rough rock surface, thinking about possible paths. But as he looked at Isa, determined but less experienced in climbing, his worry grew, because the trail along the cliff edge continued to be slippery and uneven, with occasional steep sections.

"Maybe this wasn't such a good idea," Timo said, attempting to wipe the water from his face. The rain, persistent and unforgiving, had soaked through their clothing, leaving them cold and damp.

She ignored him and said, "We should be almost there." The map was cradled in her hands, its surface dotted with raindrops. The forest around them appeared to thin out, with fewer trees as the trail ascended.

After ten minutes, she stopped. "It should be here."

"Are you sure?"

"The police officer in Mjällom indicated this point where Dancho and Jonathan likely fell."

"Mmm," Timo said and walked around. The rocky plateau stretched out before him, its rugged surface marred by cracks and crevices, overlooking a vast expanse of forested landscape.

Then he walked to the edge of the plateau, much to the dismay of Isa who called, "Be careful!"

"Don't worry... I have more experience than you do," he said and looked over the edge, leaning slightly forward to get a better view of the surroundings below. Then he turned to Isa, "I doubt it was an accident. It's difficult to go over this border. Unless you were standing extremely close to the edge."

"They left at 6 a.m. in the morning. According to Boris Krastev, Dancho chose the trail."

"Dancho had a backpack with him, right?"

Isa nodded.

"Like he was going on a long journey," Timo added.

"Exactly. But Jonathan wasn't. According to their friends, they seemed happy. No signs of distress or fear. They were just two friends going on a hike."

Timo surveyed the rugged landscape, his gaze tracing the contours of weathered rock formations and jagged cliffs that stretched out beneath them. The rocky plateau they stood on offered a panoramic view, revealing the raw beauty of the natural terrain, with deep crevices and steep inclines leading down into the valley below. "So, what could have gone wrong here? Why did they disappear?"

"Maybe they had a fight and they both fell," Isa said. "Dancho was in love with Jonathan, but who said it was mutual."

"Good point."

"I want to see where they were found," Isa said and went off.

"Lindström, be... careful!"

Before he could say anything else, she took the trail down and disappeared between the trees. The descent was challenging, the rain making the trail slippery, and the mud was clinging to their boots. As they descended, the sound of raindrops hitting leaves intensified, creating an almost rhythmic melody in the forest.

He saw her descending fast. Too fast.

"Lindström, slow down!"

In the next moment, her foot slipped on the rain-slicked trail, and Isa found herself sliding uncontrollably down the slope.

Reacting swiftly, Timo maneuvered down the trail after her. As Isa's precarious slide continued, he saw her attempts to slow down by grasping onto rocks and branches.

Timo, propelled by adrenaline, closed the gap. Just as Isa neared the edge of a cliff, his firm grip caught her, bringing her to an abrupt halt.

They sprawled on the rain-soaked ground, his arms tightly around her, her body tense with shock.

"Now... will you please listen to me?" he said trying to catch his breath.

She nodded, still unable to say anything.

"Are you hurt?"

"Just some scratches," she stammered. "Thanks... I..."

Timo interrupted, "I'll get up first, okay?"

She nodded again, and Timo rose from the damp ground. He reached out and then pulled her up and away from the edge.

As they resumed their descent, Isa remained close to Timo.

Reaching the bottom, Timo's gaze shifted from the site where Dancho and Jonathan were found and where he was standing now, to the plateau above. Through the rain and mist, he noticed another, smaller plateau to the left. It seemed like a hidden alcove in the rocky expanse. "It's not that high."

"That's why Dancho survived the fall, and Jonathan likely as well."

Timo turned around, envisioning the surroundings as they might have looked during the summer when Dancho and Jonathan were there. He imagined vibrant greenery, the scent of pine in the air, and perhaps a warm breeze rustling through the leaves. "What's over there?"

He pointed to a small cave hidden between the trees, situated next to what appeared to be another cliff, leading to a section further down.

"They looked there for Jonathan, but they never found him," Isa explained.

"And the ravine?"

"There was a report stating that they deemed it too dangerous, and they eventually gave up the search for Jonathan," Isa said.

An involuntary shiver ran through his body as the chilling air seemed to seep into his bones. "Where were the others that day?"

"They all claim to be in the cabin until noon, except for Celeste who went for a walk in the morning... alone. When Dancho and Jonathan weren't back around noon and no one could reach them, they decided to look for them, and Max found them."

"When did Celeste come back from her hike?"

"I don't know. It wasn't written in the report. Do you think she…"

"I'm not saying anything. When exactly was the emergency call made?"

"Uh… around 1 p.m.," Isa said.

"It took us two hours to get here from the cabin where they stayed—fair enough, the weather is worse than it was that day. But around the time Max went to look for them, it was raining as well. There is a bad connection along most of the trail. Only up there my phone received a signal. No one knew where Dancho and Jonathan were. Yet, in one hour, Max managed to find them and called for help. He knew where to look for them."

"Celeste?"

"Maybe, but there is no evidence. Another thing: how did Freya end up in the hospital?"

"That's… a good point," Isa said and looked at him.

"Someone must have brought her there."

"We need to go back and talk to Jonathan's family before we talk to Boris again. He's the only one who can shed more light on what happened that Sunday morning."

The rain was falling less heavily now. They still had two hours of walking and then another four hours of driving back to Gävle. It was going to be a really long day.

\* \* \*

The next day they headed to Iggön. Timo was still recovering from the 'quality time' with his chief inspector. Eight hours in the car and half a day of walking in the rain wasn't ideal. He could feel every muscle in his body protesting. The strain was more than he had anticipated, perhaps a sign of aging. On the contrary, Isa appeared cheerful, seemingly unaffected by their ride down the rain-soaked hill.

Isa had thrown him a few concerned glances as he began fidgeting with his phone again, occasionally stealing glances out of the window as the landscape blurred by. She had attempted to break the silence a few times.

"You're awfully quiet again, Paikkala. Everything okay?" Isa asked, her eyes fixed on the road.

"Yeah, just tired," Timo replied. "It was a long day yesterday."

"Oh, I see you didn't quite appreciate my sparkling company." A mischievous smile played around her lips.

An annoying, stubborn know-it-all who almost got them killed, he thought but decided to keep that particular observation to himself.

They were nearing Mrs. Gedman's house, and the quietness of the village seemed to weigh on them. Timo felt a knot in his stomach as they approached the gate to the house and his mind drifted to the other problem he had tried to tuck away unsuccessfully.

Maybe he should call Kristina. Why had she been so adamant to call him?

For a moment he considered asking Isa if he could call her, but then decided against it. He kept his gaze on the surroundings.

Iggön's streets were charming and peaceful, lined with quaint houses and small shops. The village had a laid-back atmosphere with cobblestone streets, old-fashioned lampposts, and a refreshing sea breeze. The small town exuded a sense of community, where locals greeted each other. The overall ambiance was calm and serene, offering a perfect setting for Jonathan's mother to find solace after her son's disappearance.

Timo and Isa trudged up the path leading to Mrs. Gedman's house, their boots squishing through the wet leaves that carpeted the ground. The winter air was cold and biting, but at least it was dry today, a welcome change from the previous days of rain and snow. The trees that lined the street were bare of leaves, their branches stretching up to the cloudy sky like bony fingers. As they walked, they pulled their coats tighter around them, trying to ward off the chill.

Mrs. Gedman's house, though simple, looked well-maintained.

Timo rang the bell.

"I think I could live here," Isa said and looked at the sea in the distance. The waves crashed against the rocky shore, sending sprays of salty water into the air. The sound of the sea was soothing, a constant hum in the background of their conversation. Isa drew a deep breath, then turned back to the house and smiled at Timo, who was looking at her with a grin.

"You're getting really sentimental, Lindström," he teased. "I'm not used to that."

And he was a little concerned. She was talking a lot about leaving and living a quieter life these days. He was proud of her that she connected again with her children, but it was driving her away from him.

Obviously, the doubts had been visible on his face because she said, "I'm allowed to appreciate the simple things in life, you know. But don't worry, I'm not going anywhere. You're stuck with me."

He gave her a quick nod, but he wasn't convinced.

Mrs. Gedman opened the door with a warm smile, revealing a friendly face with deep-set wrinkles that spoke of a life filled with joy but also a lot of grief. She was a middle-aged woman, with short, curly grey hair that framed her face and bright, blue eyes that sparkled with kindness. She was dressed in a cozy sweater and a long skirt, and her hands were covered with oven mitts, indicating that she had been busy in the kitchen.

"Yes, how can I help you?" she said.

Timo and Isa introduced themselves and told her they wanted to talk to her about her son.

"Jonathan?" she said surprised. It was as if someone had brought up a bad memory and a sparkle of hope at the same time. "Did you find him? Where is he?"

"We're sorry, Mrs. Gedman," Timo said. "We haven't found your son. We're just hoping to learn more about him. We believe his disappearance has something to do with another case we're working on."

Mrs. Gedman, her expression softening with a hint of surprise, moved aside to welcome them. "Please, come inside. I'll prepare some coffee for us."

Timo and Isa followed her into the kitchen.

The kitchen was spacious and bright, with large windows that let in plenty of natural light. The countertops were made of gleaming granite, and the cabinets were a rich, warm brown. The aroma of freshly brewed coffee filled the air, mingling with the scent of something baking in the oven.

Timo let the aroma fill his nostrils. He felt a sudden craving for coffee.

Mrs. Gedman led them to the kitchen table and poured them each a cup of steaming hot coffee and handed it to them. The lingering chill from the previous day dissipated as he cradled the warm cup of coffee.

But when he took a sip, immediate regret set in. He was an avid coffee drinker, some would even call him an addict, but this brew was too strong for his taste. He made a face as he swallowed, and Isa noticed, attempting to stifle a laugh.

"You don't like it," Mrs. Gedman said as she looked at him.

"Uh... I'm not much of a coffee drinker," he said with a straight face, avoiding eye contact with Isa, who was undoubtedly trying to remain serious.

Mrs. Gedman said, "So, you want to hear about my Jonathan. What can I say... he disappeared. He... every day I hope he'll be standing on the doorstep, but... he isn't."

"He was declared dead last year," Timo said and put the cup on the kitchen counter. Isa hadn't touched hers but took out her notebook and looked at the woman.

"Yes, six months ago," Mrs. Gedman said.

There was such a profound sadness in Mrs. Gedman's voice as she spoke about her disappeared son.

"Why now?"

"I don't know. I got up one day and realized he was never going to come back. I'll likely never know what happened to him, and that's... the most excruciating thing."

Tears welled in Mrs. Gedman's eyes. He had seen this so many times, but every time it struck him again with the same force. Grief, raw and unrelenting, manifested in the tears that silently traced the contours of her eyes. The weight of a mother's heart, burdened by the unresolved fate of her son.

"Can you tell us a bit more about your son?" Isa asked.

She sighed and then forced a smile on her face, as if she wasn't allowed any form of happiness. "My son was the gentlest, kindest soul. He loved music, nature, and people. Jonathan was passionate about life, always looking for the beauty in everything. He played the guitar, wrote songs and poems. Even during the toughest times, he found solace in his music."

"He was part of the creatives."

"Yes, he was. It started in high school. He felt good in this group. They had the same passion for arts, music, and expressing themselves. But as he grew older, things changed. Life happened. They were still close, but the dynamics shifted."

"In what way?" Timo asked.

"Well, they grew up. The naivety of youth faded, I guess, and responsibilities and challenges replaced it. Jonathan was always a dreamer, an artist at heart. But as he grew up, he faced the realities of life, and so did his friends. Jonathan never knew his father. He died when he was three. A freak accident at work. I always wondered if life would have been different when his dad had still been around. I don't know if I..."

She shook her head as if to dispel the thought.

"Were there any frictions between them?"

Mrs. Gedman frowned. "No." Then she shook her head. "Sorry... yes, there were."

"Between Celeste Westerberg and your son?"

"How do you know?"

"What was it about?" Isa asked, ignoring her question.

"A few months before his disappearance, she was standing on our doorstep, demanding to speak with Jonathan—we were living in Gävle at that time. They argued. It was quite brutal. They were screaming at each other."

"About what?" Timo pressed.

Mrs. Gedman hesitated before answering, "It was about their music. Celeste accused Jonathan of being too idealistic, unwilling to compromise for success. Jonathan, in turn, accused Celeste of losing her authenticity and becoming consumed by the desire for commercial fame. It was a clash of artistic views and personal values. The last time I saw them arguing like that..." She trailed off, her eyes reflecting the painful memory.

"Aria 25?"

She quickly nodded. "At that time, it wasn't called Aria 25. It was a softer, more acoustic version. Celeste immediately saw the potential, but Jonathan didn't feel it was... him. And they kept on fighting until that day."

"What do you think happened to your son?" Timo asked.

Mrs. Gedman sighed. "I don't know. An accident. Like they said." She wiped the tears from her cheeks. "You know... he was loved. I still find comfort knowing that."

"Forgive me, Mrs. Gedman, but we need to ask: did your son have a girlfriend or... boyfriend?"

Mrs. Gedman looked Isa straight in the eye. "He kept it hidden from me, but I knew. I knew he was gay. But Jonathan never felt the need to announce it to the world. It was his personal journey. And yes, there was someone. He was in love. That was clear."

"Was it Dancho Krastev?"

Mrs. Gedman furrowed a brow. "The boy who survived? I don't think so. To be honest, I don't know. I still don't know why he couldn't tell me."

"Could it be that they wanted to run away?"

"Jonathan? I doubt that."

The emotions were too overwhelming, and the woman broke down before their eyes. "How could he believe that I wouldn't support him?" she cried out.

Timo and Isa sat in silence, witnessing the raw pain and heartache pouring out of Mrs. Gedman.

"Maybe it wasn't about you, Mrs. Gedman," Timo said calmly. "Maybe it was about Jonathan's boyfriend."

The old woman looked up from her tear-stained eyes, a mixture of confusion and sorrow etched on her face.

"Who else knew about Jonathan being gay?" Isa asked.

"No one. I think he even didn't tell his friends."

"What about Jonathan's relationship with the other creatives? Jukka, Max, Boris, Freya."

"It was good... at first, but it was a known secret that Jukka, Boris, Max and Freya were doing drugs."

"Wait, Boris as well?"

"Yeah, they all tried it at one point. It was innocent at first but for Freya, it became problematic. She became an addict. Even now, when I see her family, I can't help feeling sorry for them."

"Mrs. Gedman, you helped us a lot," Timo said. "One more question, could we see Jonathan's room and maybe go through his stuff? You never know, we might find something new."

"You can see his room, but his stuff is... mostly gone. I kept the photo albums, medals, and stuff from school, but the rest I gave away."

Isa furrowed her brows. "How come?"

"When he was declared dead, I organized a get-together with his friends. I had collected all his stuff and told them they could keep whatever they wanted. I wanted them to remember him, but I also wanted them to have a chance to heal."

"That must have been difficult," Timo empathized.

"It was," Mrs. Gedman admitted. "Ultimately it was just a nice being together. It was like having Jonathan back. It was so..." Her voice broke. "It was so bittersweet. Each friend took a piece of his life with them, and I hoped it would bring them some solace. Now, only the memories linger here."

"Sorry to ask, Mrs. Gedman," Isa said, "but was there some sort of recording in Jonathan's stuff?"

"Recording? How would it look like?"

"Maybe a USB stick or a file on a computer?"

"I still have his computer. USB stick? Could be."

"Do you know what his friends took with them?"

Mrs. Gedman shook her head. "I didn't pay much attention. They were mourning, and I wanted to respect their feelings. They might have taken something, but I don't know what. You can check his computer. It's in the living room."

"Do you recall who was present?"

"Who? My God, my memory isn't as sharp as it used to be. Max, Jukka, uh... Celeste? No, she wasn't there. And there were a bunch of other school friends. I can't remember them all."

"Well, we'd appreciate it if you could share the names as they come back to you," Timo said.

"Of course."

"What about a journal?" Isa asked.

Mrs. Gedman pondered for a moment. "Jonathan liked to express himself through his music and poems, but I doubt he kept a journal. I didn't find any, but you can look around if you want."

"Thank you, Mrs. Gedman," Timo said and gave her his card. "If there is anything else you can think of, give me a call."

## CHAPTER

# 22

TIMO'S HEART RACED AS HE SPED through the empty streets, his car skidding around the corners as he made his way to the hotel. When he finally arrived, the sight before him was one of chaos. An ambulance and several police cars were parked out front, their flashing lights casting a red and blue glow over the area.

Without a second thought, he flung the car door open and sprinted towards the entrance, only to be stopped by Isa. "You can't go in there, Timo," she said firmly, her hand on his chest to keep him back.

Timo's panic rose as he struggled against her hold. "I need to see her. Please, let me in."

Isa's expression softened, but she shook her head. "It's not a good idea."

"Just tell me...," he said. His voice broke.

Timo's eyes filled with tears as he sank to the ground, his body wracked with sobs.

"You can't be here," Isa said and took his arm to pull him up.

She turned to Varg who was standing a few meters away from them, staring at the unusual scene. "Take care of him, but don't let him go inside."

Timo was in no state to argue and allowed himself to be led away. Isa then walked inside the hotel, her heart pounding in her chest. The entrance hall was a flurry of activity with officers rushing in and out, and paramedics hurrying past her with medical equipment. The elevators were crowded, and Isa had to wait for several minutes before she could squeeze herself in. She pressed the button for the ninth floor and watched as the numbers ticked by.

When the elevator doors opened, Isa stepped out and made her way through the hallway towards the room where the door was open, and a handful of police officers were standing.

Isa could hear hushed voices and footsteps as she approached the room. Her hand instinctively went to her holster, and she took a deep breath before stepping inside. The room was small and cramped, filled with police officers, all focused on the body lying on the bed. The air was thick with the smell of antiseptic and something else she couldn't quite place.

She moved closer to the bed, careful not to disturb the evidence. She recognized the victim immediately. The beautiful face, the high cheekbones. She had only met her once, on an evening that had ended in tragedy. It was as if she were sleeping. No blood, nothing that could reveal she had died a violent death.

Isa took out her notepad and started jotting down notes, trying to make sense of the scene in front of her. There was nothing else that she could make of it. Kristina Rapp had died a silent death. One she had chosen.

Suicide.

"Is there a note?" Isa said.

"There was a piece of paper in her hand," Sylvia said.

"Can I see it?"

Sylvia held up a plastic bag with the paper in it and gave it to Isa.

*"I'm sorry, but this is too hard to bear,"* Isa read aloud.

"We'll check if it's her handwriting, but nothing suggests that there was anyone else in the room," Sylvia said and looked at Isa.

"How did she die?"

Sylvia pointed to the bottle on the nightstand.

Isa walked over to the table and picked up the small bottle. It was labeled as sleeping pills. She opened it and saw that there were only a few pills left.

"It looks like suicide," Sylvia said.

Isa sighed. "Yeah."

"Who was she?"

"A police profiler... and a good friend of Inspector Paikkala."

"Oh, I didn't know... he must be..."

Isa nodded and looked at the body again. "Devastated... yeah, he is. This is not going to be easy."

"She looks so young... so beautiful. Why?"

"The prospect of a life of pain and suffering," Isa stared at the lifeless body, lost in her thoughts. Finally, she turned to Sylvia and said, "She had inherited the defective gene for Huntington's disease."

Sylvia's eyes widened in surprise. "Oh my God. That's terrible. But... how do you know?"

"I just know. She had found out recently and was struggling to come to terms with it."

Sylvia shook her head. "I can't even imagine what that must have been like for her. To know that you're going to develop a fatal disease and there's nothing you can do about it."

"It's a cruel fate. And it seems that Kristina has decided to take control of the situation by ending her life on her own terms."

Sylvia looked at Isa with a mix of sadness and disbelief. "But... suicide? That's such a drastic step. Couldn't she have sought help? Talked to someone?"

And Kristina had. Only her perception had already been skewed. And now she had settled one of her best friends—the man she had loved—with a lifelong feeling of guilt he would never be able to shake.

"Kristina was a profiler. She understood the human mind better than most. She knew what she was doing. And maybe she felt that there was no other way out."

Sylvia looked back at Kristina's lifeless body and sighed. "Or maybe even profilers can't escape the darkness within their own minds. It's a tragedy. Such a waste of a brilliant mind and a beautiful life."

Isa nodded. "Do a thorough sweep. I'll be outside... with the boss."

"Okay," Sylvia said and walked over to Dr. Einarsson who meanwhile had entered and was examining the body.

Isa stepped outside, her mind racing with so many emotions she could hardly cope with. She couldn't imagine being in Kristina's shoes, facing a slow and painful death with no cure in sight. But she also couldn't imagine taking her own life.

When she stood outside again, she saw Timo sitting in his car. She walked over to the car and got in.

He was leaning his head against the window and had his eyes closed. When she got in, he made no effort to look at her.

"Are you okay?" Isa asked and immediately realized it was a stupid question.

He let out a deep sigh before opening his eyes and turning to her. "What do you think? I'm not okay."

"I know this is hard for you," Isa said gently, placing a hand on his shoulder.

Timo shook his head. "I failed her. It's my fault. I should have..."

"Timo, you couldn't have known," Isa said.

"I should have known," Timo's voice was filled with anguish.

Isa didn't know what to say. She had seen Timo in difficult situations before, but this was different.

"Even if you had said yes to her, she had already made up her mind. This doesn't come out of the blue. It's not you. It's the terrible realization that there is nothing she could do about it."

"I backed away when she asked me," Timo's voice broke. "I have been avoiding her calls. Maybe she just wanted to talk, and I ignored her."

He put his head in his hands.

Isa placed her hand on his back. "I'm so sorry."

Then he looked up and said, "I want to be alone for a while. Can you handle it?"

"Yeah, of course, but... don't do anything stupid," she said.

He shook his head.

She got out of the car. And as he drove off, Isa stood there feeling a mix of emotions. She had never seen him so devastated. Somehow it felt the onset of change. Everything would be different. More than the tragedy of Kristina's death, she feared the impact on the team, on her friendship with Timo. She couldn't bear to lose him.

Then she walked back into the building.

* * *

When he woke up, Max was disoriented. His head was throbbing, and his vision was blurry. He tried to lift his right hand to his face, but he couldn't. He looked down and screamed. It wasn't there. Panic set in, and he looked down to see a bloody stump where his hand used to be. There was a pile of blood on the floor. He had lost so much blood.

The pain was something he had never experienced before, and he let out a scream that echoed off the walls of the basement. He felt weak, dizzy, and nauseous.

As he looked around, he could hardly make out anything. It was too dark.

There was a foul odor in the air.

He couldn't think straight. His arms were still tied to the chair with duct tape. He had to find a way to untie himself before whoever did this returned. He wouldn't survive another torture session.

Max leaned over as far as he could, trying to bring his teeth closer to the duct tape that bound his wrists to the chair. He could feel the rough edges of the tape pressing against his lips as he opened his mouth wide, biting down with all his strength.

But no matter how hard he tried; the tape wouldn't budge. He could feel the panic rising in his chest. It was too thick and too tightly wound around his wrist. Max could taste the bitter flavor of the tape in his mouth, and he could feel the strain in his jaw as he continued to bite down.

He stopped and looked at the blood on the armchair and the stump, where his hand used to be.

Without hesitation, Max began to force and wriggle what remained of his hand, using every bit of strength and willpower he had to try and loosen the tight grip of the duct tape.

At first, the pain was unbearable, but Max gritted his teeth and pushed through. He could feel the duct tape starting to give way as he continued to twist and turn his stump.

Finally, with a sharp tug, Max felt the duct tape snap, and his right arm was free.

There he was with one arm free but no means to untie his left arm. The pain was overwhelming, and he was growing weaker by the second. But he couldn't give up. He had to find a way out of this nightmare.

His eyes darted around the room, taking in every detail. There were no windows, just concrete walls, and an old armchair in the center. A flicker of hope flashed across Max's mind as he saw something glinting in the corner of the room. He strained his neck to get a better look, and his heart sank as he realized it was just a discarded piece of metal.

Max started to rock the chair back and forth, putting all his weight on one side and then the other. He repeated the motion over and over again, using his free arm to gain momentum.

As the chair began to shift and creak under his weight, Max put all his strength into one final push, and the chair finally gave way. With a loud snap, one of the legs broke, and the chair toppled over, sending Max crashing to the ground.

Pain shot through his body as he hit the floor. He quickly pushed himself up onto his knees, using the remainder of his arm to steady himself.

With his left arm still bound to the chair, Max reached out with his stump and started to push down the duct tape. It was still tight, but the chair was no longer holding him down, and he had more freedom of movement. He put his knee on the broken armchair to apply pressure and free his arm.

With a sharp pull, Max finally freed his left arm from the duct tape that bound it to the chair. He let out a cry of relief as he examined the cuts and bruises on his wrists and arms.

Max knew he had to act fast. He had to find a way out of the room before the man returned. He looked around for anything that could help him escape. His eyes fell on the broken chair leg. He picked it up, feeling the weight of it in his hand. It wasn't much, but it was better than nothing.

His thoughts were interrupted by the sound of footsteps approaching the room. He froze, his heart racing as he tried to figure out his next move. He knew he couldn't fight the man off with just one arm.

With a surge of adrenaline, Max made a decision. He would attack the man as soon as he entered the room. He waited, his grip on the broken chair leg tightening with each passing second.

The door creaked open, and a man stepped into the room. He looked surprised to see Max free from the chair, and he took a step back as Max lunged forward with the broken chair leg.

"Well, well... you're awake," the man said, a cruel smile spreading across his face. "Good. I have some more fun planned for us."

"You?" It was the first time Max saw him so clearly. It confused him for a moment but then Max swung the makeshift weapon with all his might, connecting with the man's arm. The man let out a cry of pain. Max swung again, this time hitting the man's head with a sickening thud. The man crumpled to the ground, unconscious.

Max didn't waste any time. He ran out of the room. As he stumbled up the stairs, Max could feel his strength fading, but he didn't stop.

He burst through the door at the top of the stairs and found himself in a dark hallway. He could hear voices coming from down the hall, but he couldn't make out what they were saying. He looked around frantically for a way out, but all he could see were closed doors.

He heard footsteps coming from behind him and turned to see the man he had just knocked out standing in the doorway, his head in his hands. Max took off down the hall as fast as he could, the broken chair leg still clutched in his hand.

The voices were getting louder now, and Max could see a dim light at the end of the hallway. He pushed himself harder, ignoring the pain in his body as he ran towards the light.

As he got closer, Max could see that the light was coming from a door. He burst through it, not stopping to check if anyone was inside. He found himself in a small room with a window looking out onto the street.

Max didn't hesitate. He smashed the window with the broken chair leg and crawled through it, ignoring the glass cutting into his skin. He landed on the ground outside, rolling to lessen the impact.

He looked around, trying to get his bearings. He didn't recognize the street or the buildings around him, but he knew he had to keep moving. Max started to run, not knowing where he was going but knowing he had to get as far away from that place as possible.

As he ran, Max could feel his strength fading. He stumbled and fell, hitting his head on the pavement.

And then everything went black.

* * *

"Paikkala, what are you doing?"

Timo looked up at Isa, his eyes bloodshot and his speech slurred. "What does it look like I'm doing?"

Isa shook her head in disapproval. "You're not good at this. You don't drink."

She signaled the waitress.

"How many did he have?" she asked her.

The young woman looked at him and said, "Five beers or so."

Isa sighed and turned back to Timo. "You know better than to drown your sorrow like this."

Timo glared at her. "What do you know about it? You don't know what it's like."

Isa's expression softened. "I may not know exactly how you feel, but I've lost people too. And I know that drinking yourself into a stupor won't make it any better. It was even you who told me."

Timo looked away. The few patrons who were still there at this late hour were either hunched over their drinks or slumped in their chairs, lost in their own thoughts.

Timo tried to steady himself. He knew Isa was right, but he didn't know how else to deal with the guilt and pain that consumed him.

"I just miss her," he said.

Isa placed a comforting hand on his shoulder. "I know you do. But drinking won't bring her back. You need to face your feelings and find a healthy way to cope."

"Sure... you weren't the one who let her down."

"Look, Paikkala, you've been through worse. Your father died, Caijsa was murdered."

"But this time it's my fault," Timo said.

"Even if you'd slept with her, she would have done this. Her mind had been made up already."

Timo nodded, knowing she was right, but something inside of him said he could have done more to help her. He tried to push the thoughts aside. "Just leave me."

"Paikkala, I cannot do that. The team needs you. I need you."

"Why? You can perfectly do this without me. I'll mess everything up anyway."

"Celeste is dead, Jukka is dead. Max is missing. We need to find him."

"And Kristina's death is nothing?"

"I didn't say that," Isa said in a stern voice.

"Just... leave me."

He pushed away the empty beer bottles and stood up, but the dizziness hit him hard. Stumbling, he almost fell, but Isa quickly caught him and helped him steady himself.

"Come on," she said, "let's get you out of here."

Timo didn't resist as she guided him out of the bar and into the cool night air. The fresh breeze helped clear his head a little, yet the sensation of being lost and alone persisted.

"Let's get you home," she said.

He leaned against the wall of the building and let himself slide down against it.

She sighed and looked at him. "But I'm not so sure I can leave you alone."

Timo looked up at her, his eyes glassy. "I'll be fine. Just need some time to myself."

"I don't think that's a good idea. You're not in the right state of mind to be alone."

Timo closed his eyes and leaned his head against the wall, feeling the weight of the past few days bearing down on him. He knew he needed to face his feelings and deal with his grief, but he didn't know where to start.

"Come, let's get you to my place," Isa said.

Ten minutes later they were driving to her home. In silence. There wasn't much Isa could say.

When they arrived at Isa's house, she helped Timo inside and settled him on the couch. She went to the kitchen and returned with a glass of water and some painkillers, which she handed to him.

"Here, take these. They'll help with the headache."

He took the pills and drank the water, then leaned back on the couch and closed his eyes.

Isa sat beside him. "We'll get through this together."

Timo opened his eyes and looked at her. "Thank you."

Isa smiled at him. "Get some rest. We'll talk in the morning."

# CHAPTER

# 23

"**PAIKKALA, IT'S TIME TO WAKE UP,**" Isa said and didn't hesitate to give the couch a nasty kick.

Timo woke up with a pounding headache. He was disoriented for a moment, until he remembered that he had ended up at Isa's house after drinking too much the night before. He groaned and sat up, wincing as the light filtering in through the curtains stabbed painfully at his eyes.

Suddenly, it all came back to him: Isa had found him at the bar, convinced him to come home with her, and he had ended up on her couch. He felt a pang of shame; he hadn't meant to make such a scene in public.

"Ugh," he muttered to himself, running a hand over his face in an attempt to wake himself up. "What time is it?"

"Jesus, Paikkala, you're such a bad drinker," Isa let out, walked to the kitchen, and came back with a glass in her hands.

"Drink this," she said, handing him the glass containing an unknown yellowish substance.

"What is it?"

She ignored him and walked back to the kitchen.

Timo took a sip of the drink and winced; his headache was still pounding away mercilessly. The bitterness of the drink made him suppress a gag.

"You have a hangover, and I don't have time to wait while you sober up," Isa called out. "Drink up now! We have to go."

He looked up at her. She was surprisingly harsh. Then he took another gulp of the drink, decided he would try without it and then put it on the table next to the couch.

"They found Max Westerberg," she said.

"And? Is he..."

"He's in a bad shape, but he'll live."

"Can we talk to him?" Timo asked.

"Not sure in what shape he is, but we'll try. We're going to the hospital. Hurry up!"

Timo got up, straightened his back, and tried to recall where his jacket was.

Until that moment, his mind had been fuzzy, but now he remembered everything clearly. His heart felt like it had been ripped out of his chest when he thought back to the moment he received the phone call about Kristina's death—a gut-wrenching blow. He hadn't been able to breathe or think properly ever since learning about her death.

He could only imagine how terrified she must have been in her final moments. Desperation overwhelmed him as he wished he could turn back time to prevent any of this from happening. He wished he had said yes, he wished he hadn't ignored her calls.

"I just need five more minutes," he said.

Isa hesitated for a moment before finally relenting. "All right. But I know what you're thinking, and you should stop. I don't know if you remember our talk yesterday, but I'll keep telling you, 'You are not to blame.' She made the decision to end her life long before she made the request. She would have done it regardless."

He knew Isa was right, but it didn't ease his turmoil. He couldn't stop replaying the last conversation he had with her in his mind, wondering if there was something he could have said or done differently. His reaction to her request haunted him—a mix of stupidity and awkwardness.

"Come on, Paikkala," Isa said, her voice firm yet gentle. "We need to go."

Timo stood up, grabbed his jacket, and followed Isa out of the door.

Outside, the sun shone brightly, but the air was cold. It promised to be a beautiful day, yet he couldn't appreciate it. He wished he could turn off his brain, if only for a little while.

As they drove to the hospital, Isa briefed him on what Varg had told her about Max's condition. He had been found lying on the sidewalk, barely clinging to life. Severely dehydrated, covered in blood, bruised, battered, and missing his right hand.

Timo listened to her words, but they didn't seem to percolate.

As they arrived at the hospital, Timo drew in a deep breath, attempting to compose himself. He understood the importance of being fully present and focused if they were to glean any useful information from Max.

Isa took the lead, guiding them toward the intensive care unit where Max was undergoing treatment. Their path was intercepted by a nurse at the entrance, who requested their badges before granting them access.

"Ten minutes, maximum," the nurse declared in a stern tone, and accompanied her statement with a haughty glance.

The sight that greeted them when they entered was painful. Max was hooked up to all sorts of machines, his face bruised and battered. His right arm was wrapped in bandages where his hand used to be.

Isa leaned in to speak to Max, but he didn't respond. His eyes were closed, and his breathing was shallow. Timo stood back, feeling helpless and useless. Why did he suddenly feel so numb and insensitive at the sight of this man? Even if he didn't want to show it, he always felt a sense of involvement. There were emotions in every case, but now, it was all so detached. He had never experienced that before.

A male nurse entered the room, and Isa addressed him. "Has he been conscious?"

The nurse explained, "Yes, but he's drifting in and out of consciousness. He lost a considerable amount of blood, and he's dealing with a severe infection. We haven't been successful in reducing his temperature yet. The next few hours are crucial. Only then can the doctors evaluate if he's strong enough for surgery. Whoever did this was a butcher. It almost looks like the hand was ripped off."

"Did he say anything?" Isa asked.

"Yes, when he arrived at the hospital, but it was very incoherent. He was talking about a cellar and a man, but beyond that, I couldn't understand much."

"We need to get him police protection," Timo said. "If whoever abducted him knows he survived, they may want to finish the job."

Isa nodded.

A moan came from the man in the bed. "Stop... no, please."

Isa leaned in. "Max, can you hear me? I'm Inspector Lindström."

Beads of sweat were dripping from his forehead, and he was wildly turning his head from one side to the other as if he were having a nightmare.

"He's coming," Max shouted.

His eyes were wide open, but it was as if he weren't really there, like he was watching something that only he could see.

Isa tried to calm him down. "Max, you're safe now. You're in the hospital."

But Max continued to thrash around. "No, no, he's here. He's going to kill me."

"Who?" Timo intervened. "Who is it? What does he look like?"

"Get him away from me!"

The heart monitor started beeping rapidly, indicating Max's heartbeat was increasing, and his blood pressure was getting out of control.

"You need to warn him," Max shouted and grabbed Isa's arm. "You need to warn him."

"Who?" Isa said, confused.

The door was thrown open, and a doctor rushed in. "Max, we need to give you a sedative to help you calm down and get some rest."

He turned to the nurse. "Prepare 5 milligrams of lorazepam and inject it intravenously."

The nurse nodded and quickly prepared the medication.

The doctor turned back to Max. "Now, Max, I need you to relax and let the medication do its job. You're safe here, and we'll make sure no harm comes to you."

Max's grip on Isa's arm loosened as the sedative began to take effect. He let out a deep sigh and closed his eyes, finally finding some peace.

The doctor turned to Isa and Timo. "He should be sleeping for a few hours. We'll keep him under close observation and make sure he's stable enough for surgery when the time comes. But he's in a really bad shape."

"Does his family know?" Isa asked.

"Yes, they were contacted. His parents are on their way."

"We'll have an officer outside his room," Isa continued.

"You think there is a chance...," the doctor said, surprised.

"He was tortured and escaped. Likely the perpetrator is looking to finish whatever he started. We need to protect him."

"Okay... just one thing... when Max arrived at the hospital, there was a short period, he was lucid. He said he hit the man. And he mentioned a name... Jonathan."

Isa quickly looked at Timo. "Was there anything else he talked about? Did he recognize the place where he was held? Was it a house? An apartment?"

The doctor shrugged.

"Thanks, doctor." Then Isa turned to Timo and said, "We'll have to come back later when he's awake and more coherent."

They said their goodbyes. But as Isa and Timo walked to the exit, she noticed how quiet he was.

"Look, Timo, I can't do this without you. People are in danger. We need to act fast, and I need your full attention on this. Okay?"

He nodded. "Yeah, I know."

"With Jonathan Gedman, we seem to be on the right track."

He nodded and then said, "I'll be okay... I promise."

*\*\**

With a court-issued search warrant in hand, the police headed towards Gideon's house. They pressed the doorbell but were met with an unsettling silence. The officers, empowered by the warrant, then cautiously pushed the door open. Upon entering, Varg and Sylvia, along with five colleagues, were immediately struck by a foul odor.

Varg, hand covering his nose, turned to Sylvia. "Should we get forensics in here?"

"Not just yet," Sylvia responded and pulled the plastic gloves from her pocket. "Let's see if we can find anything before calling them in."

Navigating through the cottage, they explored its two bedrooms and living room. The living room, modestly furnished with a sofa, coffee table, and a few chairs, featured a bookshelf against one wall, filled with old, worn-out books. A photo on the mantelpiece captured better times—Gideon and Mari smiling at the camera.

Advancing to the back, they entered the kitchen, where the source of the unpleasant smell awaited. The space was cluttered with dirty dishes, discarded food containers, and an overflowing garbage can, releasing an overpowering stench of rotting food.

In the midst of the chaos, a large plastic bag stood out, covered in blood and seemingly left undisturbed for some time. Varg, careful not to disturb potential evidence, approached and, with gloved hands, opened the bag. What he found made him recoil—a couple of decaying human fingers.

Sylvia immediately called forensics. "We've found body parts."

Then Varg noticed a piece of paper on the counter, with a phone number scribbled on it. He picked it up and showed it to Sylvia.

"What do you think this is?" he asked. "We should call the number and see who answers."

Sylvia dialed the number and put it on speaker.

It took a while before someone picked up, and Varg and Sylvia exchanged a quick glance. They heard a familiar recording. The same music as when Max and Jukka had disappeared.

But then the recording was interrupted, and a man's voice said, "They will pay for what they have done. This isn't over yet."

Sylvia's grip on the phone tightened as she tried to keep her emotions in check. "Who is this?"

The man on the other end laughed, a cold, mocking sound. "You'll find out soon enough," he said before hanging up.

Sylvia looked at Varg who was still looking at the paper with furrowed brows. "We need to trace that call. We need to find out who this guy is before he hurts anyone else."

But when Varg didn't say anything, she asked, "What's wrong?"

"I... somehow know this voice. I think I talked to him before."

"Who?"

"I... don't know. I can't remember where."

He put the paper down and then said, "We need to search the rest of the house."

The forensics team had entered.

"But where is Gideon?" he said.

Upstairs, there was nothing special. The bedroom was simple and unremarkable, with nothing that caught their attention. There was a second room with a desktop, laptop, and a printer.

But as they made their way downstairs, one of the officers called out, "I found something."

Varg and Sylvia hurried to where the officer was standing. He was pointing at a door in the corner of the basement. "It was locked," he said, "but I managed to open it."

The rest of the basement housed remnants of Gideon's past pottery hobby, with shelves filled with clay, sculpting tools, and unfinished projects.

Varg turned his attention back to the smaller room and gestured for the police officer to step aside. He took out his gun, pushed the door open, and they stepped inside. It was a small room, barely big enough for a single person. There was a chair in the corner next to a pile of dried-up blood. A strange mixture of gasoline and urine filled the room.

Against the opposite wall, there was a table with a series of knives and other instruments.

Sylvia shivered. "This is sick."

Varg walked over to the table and examined the tools. "This guy knew what he was doing."

"Jeezes, Jukka must have been so scared," she let out. "And Gideon Younggren did this?"

Varg sighed, let his eyes scan the room again and then said, "I don't know. But there is something not right about this."

\*\*\*

Sylvia entered Dr. Einarsson's office, nestled in the modern and meticulously maintained section of the police building. The space exuded an aura of order and organization, with no loose papers or files in sight. Much different from the desks of most police officers.

Light blue walls set a calming tone, adorned with framed certificates.

The focal point of the room was a leather chair behind the desk, flanked by two inviting seats for visitors. Sylvia's eyes wandered to a bookshelf on the wall, housing a collection of thick textbooks on forensic pathology, anatomy, and criminal law. On the opposite wall, a large whiteboard displayed a tapestry of notes, diagrams, and charts.

Compared to his predecessor, Dr. Einarsson's office was much more organized and structured.

"Sergeant Ahlgren, we keep meeting a lot," he said without taking his eyes from the paper on his desk.

"Well, you don't show up at the briefings. So..."

"Briefings are for the police team. I'm not part of the team. I only come when I'm invited."

"In a sense you are part of the team," she said.

He gave her a quick stare. "And why is it always you?"

She frowned. "What do you mean?"

"I never see you colleagues here, but you on the other hand..."

Sylvia raised an eyebrow. "Is there a problem with me being here, Dr. Einarsson?"

"No, not at all. It's just an observation."

She had to admit she could've picked up the phone and called him or asked via email to send the report, but somehow, she liked the thought of visiting him. He annoyed her beyond measure, he had insulted her and scorned her. Yet she found herself longing to be in his presence.

Sylvia nodded, "Well, I'm here to collect the forensic report of the Younggren's home. I hope you've had a chance to examine the evidence."

Dr. Einarsson leaned back in his chair, "Yes, I have. And I must say, the findings are quite interesting."

"Why?"

"The blood and the fingers are Jukka's, and Mr. Younggren's DNA was found on the instruments in the basement."

"And?"

"His DNA was only found on the tools, nowhere else in that basement. Someone cleaned it thoroughly..."

"And wants us to think that Gideon Younggren did all of this," Sylvia said.

"Correct."

"Did you find anything else?"

"No, but I can say for certain that Max Westerberg was not held there. I should have found his blood."

"So, someone is framing Gideon Younggren. But who?"

Dr. Einarsson shrugged. "That's not my job to figure out. My job is to provide the forensic evidence and let the police do their job."

Sylvia sighed. "Yeah, I know. It's not going to be simple."

Dr. Einarsson offered her a small smile. "We both know that the truth is never simple."

"Anyway... thank you for your report, Dr. Einarsson."

Why did her interactions with him always begin with civility, only to devolve into moments where he inevitably said something that irked her?

He leaned back in his chair, studying her for a moment. "You know, sergeant, I've been thinking."

"About what?" Sylvia asked, sensing that she wasn't going to like where this was going.

"About us," he said simply. "We seem to have developed a sort of... rapport, wouldn't you say?"

Sylvia felt a wave of irritation wash over her. "I wouldn't call it that," she said coolly. "We're just colleagues, that's all."

Dr. Einarsson smirked. "Sure... so tell me, why do you want to be an inspector?"

"Why do you ask?"

"I find it strange."

"Why? Because a woman can't do this job?"

Dr. Einarsson frowned. "No, because you're smart... and you can do so much better."

She didn't know what to say.

He continued, "You have the potential to do great things, Sergeant Ahlgren. But being a police inspector is not the best use of your talents."

Sylvia was taken aback by his words. "What are you trying to say?"

"This job is... dangerous, emotionally demanding. You should be doing something more... challenging, more rewarding. What does your boyfriend think about this?"

Sylvia could feel her anger bubbling up. "What makes you think you know what's best for me?"

He gave her a sarcastic smile. "I don't. But I do know that you're capable of achieving great things, if you put your mind to it."

Sylvia shook her head, "I don't need your advice, Dr. Einarsson."

"Fair enough," he said, holding up his hands. "But just remember, if you ever need someone to talk to, I'm here."

"I'll keep that in mind." Sylvia stood up abruptly. "I think we're done here... Dr. Einarsson. I'll be sure to let the team know about your report."

Without another word, she strode out of his office, seething with anger and frustration. She couldn't believe the audacity of that man. How dare he question what she did, who she was? She was a professional, damn it, and she wouldn't let him undermine that.

# CHAPTER

# 24

**ISA SAT IN TIMO'S OFFICE,** her eyes closed, a lingering headache throbbing in the background. She felt stressed out. The low hum of the office, usually unnoticed, now seemed to exacerbate her discomfort.

The door creaked open, and Varg entered. She opened her eyes, acknowledging his arrival with a wearied nod.

"Is this your office now?" Varg said. "Where is Inspector Paikkala?"

"I don't know," Isa said. "And I don't care."

That wasn't true. She was worried. She hadn't seen him for days, and he hadn't returned her calls. Maybe it was better that she left him alone with his guilt and grief. He would eventually come to realize that it wasn't his fault.

Varg looked at her with a confused expression on his face.

"Never mind," she waved it away. "What do you have?"

"The neighbors confirmed that they haven't seen Gideon for weeks. The last time, he mentioned he was going on a vacation. It was strange since he never went anywhere, but they thought not much of it. And they haven't seen any unusual activity around his house either."

Isa leaned back in the chair, rubbing her temples as if trying to soothe the persistent ache. "Vacation," she muttered, more to herself than to Varg.

"Could be a smoke screen," Varg suggested, leaning against the edge of Timo's desk. "We should dig deeper into Gideon's recent activities and connections."

Isa appreciated Varg's focus on the case. At least, someone was doing his job. "Agreed. Start by checking his phone records, recent contacts, anything that might give us a lead."

Varg reached into his pocket and pulled out a small notebook. "I've got a list of names and addresses from the neighbors. People who might know more about Gideon's whereabouts or activities."

"Do we need to talk to his ex-wife again?"

Varg shrugged. "What information did we get from her last time? She will keep on protecting him. We've been watching her home for the last week, but nothing."

"Where is he hiding? And where is Freya? Is she involved?"

"We still can't reach her. Her phone is offline."

"She's on holidays. She has to come back at a certain point. We have an APB issued for her, and we're keeping an eye on the airports and borders."

"Or she might never come back? She might be in it, together with her father."

Isa sighed, feeling the weight of the case bearing down on her. "This is taking too long, We need a breakthrough, Varg. Something to give us direction."

"What about Max Westerberg?"

"He's still in an induced coma. It seems his injuries are more severe than initially anticipated. Internal bleeding, fractures, next to an amputated hand."

"Another thing... Helena Håkansson contacted us again," Varg said. "She remembered receiving a call about six months ago from someone asking about Dancho Krastev's recording."

"Really? What did they ask? Who was it?"

"This person identified himself as Jonathan Gedman."

"Jonathan? But he has been missing for five years. What did he want to know?"

"He asked who made the recording. She thought it was strange because Jonathan Gedman was the person who would receive the recording. So she didn't provide him a lot of information suspecting that it was not Jonathan on the other end of the line."

"So indeed, it was an impostor."

Varg nodded. "But there was something else. The voice sounded familiar, like she had met this person before, but she couldn't recall where and when... and who."

Isa's mind raced, trying to connect dots and possibilities. "It shows again that we need to investigate the past. The disappearance of Jonathan Gedman is key."

"We can trace where the incoming call was coming from," Varg suggested.

"We need a warrant for that, but we won't get it. This is far too circumstantial. We just need to find another way. Talk to her again. Maybe she remembers the voice."

More questions than ever. This investigation was going nowhere. Even the boss was checking out. Timo should have been here. Maybe it was her time to shine, when all the men in her life were giving up. Just like Sylvia had said. The office she was sitting in felt like coming home, for the first time. She had never seen herself as the superintendent. She had thought about leaving, taking care of her children and settling down. But she had never thought of the other possibility. Maybe it was time.

"Did Sivert get anything from Jonathan's computer?" she asked.

"He's still busy with it. I'll check with him again."

"This should be his highest priority. And what about Andreas Lundqvist and Verner Blixt?"

"We got input from organized crime. According to them, Andreas has bigger problems than a few small drug dealers who own him money. The word on the street is that Jukka and Max are in debts, and that they are working for him to pay him back. He would never compromise that. Torturing Jukka and Max would put him in the spotlight, and he doesn't want that. I think we can assume that Andreas had nothing to do with the murder and the abduction."

"Good work. And as for Gideon and Freya, let's keep digging. They are somewhere."

As she left the office that evening, Isa's thoughts drifted back to Timo. She couldn't shake the unease, the nagging worry about his well-being. The unresolved tension lingered in the air. For now, she focused on the investigation, but a part of her was already planning the conversation she needed to have with him.

\* \* \*

"Timo, what's wrong?" he heard her voice through the loudspeaker and knew it had been a mistake to call Ingrid.

Kristina, Ingrid.

He held the phone for a moment, lying on the floor of his living room, a ritual that had helped clear his mind countless times but not this time.

He swallowed hard to stop the tears welling in his eyes. It was really a mistake to call her. Why couldn't he let her go? No matter how much distance they put between them, they always found themselves seeking each other's company—phone calls, messages.

He had been sitting outside her house, watching her, and she had let it happen. He had called her just now, and in ten seconds, she had picked up the phone. It wasn't just him. She couldn't let go either.

He tried to speak, but his voice cracked. "Kristina... she... she..."

"What happened to Kristina?"

"She's dead. She... she..." Timo couldn't finish the sentence. The words were stuck in his throat, choking him.

"Oh, Timo, I'm so sorry," Ingrid said softly. "What happened?"

"She... she committed suicide."

There was a long pause on the other end of the line. Finally, Ingrid spoke again. "That's terrible. I can't even imagine what you're going through. I didn't know she was... troubled."

Timo closed his eyes, and tears ran down his cheeks. He felt so alone, so lost. "I don't know what to do," he whispered.

"Do you want me to come over?"

Timo paused briefly before responding, "No, let's not do that. It's okay. I'll be fine."

"Are you sure?"

"Yeah, I'm sure."

Silence.

Then Ingrid said, "This is killing me... I don't think you're okay. I want..."

"Don't," he whispered. "I need to think."

"Timo?"

"I feel like I'm drowning. The control is slipping away. I can't do my job. I'm thinking about you all the time. I feel stuck... inadequate."

He heard her gasp for air.

"I know this is not what you want to hear," he said. "But this is how

I feel."

"It's the emotions talking."

Maybe she was right, but Timo couldn't help the way he felt. "I just need some time to process everything. I need to figure out how to move on from this."

"I understand," Ingrid said. "But don't shut me out."

Maybe he should. He was too dependent on her. She didn't want to commit. He was never going to be first in her world. Her children and her husband were. What was he doing?

"Can you just stay on the phone with me?" he finally asked.

"Of course. I'm here."

They spent hours on the phone, him sharing stories about Kristina while Ingrid just listened. The connection he felt was unlike anything he had experienced before.

* * *

When Freya got off the plane that afternoon in Stockholm, she never thought she would be spending the rest of the day in an interrogation room at the Gävle police station. The whole situation seemed surreal to her. A bunch of police officers had escorted her out of the airport into a police car, and two hours later she stepped into the police station. At that moment, her stress level had gone up.

What was going on? What did they know?

Everything had gone so well. Until now.

When Isa and Varg entered the room, she gave them a small smile, but they looked so serious that she found herself straightening up and feeling a knot form in her stomach. They didn't waste any time with small talk and got straight to the point.

"Ms. Younggren, we need to ask you some questions about your recent activities," Isa said, her voice calm but firm.

*Oh, God, they know.*

Freya felt her heart rate increase. "What do you mean?"

"Where were you the last two weeks?" Varg asked.

"Uh... holidays. I was in Ecuador, traveling the Andes."

Isa raised a brow. "Alone?"

"Yes... no, I mean I took a guided tour. We were about ten people from all over the world. What is this about? What did I do wrong?"

"Why didn't you contact anyone?"

Freya's eyes widened. "Did something happen to my parents?"

"Please answer the question," Isa said and looked her in the eye.

"I lost my phone and... my brother knew where I was."

"Your brother repeatedly tried to contact you. He didn't know where you were, only that you were somewhere... on an extensive holiday."

She knew that.

"I sent them an email before leaving with all the information," Freya said.

"He never received any information from you," Varg said in a stern voice.

"Seriously... what is this about? I can prove that I was there. I have a boarding pass. A dozen people saw me. Why do I need to prove this?"

Isa ignored her questions. "Why this holiday?"

"I... that's personal."

Varg put a bag with a pill bottle on the table. "What is this?"

They knew.

"You took this from my bag?" Freya stammered.

"What is it?" Varg repeated.

"My sleep medication."

A sarcastic tone crept into Varg's voice. "Sleep medication? How do you explain the capsules with a strange yellow substance we found mixed in?"

Freya's eyes widened, panic and shock coursing through her body.

"I... I have no idea how that got there. You have to believe me."

Isa leaned forward, locking her eyes on her. "We saw him... waiting for you at the exit. One of Andreas' men. You are working for him. Already for years."

Freya's shoulders slumped. "No, you have to believe me. I am the victim. Because of him... And Jukka, Max... and Boris. They are to blame."

"Jukka is dead. Max is in the hospital, and your father is missing. Someone used his home to torture and kill someone."

"Uh... what?"

"What is in the pills?"

Freya looked at her hands and doubted for a moment if she would reveal everything she knew. There was still so much anger and resentment about what they had done so many years ago. Because of them, she was an addict. And she would be the rest of her life. There was no escape. Never. The overdose was still fresh in her mind. After that, nothing had ever been the same. She could have died. But her so-called friends had decided just to dump her on the footsteps of the hospital that same day when Jonathan and Dancho had gone missing.

Max and Jukka had gotten what they deserved.

Isa opened the file in front of her and showed her a picture of the blood stains found in the basement of her father's home, the instruments covered in blood and the bagged fingers. Then she pulled a picture of Jukka Ulfsson's dead body.

Freya felt a wave of nausea wash over her as she saw the gruesome images. She couldn't believe what she was seeing, and she felt a cold sweat break out on her forehead.

"Is this a message? Or are you in on it? Did he have to pay?"

"I... I don't know anything about this. I swear," she stammered.

"What's in the pills?"

She ran her hands over her face and then said, "It's an experimental drug. Andreas got to know about it via one of his 'acquaintances' in

Colombia and wanted to try it out. See if he can find a market for it over here."

"And you were the courier?"

"Yeah," Freya said. "I'm always the one taking the risks."

"And why is that?" Isa said.

"I'm the addict. Max and Jukka made sure to stay away from using drugs. They focused on collecting the money, but they got into trouble. I was always the one to fix it."

"What about Boris?"

Freya threw her head backwards and let out a sarcastic laugh. "Boris? He was the smart one. He stayed away from the drugs already a long time ago. After the incident at the hiking trip, he made sure he never came into contact with drugs again."

"What incident?" Isa asked.

She took a moment to reflect and then said, "Because of him, I almost died. There was a time I would have done anything for that man. He betrayed me when he left me to die on the footsteps of the hospital. That morning, we decided to get high, but I was too eager, and I was too depressed... things got out of hand. When Max, Jukka, and Boris realized what was going on, they got into a panic. Maybe I should be happy that Boris realized I needed to go to a hospital. But they were scared, and they decided to drive over there and just dump me."

Isa frowned. "It looks to me that Boris saved your life. Why would you resent him?"

"Because he was the only one, I trusted. After the incident, he didn't want to have anything to do with me. I looked up at him. I loved him. But he betrayed me."

Isa leaned backwards in her chair. "What do you still remember of that day?"

"Not much. I was high all the time. But what I do remember is that there was a lot of tension. Between Celeste and Jonathan. They were fighting most of the time. I think it was about music. Jonathan was a great composer, but he could be stubborn at times. He also had no sense of marketing his work. Celeste was so much better at it."

"Could they have been fighting over 'Aria 25'?"

"It's blurry," Freya admitted. "But I do recall Jonathan being furious. He accused Celeste of trying to take credit for the project. There were heated arguments, but I never thought it would lead to something like this."

"Like what?" Varg asked.

"I don't know, but Celeste was determined. She wanted 'Aria 25' to be a success, and Jonathan's resistance wasn't helping. I just thought it was artistic differences, you know? Celeste knew from the start that they had a hit, but Jonathan was so resistant to compromise. He believed in the purity of his artistic vision, while Celeste was more pragmatic. She wanted to market 'Aria 25' to a broader audience, make it accessible, and turn it into a commercial success. They clashed over the direction of the project, and it became a power struggle between artistic integrity and commercial viability. It wasn't just about the music; it was about control, recognition, and, ultimately, success. Celeste was determined to see her vision realized, even if it meant sidelining Jonathan's artistic ideals. And she was right... it became a success."

"With you on vocals," Isa added. "And Jonathan out of the picture."

"I didn't mean..."

"Was Celeste responsible for his disappearance? She went to look for them."

Freya shook her head. "Of course not!"

"Six months later she's on top of the world, and then... a psychiatric hospital. Was she feeling guilty?"

She didn't know what to say. Every word voiced so clearly what she had thought all those years. She didn't know for sure, but it seemed like the pieces of a puzzle were falling into place, revealing a disturbing picture. The inspector's questions touched on the suspicions and uncertainties that had lingered in her mind for years. Celeste's sudden rise to success after Jonathan's disappearance, her subsequent mental health struggles, and the unresolved tension between them all hinted at a more complex story. Isa's probing was bringing those buried doubts to the surface, forcing her to confront the possibility that Celeste might have been involved in Jonathan's vanishing.

"Or did you do it together?" Isa asked.

"No, no. I respected Jonathan. Sure, he wasn't the easiest person to get along with, but he had talent. Celeste, she loved him. I don't know what happened to him. And how could I? I was fighting for my life."

Freya could feel the stress mounting.

"Jonathan and Dancho," Isa said, her gaze fixed on Freya.

"What about them?"

"Were they a couple?" Varg jumped in.

"A couple? I don't think so. Jonathan was gay... we all knew that, but Dancho... he was just an annoying... sorry, but he was Boris' little brother who just hung around. I don't think there was anything between them. I don't think Dancho liked men."

Isa scribbled something down on her notepad. "Your father... how was he in the last few weeks?"

"What do you mean?"

"Was there anything strange in his behavior?" Isa inquired, while she kept her gaze on Freya.

"Do you seriously think he has anything to do with Jukka's murder and what happened to Max? This is not him. Andreas did this to them."

"Please answer the question," Isa said in a stern voice.

"No, he was fine... like he always was. He..."

But there had been something. A subtle change, a shift in demeanor that Freya couldn't quite put her finger on. The realization settled, and she hesitated before admitting, "Well, maybe there was something, but I didn't think much of it at the time. He was just more... distant, preoccupied."

"Distant and preoccupied?"

"Yeah, he was spending a lot of time in his study. And he went out much more than before."

"Where to?"

"Don't know. And there were some strange phone calls. A bit mysterious. I asked him about it, but he brushed it off, said it was work-related. But it felt off, you know?"

"Work-related? Did he give any specifics?"

This was taking too long. All those annoying questions. It had started subtly, like it always did.

A subtle itch at the back of her consciousness.

But it didn't take long.

Soon Freya's heart began to race, a frantic rhythm matching the panic. She could almost taste the bitter sweetness of the substance, could feel its seductive embrace calling out to her from the depths of her addiction. It was a primal need, consuming her thoughts until it was all she could focus on.

"Can I just go?" she said as the familiar ache settled into her stomach.

"Did he give any specifics?" Isa repeated.

"No, just that it had to do with his business. I tried to get more information, but he was evasive. It did seem like he knew the person. So I let it go."

Varg interjected, "Any idea what kind of business he was talking about?"

"Jesus, I don't know. He used to be in real estate, but... he had to sell his business because..."

And then it all came flooding back.

Because of her, he had to sell most of his assets to help with her addiction. They were struggling financially, and the stress took a toll on their and her parents' relationship.

Because she wasn't brave enough, because she had no spine to withstand the pain that would soon engulf her entire body.

The craving.

It was a bitter pill to swallow as she was confronted again about the consequences of the choices she had made.

"Your father has been missing for days. Where else could he be hiding?"

Her mind was jumping around. She couldn't think straight. "How long is this going to last? I really need..."

"Where could he be hiding?" Varg asked.

They weren't going to let her go.

"I don't know. He doesn't have any friends or other family. I don't feel too well. I need..."

"Your brother's? Your mother's?"

She shook her head.

"Okay. Ms. Younggren, you understand we need to arrest you for possession of drugs and trafficking. You still don't want a lawyer?"

Arrested? The walls were closing in. No, this couldn't be. She needed a fix. And quick.

"Ms. Younggren?" Varg asked.

"Yeah, I want a lawyer."

In no time, she would be out. Andreas always took good care of his employees.

But until then it was going to be painful.

## CHAPTER

# 25

ISA PUT HER HANDS ON HER HIPS and looked at him. He kept staring at the paper on his desk and ignored her. "You have nothing to say?"

He looked up, surprise evident in his expression, before giving her a cold gaze. "About what?"

"Timo, you disappeared for days. We have a case. We need you."

"And you managed, no? You don't need me."

"Of course, we managed. That's not the point. We are a team, and you are the leader."

He didn't move a muscle and looked at her with his piercing blue eyes. His eyes, which she had always found so mysterious and beautiful on one hand, and scary on the other hand. It was like they cracked one's soul completely open. All her thoughts, aspirations and secrets were lying in the open.

She always felt a sense of vulnerability under his gaze, and she quickly looked away. She cleared her throat before speaking again. "Look, Timo. I know you're hurting but you can't just disappear like that without any explanation. We're a team, and we rely on each other. We should help each other."

He leaned back in his chair and folded his arms. "I've lost someone."

Isa's frustration flared at his dismissive tone. "Yeah, I know. And we lost Mila and Lars almost a year ago. I lost Alex. You lost Caijsa. We all lost people."

"And we all stayed professional?" he said with a sarcastic tone in his voice. "You couldn't handle Alex's death... you still can't."

"That's not fair!"

This was getting out of control. Before any of them said something they regretted, someone needed to call a time-out.

And he did by saying, "I'm sorry."

She calmed down.

"You told me there is no place for emotions in our job," she said.

He looked down at his hands on the table and then said, "And that's why I had to take myself out of the equation for a moment. I couldn't handle it. But I'm here now."

Suddenly, a wave of anxiety enveloped her, and she didn't know why. Something was lingering in the background. Something big, something that would change their lives forever. For a moment, she doubted if she would tell him the stalker was back, but she kept quiet. She could handle it.

"Freya Younggren has been released," Isa said. "We're keeping an eye on her."

"You think she'll lead us to her father?"

"Maybe. We have an APB on him."

"Good. What about Max?"

"His second surgery went well, but they still keep him in an induced coma. Not sure when we will be able to talk to him."

Leaning back, he said, "Too bad. He might be able to tell us more about who attacked him. We should be lucky he's still alive."

"This is linked with Jonathan Gedman's disappearance. But how? And how is this linked with Celeste Westerberg. It can't be drugs."

"I wonder..."

"What?" Isa asked.

"Why would anyone have a sudden breakdown?"

"You mean Celeste?"

He nodded.

"It was not sudden," Isa said. "Her family claims that it was a process of years. Her perpetual perfection, the pressure she put on herself. And the stalker..."

"Do we know the stalker was even real?"

Isa frowned.

Timo continued, "Dr. Holmberg doubted it. Zelia Flodin doubted it. Her family dismissed it, but at the same time they were eager to go with the story."

"I don't know, Timo. What do you think happened?"

"There was no stalker, but Celeste witnessed a murder."

"Murder? Jonathan Gedman?"

"Or she participated in one," Timo said.

"They killed him?"

"Maybe," Timo said. "We need to find out what happened that day."

At that moment, they heard a knock on the door and Varg came in.

"Sorry to disturb you but Ms. Alva Stendahl is here," he said. "She asked for Inspector Lindström."

Isa stood up. "Why?"

"She didn't want to say."

"Alright, let's go talk to her then."

* * *

The last time they had seen Alva, she was covered in paint smears, a stark contrast to her current well-chosen, beautiful, and sophisticated appearance as she stepped into the room, exuding an air of confidence and grace. Every detail of her ensemble seemed meticulously selected to accentuate her flawless appearance, commanding attention effortlessly.

"Ms. Stendahl, what brings you here?" Isa asked.

Alva, holding a small leather-bound diary, extended it towards Isa. "This belonged to Celeste. I found it in her things."

She accepted the diary, flipping through its pages while Alva observed her with keen interest.

"It's hard reading," Alva remarked.

"Why?"

Alva hesitated before responding, "It's just... hard to read about someone's personal thoughts and feelings after they're gone. It's like you're invading their privacy."

"I can imagine."

"And... I didn't want to believe it, but the pressure she was under was unbelievable. No wonder she had a breakdown with that family of hers. I blame them."

Concern flashed across Isa's face. "What do you mean?"

Alva looked down at the floor, choosing her words carefully. "Celeste was really struggling with the pressure from her family to be someone she didn't want to be. They disapproved of her love life... of me. She pushed herself to get to a level in her art that no one could ever attain. Just because her father and mother didn't think she was good enough. Celeste was so torn between her own desires and their expectations. It was a constant battle for her."

"We had no idea it was that bad."

"Neither did I, until I found this diary. She wrote about it a lot," Alva said, gesturing to the small leather-bound book in Isa's hands. "And she wrote about Max. I knew it. The man is a pervert. He was in love with his sister. He tried to rape her."

"That's..." Isa didn't know what to say, and she continued by asking, "And did she mention anything about a stalker?"

"No." Alva glanced at her watch. "Anyway, I'm not sure it will help you, but you can keep it."

"Thank you."

"I have to go... it's the exhibition of my latest sculptures."

"You sculpt as well?"

Alva nodded, offering a bright smile. "Painting, sculpting... whatever helps me."

"Helps you?"

"Not to let the demons in again. Drugs and alcohol, remember." Alva's intense gaze remained fixed on Isa as she spoke, emphasizing each word.

"Thank you for bringing this to me," Isa replied, trying to keep her voice steady. "I'll take a look and see if there's anything in here that might help with the investigation."

Alva nodded, still gazing intensely at Isa. "Of course. I hope it helps."

Isa put her eyes back on the diary in her hands. "Good luck with the exhibition."

Alva gave her a smile before turning to leave, leaving Isa to ponder the strange encounter.

\* \* \*

Isa took a deep breath and stepped out of her car. She had been dreading this moment for days, but she knew it had to be done. Her son Felix had left his backpack at her house during his last visit, and she had promised to drop it off at Viktor's house on her way home from work. She rang the doorbell, and after a few moments, the door opened.

"Isa?" Viktor said. "What are you doing here?"

"I have Felix's backpack," Isa said, holding out the bag. "He left it at my house."

Viktor took the bag and stepped aside, gesturing for her to come in. "Thanks. Can I get you anything? A glass of wine, maybe?"

She hesitated for a moment before nodding. "Sure, that sounds nice."

"Sorry... Felix is staying with a friend and Olivia is at my mother's," he said.

"No worries," Isa said and put her coat on the peg. "I'll see them next weekend."

As she walked further inside, she took in the cozy ambiance of Viktor's home. It was a small but inviting space, with an open plan living room and kitchen area to the left, and a narrow hallway leading to the bedrooms on the right. The soft cream walls and polished hardwood floors added to its warmth.

Despite its modest size, the house felt lived-in and welcoming, with family photos adorning the walls and scattered toys hinting at the presence of children. Isa noticed a few boxes still waiting to be unpacked, adding a sense of anticipation for the home's future transformation. The kitchen, with its clean lines and modern appliances, exuded a sense of practical elegance. Pots of fresh herbs on the windowsill filled the air with the delightful scent of basil and thyme, adding to the homey atmosphere.

She couldn't help but admire the care and attention to detail evident in the house's decor. Yet, beneath her appreciation, a subtle pang of envy tugged at her heart, recognizing the new beginning that Viktor and the children were embarking on.

Viktor poured two glasses of red wine and handed her one. They sat down on the couch, and Viktor took a sip of his wine.

"So, how have you been?" he asked, looking at her over the rim of his glass.

She settled onto the couch, her eyes still darting around the room. "I've been busy with work. Big case."

She felt nervous. Why was she sitting here anyway?

"I heard. The abductions. Any leads?"

She took a quick sip of her wine. It wasn't bad, but then again Viktor had always been good at selecting quality bottles. But a subtle reminder whispered in her ear. Moderation. After the pain of Alex's death had pushed her in a direction where alcohol had become both solace and a slippery slope, she knew that every sip needed to be taken with caution. She was thankful to Timo for having pointed it out to her before it had become a problem.

She turned to Viktor and said, "No, no leads yet. But we're working on it."

Viktor took another sip of his wine. "I'm sure you'll figure it out."

"And you? How's the new job at Tech4You?"

Viktor smiled. "It's great. I'm really enjoying it. The team is fantastic, and the work is challenging but fulfilling."

She nodded and raised the glass for another sip of her wine.

His blue eyes sparkled in the dim light, and his soft features were more defined than she remembered. He seemed more confident, more self-assured. His new job was doing wonders for him.

And he had clearly been hitting the gym, evident in the subtle increase in his broad-shouldered, muscular frame.

Maybe if things had been different, if they had worked harder at their marriage, they could have been happy together. But it was too late for that now. They had both moved on.

"Felix seems to love the new class," she said.

"Yeah, he's got a few new friends. Some older kids. But he loves the projects. It was a good idea to advance him."

"I agree," Isa said and looked at her hands.

She felt nervous again.

"I'm so sorry about Olivia," he said softly. "She needs more time. Ellen and her... they just clicked. It'll take some time before she gets over it."

"That is fine. It isn't easy for her. You and Ellen... there is no way you're getting back together again?"

Viktor sighed, taking a deep breath. "Ellen and I have moved on. I haven't talked to her in half a year."

"I'm so sorry," Isa said.

He looked at the glass in his hand and then put it on the table. "I think it was my fault."

"Why?"

"Because... I was so caught up in work and my own ambitions that I neglected our relationship. I wasn't there for her. She tried to tell me, but I didn't listen."

"Somehow, I can't see you ignoring anyone's feelings. When we were married you were always so considerate, so caring."

Viktor looked at her, his expression pained. "Isa... she was right."

A puzzled expression creased her forehead. "About what?"

"About you."

She held her breath. That moment she forgot she had left them; she forgot all the regrets and the pain. She only saw Viktor, the man she had once loved so deeply.

"She told me that I was still in love with you. I didn't want to believe her at the time, but now..."

He trailed off, and Isa could see the regret etched on his face. Her heart was beating faster than ever before.

"Viktor," she said softly.

"I know it's too late," he said quickly, almost as if he was afraid of what he was saying. "I don't want to make things awkward. I just had to tell you. I've been carrying it around for too long."

Isa felt tears prick at the corners of her eyes. "I've missed you."

He took her hand. It was warm and strong, just like she remembered.

"I've missed you too," he said.

An array of feelings swept over her like a storm. It was like a floodgate had opened, and all the love and passion that she thought was long gone came rushing back.

Viktor leaned in closer, and she could feel his breath on her face. She closed her eyes, savoring the moment, and then he kissed her. It was like coming home. His lips were soft and warm, and she could taste the wine on his tongue. They kissed like they hadn't in years, and it felt like the world had stopped spinning just for them.

When they pulled apart, Isa felt like she was in a dream. This couldn't be happening, not after everything that had happened between them. But it was happening, and it felt right.

"I'm sorry," he stammered. "I shouldn't have..."

Isa cut him off with a smile. "Don't be sorry."

They sat in silence for a few moments.

"I don't know what this means," Viktor finally said.

"I don't know either. I'm sorry, Vik. I truly am. All those years I left you alone."

"It wasn't your fault," he whispered.

"Don't make excuses for me. It was my fault. I needed time and I was scared but I could have reached out earlier. I'm happy and so grateful that Felix wants to spend time with me, but I still feel I'm not worthy. I have so many doubts. This kiss is... it brings back a lot of memories. Good, exciting memories of the two of us, but also a lot of shame and guilt. I don't want to hurt you. Not again."

Viktor looked at her intently. "You don't have to feel guilty or ashamed. We both made mistakes. All we can do is decide what we want for our future."

"And what do you want?"

"I don't know," he said simply. "I do want to see if we can rekindle these feelings, we obviously both still have."

Isa got up and looked at him. "I need to think. I... this is going too fast."

"Is it Timo?" he blurted out as he followed her to the hallway.

She quickly turned around. "No, of course not."

"Is it Alex?"

And that question shocked her even more than the previous one. She stood frozen, looking at the wall. After a moment of hesitation, Isa finally turned to face Viktor. "No, it's not Alex."

"I find that hard to believe. Just his name is enough to throw you off balance."

"I really need to go," she said and took her coat from the peg. But tears were already forming in her eyes.

He put his hands on her shoulders as she stood with her back towards him. She quickly turned around to face him, tears streaming down her face. He saw it and wiped them away with his fingers. Soft, gentle fingers.

"You are traumatized," he said. "You will never get over him if you don't find help. I'm here if you want to talk, but... I think this goes so much deeper. You need professional help."

The image of Dr. Wikholm came to mind. She had tried. At least that's what she had told herself. Maybe not hard enough.

"I don't want to get over him," she whispered. Her voice broke.

Viktor looked at her with concern. "You can't let Alex control your life like this."

"I know," she said, wiping away her tears. "But it's not that simple."

"I understand," Viktor said, pulling her into a hug. "But you can't keep living in the past."

Isa closed her eyes and rested her head on his shoulder. She didn't want to let go, but she knew she had to. She pulled away and looked up at him. "I need to go."

He gave her another smile, and she left.

\* \* \*

Isa was lost in thought as she drove home. She couldn't believe what had just happened with Viktor. The kiss had been unexpected, but it had felt so right. And yet, there were still so many unresolved issues between them.

As she drove, she thought about Alex. He was always there, lurking in the back of her mind, even when she didn't want him to be. She had tried to move on, but it seemed like she couldn't escape him.

Maybe Viktor was right. Maybe she did need professional help. She had tried therapy before, but it hadn't worked. Maybe she needed to try again. Timo had told her time and time again, when things got difficult, she backed off.

When she got home, she sat in her car for a few moments, just trying to collect her thoughts. She knew she needed to talk to someone, but she wasn't sure who. She didn't want to burden Timo or Viktor with her problems, and she didn't have any close friends she could confide in, besides Ingrid who was going through her own turmoil at the moment. She hadn't told Timo yet, but Ingrid had told her that her marriage was getting increasingly on shaky ground. Her friend hadn't been able to get Timo out of her system and was that close to giving up on her marriage.

She couldn't tell Timo because she didn't want the two of them together.

Maybe Viktor was also right about Timo. Alex and Timo. Her secret crush on her boss wasn't helping. Alex, Timo, and Viktor. Why was she in that situation again? The men in her life and her love life.

She would call Dr. Wikholm in the morning and set up an

appointment. She knew it wouldn't be easy, but she was willing to try again.

As she entered the house, she realized how much had changed in the past few hours. Trying to clear her mind, she decided to take a hot shower and get some rest. Tomorrow was a new day, and she was ready to face it.

As Isa closed the curtains in the living room, she didn't notice the sound of a car pulling up outside her house. The darkness outside was silent, except for the sound of the engine as it idled in the street. She went to bed, unaware of the presence outside and drifted off into a restless sleep.

The car remained parked there, watching and waiting in the darkness.

*  *  *

"What did you learn?" Timo said, opening the door and welcoming his mother into the lake house.

"A good evening to you too," Valesca replied in Russian, planting a kiss on her youngest son's cheek.

"Sorry, Mom," he said, quickly closing the door.

"I see not much has changed," she remarked, casting a critical eye over the lake house's interior.

"Maybe one day," he chuckled. "If you feel like doing some interior design... go ahead." And he immediately realized she might just take him up on that.

"And?" he prompted as he took her coat.

"Eriksson is gaining influence. He's strategically placing his confidants, such as the new chief prosecutor, and making moves to expand his power within the Social Democrats. It seems like he's trying to consolidate his control," Valesca said. "I talked to Prime Minister Hult during the New Year's gala. It's clear he's not happy. He wants to get rid of Eriksson, but... he almost looked afraid."

Timo's expression turned grave. Commissioner Eriksson was a dangerous man, and he had to be stopped before he did any more damage.

"Eriksson needs to be punished for what he has done."

"Be careful, Timofey. Eriksson is not someone to be underestimated."

"I will," Timo assured her, dropping into the one-seater next to the small table in the living room. "I can't do anything anyway. Hult is the only one who can push back."

"I don't think he can and will. Like I said, he looked scared. Eriksson has something over him."

"Leif Berg. They all had something to do with Berg's death." He sighed and let his hands run over his face.

"What's going on?"

"Nothing," he replied, looking up at her.

"Timofey, I'm your mother. I can see immediately when something is wrong."

"A good friend of mine died recently," Timo said, a heavy sigh escaping him. His gaze dropped.

She walked over to him and placed her hand on his shoulder. "I'm sorry, Timofey. Anything I can do?"

"No. You don't know her. I'll be fine. It was just... unexpected."

She dropped onto the sofa, facing him. "Take care of yourself. I see how you're isolating yourself again. This is not healthy."

"I just... I'll be okay. Give me some time. How's my dear brother Fredrik, by the way?"

"Fredrik is doing okay. He's a bit sleep-deprived these days."

"I'd never expected him to leave Pam and the kids for Sandra Arvidsson."

His mother sighed. "And the baby he has with her. But he did... and now Pam is going after him with everything she's got. Her lawyer is asking for sole custody of the kids."

"I never liked Pam, but I can understand her."

Valesca frowned. "Really?"

"I mean, it's not like Fredrik's behavior was acceptable. She's hurting. But I don't think it's fair for Pam to take away his rights as a father either."

"I don't think Sandra will make him happy," Valesca said.

"Fredrik is restless... always has been. Look at his career. Now he's working for the Sweden Democrats. Before he was working for Leif Berg, Minister of Justice, a Social Democrat. He's not true to himself and his values."

"He's not your father. Fredrik is an opportunist. Yrjo was an idealist."

As she mentioned his father, his stomach tightened. He knew now Yrjo wasn't his father. It made him sad that every time he heard that name, he had to associate it with 'not my father'. She still refused to give him a name, and somehow, he had given up. He would never know who his real father was.

"A year ago, I would never have thought that all our lives would be so turned around," he said and sighed.

His mother looked outside. A deep darkness had descended over the snow-covered trees and lake.

"You know, Timofey, sometimes life takes unexpected turns. It's how we react to those turns that define us," Valesca said, still looking outside. "It's important to remember that we have a choice in how we respond to these situations."

"It's just hard sometimes."

"I know," Valesca said, turning back to face him, and smiled. "But remember, you're not alone. You have family and friends who care about you."

He was shocked by her words. Like she knew exactly what he was going through. The pain, the guilt, the shame. It was all there.

"I missed you at Christmas and New Year," she continued. "Why didn't you stay with me in Helsinki?"

"Big case... no time," he said. Not really in the mood to spend time with his overly dramatic mother and her sister Lilia.

"Are you dating again?"

"Mom," he let out. "Don't start."

"It seems it's only your brother who's providing me with grandchildren."

Timo chuckled. "I'm not really thinking about that right now. I have other things to worry about."

"Ingrid?"

He held his breath and then said, "No, that is over."

She looked at him with her icy blue eyes. Sometimes they were a lot alike. Many people had told him that he could get the world with those eyes.

"But is it really over?" she said.

"It was a mutual decision. So, yes, it is."

Of course, it wasn't. Neither Ingrid nor himself could really let go. The endless conversations over the phone, his weekly drives to her home, just to see her.

"Don't forget that life is short."

He wasn't sure what she wanted to say. She hadn't been particularly supportive of Ingrid.

She got up, walked over to him, and gave him a kiss on the forehead. She looked him straight in the eye. "You are a beautiful, smart man, Timo, but I worry that you are wasting your talent. You can do so much more. I know you don't want to hear it, but you're wasting away in this God-forsaken city. And you are taking the sorrow of the entire world on your shoulders. You need to get out of this cycle. A change of scenery would help. Just saying... I'm here when you need me."

"Mom, I...," he started, and then the lump in his throat prevented him from continuing.

Where had this mother been all of his life? Or did he just see her in a different light? Had she always been there?

But it was true. He needed her more than ever.

"Look, I've been thinking about traveling for a while," she said. "I want to see more of the world before it's not possible anymore."

"Mom, you're still young."

"Well, things can go fast. Look at your father... in the prime of his life. Anyway, my two sisters, Lilia and Natalia don't want to come with me."

"Lilia... how is she doing?" he said suddenly. "I was shocked to hear George broke up with her. He's my friend, but I don't understand. I haven't talked to him in months. It's so out of character for him."

"I know it's strange," she said and turned away from him.

But he knew she was lying. For months, she was avoiding the topic. She knew more.

"Anyway," she continued. "I would like you to come with me."

"Mom, I can't just leave," he let out.

"Take a sabbatical."

"Sabbatical? No one takes a sabbatical in the police force."

"Think about it. It'll be fun. You and me. Much needed and overdue quality time with my youngest son."

She smiled at him and then took her coat.

He wasn't too sure about spending so much time with her. He had missed her, but at the same time, their characters often clashed.

No, this wouldn't be a good idea.

\* \* \*

Perhaps he had heard the faint hum of the car engine in the background as he stepped onto the sidewalk, or perhaps not. Either way, it was too late when he finally turned around. The vehicle struck him with such force that he was launched into the air, catching a glimpse of his papers, previously nestled neatly in his briefcase, scattering like autumn leaves caught up in the wind. His body smashed against the windshield, shattering the glass, before being flung to the side and ultimately crashing onto the pavement below. The car's wheels screeched as it sped away without so much as a brake or a pause. He could hear the sound of heavy footsteps and raised voices emanating from the building before everything went dark, and he lost consciousness.

* * *

Timo looked tired. His T-shirt was wrinkled, and his hair was all messed up like he had just stepped out of bed. He sat down next to her and asked, "How is he?" His concerned eyes met hers.

Isa shook her head. "I don't know. They won't tell me anything. They're still operating on him." Her voice was trembling.

He looked around.

The waiting room was filled with a cacophony of sounds, the beeps of the machines, the muffled voices of doctors and nurses hurrying down the hallway, and the occasional sound of a patient being wheeled past.

Timo put his hand on her shoulder and said, "It's going to be okay. He's strong. He'll make it." But he could feel the worry gnawing at his own gut.

Isa's gaze fell to the floor as she muttered, "It was the stalker. I just know it was him. Witnesses said that the car hit Viktor on purpose and then fled the scene. It's all my fault."

"Lindström, you can't blame yourself."

"I know but...," Isa said. "He's... important."

"Where are the kids?"

"With my parents. I'll pick them up later."

"I know you don't want to talk about it right now, but did any of the witnesses see the license plate or the driver? Can they give a description of the car?"

"I know time is crucial. Varg has been questioning the witnesses. He should know. I just hope... he can't die." She put her face in her hands and started crying.

He felt useless as he sat down next to her and put his hand on her back.

Just then, a doctor walked up to them. "Are you here for Viktor Clausen?"

"Yes, how is he?" Isa asked, wiping her tears away.

"The surgery went well," the doctor said. "He has a fractured leg that needed surgery for realignment. We inserted four screws and a plate. There was no internal bleeding as we originally suspected. He also has two broken ribs and a concussion, but he will be fine. He was very lucky."

Isa let out a sigh of relief and Timo smiled, feeling a weight lifted from his shoulders.

"Can we see him?" Isa asked.

"Not just yet," the doctor said. "He's in recovery right now, and we want to monitor him closely for the next 24 hours. But we'll let you know as soon as he's ready for visitors."

"Thank you, doctor," Timo said.

As the doctor walked away, Isa let out another sob.

"Isa, I'll talk to Varg. Okay?"

She nodded.

"Are you going to be fine?" he said.

"Yeah, go and get whoever did this to the father of my children," she said. There was a lot of buried anger in her voice.

* * *

Varg sat in Timo's office, looking at the serious face of his boss.

"We should have taken this more seriously," Timo said.

"There was nothing... no indication that this could happen," Varg replied.

"I know, but we can't afford to make any more mistakes like this. Viktor could have died. Any CCTV from the accident?"

"No, few witness statements. Black car. A witness says it was an Audi, another one a BMW. So, we don't really know. It was dark and snowy. I only have part of a license plate: ML... something and then a last digit 7. At least, that's what the three witnesses could agree on."

"Check the databases and see if there are any cars matching that description and license plate number. Maybe we get lucky."

"Yes, sir. I'll also check if the car has been seen on CCTV in the area."

Timo nodded his head and rubbed his chin. The stubble scratched against his hand. He felt the energy leave his body with every second. Isa, Kristina. He let them both down. How could he still be sitting here and pretend everything was fine? That he was in control.

He looked at Varg.

Varg avoided eye contact, fidgeting in his seat.

"You can go," Timo said.

"What about Mr. Westerberg?"

"This is your priority now," Timo said in a stern voice.

"Oh, okay... sir," Varg stammered and left the room.

Timo leaned back in his chair, closing his eyes for a moment. He heard the distant sounds of the city outside his window, the honking of cars and the murmurs of people passing by. But his mind was elsewhere.

He couldn't shake off the feeling that he had failed everyone. He had failed to protect Isa, and he had failed to provide comfort to Kristina.

They trusted him to keep them safe, and he had let them down. He felt like a complete failure, and he wasn't sure if he could continue working as a police officer.

He glanced around his office, taking in the familiar surroundings. He had been working in this office for almost two years, off and on, but it had never felt like home to him. Not really. He needed to get away, to clear his head and figure out what to do next.

He stood up and grabbed his coat, deciding that he needed some fresh air. As he made his way out of the building, he couldn't stop thinking he might not be coming back. The thought made him feel both relieved and scared.

He stepped out into the cold air and walked aimlessly through the streets of Gävle. Snow was falling. Snow, rain. It was a strange season. Just like him, nature couldn't decide.

He wondered what his life would be like if he left the police force. Would he be able to find a new purpose, a new sense of meaning?

As he walked, he came to a park and sat down on a bench. He watched as a group of kids played in the snow, laughing and shouting. Their carefree attitude made him feel envious. He wished he could go back to a time when life was simple, and he didn't carry the weight of the world on his shoulders.

Maybe he should take his mother up on her invitation to take a sabbatical and travel the world with her.

At thirty-seven, he found himself in a full-blown mid-life crisis.

The snow continued to fall around him.

He closed his eyes.

After this case, he would make a decision.

Then, the intrusive ring of his phone shattered the serenity.

"Paikkala," he answered.

"Sorry to disturb you... it's Sivert," came the voice on the other end.

Timo's brow furrowed. Sivert rarely reached out to him; the man harbored an evident fear of him. "What is it?"

"Jonathan Gedman's computer. I should have started earlier, but there was..."

"Get to the point."

"Jonathan had a boyfriend," Sivert said.

"Dancho Krastev."

"Not Dancho Krastev. There are so many emails and love letters. They were planning to get married."

"Sivert, who are they?"

"Jonathan and... Lukas Stendahl."

## CHAPTER

# 26

"AND WHO ARE YOU AGAIN?"

Stoyanka looked at the well-dressed man sitting quietly on the couch in the living room. On this Saturday morning, she had heard the door ring and had found him on the doorstep of the house asking for Boris.

"I'm an old friend of your nephew," Lukas said without any emotion and put his hands in his lap. "We used to call him Bulgari."

Stoyanka's eyes narrowed, and a stern expression crossed her face. "I don't care what you used to call him. His name is Boris."

"Yes, of course. Sorry about that. By the way, thank you for the coffee and cookies... you shouldn't have bothered."

There was something about him. Her 'being cautious' radar hadn't completely set in yet, but she didn't feel comfortable. The politeness in his tone seemed forced. Maybe she shouldn't have let him in. Radu was in his cabin again and Boris hadn't come in yet. He was late today.

"And why do you want to speak to him?"

"Jukka Ulfsson and Max Westerberg," he said.

She was taken aback. "I heard what happened."

"Yes, it's terrible. I was wondering if we should do something special for them. Something to remember Jukka and help his family. We should also support Max's family. They went through a lot."

Stoyanka studied Lukas for a moment, assessing his sincerity. The tragedy had affected everyone, and the idea of doing something for the grieving families seemed genuine. Yet, a lingering suspicion kept her guard up.

"Why do you think Boris would be interested in this?" she asked with a deep Bulgarian accent.

Lukas leaned forward and took a cookie from the plate. "Boris was close to Jukka and Max. I thought he might want to contribute or, at the very least, be informed about it."

Stoyanka crossed her arms. "Boris has a lot on his mind. I'm not sure if he's up for getting involved in anything right now."

Lukas nodded understandingly. "His brother."

A second time, she was shocked by his words. It wasn't the words, but the way he had said them. There was a depth, an understanding, as if he knew something more about Boris' past than he should. Her suspicion grew with evert second.

"How is Dancho doing?" he continued.

"Fine. As well as he can be."

"There are stories of people who suddenly wake up after years of coma... or who step by step regain consciousness. It's a miracle, really," Lukas said, his gaze fixed on Stoyanka.

She shifted uncomfortably in her chair. "Dancho's condition is stable, but the doctors haven't given us much hope. This is the way he will stay for the rest of his life."

Lukas nodded. "The accident was a tragedy."

Stoyanka's eyes narrowed. "You seem to know a lot about my family. Why is that?"

Lukas leaned back, maintaining an air of nonchalance. "Boris was like a brother to me once... they all were my friends at one point."

"Then why can't I remember Boris ever mentioning you?"

"I wasn't so... prominently present as the others. I was shy, and I wasn't really talented like the rest of them. I kept to the shadows, so to speak." Lukas looked at his hands for a moment and then continued, "Boris and the gang were quite a remarkable bunch. Talented in ways that drew attention. Artistic, daring, always pushing boundaries. Me? I was more of a spectator, quietly admiring their skills from the sidelines."

Stoyanka's suspicion persisted. "So, why do you want to reconnect now, after all these years?"

Lukas sighed, his gaze drifting momentarily. "Life has a way of making you reassess things. The passing of time makes you reflect on what's truly important. When I heard about Jukka and Max, I couldn't help but feel a need to revisit the connections of my past. To pay my respects and maybe find solace in shared memories."

Stoyanka eyed him warily. "Well, you've delivered your message. I'll let Boris know about it."

"If he's not interested, that's fine. I just wanted to extend the invitation."

"As I said... I can't help you. Boris isn't here. Maybe you should come back later or try to catch him at his house. Anything else?"

Lukas shook his head. "No, that's all. Thank you for your time. But can I ask you a favor?"

"What?"

"My ride will pick me up in thirty minutes. Can I stay here until then?

It's really freezing outside."

Stoyanka hesitated, her suspicion lingering. "Thirty minutes, and then you leave."

"Absolutely," Lukas assured her, a smile playing on his lips.

\* \* \*

"Lukas Stendahl is not home," Varg's voice sounded through the speaker. "Do you want us to go inside?"

Timo sighed. "No, we don't have a warrant."

"But people could be in danger."

"Who? No one else has been reported missing." Timo dropped in his chair and looked at the people in the room. Sylvia, Isa and Sivert. No one was happy being called out on a Saturday morning, but they all felt there was finally a breakthrough.

"We'll issue an APB," Timo said. "Come back to the station."

"He's trying to flee," Sylvia said. "We should keep an eye on airports and highways."

"Wait a second... we don't even know if he's the one who abducted Jukka and Max." Isa was leaning against the wall. "The only thing we know is that he was Jonathan Gedman's lover."

"It makes perfect sense," Sylvia started. "He's out for revenge. He thinks the creatives are responsible for Jonathan's disappearance."

"But it doesn't make it true," Isa interrupted. "We need concrete evidence before we start chasing him down like a criminal."

"I found emails from Dancho Krastev on Jonathan's computer," Sivert said. "Sweet declarations of love, but it was clearly not mutual. Jonathan's replies were polite but distant."

"So, Dancho could be involved too," Isa said. "What really happened that day?"

Timo closed his eyes. If he could only block the noise and the worries and hear his own thoughts. The rational, factual part of his brain fought to maintain focus. This wasn't about drugs. This was about love and revenge. Sylvia was right. Lukas Stendahl was looking for answers. The love of his life was gone, and no one knew what happened to him. Living with that knowledge would turn any man desperate, potentially dangerous.

"Dancho Krastev, Boris Krastev," Timo said. "Besides Freya Younggren, they are the only ones left who might know what happened that day. He's going after them."

"But Dancho is in a coma," Isa said.

"It doesn't matter... this is a heartbroken, desperate man," Timo said, got up, took his jacket from the back of his chair, and walked to the door. "We need to be fast. He has nothing to lose anymore."

*  *  *

He looked at the man in the bed. A silent figure. The sound of the breathing machine in the background. The anger and resentment were flooding every cell in his body. How he hated this man in front of him. He had no right to claim the man he had loved with every part of his being. Jonathan. He saw his face so clearly. His voice, his smell. They were all there. Even after five years. Five, long excruciating years.

They had made plans. And then that stupid boy had messed it all up. Jonathan was never supposed to be on that hike. Lukas vividly recalled the call that Saturday night. Jonathan practically pleaded for Lukas to come and rescue him from there. He'd had his fill and wanted nothing more to do with the creatives. He wanted to go on his own path, together with Lukas.

Lukas had promised him to come and pick him up. He hadn't asked much. Maybe he should have, but it had always been better to let Jonathan's artistic soul vent for a while. Drama and deep feelings were something he strangely loved about him.

When he arrived that Sunday morning, it had been too late. No one knew where Jonathan was. Lukas was furious. Furious at the boy who had enticed Jonathan on that ill-fated journey. Furious at his so-called friends who were strangely unaffected by the disappearance of two of them. Furious at himself for not being there sooner. He had searched for Jonathan for months, turning every stone in the hopes of finding him. Years had gone by without any hope, until that day, six months ago, when Jonathan's mother had called. The announcement of his death declaration had hit him like a tidal wave, but it hadn't prepared him for what had happened next. The recording. He had found it in Jonathan's things.

And he had confronted Celeste with it.

Celeste. He had believed in her once, but that day he could only see a spoiled little brat who always got her way. Who had used the death of his lover to ensure her own success.

But it got worse. She was even so audacious to mention she had seen the fall. She had seen Jonathan falling down the cliff and she had done nothing. The guilt and shame she had carried with her for years. Poor little rich girl. She wanted to come forward and confess. She had even told Jukka about it.

But as her manager he had advised her to keep it quiet. He wanted her to succumb to her fears and doubts. And it worked. The mentally vulnerable Celeste was again a shadow of the strong woman she had been.

But he wanted more. He didn't believe her. Maybe she was the one who had pushed him down the cliff, maybe they all had something to do with it. What started as a thought, soon became an obsession.

They knew where Jonathan was. And he would get to the truth, no matter what.

"I know you killed him," he said and looked at Dancho.

The breathing machine continued to hum in the background.

"Jukka and Max knew nothing. Collateral damage. Celeste took her own life. I should have played it differently... I know. She was the only one who knew more... except you."

Lukas moved closer.

"I know you are awake. You might fool your family, but not me. I was so blinded about my anger for Celeste and the others. I had never considered you until I realized it could only have been you."

Another step closer.

"Did he reject you?"

Another step closer.

Anger burning.

"You... ridiculous, little boy. Why on earth would he ever be interested in you?"

He could hardly breathe.

"Answer me!"

Dancho opened his eyes. And for a moment, he was shocked.

"So, I was right," Lukas said in an ironic voice.

But Dancho kept looking straight ahead, his body still, the breathing mask covering his nose and mouth.

Lukas was now standing next to him and looking in the brown eyes that were fixed on the light bulb in the ceiling.

"Say something!" Lukas demanded, his patience wearing thin. He wanted to shake the truth out of Dancho, to force him to acknowledge the pain he had inflicted.

But Dancho remained silent, his eyes betraying nothing. Lukas, frustration reaching its peak, grabbed the breathing mask and pulled it away from Dancho's face.

"Answer me!" Lukas shouted, the words reverberating through the sterile room. "You pushed him, but it didn't go quite as expected, did it?"

Dancho gasped for air, his breaths shallow and strained.

The tears started to flow as Lukas continued, "He must have been so scared. He... I..."

And then the resentment reached a peak and he put his hands around Dancho's neck and pressed.

Memories rushed back. Lukas first saw Jonathan during a school concert, a moment etched into the fabric of his soul. He was playing the guitar. Such an intimate, vulnerable song. It spoke to his soul. Then, in the middle of the performance, Jonathan suddenly looked at him.

Their eyes locked, and time seemed to freeze. In that instant, Lukas felt a magnetic pull, an invisible force drawing him closer. Jonathan's gaze held a mixture of vulnerability and strength, a paradox that ignited a spark in him. Love unfurled its delicate wings, and in the midst of the concert hall, their connection was forged.

"Lukas, step away from Dancho," a deep voice sounded through the room. He turned and saw the police officers.

Timo had his gun drawn and aimed at Lukas, just like Isa and two other police officers.

Timo's gaze shifted between Lukas and the struggling figure in the bed. Dancho coughed and gasped for air.

"Last warning... step away from the bed," Timo repeated. "You want to find out what happened to Jonathan. This is not the way."

*I am here, my love. I'll always be here.*

*Remember me.*

"Lukas," Boris yelled. "He can't help you."

Boris' sudden appearance startled Timo. His eyes narrowed, and a frown creased his forehead.

Lukas, torn between the memories of Jonathan and the present reality, slowly stepped back, his hands raised in surrender.

He looked straight at Boris. "But you know... you..."

For a moment, Boris looked to be frozen in time. Then Boris slowly shook his head. "I don't know... I'm sorry."

*Find me.*

## CHAPTER

# 27

THE INTERROGATION ROOM WAS SMALL and poorly lit, with cracked, gray walls and a single metal table and four chairs in the center. A two-way mirror dominated one wall, through which the police officers could observe the suspect without being seen. Lukas sat with his hands in front of him, cuffed to a metal bolt in the table, his head lowered, and his eyes fixed on the table in front of him.

Timo sat at the other side of the table; his arms crossed over his chest as he stared down at Lukas. Isa sat beside him with her eyes fixed on Lukas.

Timo cleared his throat, breaking the silence. "Lukas, we saw the tapes. Jukka and Max. You taped everything."

No reaction.

"I know you wanted justice for Jonathan. We just try to understand why and how this all started."

Lukas looked up, tears streaming down his face. "They... know what happened to him."

"How did you find out?" Timo asked.

Isa cast a quick glance at Timo. Impatience and irritation marked his demeanor, not an ideal state to start an interrogation.

Isa intervened. "Tell me about Jonathan."

Lukas' eyes darted back and forth between Timo and Isa.

"It must have been hard all those years not knowing what happened to him," she continued.

From the corner of her eye, Isa saw Timo tapping his finger on the table. He stopped when she gave him another angry look.

She turned her face to the mirror. She knew that Sylvia was following everything from the other side.

"I thought he... he didn't want to be with me anymore. That he ran away, left me. That I was to blame." Lukas' voice cracked as he spoke. "It didn't make any sense, but... what was I to think?"

"When did you suspect the group had anything to do with it?"

"It had always been there. The doubt. That morning when I arrived at the cabin, they were behaving strangely."

"How?"

Lukas hesitated for a moment. "They were whispering, exchanging glances. It was like they shared a secret, something they didn't want me to know. I confronted Boris about it, but he dismissed it as creative tension."

Isa glanced at Timo, who leaned back in his chair, watching Lukas intently. "Freya had an overdose. Maybe they wanted to keep that a secret."

Lukas bowed his head again as if he needed a moment to collect his thoughts. "But when Celeste came back, she was visibly nervous and upset. Max asked her about it, but they broke into a fight. She was telling him how he was suffocating her, that he needed to leave her alone, and that he didn't know how to behave around her. He loved her... but not like a brother... that was clear."

"Did you see any inappropriate behavior from Max?"

"Yes. He kissed her on the lips and once I saw him come out of her bedroom in the middle of the night when the entire gang was staying at their place. He looked angry and... embarrassed to see me. But I think that's not why they were fighting. I think Celeste told him about what had happened to Jonathan."

"And what happened next?" Timo asked.

"Boris and Jukka suddenly decided to leave."

"They left before Dancho was found?"

"Yes. Afterwards, I understood why. They drove Freya to the hospital. Because I kept insisting, Max and I started to look for Jonathan and Dancho. Max found Dancho at the bottom of the cliff and that was it. No Jonathan anymore. Days after days I scanned the area, thinking he was lying there somewhere all alone... but nothing."

"And then you found the tape," Isa said.

Lukas looked up and said, "Jonathan's mother invited me. I think she knew of the two of us... or at least she suspected it. She wanted to have him declared dead. This was such a shock. My mind went blank. I wasn't ready to give up on him yet, but she was."

"I can't imagine what that must have been like for you," Isa said, her voice soft.

Lukas paused, gathering his thoughts. "It felt like the ground was ripped from beneath me. I was still holding on to the hope that Jonathan might come back one day, that he was still out there, somewhere. But his mother... she couldn't bear the uncertainty any longer. She thought it was time to let go. And she was giving away his things. I still don't know how she managed to do that, but I am grateful."

Timo's eyes were still fixed on the man in front of him. "We found

Gideon Younggren in your cellar. Dead."

"It's unfortunate, but he should have listened. He was an ally, until he chickened out. He wanted revenge for his daughter. I didn't really care for her, as long as he helped the cause."

"And that was?"

"Finding Jonathan."

"Three people are dead. That's a hell of a price to pay for the cause."

"Two people," Lukas said.

Timo gave him a sarcastic grin. "I'm sure we will be able to prove that your meddling pushed Celeste over the edge. And if we dig a bit deeper, I'm sure we'll find out you were her stalker. And it didn't start six months ago, but five years ago."

Lukas frowned. "Uh... what? I don't know anything about stalking."

"And the stalking of my chief inspector," Timo continued. "Why?"

"I don't know what you are talking about," Lukas said.

"Fine," Timo said. "Have it your way."

"Coming back to the recording," Isa said. "When did you start to realize what it was?"

Lukas gave her a mocking smile. "Almost immediately... not all the details and the full extent. That came later, but that the creatives had something to do with it... yes."

"You called the studio."

"I learned it wasn't Jonathan who made the recording, but someone made it for him. I must admit it put me in a downward spiral."

"Downward spiral?" Timo raised an eyebrow.

"I confronted Celeste first. She denied everything, tried to spin a tale about protecting Jonathan. But I saw through it. She was more concerned about her own reputation than finding Jonathan. But she did reveal she was there and that she stole the song. And I got more and more convinced that that entire group had a lot to hide."

"First Celeste, then Jukka and Max. Why didn't you go to the police?"

"I was angry, confused, and hurt. Besides no one would be able to give me what I wanted... revenge."

"You used the recording to blackmail Celeste," Isa took over. "You sent it to her phone."

Lukas nodded. "I never meant for her to die. I thought she knew it was me. I wanted her to confess, but..."

"I doubt you feel sorry about that," Timo said. "It was a great performance... your tears after she died."

Isa threw Timo another angry look. "And Jukka Ulfsson?"

Lukas hesitated, the weight of his actions bearing down on him. "I wanted answers. And Celeste died before she could give any. Jukka was my next target. Gideon stole the van. I know somebody, Ornar, at the emergency center. Amanda would be working that evening. Gideon and I attacked him in the kitchen." Then he let out a sarcastic grin. "He didn't even realize what was happening to him. He was so stoned."

"Why the drama? We could have helped to find Jonathan."

"I wanted you to notice, but I also needed time to get the information I wanted."

"You wanted to be the judge and jury. It doesn't work like that. You cannot take matters in your own hands."

"I had to. The police weren't going to do anything. For them, it was an accident, even if his body was never found."

"And what did Jukka Ulfsson tell you?" Timo asked.

"You saw the tape. He was crying like a baby. Oh, Gideon loved it. He was confessing everything about their drug business. How he, Max, and Freya had been running it for years. How Freya had not been the victim like Gideon had thought, how she had actively participated in spreading the drugs that had impacted her life so much. You could say that he wasn't too pleased."

"What exactly are you saying?" Timo asked.

"Nothing... just that Gideon was an active participant in the torture of Jukka."

"You set him up," Timo said, his blue eyes fixed on Lukas. "You used his house. You left his prints everywhere. He was a scapegoat."

"And he had to die," Isa complemented.

"He was scared. He wanted to stop. I couldn't let that happen."

"And Max?"

"He found Dancho. I thought he had removed evidence to protect his sister."

"Did he tell you that?"

Lucas looked at his hands and said nothing.

"Why did you decide to confront Boris and Dancho?"

"Max said Dancho was always hanging around Jonathan. Then I realized Dancho made the recording. I wondered how he'd react if Jonathan said no to him. It all clicked into place."

"Did it?" Timo said.

Lukas shifted uncomfortably in his chair. "Of course, it did. There was a struggle. Dancho killed Jonathan and got rid of his body."

Timo shook his head. "And then ended up in a coma? How? I don't buy it."

"He's not in a coma. He plays it very well and his family is protecting him."

"And he's fooling the doctors too? Come on! There is no reason to assume he is conscious."

Lukas glared at Timo. "You don't understand. He's faking it. I saw it in his eyes when I confronted him. He knows what he did."

Timo leaned back. "We'll need evidence to support your claims. You can't just accuse someone without proof."

Isa chimed in, "What about Boris? What does he have to do with all of this?"

"He knows... he has always known."

* * *

Stoyanka sat quietly beside the bed, her fingers delicately gliding over Dancho's forehead. The rhythmic hiss of the breathing mask echoed in the room. Her gaze was intense. She couldn't let her eyes waver from his face. The soft glow of a bedside lamp cast shadows, playing on the contours of Dancho's features. The room was wrapped in an almost tangible stillness. As her fingers traced the lines of his forehead, she found herself lost in a sea of thoughts.

"How is he?"

She turned around and saw Boris standing in the doorway.

"He's okay," Stoyanka replied in Bulgarian. She withdrew her hand, her fingers lingering momentarily in the air before settling back on her lap. The shadows seemed to deepen around them. "The doctor said he didn't sustain any lasting injuries."

Boris took a step forward, his eyes fixed on his brother. "Do you think he can hear us?"

Stoyanka sighed, her gaze returning to Dancho. "I don't think so."

Boris approached the bed. "I just..."

He sighed.

"I just wish he would wake up," Boris finished his sentence.

He reached out, his hand hovering over Dancho's. He hesitated for a moment before gently placing his fingers on his brother's motionless hand. Stoyanka watched the silent exchange.

Dancho opened his eyes.

Boris froze for a moment. "It's always so shocking when he opens his eyes. It's like he's still there. Maybe the doctors should have another look at him."

Stoyanka placed a comforting hand on Boris' shoulder. "Maybe... but we heard it time and time again. This is just a temporary reaction. The doctors said there might be occasional movements or responses, but it doesn't necessarily mean he's fully conscious or aware of his surroundings."

"We should at least try," Boris replied and looked at his brother again. The eyes exhibited a rhythmic movement, gliding up and down in a cycle, as if searching for connection.

"I don't want you to get your hopes up," Stoyanka said. "We've been through this before."

"But..."

She took his hand and moved closer to him, both of them sitting on the edge of the bed. "I didn't want to tell you but your dad... he's not doing well. This would only stress him more."

"What's wrong with him?"

"There is a reason why he spends most of his time in that cabin. There are too many ghosts. Your mother, your brother. He's not coping, he hasn't been coping for years."

"Why didn't you tell me?"

She gave him a smile. "You shouldn't have to worry about that. You have your own life to lead."

He sighed and shook his head, "Auntie..."

"Boris, you need to go to the cabin and get your dad. Talk to him. He'd appreciate that."

Boris nodded, tearing his eyes away from Dancho's face. "You're right. I'll go."

Stoyanka offered him another sympathetic smile. "I'll stay here with Dancho."

Boris squeezed her hand and turned to leave the room, but he stopped at the door and said, "We need to protect him... no matter what."

She nodded and as she heard his footsteps on the stairs going down, she turned to Dancho. Stoyanka's gaze fixed on him again and let her hand glide over the side of his face. The eyes were still moving up and down.

"It's just you and me now," she said.

Stoyanka reached for the tube of the breathing mask and let it go through her hands. The room seemed to tighten.

*No. No.*

"It's interesting... how your own brother believes you are responsible," she said, taking a deep breath before continuing, her gaze fixed on the man in the bed. "But we both know who really is."

In the next moment, she decisively squeezed the tube shut, and Dancho started to gasp for air.

*Stop. Stop.*

She released it and looked at him, a sarcastic smile on her face. "It's too bad Mr. Stendahl didn't push through. He should have killed you, but he was weak. Like most of your kind are."

The accusation lingered in the air as she observed his still form, the shadows in the room deepening with the weight of her words. "I know you are in there, seeing and hearing everything. Locked in your own body... but not for long anymore. Five years is enough, and I cannot take that risk anymore that you'll get better one day. One of these weeks, your breathing will get worse... I'll make sure of that. And worse. And then you'll die."

*Why keep me all these years? Why torture me? Just kill me.*

Stoyanka got up. "They will never find him. Down the next cliff. His flesh devoured by wild animals. His bones scattered around." She sighed. "If only I had had more time and finished the job. You both had to disappear, but I did not have enough time. Now I got stuck with you... and it's your fault."

*It's your fault. You killed him.*

"You shouldn't have written that letter. The letter I found on the kitchen table that morning after you had left. Luckily, your father didn't see it. How could you think we'd be okay with you running away... with a man? The filth, the humiliation. You are no family of mine."

She started laughing.

As her laughter echoed through the room, Stoyanka's expression shifted from cruel satisfaction to a twisted sense of amusement. She circled the bed, her eyes never leaving Dancho's face.

"You wrote about love and freedom in that letter, about embracing your true self. Pathetic." She spat the word with disdain. "Love is for the strong, not the weak. You betrayed us, your own family. You are just like your mother. Emotional, selfish, and naive."

A twisted smirk played on her lips. "And the funny thing is... he didn't even want you. I learned that today. Pathetic little shit!"

Stoyanka picked up a framed family photo from the bedside table, examining it with a sneer.

"The prodigal son, gone astray." She tossed the photo aside, and it clattered against the floor. "You thought you could escape our traditions, our expectations. But you see, you were never meant to be free."

Stoyanka leaned in, her face centimeters from Dancho's. "You made your choice, and this is the consequence."

She moved to the door. "I'll need to do this more carefully from now on. There's too much focus on you and this case... but rest assured, I'll be keeping an eye on you."

*No. Please. Don't do this.*

\* \* \*

The first time Dancho laid eyes on Jonathan was a moment frozen in time. He had tagged along with his older brother, Boris, to one of the gatherings of the creatives.

Jonathan stood there, a luminous figure in the chaotic swirl of artists. His presence was magnetic, drawing Dancho's attention like a moth to a flame. Dancho was still a teenager, grappling with the turbulence of his emotions, and in that moment, the world around him faded into the background.

As Jonathan spoke, sharing his thoughts and ideas, Dancho found himself captivated not just by the words but by the soul behind them. There was a vulnerability in Jonathan's gaze, a tender strength that resonated with the tumultuous emotions Dancho was wrestling with. It was love at first sight.

But this love, these feelings, he didn't dare to share them with his family—a fear rooted in the homophobic reactions he had witnessed before. The mere thought of revealing his true self, of admitting that he was gay, filled him with an overwhelming sense of fear. The atmosphere at home had been tainted by prejudice, leaving him in a constant state of unease.

Jonathan's interest in him became a beacon of both hope and confusion. The camaraderie shared during those creative gatherings seemed to transcend the boundaries of friendship in Dancho's eyes. He longed for acceptance, for the possibility that someone he admired could reciprocate his hidden feelings. Little did he know that Jonathan's kindness was born of genuine friendship, not romantic love.

The obsession grew.

Dancho, in his naive yearning for acceptance and love, had embarked on a journey fueled by his emotions. His aunt's constant belittling had worn him down, the relentless criticism echoing in his ears like a cruel refrain. Her words, a harsh commentary on his perceived shortcomings, painted a portrait of a person he was not.

In the midst of this emotional turmoil, Dancho found solace in the connection he believed he shared with Jonathan. Naively, he poured his feelings into love emails, hoping to bridge the gap between them. Unbeknownst to him, his actions were tinged with a blindness to Jonathan's true feelings, a rejection he was not prepared to face.

As the weekend trip approached, Dancho's resolve solidified. The constant barrage of his aunt's words had pushed him to a breaking point, and the decision to escape from the stifling environment became his beacon of freedom. He had written a letter, a desperate plea for understanding and a request for Jonathan to join him on this journey to escape the oppressive atmosphere at home.

In a moment of hopeful anticipation, Dancho placed the letter on the kitchen table, a strategic move to ensure that his family would discover it only after he had left. But fate had other plans, and Stoyanka discovered the letter, fueling her anger even more.

The weekend unfolded with an undercurrent of tension that cast a shadow over the once vibrant camaraderie of the creative group. Celeste and Jonathan, once united in artistic endeavors, found themselves entangled in continuous arguments that echoed through the cabin. Boris, more interested in indulging in drugs with his friends Jukka and Freya, distanced himself from his brother.

The artistic freedom that once flourished between them had given way to greed and anger, leaving Dancho yearning for an escape from the toxicity that now permeated their once harmonious gatherings. Attempts to approach Jonathan were met with a noticeable distance, and the camaraderie that had bound them seemed irreparably fractured.

As the weekend reached its climax on that fateful Saturday evening, a final showdown unfolded between Celeste and Jonathan. Accusations flew, each blaming the other for a lack of understanding. In the aftermath of the heated confrontation, Jonathan sought solace in solitude to clear his head. In his naive longing for connection, Dancho proposed joining him on a hiking trip the next day.

Jonathan hesitated; his reluctance clear as he expressed his reservations about fueling romantic ideas. But Dancho, either unable to comprehend or unwilling to accept the reality, clung to the hope that this shared excursion could mend the rift between them.

As Dancho and Jonathan ventured on their hike the next day, the weight of Dancho's emotions hung in the air. When they reached the plateau and decided to take a break, Dancho mustered the courage to confess his love for Jonathan again. But the response he received was not the one he had hoped for—Jonathan rejected him.

Amid this emotionally charged moment, their eyes caught sight of Stoyanka. The evening before she had arrived at the cabin and had stayed in the car for most of the night, not really knowing what to do. But when she saw Jonathan and Dancho leave that morning, she followed them.

The confrontation with Stoyanka escalated quickly. She accused Jonathan of manipulating Dancho's mind, insinuating that he was the reason Dancho believed he was gay.

The heated discussion spiraled out of control.

Stoyanka stormed towards Jonathan, forcefully pushing him closer to the edge. Dancho, alarmed, rushed to intervene, desperate to prevent the escalating conflict. In the chaos that unfolded, Jonathan, teetering on the edge, lost his balance and plummeted over. Dancho reached out and tried to help him, but Jonathan, in a moment of panic, pulled him down with him, and the two figures disappeared over the precipice.

When Dancho woke up, he felt disoriented. He couldn't move, and the sound of footsteps drew near. Panicking, he tried to understand what was happening.

Dancho lay there, unable to see clearly, but the vivid sounds painted a gruesome picture. He heard her cruel actions, the life being choked out of Jonathan, and her laughter that filled him with dread. She carried away Jonathan's lifeless body, leaving Dancho alone. It seemed like hours had passed. Hours of fear and desperation not knowing what she would do to him. Then he heard Max's voice calling his name, just before passing out a second time.

Dancho woke up in the hospital, his surroundings a blur of white and sterile scents. Panic set in as he tried to move, only to realize he couldn't. His body felt unresponsive, disconnected. He could hear the hustle and bustle of the hospital, distant voices, footsteps, and the steady beeping of machines. The realization dawned on him like a heavy weight—locked-in syndrome.

Every sound, every conversation, registered in his mind, but he couldn't communicate. A profound sense of helplessness enveloped him. As the days passed, he understood the extent of his vulnerability. Stoyanka, the woman who had orchestrated Jonathan's death, was now his caregiver.

The irony was not lost on him. Trapped in his own body, he saw her mask of devotion, admired by those around him. Stoyanka isolated him subtly, controlling the information flow, cutting ties with doctors, and creating a facade of undivided care. Dancho was at the mercy of the very person he knew would not hesitate to kill him.

The bedroom at home became a prison, and Stoyanka, the warden with a deceptive smile. The once-familiar walls now closed in on him. Every day felt like a countdown, a slow march toward an inevitable fate—the end orchestrated by the very person entrusted with his care.

As he lay there, helpless, Dancho couldn't escape the haunting realization that she would kill him eventually. The extent of her hatred became shockingly clear. She told him over and over again what a despicable human being he was. She blamed his mother, her own sister, for being so soft and lenient. The envy, the resentment that his father had chosen his mother over her. This was her family. Her perfect family and he was no part of it anymore.

He could only wait and hope his ending would be quick and not be too painful.

# CHAPTER

# 28

TIMO WAS LOOKING THROUGH THE LARGE WINDOW of his house. "Lukas Stendahl was charged with the murders of Jukka Ulfsson and Gideon Younggren?"

"Yep," Isa said.

"Not Celeste Westerberg," he said, still with his back turned to her.

The water of the lake seemed so bright, and he squinted his eyes.

"No. Not yet. It's not straightforward to prove there is a direct link between his stalking and her suicide. She was mentally fragile."

"And Jonathan Gedman is still missing," Timo said and walked to the kitchen. A steamy cup of black coffee was waiting for him.

"The police in Mjällom are reopening the case."

"After five years?"

"Mrs. Gedman doesn't have closure. Maybe this time they'll find him."

Timo sighed, picked up the cup and then put it down again while he stared aimlessly out of the window. He felt tired. It was like the energy was drained out of him.

"What's going on?" Isa said and crossed her arms.

"What do you mean?" He turned to Isa, his brows furrowing in confusion. He took a sip of his coffee.

"You seem nervous," she said and walked over to where he was standing.

He had made a decision. It had been a hard one. For almost two years he had called Gävle his home, but in the last weeks the cry to do something else had sounded louder and louder until he could no longer ignore it.

Timo set his coffee cup down on the counter and took a deep breath. He looked into Isa's eyes, the weight of his decision evident in his expression.

"You're right, Lindström. I've been feeling restless lately," he admitted, his voice tinged with a mix of uncertainty and determination. "I've made a decision, and it's not an easy one. I've decided to leave Gävle."

Isa's eyes widened, and her arms fell to her sides. "Leave? But... why?"

"I... can't do anything here anymore. I feel useless. I'm not happy. It's not you nor the team."

"If you don't want to be superintendent..."

"It's not that," he said and looked her in the eye. He saw desperation. Sadness. Disbelief.

"I'm sorry," he said. There were no other words he could think of to say.

"How can you leave us?" she asked. It was as if she had to quench the growing anger and disappointment.

"You can lead this team. You don't need me."

"How can you say that? Since you arrived here, everything started to make sense. You... I... You are my friend. Please, think about this."

"I thought about it... for a long time."

"Is it Ingrid?"

"No... although it's not working. I need to create more distance between Ingrid and myself. But it's ultimately about me. I need to figure out what I want to do with my life."

Isa put her hand over his. "Look, Timo. I know a lot has happened in the last months... year, and it takes time to recover from the trauma, but here you have friends. I am your friend. What will you do?"

"I'm taking some time off to travel," he said. "With my mother."

"Your mother? Are you serious? This is the woman you can't spend five minutes with without getting upset and frustrated. You told me it's all about her. How can you then..."

"Maybe that's exactly what I need. I just don't want it to be about me this time. I just want her drama, because in the end it's so insignificant and that's okay."

Isa let her head down. There was no way she'd be able to convince him that he was making a huge mistake. It was now or never. She had to tell him how she felt, really felt about him. He wasn't just a colleague and a friend. Viktor was right. Alex, but also Timo. But as she stood there, the weight of his decision heavy on her mood, she couldn't. She didn't want to burden him with yet another drama. He was still in love with Ingrid.

"When?"

"I handed in my resignation yesterday," he said. "I'll leave in a month from now."

"You're leaving the police force altogether?" Isa exclaimed, unable to contain her disbelief and frustration.

Timo nodded, his eyes meeting hers. "I've made up my mind,

Lindström. This is what's best for me."

Isa's emotions erupted, and she couldn't hold back any longer. "How can you do that?" she yelled, her voice echoing through the room. Her anger and hurt reverberated in her words.

Timo's brows furrowed. "I've thought long and hard about it. I need a fresh start, away from all of this. Away from the memories that haunt me."

"But you're throwing away everything you've worked for!" Isa argued, her voice trembling with a mixture of passion and disappointment. "You're an incredible detective, Timo. You have a gift for solving cases, for making a difference. Don't you see that?"

Timo's gaze softened, but his determination remained steadfast. "I appreciate your faith in me, Lindström, but this is about more than just my career. It's about my happiness, my sanity."

Isa took a step closer, her eyes filled with tears. "What about us? The team... me."

Timo's expression turned painful as he reached out to touch her arm. "I care about you deeply, you know that. And the team. But I can't move forward until I put my past behind me. I need time to heal, to find myself again."

Isa's anger gave way to a profound sense of loss and heartache. She shook her head. "You're making a mistake, Timo. You're running away from everything that matters."

Timo's voice wavered with emotion. "Maybe I am."

"Does Ingrid know?"

"Ingrid... I'm not..."

"Oh, stop pretending, Timo," she said. "I know you and Ingrid have been talking a lot. You've never been able to let her go. If you don't want to stay for me, then stay for her."

"I can't," he said.

Isa couldn't bear to hear any more. The weight of her unspoken feelings and the weight of Timo's decision crushed her spirit. With a mixture of anger and sadness, she turned away from him, storming towards the door.

"This is goodbye, Timo," she said, her voice laced with bitterness. "I hope you find what you're looking for."

And without another word, she left, her heart shattered, and her mind filled with the realization that their paths had diverged.

Still, she couldn't bring herself to saying the words she wanted to say.

* * *

Sylvia meticulously organized her papers in the now-quiet meeting room, the lingering discussions of the just-concluded meeting still resonating in the air. As she focused on the task at hand, the soft creak of the door drew her attention. Dr. Einarsson entered.

"How did it go?" His voice sliced through the room.

Sylvia lifted her gaze, meeting his eyes. "What? The meeting?"

"No, your exam."

A frown creased her forehead, and she rose from her seat. "Not too bad."

"That's good," he said, offering a brief smile.

She mirrored it and then said, "It's always a bit nerve-wracking, but I think it went as well as can be expected."

He nodded, but his usually calm demeanor seemed unsettled as he hovered near the doorway, lost in thought.

"Is there something you want?" Sylvia asked.

"I want to apologize... for the other day. I didn't want to be so blunt. I was out of line. I shouldn't have said what I said."

She looked at him with big eyes. "Uh... it's fine... I understand."

He looked down and then said. "I'm not sure you do. I mean... I said it for a reason. I like you. I think you are a great detective, but I don't want anything to happen to you."

Sylvia was taken aback by Dr. Einarsson's confession. She had suspected that he had feelings for her, but she never expected him to be so open about it. She didn't know how to respond.

"Thank you," she said, not sure what else to say.

Einarsson looked at her for a moment, then nodded and walked away. Sylvia stood there, feeling a mix of emotions. But if she were honest, she felt the same.

"Dinner," she said quickly.

He turned around. "What?"

"Dinner. Friday 8 p.m."

He smiled and nodded.

\* \* \*

"You look bad," Viktor remarked, stretched out on the sofa in the living room of his mother's house.

"Well, I got some bad news today." Her gaze dropped to her hands, fingers intertwined in a restless dance.

Viktor, trying to lift himself up, offered, "Oh, sorry... anything I can do?"

"No, I'll be okay."

"Thanks for helping out with the kids. They should visit you more often, but Mom... well, she's adamant about taking care of them."

"Of course," Isa replied, aware of the subtle tension with her former mother-in-law.

Changing the subject, Viktor asked, "How was Olivia?"

"Moody... but okay. We didn't fight."

"Good," he said, a smile playing on his lips.

Isa locked her gaze on him. "I'm also here to tell you that we found the car that hit you."

Viktor's interest piqued. "Who?"

"The car was stolen a few days before your accident. We're still looking for the driver. I'm sorry."

"Don't be sorry. It's not your fault."

"I need to apologize. I think it's because of me you got hurt. That stalker is behind it all. I can feel it."

"Is someone investigating this?"

"Yes, but they have not been able to find him," she said and sighed. "Lukas Stendahl claims it's not him. And I tend to believe him. Why would he focus on me?"

"Isa, this is serious. I don't want you to get hurt."

"Or you and the children." She got up and paced around the room before settling on the edge of the couch where he was lying. "Maybe it's best I disappear for a while."

"Isa, don't do that," Viktor said.

He struggled to sit up on the sofa, wincing in pain as he adjusted his position. He reached out and grabbed Isa's arm. "We can't let fear dictate our lives. Disappearing won't solve anything. We need to face this head-on, together."

He sounded so convincing, so strong. She liked the new Viktor.

"You're right," she said. "I can't let this stalker control me, but I'm so tired. I just want to give up and with Paikkala gone I don't know if I'm willing to stay here and keep going as if nothing has changed."

"Timo is gone?"

She nodded.

"Why don't you take over the team?"

"Viktor... no, just leave it."

"Just think about it. If anyone can do this, it's you."

She gave him a quick smile.

The doorbell echoed through the house, prompting Isa's question, "You're expecting someone?"

Viktor glanced towards the door. "It's probably Felix's new friend. Do you mind getting the door?"

Isa nodded, making her way to the entrance. As she swung the door open, she found herself face-to-face with a young man—Oliver Pilkvist. His blue eyes met hers, and recognition flashed across her face. Timo had shared stories about the thirteen-year-old who had been rescued after a harrowing ordeal.

Oliver, now looking more mature, greeted her with, "Good day, Inspector Lindström."

Surprised, Isa responded, "You know me?"

"Of course, after your colleague Superintendent Paikkala saved me, I know everything about the Gävle police department."

Uncertain about Oliver's sudden appearance, Isa asked, "What are you doing here?"

"Felix." He gestured towards the boy who had just come down the stairs. "We're practicing for the chess tournament. You do know that he's participating, right?"

Felix interjected, pushing past Isa, "Oliver, come. We can go to my room."

As they ascended the stairs, Isa turned to Viktor. "Oliver Pilkvist is his new friend?"

Viktor, seemingly unconcerned, said, "Is there a problem?"

Curiosity and unease lingered in Isa's thoughts. "I wonder. There's something about Oliver that feels off to me. Maybe it's my instinct or the timing of his sudden appearance. There's just... something."

"Now you're being paranoid. He's just a normal kid."

"I guess so," she replied, a sense of doubt lingering. "I'm off then. See you on Saturday."

Viktor waved goodbye with a smile as Isa left, leaving the feeling of uncertainty to linger in the room.

\* \* \*

Timo took the book, 'The Search for a Serial Killer', in his hands. Kristina Rapp. It was her first and only book, a culmination of years of investigation and dedication. He felt a pang of nostalgia as he recalled the time he had spent working alongside Kristina. Those years in the Stockholm police force. A time he looked back at with mixed feelings.

He carefully placed the book in the cardboard box on his desk, alongside other remnants of his career in law enforcement. The box was a repository of memories, both good and bad.

His mind wandered back to the day Finn Heimersson had taken over as superintendent, a turning point in his career. Initially, he had been filled with frustration and anger at being passed over for the promotion. But now, with the benefit of hindsight, he saw things differently. Perhaps it hadn't been a bad thing after all.

Sure, Finn hadn't been the right person, but Finn was dead and the friendship they had shared—or at least what he thought was friendship—along with it.

Timo realized that the path he had been on, the relentless pursuit of criminals, the constant exposure to darkness and violence, had taken its toll on him. It had consumed his life, leaving little room for personal happiness and fulfillment. He had become jaded, worn down by the weight of the job.

As he looked at the cardboard box, filled with the artifacts of his career, a sense of clarity washed over him. This wasn't the life he wanted anymore. The high-stakes nature of the job, the constant danger, it had all become too much. The loss of friends and loved ones.

He would leave it all behind. He would walk away from the badge, the investigations, and the constant adrenaline-fueled chase. It was time for a fresh start, a chance to rediscover himself outside the confines of law enforcement.

It was funny to realize that not so long ago he had craved those very challenges he was now eager to escape.

He closed the lid of the cardboard box, sealing away the remnants of his past. The weight on his shoulders lifted, replaced by a newfound sense of freedom. He knew that this chapter of his life had come to an end, and a new one was waiting to be written.

"You are already packing, sir?" Sylvia stood in the doorway. "You'll still be with us for a month, right?"

"Yes, but this moment is as good as any other," he said. "I don't have much stuff anyway."

"Forgive me for asking, but why are you leaving?"

"It's time to give the new blood a chance. Passionate police officers like yourself. Speaking of which, congratulations to you and Varg on making inspector. I just received the news."

She looked at him surprised. "Oh... that's great news. Thank you, sir."

He had watched her grow and develop as an officer, witnessing her dedication and determination firsthand. Her promotion to inspector was well-deserved, and he knew she would excel in her new role.

"I have full confidence in you, Inspector Ahlgren," Timo said. "You and Varg will do well."

Sylvia's expression softened. "Thank you, sir. Your guidance and support have meant a lot to me. It won't be the same without you."

"Thank you," he said and then turned his attention to the box, but Sylvia kept standing in the doorway.

"Did you want anything else?"

"There is a certain Stella Åkesson who wants to speak with a senior investigator. She didn't want to talk to me. She claims she knows Alva Stendahl and Celeste Westerberg."

"Really?" he said. "Well, I'll have a talk with her. Where is she?"

"In interview room two."

*　*　*

Stella Åkesson seemed nervous and unsure. She was a young woman with wavy chestnut hair and hazel eyes reflecting a hint of anxiety. Her fidgeting hands, twirling hair, and occasional hesitation in her words revealed an inner struggle, showing uncertainty about how to behave.

Timo's piercing blue eyes focused on her as she spoke, making her feel smaller with each word. "So, Ms. Åkesson, you wanted to talk to me."

"Yes, I... I heard about Celeste Westerberg's death."

"Did you know her?"

She shook her head. "I talked to her only once. I don't think we would have been friends."

"Why not?"

"Because I slept with her wife. I was Alva Stendahl's mistress for a while."

"I see," Timo said. "But we already know Celeste filed for divorce because Alva had been unfaithful to her."

"I know but..."

"What is bothering you, Ms. Åkesson?"

"Are you sure it was suicide?"

He looked at her surprised. "Do you think it might be something else?"

Stella's eyes darted nervously around the room before meeting Timo's gaze. There was a mixture of concern and doubt etched on her face as she gathered her thoughts.

"I can't say for certain... but I know Alva... unfortunately. She might have something to do with Celeste's death. Maybe she didn't kill her, but... look, I ended my relationship with Alva because it was suffocating. She made my world so small."

Stella's voice trembled, her hands tightly clenched in her lap.

"Alva... she was... she is a master manipulator," Stella began. "She had a way of twisting the truth, making me doubt myself at every turn. It was like living in a constant state of confusion and second-guessing."

Her eyes locked with Timo's. As she continued, her voice gained strength. "I started to notice the patterns, the subtle ways she would gaslight me. She would belittle my opinions, make me question my own sanity, and then she played the victim. It was a never-ending cycle that left me feeling trapped and powerless. She made me doubt my own worth, my own judgment. And when I finally gathered the strength to end the relationship, it was like a weight lifted off my shoulders. But the scars, the emotional toll, are still there."

"You think it was a pattern," Timo remarked.

"It wasn't the first time. I think she did the same to Celeste. Well, I'm absolutely sure she did."

"Why?"

"It was the only time I talked to Celeste. It was just after Alva and I broke up. I attended a concert, and Celeste was there too. We started talking. I could see the pain in Celeste's eyes, the same pain I had experienced. We connected over our shared experiences with Alva, the manipulation, the emotional abuse. It was like looking into a mirror and seeing my own struggles reflected back at me."

"We have no evidence that Alva is responsible for Celeste's death."

"Not directly. It's always subtle. Like in my case, she started stalking me..."

But Timo hadn't heard the rest. It all fell into place. Alva was the stalker. Alva was Celeste's stalker. She was Stella's stalker.

And she was Isa's stalker.

He got up. "Sorry, I need to go. Thank you. This helped a lot. Inspector Ahlgren will take care of you."

# CHAPTER

# 29

ISA PUT THE KEY IN THE LOCK and stepped inside. It wasn't exactly the day she had hoped for. Her day off had started with Timo telling her that he wanted to leave. Then there was Oliver Pilkvist who had let her leave Viktor with a nagging strange feeling of danger. The entire drive home she had contemplated how she could get him away from her son. Oliver was a strange boy. Timo had even come that far to say that he was a psychopath in the making. He had felt it after his visit to Oliver's mother, after both Oliver and he had survived the ordeal of being kidnapped and used in a perverted game of hunter and prey. Claiming a thirteen-year-old boy was a danger to society was maybe a stretch too far, but she trusted Timo's intuition. It was one of his strong points.

Timo. How she would miss him!

She placed the keys in a porcelain bowl on the table near the door, hung her coat on the peg, and kicked off her shoes before walking from the hallway to the kitchen.

The warmly lit kitchen greeted her, filled with the scent of a meal she had prepared earlier. Isa's eyes settled on the wooden table in the center of the room.

The room hummed with the refrigerator's gentle whir and the ticking of a clock on the wall. She found some comfort in the peaceful atmosphere.

Moving with ease, she prepared herself a cup of tea. The sound of boiling water filled the air as she selected a teacup and saucer. Soon, the aroma of chamomile enveloped the kitchen. Isa settled at the kitchen table, cradling the warm cup in her hands.

As she sipped her tea, thoughts of the day swirled in her mind. The unease regarding Oliver Pilkvist and her determination to protect her son lingered.

Suddenly, she jumped up. A strange noise came from the living room, sounding like footsteps. Maybe the noise had been there before, but with her mind settled on Oliver, it hadn't really percolated.

The gun was in the safe, hidden in the living room. She had learned her lesson. Before, she had been careless, leaving it sometimes on the living room or kitchen table. But now, she was defenseless. What if the stalker had suddenly decided to take it to the next level?

She opened the cupboard and took out a knife. This might be risky. Perhaps she'd better leave the house and call her colleagues.

But where was her phone? It wasn't in her pocket. The realization hit her that she had left it behind on the table during her visit with Viktor, completely forgotten in the midst of her distressing encounter with Oliver.

Silence engulfed the house, amplifying her unease. With the knife in her hand, she walked over to the living room.

A chill hung in the air, causing her to shiver involuntarily. Her eyes scanned the room, searching for any signs of intrusion or disturbance. And that's when she noticed it—the large window leading to the garden stood open.

Alarm bells rang in her mind as she assessed the situation. She was sure she hadn't left the window open. It was too cold outside. Fear clenched at her heart, intensifying her sense of vulnerability.

Someone was inside her home.

Isa's grip tightened on the knife, her instincts urging her to be cautious. She moved up to the window, looked outside but saw nothing. A pristine white layer of snow, untouched. There were no footprints. Nothing.

She closed the window but when she turned around, she jumped up. Someone was sitting on her couch. Hands nicely folded in her lap, Alva Stendahl was looking at her.

"What are you doing here?" Isa said. But the moment she had spoken those words, she knew.

Alva's lips curved into a cold smile. "The door was open."

"No, it wasn't," Isa said. Her hand was so tightly wrapped around the handle of the knife that it started to hurt.

Alva held up a key and then said, "You lost your key a few days ago, and then you found it back."

"How..."

"Never mind. You knew that placing new locks on the doors wouldn't stop me."

"What do you want?" Isa's mind raced, her survival instincts kicking into high gear. She knew she had to stay focused and find a way to escape. The back door was out of the question, as she had locked it and secured the key in a drawer in the kitchen. The front door became her only chance for freedom.

Her grip on the knife tightened as she slowly started backing away from Alva, her eyes fixed on the path that led to the front door. Every step she took felt heavy with trepidation, aware that any sudden movement could provoke a dangerous response.

"What do you want?" Isa's voice trembled, but she refused to let fear overpower her determination.

"You know very well what I want. We've been dancing around this for weeks. I want you."

"Me?" Isa said. "What do you mean?"

"You're good... you can be honest now. Viktor isn't here. I scared him away, so we could be alone. He won't bother you anymore."

Isa frowned. "What? He isn't..."

"But if he comes near you again, I'll have to hurt him... again, probably kill him."

"You ran him over with a car."

"I had to... just like I had to burn Alex's sweater. Now you can really move on."

The sweater. It was all she had. Lost. Forever.

"You did the same thing to Celeste," Isa let out. She could hardly catch her breath. In that moment, Isa's instincts screamed at her to flee, but Alva kept watching her like a hawk. Like a lioness, which was about to jump on her prey. She just wanted to play with it a while longer, because that was the excitement Alva longed for.

"I don't want to hear that name anymore. She betrayed me."

"Yeah... after all you've done for her."

"I kept her safe. I was there all the time. That ungrateful woman."

"You were her stalker."

A faint smile appeared on Alva's face. All that time, she hadn't moved a muscle. The hands were still nicely folded in her lap. She was sitting straight like a good schoolgirl was told to do, looking right at Isa. "Yes, I was. I fell in love with her when I was eighteen. My father, who was a real bastard and couldn't get his hands off me, took me and my brother to a concert. Such a beautiful woman and so talented. I was totally fascinated. I tried to talk to her that evening, but I couldn't. It was strange. I had seen her before, in school, and with Lukas, but the click hadn't been there. Until that moment. The days after the concert, I started collecting everything I could find out about her. She was a rising star, a high potential, and there was no doubt. Celeste made me dream. She made me forget my shitty life."

"And you started following her," Isa said and stepped closer to the door that would lead her to the hallway and to safety.

"I wouldn't do that if I were you," Alva said. "I'm an expert in martial arts. I'll snap your neck in no time... and I don't want to do that."

Isa held her breath.

"You look so much like her," Alva continued. "That passion, that energy."

"The madness?"

"The madness... yes, maybe. She wasn't that mentally stable."

"But you used that to get close to her."

Alva shook her head. "No... not at first. I took my time to observe her."

"And?"

"She was unhappy. They put her under so much pressure... and then that disgusting brother of her who continuously assaulted her."

"Is that even true? The diary... you made it."

Alva let out a sarcastic puff. "I have plenty of photos and recordings. That's what happens when you have bugs planted in her apartment. The diary is real. It's her handwriting... no?"

"But you put the stories in her head. She couldn't think for herself anymore."

The entire time, Isa had listened to her story while standing with the knife in her hand, moving closer and closer to the door. On one hand, she wanted to get out of there as soon as possible. On the other hand, the police officer in her couldn't just leave without hearing the entire story.

* * *

Viktor opened his eyes. There was a phone ringing somewhere. After Isa had left, he had taken a painkiller and had fallen asleep on the couch. He pushed himself up and scanned the room, only to find the phone lying on the table next to him.

Viktor's groggy mind began to clear as he realized the phone ringing was not his own. Isa must have left it behind. He reached over and picked it up, glancing at the display to see Timo's name flashing on the screen. The persistent ringing continued, urging him to answer the call.

"Hello," he said.

"Lindström... uh, who's this?" he heard Timo say on the other side of the line.

"Viktor."

"Where is Isa? Can you get her for me?"

"Uh... she's not here. She left her phone here by mistake."

"Shit. Where is she?"

Viktor started to feel a sense of worry creep into his voice as he replied, "I'm not sure. She left a while ago. Is something wrong?"

Timo's voice on the other end sounded tense. "I'll try to catch her at home then."

"Timo... it's the stalker, isn't it?"

"Yeah. I hope we're not too late."

* * *

"What happened?" Isa said.

"It was fantastic," Alva said and got up. Isa jumped back, the knife still aimed at Alva. "After the hiking incident and the pressure from her hit single, fragile Celeste finally succumbed to pressure. The day after she checked into the hospital, I checked in too."

"How could you fake this for so long?"

"Fake it? There are plenty of traumas to dig into. Sexual abuse, drugs, alcohol... you name it, I can tell you all about it."

Isa shook her head, a mix of disbelief and anger coursing through her veins. "You're sick. How could you manipulate someone's life like that? How could you toy with their emotions and inflict so much pain?"

Alva smirked, her eyes glinting with a twisted sense of satisfaction. "Oh, Isa, you have no idea what I'm capable of. People are so easily deceived, so easily broken. It's a game, and I always win. Celeste was a troubled woman."

"Her parents were right. You gaslighted her for years."

"I wanted to protect her."

"Protect her? By destroying her? Manipulating her emotions, making her doubt herself at every turn? That's not protection, that's abuse!"

Alva's smile widened, her voice dripping with cruelty. "Oh, Isa, you don't understand. Celeste needed me. She needed my guidance, my control. I shaped her into someone stronger, someone who could withstand the harsh realities of life. It was all for her own good."

Isa's grip on the knife tightened even further, her voice trembling with rage. "You twisted her reality, destroyed her sense of self. That's not love, Alva. That's sick and twisted."

Alva's expression hardened. "Love is a fickle thing. Sometimes it requires sacrifice, even if it means tearing someone apart to make them whole. Celeste owed everything to me."

"Celeste found the strength to break free from your manipulation. She stood up to you, and she paid the ultimate price for it," Isa said.

Alva's smirk faltered for a moment, a flicker of irritation crossing her face. She regained composure quickly, leaning in with a chilling calmness. "You don't understand. Celeste was weak. She needed someone to guide her, to make decisions for her."

Isa shook her head. "That's not love, Alva. Real love empowers, supports, and nurtures. What you did was an abuse of power and a betrayal of trust."

"I am disappointed. I thought you were different."

"How can you claim you know me?" Isa said surprised. "You've seen me what... twice."

"We connected over a poem."

"Poem? I merely recited a few lines from a book that's dear to me. That's not connection."

"That's enough. I knew you were better than Celeste. She betrayed me. You would never do that." Alva's smile widened as she continued, "And Isa, I'm a stalker. I know more about you than you think."

"You restarted your manipulation after she had handed you the divorce papers."

"Little did I know Lukas had the same plan. It made it a bit... confusing."

"She killed herself," Isa said.

"That... wasn't the intention."

"You're saying Celeste's death wasn't your intention? But you drove her to the edge. You pushed her to the point where she saw no way out. How can you stand there and pretend you didn't have a hand in her despair?"

Alva's gaze turned cold, her tone devoid of remorse. "I won't take the blame for her choice."

"You wanted her back. And in the end, you failed."

"Well, that's Lukas' fault... and I have you now," Alva said with a grin on her face.

"And what are you going to do? Make me love you? You have a distorted idea of love. Love is not about control or manipulation. It's about trust, respect, and genuine care for another person. What you're doing is not love—it's a sick obsession."

Alva looked at the floor for a moment and then said, "I know. I want it all to end."

"Then give yourself up."

"No... not like that," Alva said. "I'll take you with me."

"What do you mean?"

* * *

"Alva Stendahl is not home," the voice said through the loudspeaker.

Timo turned the steering wheel. "Okay, I'll be at Lindström's house in five minutes."

"Sir... we found a note on the kitchen table," Varg said.

"Read it to me." Timo's grip tightened on the steering wheel as he listened intently to Varg's words.

"This isn't good. It's a goodbye letter."

"Varg, read it!"

*"To those who may find this, I have carried the weight of my pain for far too long. The darkness within me has consumed every trace of happiness, leaving only despair in its wake. The world was never kind to me, and I was never kind to myself. In my final act, I release the burdens that have plagued my soul. I seek solace in the void that awaits, where I hope to find the peace that eluded me in life. To Isa, know that I wanted us to be bound forever. In death, we shall be united, our souls intertwined in eternal darkness. Farewell, Alva."*

"She's going to kill herself and Isa with her," Timo said. "Stay at the house and secure the area, Varg. Notify backup and tell them to meet me at Inspector Lindström's home."

He pressed harder on the accelerator. Doom scenarios were racing through his mind. Isa was an experienced police officer. She could stand her ground, but Alva Stendahl was a cunning manipulator.

He wasn't sure if he'd be there in time.

\* \* \*

Isa understood Alva's intentions all too clearly. This was the moment to act; there was no room for negotiation. Her mind raced, knowing her life hung in the balance.

With a burst of energy, Isa made a dash for the hallway. The front door offered her only chance of escape, but Alva was faster. In one swift move, she seized Isa, throwing her off balance, causing the knife to slip from her grip.

They grappled desperately, locked in a struggle for control. Isa fought back with all her strength, trying to break free, but Alva's grip was unyielding. Instinctively, Isa sought a way out, launching herself towards a nearby table in search of a weapon.

Their struggle intensified as Alva reached for the knife. Fear and adrenaline fueled Isa's efforts as she fought for her life, refusing to let Alva gain the upper hand. Their hands wrestled over the knife, each woman driven by a primal urge to survive.

"I need you to die," Alva screamed. Isa tightened her grip, refusing to surrender, even as her heart raced with fear.

Their faces were so close.

Suddenly, she heard someone pounding on the door, their voice calling out Isa's name.

"Isa, Isa!" the voice echoed, growing louder and more frantic with each plea. She recognized the voice. It was Timo.

"Help," Isa cried out, but just as help seemed within reach, Isa's guard slipped, and Alva's blade found its mark. Pain surged through Isa as the knife pierced her flesh, bringing with it a sense of despair.

As darkness closed in, she realized her fight had reached a tragic end, her final thoughts consumed by the harsh reality of her mortality.

She heard the shatter of glass and a desperate voice still crying her name.

## AND THEN EVERYTHING WENT BLACK

**BOOKS IN THIS SERIES:**

THE FIND
EVIL BENEATH THE SKIN
RETRIBUTION
THE STORM

**AND... THE STORY CONTINUES**

**COMING SOON:**

**BOOK 6 – DARKENED HEART**

Printed in Great Britain
by Amazon